A FAMILY IS TORN AS
A NEW NATION EMERGES
FROM THE PAIN AND
STRIFE OF WAR

Revolution splits the American colonies, and the
wilderness is ravaged by war. In the lands of
the frontier, Owen and Ella Sutherland see the
company they have built threatened, and their
own son turn against them, as old friends become enemies in the fight for a new nation's
freedom.

REBELLION

The Fourth Powerful Novel
in the Northwest Territory Series

THEY LIVED, LOVED, FOUGHT, AND DIED AS AMERICA WAS BORN

OWEN SUTHERLAND. The founder of a fur-trading empire, he must jeopardize his home and family and risk his life to aid the rebellion...

ELLA SUTHERLAND. She will fight beside her husband to preserve the life and the family their love has created...

MANOTH. Shamed by Owen Sutherland, he will lead the dreaded Seneca in a quest for bloody revenge...

JEREMY BENTLY. Owen's stepson, he returns home to the colonies with a young English bride and a loyalty to England too strong to break...

PENELOPE GRAVES. Her fearless spirit and her love for Jeremy must face the ultimate test in the wilderness...

HUGH MEEKS. A cutthroat pirate hired by Sutherland's enemies, he will lie, cheat, betray, and murder to feed his boundless greed...

SALLY COOPER. She must learn her own heart before she can lose it to the man she loves...

TOM MORELY. Stubborn as he is brave, he will sacrifice all for his friends—and wait forever for one woman...

PETER DEFRIES. A boisterous Albany Dutchman, he uses his wits and brawn to fight the British everywhere and every way he can, on land and sea...

By Oliver Payne from Berkley

NORTHWEST TERRITORY SERIES

Book 1: *Warpath*
Book 2: *Conquest*
Book 3: *Defiance*
Book 4: *Rebellion*

NORTHWEST TERRITORY · BOOK 4

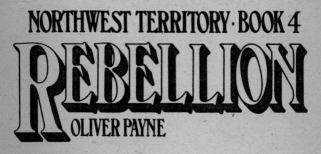

REBELLION

OLIVER PAYNE

Created by the producers of
Wagons West, The Australians, and
The Kent Family Chronicles Series.

Executive Producer: Lyle Kenyon Engel

BERKLEY BOOKS, NEW YORK

REBELLION

A Berkley Book/published by arrangement with
Book Creations, Inc.

PRINTING HISTORY
Berkley edition/October 1983

Produced by Book Creations, Inc.
Executive Producer: Lyle Kenyon Engel

ISBN: 0-425-06271-6

To the Monsons

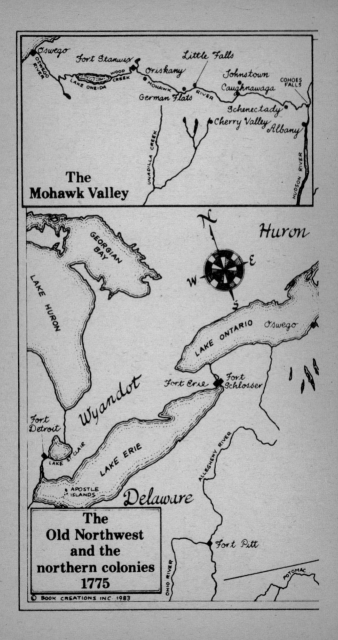

The
Mohawk Valley

The
Old Northwest
and the
northern colonies
1775

© BOOK CREATIONS INC. 1983

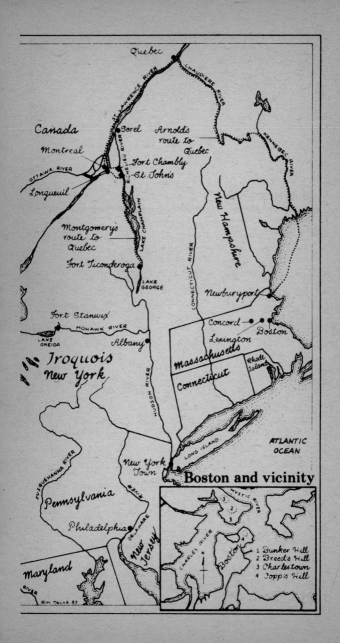

Quebec

CHAUDIERE RIVER

Canada

Montreal

Sorel

Arnold's
route to
Quebec

Fort Chambly

St. John's

KENNEBEC RIVER

OTTAWA RIVER

ST. LAWRENCE RIVER

RICHELIEU RIVER

Longueuil

Montgomery's
route to
Quebec

LAKE CHAMPLAIN

New Hampshire

Fort Ticonderoga

LAKE
GEORGE

Fort Stanwix

MOHAWK RIVER

CONNECTICUT RIVER

Newburyport

LAKE
ONEIDA

Concord

Boston

Iroquois
New York

Albany

Lexington

Massachusetts

HUDSON RIVER

Connecticut

Rhode
Island

SUSQUEHANNA RIVER

LONG ISLAND

ATLANTIC
OCEAN

New York
Town

Boston and vicinity

Pennsylvania

DELAWARE RIVER

MYSTIC RIVER

Philadelphia

New
Jersey

CHARLES RIVER

Boston

Maryland

RIVER

1 Bunker Hill
2 Breed's Hill
3 Charlestown
4 Copp's Hill

RON DELLE 83

I am certain any other conduct but com-
pelling obedience would be ruinous and
culpable....I know I am doing my duty,
and therefore can never wish to retract.

—*King George III*
July 1775

If we tamely give up our rights in this country...we shall be stamped with the character of bastards, poltroons, and fools, and be despised and trampled upon...by all mankind.

—*Benjamin Franklin*
February 1775

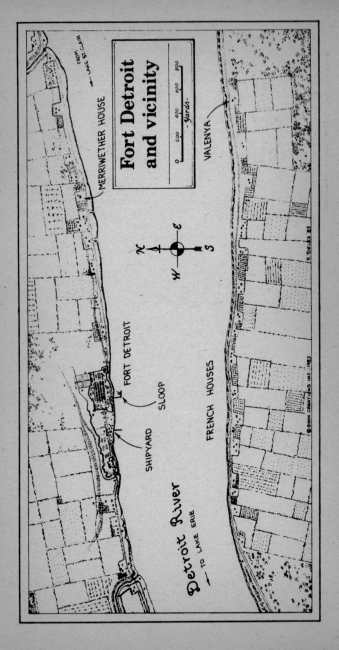

Fort Detroit
and vicinity

0   200   400   600   800
       - Yards -

FROM
LAKE ST. CLAIR

MERRIWETHER HOUSE

VALENYA

FORT DETROIT

SLOOP

SHIPYARD

FRENCH HOUSES

Detroit River
TO LAKE ERIE

© BOOK CREATIONS INC 1983

R. DELEE 83

Whig and Tory

chapter 1

THE PIRATE

Hugh Meeks snorted and laughed, saying, "Ain't it a fine day for a brawl, Farley?"

He cackled again and jabbed an elbow into the ribs of his slender, aging companion, who staggered, coughing, false teeth clacking furiously. The seedy clerk, Farley Jones, and shipmaster Hugh Meeks stood on the deck of a sloop tied up at the landing of Fort Detroit, in the heart of America's northwest wilderness. They were watching a crowd of three hundred frontiersmen and Indians gather on an expanse of open ground just outside the fort's western gate. A British flag above the stockade wall snapped in the fresh breeze. It was a clear, crisp December morning in the year 1774.

Jones tried to ignore Meeks, for he wanted no part in what was about to happen. If this treacherous pirate with the guile of a serpent had his way, there would be cracked bones and caved-in heads among the folk of Detroit, white and red alike. Giving the shipmaster a sidelong glance, Jones wondered where their employer— the Boston merchant Bradford Cullen—had found such a hulking roughneck.

Surely the wharves of New York or Boston could not have bred the likes of Meeks, whose savage temper bullied fierce sailors, and whose wit and seamanship won their admiration and respect. More likely it was the West Indies, the old Spanish Main, or the buccaneer haunts of Barbados that had nurtured him. Cullen must have discovered Meeks in the sugar trade between New England and the Caribbean.

Jones noted a flurry of movement a hundred yards off, near the fort's gate. Owen Sutherland was coming. Fear and anticipation rose in the clerk. He hated this man just as violently as did Cullen, whose fur-trading firm had for years been in bitter conflict with

3

Sutherland, leading partner in the flourishing Frontier Company. In the past, Jones had served Cullen out here at the center of the northwestern fur trade, and had been outwitted and defeated more than once by Sutherland and members of the Frontier Company. This morning he expected to see Meeks take some measure of revenge for those defeats, and the very thought of watching Sutherland bleed thrilled him.

Jones felt the cold eyes of his companion, and he looked around to be met by that cunning, squinting stare that always caught him off guard. His left eye half closed, the other glinting with cruel mischief, Meeks was a deceiver whose very gaze made a man shiver. The clerk's elation faded.

Coming close, Meeks said, "Will ye not skip along with us and have a lick at them rebels, matey?" Jones managed to wrench away and looked again toward the land, where he saw the tall form of Owen Sutherland, dressed in buckskins, moving through the parting crowd.

Meeks's voice almost whispered in the clerk's ear. "Ye'll have a chance at the Scotch bastard when he's down, I'll see to that! He won't even know it's ye—after I'm through with him."

Jones wheezed, plunging his hands into the pockets of his frock coat to avoid taking the heavy belaying pin Meeks was offering. As thick as the clerk's arm, the wooden club seemed puny in the sailor's meaty hands. Meeks offered the pin again, and when Jones shook his head, he winked and said, "Don't ye crave to delight yer master, Mr. Cullen? Don't ye? Pipe up! Ye'd make a reputation with a fella who'll be the powerfullest gentleman in the colonies one day! Ye may lay to that!"

Jones would not reply. Meeks gave a dry, grating laugh, turning away to observe the mob and Owen Sutherland. The clerk seethed, longing to scream that Meeks was the one always licking Cullen's boots. Meeks was forever fawning before the merchant, seeking advancement, and building his own reputation. Jones wanted to say this, but did not dare irk the brute.

At forty-five, ten years younger than Jones, Meeks was a remarkable contrast to the bent, sickly clerk. Ruddy and clean-shaven, his square chin jutting forward, Meeks rocked on his heels, placidly examining the frontiersmen ashore the way a feudal lord might contemplate condemned prisoners. Unlike his companion and most men of the day, who wore their hair long, in a queue, Meeks had his gray hair cropped close to his scalp. A sharp early-winter wind flapped the man's coat collar, but he paid the chill

no mind. Jones, watery-eyed and sniffling, bundled a tattered scarf
more closely about his own neck, and took note of that eerie white
scar running from the seaman's left earlobe down his neck. It
seemed to be a burn, a rope burn, and it stood out more starkly
when Meeks was excited or drunk and red in the face.

Meeks was muttering distantly, "Been too long since I swung
a pin. Last time was off Jamaica—aye, Jamaica it was, an' we
took a smart Portugee brig full to the gunnels with slaves. Sold
good, they did, them that lived. . . ."

As Meeks spoke, Jones guessed a noose had indeed been at
work on his throat; Bradford Cullen had known what he was about
when he engaged Meeks to go up against Sutherland. It just might
be that Meeks was the man to even things out between Cullen and
Sutherland.

Unlike the people on land, Meeks and Jones were not soldiers
or frontiersmen; but like these people of the northwest territory,
the two men made their living from the lucrative fur trade that
harvested pelts from Rainy Lake in the west to the Iroquois lands
on the frontiers of New York Colony. Having docked their sloop,
Helen, at Detroit only two days ago, Meeks was new to the northwest. He had recently been hired by Cullen mainly to run this
vessel across Lake Erie, through the broad straits at Detroit, and
up to distant Fort Michilimackinac, carrying fur and trade goods.
Cullen's other use for Meeks was to take on Owen Sutherland,
for the merchant had resolved—once and for all—to put an end
to his rival.

Jones wondered whether Meeks underestimated these frontier
folk, thinking them less hardy than seamen. If he did, he was
wrong; even a heavy belaying pin would not intimidate the likes
of Owen Sutherland. The Scotsman thrived on danger and had
fought his way to prosperity despite Indian wars and Cullen's
intrigues. Sutherland was the most important trader at Detroit,
which was the hub, the emporium, for half the continent. Each
winter and spring thousands of Indians brought in their pelts, and
hundreds of whites made a living buying the furs with manufactured goods and rum. These folk were all tough, resilient, and the
clerk knew Meeks would have his hands full if he fought Sutherland.

Just how Meeks would carry out Cullen's orders and attack
Sutherland, Farley Jones did not know. There was not another
man in this country fearless enough to challenge the Scotsman
face to face. But then, Meeks was no duelist; he was a brawler,

shrewd and cruel. Furthermore, the noisy, anxious crowd was smitten with a dangerous anger—anger that split them into two camps.

A former officer in the famous Black Watch Highland Regiment, Sutherland had just come back to Detroit after attending the first Continental Congress in Philadelphia. Sent there as a delegate by frontier folk of every political shade, Sutherland had been trusted to listen closely to representatives from the colonies, and to inform the people of Detroit about the state of the hostility between Parliament and America.

For months, perhaps years, lines had been drawn between those who favored Parliament—the loyalist Tories—and those who demanded more American rights and liberties—the rebellious Whigs. As Jones observed the growing crowd, he recognized familiar faces from the past and knew who was on which side. There was ready hatred among these people, with each party blaming the other for whatever unfavorable conditions beset their country. If Meeks did his work well, raw nerves might be touched and the crowd goaded to sudden violence.

Jones watched as the dozen sailors of the *Helen*, all handpicked by Meeks, assembled near the gangplank and took belaying pins from their master. Even more imposing than usual in the big greatcoat he wore, Meeks was alight with good humor as he spoke a word to each man and clapped their shoulders before sending them down, one by one, to mingle in the crowd. With clubs secreted in coats or breeches, these rogues knew their orders.

Meeks leered at Jones, cackled once more, and slid a belaying pin out of sight inside his greatcoat. Then he strode down the gangplank and onto the landing. Jones watched him go, brass buttons polished, buckles shining, even his stockings clean. The seaman almost looked the part of the respectable citizen anxious to hear news of the colonies and Congress, except that his rolling gait made the cutlass sticking out from behind his greatcoat swing like a devil's tail. As he pushed into the crowd, men moved aside, women looked away, and he was given ample room near the platform where Sutherland would address the people.

Not far from Meeks a loud argument was going on, and Jones noticed one of those involved was the former soldier, Jeb Grey. A settler and partner in the Frontier Company, this immense Jerseyman was an outspoken opponent of Parliament and a supporter of Congress. He would be close to Sutherland when fighting broke out and would be a tough man to contend with. Jones felt even more uneasy to see Tamano, the big Chippewa warrior; in his company was the young Sioux brave, Little Hawk, who in past years had often made fun of Jones and earned the clerk's hatred.

These Indians, friends of Sutherland's, were partners in the trading company. With them were their wives—Tamano's pretty Lela, and Little Hawk's cheerful, plump White Dove. Standing with Jeb Grey and his wife, Lettie—a portly, robust woman who had married Grey after her first husband was murdered by white renegades in the pay of Bradford Cullen—these Indians had children at their sides. The parents seemed not to anticipate serious trouble, and what would happen to the young ones when it began, Jones did not care to guess.

At least one of these young people familiar to Jones was now full-grown, and the clerk spat in anger to see him: Tommy Morely, son of Lettie Grey, had been a boy when Jones last served at Detroit. Like Little Hawk, Tom had been a bane to Jones, teasing him and causing all sorts of trouble for the sour, vengeful man. Now almost twenty, Tommy was as tall as Jeb, his stepfather, though not nearly as wide. Handsome and dark, Tommy seemed unaware of the argument going on. He was watching for Sutherland or for someone in Sutherland's party, which was now approaching the platform.

Jones saw Tommy smile broadly and tip his flat, wide-brimmed hat to a young woman coming through the crowd just ahead of Sutherland. Laughing as she played with a boy and a girl at her side, Sally Cooper inclined her head to Tom. Once again Jones was amazed to recognize an adult whom he had known formerly as a child. Pretty and fresh at nineteen, Sally had been raised as a foster daughter by the Sutherlands, and was now walking hand in hand with their younger children.

Even dried-up old Jones saw how Tom Morely was charmed by this girl, and it was no wonder, for she attracted considerable attention from all the men around her. "Just like an Injun!" Jones thought with scorn and licked his thin lips as he contemplated her uncovered head and the calf-length, maroon skirt she wore. Sally's long, auburn hair was tied back with a ribbon, and in the way of many frontier women, she wore no bonnet, as a more modest woman of the colonies would have.

Jones knew Sally had once been a prisoner of Indians, and he decided that this captivity had caused these mannerisms he considered uncouth; yet they fascinated him. He wished the crowd were not so dense so he could get a better look at Sally's shapely legs. No doubt the Morely lad was getting an eyeful.

As far as Jones was concerned, Meeks and his men could do whatever they liked to the young Sioux Indian and Morely. He would be happy if those two were battered senseless or done for, never mind what happened to Sutherland.

The clerk was sure that the partisan violence running rampant in eastern settlements and cities could be stirred up here in Detroit, for people had brought their traditional likes and dislikes out with them. Most in the surging crowd had already heard that the Continental Congress had called for a total embargo on goods from Britain, and there was much anger here over the prospect of essential British trade supplies being cut off from the northwest. Many would be ruined if that happened. Yet on the other hand there were others who raged against Parliament's new plans to seal off the frontier at the Allegheny Mountains and forbid all future settlement of Indian lands.

Doubts, rumors, lies, fears, ancient mistrust, and new resentments burned and quickened in the hearts and minds of people in Detroit. No one knew whom to believe, whom to obey, and what would happen to them if riots and mob brutality in the East broke out into a full-scale rebellion against the crown. That was why they so tensely awaited Owen Sutherland's message, for they trusted him above all others and wanted to hear his opinion on such matters as the acts of Congress and the colonial agreement not to import British goods.

If Sutherland hinted he might side with the Congress, Meeks would have an opening to swing much of the Tory crowd to his side and assault the Scotsman. It would then be a sharp fight, for many would stand by Owen Sutherland.

Jones saw another Sutherland ally: Dressed more like an Indian than a white man, with feathers and a red *voyageur* waistband, was stocky Jacques Levesque, a French-Canadian partner in the company. With him was the stout merchant, Jean Martine, and Angélique—Martine's pretty, raven-haired daughter, and Levesque's wife. The native French of Detroit liked Sutherland, too, even though they despised the *Anglais* for having conquered New France and taken it into the British Empire. It was uncertain on which side the French would stand in any general battle fought among the *Anglais*.

Jones looked along the deck to the narrow door of his cabin. It was open, and that was good, for if things got too hot, he could make a quick retreat and lock himself in. If heads were to be cracked, Farley Jones intended keeping his own safely out of reach.

As Owen Sutherland made his way through the human corridor that led toward the platform of planks that had been built on a rise overlooking the blue, rushing river, he turned over and over the words he would say to the worried residents of Detroit. He hardly noticed the many new faces in the crowd, for his mind was full with the crisis breaking over the three million people in British America—a crisis that affected remote Detroit as much as it plagued rebellious Boston.

That city's port had been forcibly closed to commerce and its provincial assembly forbidden by Parliament to meet until the Massachusetts Bay Colony had been punished for violent disobedience to London's rule. Objecting to Parliament's harshness, the colonies were speaking out in support of Massachusetts, showing a unified front that astonished the entire British Empire.

Everyone collecting here on the grass above the wide Detroit River had heard of the four thousand English soldiers quartered on unhappy Bostonians because of colonists destroying British tea rather than paying duties on it. Civil conflict was breaking out— bloody riots, attacks on government officials, and counterraids by loyalist supporters were forcing matters to a destructive climax.

The question was no longer one of intellectual theory, but rather which side an American took when the fighting broke out in his own community. There were many who already stood on one side or the other simply because a disliked neighbor had chosen the opposite position. There were others who hated all authority or whose poverty had driven them to desire a change of rule, no matter how turbulent the change. They had nothing to lose. Then there were those who were prosperous and had much to lose. Most of these wanted peace for its own sake, even if the rule of law kept the British bootheel on America's neck.

It was time for a decision, and Owen Sutherland had made his. He was no longer neutral.

Hands reached out to touch him, to grasp his own, and words of encouragement and greeting were on every side from dozens of familiar faces. But Sutherland knew that in the next few moments he would have many enemies where there had been friends. He might be despised and cast out by those very folk whose respect meant much to him. Even Tamano might turn his back, for surely many Indians would consider him their enemy.

Sutherland was taller than most men, with light-gray eyes and a head of curly black hair, and he was still lean and graceful at forty-seven. His commanding presence gave no hint of the turmoil he felt. He half turned, sensing someone by his side. Ella was at his shoulder, and lightly touched his hand. She alone knew the decision he had made in the long journey home from Philadelphia. Though English-born, Owen's beautiful fair-haired wife had lived in America for almost half of her forty years and shared his vision of united colonies with their own government that represented all people fairly. They would no longer be a subjugated, disjointed number of quarreling colonies without a voice to shape their destiny. They would govern themselves for their own good, not for the benefit of merchants and lords at home in Britain.

As he reached the wooden platform and prepared to go up the steps, Sutherland took his wife's hand in his; their children, Benjamin and Susannah—ages ten and eight—clutched at his waist. At that moment his name was shouted and the crowd began to applaud. His heart skipped.

"What will they say after they hear me?" he asked Ella, the noise of the crowd almost drowning out his voice.

She drew a shaking breath. "Many will think you damnably wrong. The rest will know you are bound by love for our country. But, Owen"—she gripped his arm—"have you seen the men from Cullen's ship? They're in among the crowd."

He took her hand again and said, "I've seen them and know who they are." He released her hand and eased the children back with a kind word. His eyes met Ella's. "Have a care. If worst comes to worst, get the youngsters away immediately."

Ella promised with a nod and drew the children to her as Owen turned and stepped up onto the platform, the claymore hanging at his side seeming to be part of him. As he stood before the shouting, cheering mob, he slowly raised his hands. In that moment he was grateful for the presence of friends so close by, even though Tamano and Levesque would be distressed to hear him speak, to learn that he had chosen to support the Continental Congress against Parliament. Congress had shown little love for Indians or Frenchmen. Still, Sutherland knew they would stand by him if there was trouble today.

"Friends," he began, his deep voice lifting over the crowd and echoing off the rough timber walls of Fort Detroit. "You asked me to go to Philadelphia and to inform you of the unhappy struggle afflicting our country.

"This is no time for ceremony, flowery talk, persuasion, or for flattery; I'll tell what I know and what I believe, and you can take it or leave it, like it or not."

He paused, looking over the crowd, seeing Hugh Meeks in its midst, and marking him as Cullen's man. Sutherland already knew about Meeks, because nothing of importance at Detroit escaped him. For a moment he held the surprised Meeks's gaze, the seaman half closing that left eye but unable to assume the squinting pose that disarmed so many.

Then Sutherland released Meeks and delivered his message to the crowd.

"Parliament insists Americans bend our knees to plead forgiveness, and the lords overseas will not rest until we've been humiliated and subjected to a permanent loss of liberty. The punishment of Massachusetts, with the closing of Boston harbor and the virtual military rule of General Thomas Gage, is but a first step of the master plan for complete tyranny over all of us, and we'll be sheared like sheep and kept docile only to profit London!"

Congress party supporters shouted in agreement, and a group of them began to blare the popular song, "Revolutionary Tea." This impudent ditty, coming as it did from advocates of the Boston Tea Party, sparked anger among the loyalist majority, who shouted down the song and called upon Sutherland to continue his message. The laughter of the men backing Boston and the Philadelphia Congress died away, and Sutherland went on.

"In Philadelphia, leading men from twelve American colonies have spoken out! These, the best men of our land, have debated these matters. Conservative and radical alike have reached an agreement for the sake of unity and the liberty of all."

As Sutherland spoke, an undercurrent of approving mutterings or angry objections passed through the crowd. Some of Meeks's crewmen, handing a bottle of rum around, tried to shout insults at Congress and at Sutherland, but a sharp look from their master told them to bide their time. Their moment would come soon enough.

"There exists a new government within a government—a body of elected committees approved by Congress—and every city, county, town, and village has chosen respected men to regulate court justice and enforce nonimportation. These committees have

taken full charge of law and order in most colonies, and any who
speak in favor of the crown, any who attempt to buy or sell British
tea, hats, furniture—anything that must be imported—are in danger of arrest or even banishment from their communities."

Someone cried out shrilly, "And a coat of tar and feathers, if
the rascals survive ridin' the rail!"

The crowd rumbled, a few agreeing that tar and feathers was
fitting punishment for any who opposed Congress. But the majority
complained that the tyranny of Parliament was being traded for
the tyranny of the mob. Abruptly, feelings ran very high, the mood
fast turning ugly. Shouting and insults mounted to a crescendo.
Sutherland stood quietly, noting a dozen soldiers of the fort's watch
being assembled near the gate in case fighting broke out.

Once more he thought it had been a mistake for his family and
those of his friends to have been brought here. He leaned over to
Ella and asked her to take the children away. Trying not to reveal
fear, Ella pushed her youngsters through the crowd past Jeb Grey's
family toward Tamano's group. A look from one to the other
confirmed that all the children and women should get into the fort,
and other folk soon had the same idea.

Before Ella and the rest had gone far, though, the angry crowd
hemmed them in, trying to get close to the speaker's platform to
shout Owen down or to hear what he said. Sutherland noted Ella's
distress and touched his claymore hilt.

Suddenly a grating voice lifted above the rest, demanding, "An'
be ye a bootlicker of the Congress party, Mr. Sutherland?"

The crowd hushed. Many wanted to hear that answered, for
Sutherland's opinion meant much to them. The Scotsman looked
reluctantly away from Ella and stared at the speaker—Hugh Meeks.
This time the man was posed, squinting, prepared for Sutherland's
response.

Before Sutherland could reply, Meeks pressed, "If ye be for
the king, then ye favor doin' away with this traitorous embargo!
If ye be true to yer brother traders all around us, who sent ye to
Philadelphee, then ye must wish a pox on them Congress rats what
care not a farthin' for us, but only want power for themselves!
What d'ye say to that, Mr. Sutherland?"

A few others, mostly Meeks's seamen, shouted in support,
calling for a definite answer and no lawyer's talk. Sutherland
hesitated, for Ella was still unable to get out of the mob, which
was pushing even closer to the platform. He wanted to keep things
calm at least until bystanders were clear of danger.

"I oppose anyone who denies me freedom or liberty," he said

to the crowd, "whether they be a committee supporting Congress or a lord in Parliament."

"An' who, at this delicate moment, do ye back, then?" Meeks went on, grinning out of one side of his mouth.

Sutherland said, "I stand for the rights of everyone out here. Those rights must be protected by the government in power, but the fact is that Parliament is no longer in power in most of British America and will never be again unless she respects the liberty of all Americans."

The crowd seethed at that, some cheering, others growing furious, then shifted visibly, separating into two groups on opposite sides of the slope. On the right were the loyalist folk, aroused to hear that royal governors and loyalists were without political strength save in the city of Boston, where Gage and four thousand men were fortified against a hostile population. On Sutherland's left were those who agreed with Congress—Jeb Grey and Tom Morely among them. This second group was outnumbered two to one, but it was determined not to yield to the strength of the loyalist party.

Sutherland said loudly, "I told you there is no use for ceremony or for flowery language this morning; it's enough to say British rule in America will never be the same again." Loyalists shouted and shook their fists; supporters of Congress stood with arms folded, smug and pleased to hear this.

"Britain will never again control the colonies without intelligent change of policies unless she resorts to force, to sending the army—"

"Let her send the army, then!" roared a smallish man, well-dressed and prosperous, whose face was purple with rage. "And the navy, and the constables and hangmen of London if need be to bring this country back to its senses!"

Dawson Merriwether, a middle-aged Virginia merchant, had prospered in the Indian trade and despised the idea of commerce with Britain being cut off as Congress had decreed. Merriwether, a dashing image of wealth in a lavender coat and silk stockings, shook his hat at Sutherland and cried, "Sir, you speak as though the rebellious scoundrels of Congress have already defeated Parliament! Can you, a former British officer, dare to believe that any colonial militia rabble could challenge the Empire and triumph?"

Loyalists applauded, and a few Redcoats standing nearby made loud jest of the fighting abilities of Americans. Their barbs, however, were returned with taunts from loyalist and Congress party advocates alike, and the soldiers shut up lest they become the targets of the mob's anger.

Standing in the crowd, a plain, middle-aged woman, beautifully clothed and carrying a folded parasol, gaped at Dawson Merriwether, fear in her eyes, as he addressed the people. Claudia Merriwether was worried that her husband was so incensed and outspoken about the Continental Congress. Sutherland took note of Claudia and wished she would depart to safety. One by one, other women and children were leaving the crush of folk, for there was a tension in the air that foreboded harm. Bravely, she stayed by her husband, though she was clearly terrified.

Sutherland spoke again. "To overcome the popular movement sweeping America would require fifty thousand soldiers and the entire Royal Navy! Britain has fewer than half that number of troops in all the world, but even should she raise such an army, and garrison every village in America, still the movement would not be snuffed out. The colonies are too large, the people too scattered for Redcoats to conquer and subjugate us for very long. The cost of governing America by military rule would be ruinous to Britain."

Merriwether screeched, "You speak too easily, sir, of bloody civil war—and civil war it will be if Congress party stooges attempt to bend us to their own brand of despotic rule! I for one will fight to my last breath, no matter if Parliament's clumsiness also angers me!"

This set off the crowd, and the Congress party howled in derision, some striking up "Revolutionary Tea" again. At her husband's insistence, Dawson Merriwether's wife drifted off, and Sutherland was glad to see her out of harm's way. Taunts were hurled at Merriwether, who ignored the insults and declared himself unswervingly behind Parliament, royal governors, and the rule of established law.

Merriwether then demanded to know if Congress intended to foster war that would ruin America, and Sutherland had to reply, "I do not want civil war, nor does any man who was at the Philadelphia Congress!" He was distracted to see Ella give up trying to get through; she huddled the children close to her, with Sally, determined and plucky, at her side. Most other families had left the crowd, which was now almost all male and increasingly surly. If Sutherland could not pacify them, it would do no good to leave the platform and try to get his family away. Fighting might erupt at any moment, and the scene become a rampage.

Sutherland said loudly, "The hour has come for a free America—"

"Ye mean *independent* America?" Hugh Meeks blared, and the silence that came over the crowd was oppressive.

Sutherland said, "I do not favor independence, but rather a government in America equal to that of Parliament." Someone threw a bottle that struck him squarely on the chest. He did not flinch, knowing it had come from one of Meeks's tipsy followers. He was glad to see Merriwether and a few others chase the fellow to the outskirts of the crowd.

"It may soon be," he said with a slight smile, "that America will become so great and powerful that Parliament will be forced to sit in Philadelphia, and Britain will become our colony."

That got a hearty laugh, easing the tension. Most men here resented England's haughtiness, though they differed in how to voice opposition to blundering British rule. In this moment Sutherland looked again for his family. It startled and angered him that they were surrounded by Meeks's crewmen, who obviously prevented their departure. Shock rippled through him. He glanced at Jeb Grey and Tom Morely, who caught his meaning and took note of Ella's group. Pushing through the crowd to join her, Tom went to Sally's side, taking the girl's arm. One of Meeks's men must have said something, for Morely turned to him and poked a thick finger against his nose. The sailor, stung and surprised, stepped back, then came toward Tom, who nonchalantly rapped the man a blow between the eyes, dropping him to his knees.

The other toughs moved as one, but Jeb was there, too, and Sally snatched a tomahawk from Tom's belt, threatening with it, so that the seamen thought twice and looked around for Meeks, who was busy heckling Sutherland.

Ella hurried her family and Sally away just as Meeks bellowed, "Answer, Sutherland: Be ye for or against that mangy, rebel-kissin' Congress?"

Without hesitation, Sutherland answered, "I stand for the Congress and for a united America!"

"Rebellion!" someone shouted, but Sutherland spoke in quick reply.

"Not rebellion, friends! Though you may call it revolution—revolution of the political wheel; revolution from tyranny and Parliament to the wheel's proper place in the natural order of things!"

"Treason!" Meeks shouted and looked for his men to support him. The soldiers advanced down from the fort, moving slowly, ready for an outbreak.

Sutherland cried, "It would be treason to my king and country if I ignored the tyranny of Parliament, which grinds our free people into the dust! It would be worse than treason to wait placidly while our chains are forged, as they are being forged at this very moment in hostaged Boston!"

"Rebel!"

"Get down, Sutherland, before we drag you down!"

"He should be strung up!"

Sutherland stood, feet apart, as the crowd of loyalists surged close, the followers of Meeks in the fore. Congress party supporters, with Jeb and Tom, moved together in response, both forces collecting before coming to blows. Sutherland did not want this. He shouted above the tumult, "Stand fast! Stand fast, before it's too late!"

chapter 2

AN ENEMY'S TERMS

Dawson Merriwether jumped up on the platform, waving his arms and calling frantically for calm, but a belaying pin flew from the crowd and knocked him brutally to his knees. Sutherland whipped out his claymore and fended off another pin. He hauled the stunned Virginian to shelter under the platform, then climbed up again to shout for order. But clubs and stones were flying, and the soldiers were suddenly set upon by Meeks's men. Others began to clamber onto the platform. These were not men from the *Helen*, but angry traders and their employees who hated Sutherland's stand. Jacques Levesque sprang up to his friend's aid.

Sutherland sheathed his sword and took on these men with his bare fists. It pained him to see former comrades in the trade suddenly become fierce enemies—but it hurt more when one caught him a stinging blow to the ear. Sutherland pounded them, his temper getting the better of him, and with Levesque at his side, he bloodied heads and blackened eyes. All the while he wanted to get at Hugh Meeks, but the man was nowhere in sight.

More loyalists and a few seamen battled their way onto the platform, almost overwhelming Sutherland and Levesque. Then, with a war whoop, Tamano stormed into the fray, with Little Hawk fighting beside him. Others of the Congress party, including Jeb Grey and Tom Morely, collected into a tight knot, and in a rushing assault, drove the loyalists back into the ranks of twenty more startled regulars who had been mustered out to stop the riot.

The meadow swarmed with brawlers. The soldiers, being the most visible targets, took on fighters from both sides and absorbed the brunt of the anger. Sutherland leaped from the platform and fought his way through a tangle of grappling men, seeking out Hugh Meeks. Few could match Sutherland for raw strength and fighting ability, and one loyalist after the other went down before him. Then he saw Meeks, delighting in the fracas, knocking heads and whacking away with his belaying pin. The seaman clubbed Jean Martine, then spotted Sutherland. They made for each other as though no one else stood between them.

Meeks unsheathed his cutlass, a devilish grin on his face, and Sutherland brought his claymore to bear. Nearby fighters were transfixed as these two squared off with cold steel, just yards from each other. At the last moment, Meeks hesitated, as though something kept him from attacking. Sutherland thought it might be a ruse to throw him off guard.

Suddenly, into the melee burst fifty fresh soldiers, long bayonets flashing in the sunlight, their hoarse battle cry like a roaring wave as they drove into the breach, driving back Whig and Tory alike. They used musket butts to good purpose, but it was the threat of the bayonet—the weapon that had conquered the Empire—that cowed the mob. In the rush of scarlet and steel, Sutherland was cut off from Meeks, and confusion was everywhere. Meeks disappeared to avoid the soldiers, and most of the people fled, many dragging injured friends away. Others, too slow to recover their senses, were arrested on the spot. The dazed Merriwether was helped off by employees of his firm, but he was not seriously hurt.

Bloodied and bruised, Sutherland climbed back onto the platform and called down for the officer of the day to get a surgeon for the wounded. Lieutenant Mark Davies, a stern, tall man of thirty, was almost hysterical as he tried to reassemble his men. Wiping the blood from his painfully cut lip, he heard Sutherland shout to him and turned in fury. His white wig was askew, exposing cropped red hair.

"You damn rebel!" the officer howled. "You began this rabble-rousing, and you and your traitorous kind will pay for it! Men, arrest him!"

Though surrounded by six bayonets pointing at him, Sutherland bristled. The officer clumsily struggled onto the platform, stepped forward, and swung the hilt of his sword at Sutherland's face. In a flash, Davies found himself lifted bodily, high over the Scotsman's head and looking down at his dumbfounded men. Shaking the astonished lieutenant like a sack of rags, Sutherland shouted at a young soldier with a bayonet.

"Hold up that pig-sticker, Private, and catch this dolt by the arse!" He made as if to throw the officer, and the private pulled back his bayonet lest this wild man actually make him run his superior through.

With a disgusted growl, Sutherland tossed the lieutenant onto the platform, and Davies rolled awkwardly, tumbling off the other side, dazed and shocked. Sutherland jumped down and motioned to the private.

"Take me to Captain Lernoult. About face! Quick march!"

The soldier, confused and startled, half obeyed, half appealed to Sutherland, "Please, sir, Mr. Sutherland, sir . . ."

But the Scotsman was already striding up the slope to the water gate, through the fight's debris, stepping over groggy rioters. The private glanced back at his lieutenant, who was sprawled on the ground. Then he hurried after Sutherland, acting as though he were the trader's guard.

At the gate, Ella and the children flew into Sutherland's arms. He quieted them and said he would be back to their home across the river by nightfall. Ella knew it was best he confront the commander right away, but she feared for him.

"Go over to Valenya, Ella," he said, touching her cheek where a tear streaked it. "Captain Lernoult is sensible. But I likely won't be in time for supper."

Ella felt at a bruise under his left eye, and he winced, trying to smile. She shook her head but said nothing. Lettie Grey came to them with her husband Jeb and son Tom, both of whom sported a few lumps. Her ruddy face flushed, Lettie seemed more excited than upset at her men's injuries, and taking these two by the arms, she said to Sutherland that it had been a stand to be proud of.

"Them Tories'd be runnin' to ground yet if the soldiers hadn't interfered, Owen! Thee done us right proud today with thy fine talk, and to be sure thy Congress party can count on us to fight when the likes of Cullen's crew start raisin' hell!"

Jeb, beefy and fair-haired, grinned and put an arm around his wife, who still spoke in the accent of northern England, her home until fifteen years ago when first she came to America with her late husband. Jeb said she was underestimating the Tories. "If the soldiers hadn't come down when they did, I was about to call on you, darlin', to play a tattoo on one of Cullen's sailors for me!"

Sutherland's guard cleared his throat in embarrassment, and the Scotsman took leave of the others. The private followed him into the fort's parade ground, where many people were helping friends and relations to limp homeward or nurse wounds. As Sutherland made his way toward the commandant's whitewashed residence, Detroit seemed changed somehow. After years living at the straits, honored and respected by the military, this was the first time Owen Sutherland felt he did not belong here.

Where once there had been friends and companions in arms, there were new officers, new soldiers, even new trade regulations. He was hardly known to many Redcoats here, and few knew that he had saved the fort and helped make peace during Chief Pontiac's great uprising. To most soldiers, twelve years after Sutherland's heroism in that terrible war, he was only another leading trader.

As he stepped onto the porch of the officer's residence, he heard a commotion at the western gate and turned around. The furious Lieutenant Davies came rapidly into the fort, his nervous men quick-stepping behind as he made straight for the commandant's house.

"You'll have my written report within the hour!" cried Lieutenant Davies. He almost stumbled out the door of the commandant's office, then turned to shout back, "But, by thunder, Captain, if my request for an immediate transfer is not granted, I'll resign my commission forthwith, and then we'll see whether General Gage approves of rabble-rousers being let off unpunished!"

Straightening his wig, Davies stormed away, leaving the front door wide open until a sentry discreetly closed it.

Inside Captain Richard Lernoult's office, Sutherland sat waiting for the fort's commander to speak. Weary and nettled, Lernoult leaned on a small writing desk with his eyes closed, fingers tented to his lips. His wig was nearby on its stand, and he was without his scarlet coat, which hung behind the door. Sighing and leaning back in the chair, Lernoult opened his eyes. In his white blouse, and without his stock, he looked more like a harried businessman than military ruler over one-third of the British Empire in America.

Lernoult was about five years younger than Sutherland, short and slim, with a lithe body hardened by years of wilderness warfare. His dark hair was short, and his brown eyes were bloodshot, shadowed by the responsibility of keeping peace in the past unhappy months at Detroit. The constant irritations caused by civil conflict had worn on his nerves, but so far he had been fair in mediating or preventing difficulties. Admired and respected by his subordinates, Lernoult seldom came into opposition with other soldiers. Now, however, he had set young Lieutenant Davies against him by declining to punish Sutherland severely, and imposing only a token fine.

Sighing again, Lernoult said, "Davies would have been troublesome just now no matter what I did to you, short of arresting you and clapping you in irons for the winter, Mr. Sutherland."

Lernoult earlier had flatly objected to Davies's demand for Sutherland to be brought to trial because of the riot and the physical abuse the lieutenant had suffered. Lernoult had seen the outbreak from the fort's ramparts, noting that hotheads had begun the brawl, not the Scotsman.

Sutherland replied, "Perhaps I should apologize to Davies for having treated him so roughly, Captain, but in the heat of the moment, he went for me."

Lernoult rubbed his eyes, the strain he was under showing in his pallid face. "I'm surprised Davies did not call you out for a duel, Mr. Sutherland, but apparently he has more sense than that." Lernoult laughed to himself, musing, "Davies probably assumed you'd choose Indian axes to duel in a birch boat—though you may lay to it that he's a capable woodsman, and the Eighth Regiment has no better liaison with the Indians than he."

They spoke at length, Lernoult asking about affairs in the East and about Philadelphia in particular. The officer even invited Sutherland to dine with him.

After the meal Sutherland reached into a pocket of his buckskin shirt and drew out a wallet with British five-pound notes. Counting out several and handing them over to Lernoult, he remarked, "Perhaps doubling the fine to buy grog for your troops will ease some of the bitterness, Captain."

"The rank and file will drink your health, Mr. Sutherland; would that it were so easy with Davies." Getting up along with Sutherland, he walked to the door. "I intend to grant the lieutenant's request—so he'll have his transfer, and that'll keep you both apart."

Sutherland departed, stepping into the soft sunshine of a cool afternoon. He was anxious to get back to Valenya and went quickly out of the crowded fort toward the river, where he had left his canoe hauled up on shore. Before going home he would visit Dawson Merriwether, who lived a short distance upriver. Sutherland hoped the fellow had not been badly hurt, and he would try to make amends before matters between them became too serious.

As Sutherland reached the water's edge, passing the wreckage of the platform the loyalists had torn apart, he took note of the ship *Helen*. She was a trim, clean vessel, newly painted and well rigged, showing Sutherland that Meeks was a first-class master who knew his business. A few sailors with bandages around their heads or arms in slings were lounging on deck, but Meeks was not in sight. Wrath burned within Sutherland, and he was barely able to restrain himself from going aboard and challenging the man. He thought better of it, for another serious conflict between Whig and Tory would only intensify hatreds here and would surely lead to more fighting. Yet if Meeks pushed matters the slightest bit further, he would find Owen Sutherland at his throat.

Sutherland realized abruptly that his canoe was not on the beach where he had left it. Then he heard his name cried in a nasal, shivering voice, and he saw Farley Jones beckoning from the deck of the *Helen*. There, tied up under the vessel's stern, was Sutherland's canoe.

That was more than he would take. Without hesitation, he crossed the beach to the landing, and as men nearby stopped to watch, he strode up the ship's gangplank, hand on his sword hilt. Jones met him, teeth clacking as he said, "It wasn't my idea to move the canoe, but Master Meeks wanted to be sure you didn't leave without seeing him—"

Sutherland pushed by, saying, "I'll see him now."

Other sailors moved as though to slow Sutherland or to keep him from breaking down the cabin door, but at the sight of his rage they hesitated as he passed. Sutherland went to the low cabin door, rammed it open, and stepped inside, ready for anything.

"Welcome, Sutherland." Complacently grinning, Hugh Meeks sat at a folding table in the center of the small cabin, which was as neat and orderly as the rest of the vessel. There were two glasses and a flask of brandy on the table, as though he had expected Sutherland's arrival. Meeks had assumed his squinting pose.

Sutherland closed the door and bolted it, leaving the uneasy crewmen outside. "Put the canoe back, or strap on your cutlass."

Meeks leaned back on two legs of his chair and spoke softly, almost sweetly. "Beggin' yer pardon for makin' so bold with yer boat, but I had a notion to meet ye, face to face like, and as ye can see, I made some headway against the wind, eh? Will ye splice the mainbrace with an old salt?"

"Stow it, Meeks." Sutherland dragged a chair over and sat down. "What do you want?"

The shipmaster chuckled and poured two glasses of fine brandy. Clinking the bottle on the table, he offered Sutherland a glass but was refused. The leering squint left him, exchanged for a brooding solemnity.

"By the powers, Sutherland, but ye're hard on a lad what desires to make yer acquaintance on peaceful terms!" He downed the drink in one gulp, smacked his lips, and said with a cackle, "Aye, that were a lively tussle we had this mornin', though it'd been livelier had you and me come to grips!"

"We might yet." Sutherland's legs were stretched out before him, his arms folded. "If you don't make your point soon, we surely will."

Meeks chuckled again, then downed the second brandy. He put the glass on the table and nodded to a brace of pistols and the sword belt hanging on the wall near his cot. "If I'd wanted ye dead, Sutherland, I'd have come for ye, soldiers or no. I want only to talk just now about our mutual acquaintance, Bradford Cullen; so if ye'll be gentleman enough, I swear yer Injun boat'll be laid by directly where'er ye choose."

Sutherland said nothing. Meeks grinned and squinted. The ship rocked gently in the drift of current from the river, and Sutherland heard men whispering outside the door.

Meeks wiped his chin. "I be under strict orders from Mr. Cullen himself to speak private-like, and pass along his terms . . . his truce terms, ye might say."

"You're wasting my time, Meeks." Sutherland stood up. "Cullen and I'll never come to terms, not till I've seen him permanently in irons."

Meeks groaned and waved Sutherland to sit, but got nowhere. Then he became cold, the half-closed eye glinting in sunlight from the cabin's windows. "It don't do no good to go off without hearin' these generous terms, Sutherland, not in such touchy times it don't. See here, Mr. Cullen's offerin' ye half share in governin' the northwest—aye, the whole northwest! Nothin' less. And he's the lad what can deliver the very same into yer hands."

Sutherland knew Cullen had curried considerable influence in Tory circles, and that belief was confirmed when Meeks said the wealthy merchant was well in with General Gage and British members of Parliament. Meeks said they were willing to make him governor at Montreal, administrator of all Lower Canada, the Great Lakes, and the enormous country west of the Ohio River. In turn, the Tories wanted Cullen to guarantee that the northwest and the lucrative fur trade would be closed to Whig agitators who wanted to break with British influence.

Pouring another brandy, Meeks went on, "My employer's a crafty one, he is, and he knows when he's about licked. Yer company's just about got him licked in the northwest fur trade, but the tables'll be turned if ye lean too far to Whiggism and rile the Tories."

"Why does he want to make a pact with me if he's so sure the Tories will dominate the northwest?"

"That's just it. He knows he can't dominate it without a hard, costly fight against ye; but if ye was to throw in with him and the Tories—with the loyal folk who the king has taken to his bosom— then Mr. Cullen'll guarantee, in writin', to give ye the lieutenant-governorship right here at Detroit!" Meeks cackled and drew a deep breath. "A pretty ripe plum that'd be for a man with yer connections in the trade, eh? Ye'd be richer than a prince within five years!"

"Meeks," Sutherland said slowly, "Cullen may be cozy with Tories and generals, but it won't be Tories and generals who'll have the final say in the colonies, nor in the northwest. I want no part of his conspiracy. Tell him he'll have to get past me before he'll rule out here."

Meeks nodded, smacking his lips and saying, "Now here comes a blessed hard thing for the likes of me; a blessed hard thing, Mr. Sutherland." His expression darkened as he squinted at the Scotsman. "There be more to Mr. Cullen's message: If ye won't make terms with him"—his face became pinched, eyes aflame, despite his sugary voice—"then Mr. Cullen'll take steps to condemn all Whigs at Detroit, discredit 'em so bad that loyal folks'll lynch 'em and leave 'em dryin' on execution dock."

Sutherland almost went for him, but Meeks held up his hands, saying, "You may lay to it that this old salt ain't speakin' for hisself—not as yet—but for our Mr. Cullen, who be the crustiest, vengefullest lubber I ever laid eyes on!" Favoring Sutherland with a sly wink, Meeks softened once more and said, "Now, let's have that drink, and we'll talk square and sensible, by the powers!"

Sutherland unbolted the door. "There's no more to say."

Meeks's expression altered from cunning to threatening.

"Mark me, Sutherland, ye're on the wrong side in this game! Cullen's had all he'll stomach of yer interference. This is his final offer!"

Sutherland opened the door. Three big seamen stood in the

way. He said to Meeks, "Tell your dogs to get my canoe ready."

"Get it yourself," Meeks hissed.

Sutherland drew the claymore, a steely, rasping sound that surprised the three crewmen. They growled and showed knives and pistols.

They were all distracted by a voice calling from shore. "Owen! Owen Sutherland!" It was the blacksmith, Bill Poole, a New Englander who led the local Sons of Liberty. Sometimes known as Liberty Boys, these men were violent radicals organized in a fraternity to oppose Parliament and Tories. "Fetch Mr. Sutherland, you there," Poole shouted at Jones, who was near the gangplank, "or we come aboard!" Staring wide-eyed at the cabin door, where Sutherland confronted Meeks and the crewmen, the clerk made a shivering sound of relief to hear Meeks grumble and relent.

"Isaac," Meeks said, and one of the men at the door glanced around, though keeping a pistol aimed at Sutherland.

"Cap'n?"

"Give this Injun back his boat—where he wants it." Meeks sat back. "Mr. Cullen would fault me if'n I cross swords with ye afore he wants it. He'd rather ye were with him, but if ye won't join now, we got our ways to persuade ye."

Sutherland pushed past the men at the door; they moved reluctantly and muttered as he sheathed the sword. Farley Jones slipped out of the way, and Sutherland descended the gangplank. He wondered just what Cullen was up to. The offer of alliance might be genuine, or it could be an attempt by the Boston merchant to draw him into some intrigue that would drive a wedge between him and others in the Frontier Company. Whatever Cullen had in mind, if the man tried to wrest control of the northwest, it would be all-out war. Since Hugh Meeks was the tip of Cullen's lance, Sutherland intended to watch him closely.

As Sutherland stepped on shore, he was met by burly Bill Poole and a half-dozen men known to be members of the Sons. Grateful for their concern, he shook Poole's hand, asking what he wanted.

A short, black-bearded man who had a barrel chest, with curly hair over his arms, Poole was respected in the settlement but known for his terrible temper. His keen, glittering eyes seemed to observe everything, and though he was poorly educated, he was intelligent and completely honest. Glancing from Sutherland to the ship, Poole spoke in a deep, slow voice.

"I heard you went aboard with fire in your eye, and we feared for your safety, Owen." The others spoke in agreement. Like

Poole, who was from Connecticut, these Sons of Liberty were mostly New England Yankee artisans—tanners, shoemakers, a hatmaker, and an apprentice wheelwright. They were all decent men, though headstrong and easily stirred to a fight over politics, particularly when it came to the hated British regulations controlling what colonials could manufacture and sell. They were all in the same situation, having come out west in the hope of making a new start. They had dreamt of a wild, untouched country, free of severe regulations and controls, but they had been misinformed. All supported the trade embargo, and each had a share of bruises and cuts from the morning's brawl.

"Don't worry about me, lads," Sutherland replied, watching a member of the *Helen*'s crew haul his canoe to shore. "I just had a chat with Cullen's man."

Poole grinned. "We thought you were gonna end what you and Meeks started today, and we didn't want to miss anythin'!" They all guffawed, and then Poole became more serious. "Actually, Owen, we been talkin', and we want to meet with you right away. Will you come to the smithy? It's urgent."

Sutherland wanted to get home to Valenya, yet he respected these men and knew them as important leaders in the small Whig faction at Detroit. He agreed to go to Poole's little shop on Saint Germain Street, near the fort's vegetable garden and the stable for officers' mounts. As they walked together, Sutherland saw several new clapboard buildings in the fort, all painted white. Most were workshops that replaced the old French log cabins, which were deteriorating.

Poole's smithy stood at the back of a building he rented, and the group went to it through a front room, where all sorts of ironwork from axes to hinges were on display. Hung on walls, standing on the floor, or laid upon shelves, the fruits of two years of Poole's labor were here for buyers to inspect. Upstairs, Poole and two others lived in a small apartment. One was an unmarried French *habitant* he had hired, the other a twelve-year-old apprentice who supported a widowed mother, his father having been a soldier killed by Indians. All the blacksmith's savings and tools had gone into this business, but he could not yet afford to send for his wife and three children waiting at home in New Haven. As Sutherland went into the shop, he complimented Poole on his accomplishments in such a short time, saying Ella and he would come to buy next week.

"Thank you, Owen. It's seldom enough I have a customer these days, for the Tories are reluctant to come lest they be accused of patronizing a radical Whig. And the Whigs are too impoverished by government restrictions."

Poole led the way into the large smithy. A new fieldstone forge stood in the center, its massive chimney reaching up through the roof. Behind it was an enormous bellows made of a whole oxhide, which forced air into the charcoal fire, making it fierce enough to soften iron.

Poole's axes were valued greatly from Michilimackinac to St. Louis, but he was forbidden to ship them to Spanish territory or even back to Niagara. To prevent industrious colonials from man-ufacturing goods that would be cheaper than British goods, British regulations forbade the trade of certain items between colonies. Also, rules against direct colonial trade with other nations severely hampered ambitious men such as Poole, who had the ability and the will to expand his business far beyond the local market. The heavy hand of Parliament was on his neck at every turn.

The men gathered in the forge room, which was lighted by several good glazed windows. In one corner, the boy apprentice clanged away at nail rod, using only a few deft hammer blows to shape a point and cut three-inch nails one after the other, seven to the minute.

Poole asked the lad to hold off while they talked, and the clanging stopped, leaving the room hushed as the men found places on workbenches and overturned crates, or leaned against the plank walls. Each knew they must keep their discussion secret, lest a spy betray them and accuse them of plotting treason against the king. They latched the doors and checked the windows for any sign of loyalists walking nearby. As Poole pondered what he would say, Sutherland examined a rotatable gridiron used for cooking, then said Ella would like to have one.

Poole answered, "So would every wife from here to St. Louis; however, I'm only allowed to sell one a month in the settlement, and duty officers won't let me ship 'em out in quantity. They do this so I can't compete with Britishers. I tell you, Owen, things ain't no better for me than they were back in New Haven." Toying with a heavy set of four-foot iron forge tongs as though they were weightless, Poole continued, "In fact everything's dearer out here than at home! It galls me, and I've had all I'm gonna take of poxy Britishers tellin' me what to make and sell and to who!"

Sutherland said, "This isn't why you asked me to meet with you, is it?"

The rest became attentive as the smith cleared his throat and rested the tongs against an anvil.

"Owen, the Sons've asked me to represent them to you, and make it clear we're gonna combine our strength." He began to tap his foot, looking down at the floor as though the words were to be read on the boards. "There's more men here feel as we do, even some Frenchmen, though they ain't many yet, and if we can organize the way the Sons're organized down in the colonies—I mean if we make our move at the right time—there ain't enough troops here to stop us takin' over."

Poole hesitated, anxious for Sutherland to speak. Instead, Sutherland drew out his long-stemmed white clay pipe and a pouch of tobacco. Other pipes came out as Poole, his body leaning forward, thought a moment before going on. Sutherland passed the pouch, and pipes were filled. A man went to the windows to check for eavesdroppers.

Poole slapped his hands together. "Damn it all, Owen, you're the speechmaker, not me! What I'm sayin' is that soon enough there'll be a reckonin' between the government troops and us, and when that happens, I want to be ready for it so the Sons out here ain't all clapped in chains like so many nigger slaves! Why, I know from my old neighbors at home that the Connecticut committee alone would send us a couple hundred Sons, armed and supplied, to establish Congress's rule out here."

Poole's followers gave their assent, saying their own colonies also would send out militia companies to enforce the trade embargo at Detroit and other western posts.

Sitting back against the anvil, Sutherland heard them out, all the while quietly smoking his pipe. When they were finished, he asked what they wanted from him.

Poole said, "Lead us, Owen! Speak for us to the other traders and the Frenchies and even the Injuns if we gotta talk to 'em heathens. Persuade 'em to back us—back us or keep out of it if they know what's good for 'em."

A Massachusetts man said, "Owen, you know local committees are springing up all across the colonies, asking colonists to stop trade with Britain until Parliament stops enslaving us. But most Detroit folk are still willing to buy British. To my mind, that's downright unpatriotic, and we've got to do something about it!"

Poole asked, "Will you lead us? These Frenchies and redskins'll listen to you, even if the white traders and merchants'll need some strong persuadin'."

Someone else shook his fist, saying, "We'll persuade 'em good, and they'll stay persuaded, just like Sons do it at home, with a tar suit and a ride on the rail!"

They all spoke at once, and Sutherland disliked their threatening tone. Looking right into the blacksmith's eyes, the Scotsman was grim and hard. When they became quieter, he said, "Represent you to whom, Bill? To the likes of Mr. Merriwether, who won't be scared off? Lead you to where? To tar and feather everyone who doesn't agree with us?"

"If we must!" Poole cried, slamming his fist on a worktable so that a box of bolts jumped from the force. "If we have to tar and feather mangy dogs that support Parliament, then we'll do it! We got to take a stand for our liberty! We'll make a blacklist of Tories, like all the Sons're doin', like Congress said we should, and them what gets on it will be sorry!"

The men shouted in angry agreement, but when Sutherland stood up they became quiet. He paced, then turned back to glare at them.

"You'll soon become like any mob, thirsty for blood and drunk with power, and once you're unleashed, innocent people will be in danger from your bile and spite!"

He looked each one over, and they had to avert their faces from his cold eyes. Only Poole stared back as Sutherland spoke in a voice trembling with anger and pent-up emotion.

"What's coming over this country can be glorious, or it can be evil! The triumph of our cause will be glorious, but if the mob rises to power, then our revolution is lost! Triumph will be swept away in evil, and we'll be no better than the tyrants we depose!"

He tossed his pipe, which had gone out, onto the anvil. It rattled in the silence. "I won't lead a mob—"

Poole roared, "Lead us against our oppressors, Owen! They're our enemy and your enemy!"

"The mob is my enemy!" Sutherland declared, fury surging. "Any mob, Whig or Tory! I'll fight it! I'll fight you, any of you, who threaten me or my friends!"

Poole's hands opened and closed, his eyebrows lowering.

The Scotsman said, "I'll back a trade prohibition, and I'll go to the second Congress in Philadelphia next spring. If the British strike at us, I'll defend myself. But if you Liberty Boys start terrorizing Detroit, then you'd better run me out first, for if you don't I'll organize a force that'll cut you to ribbons and leave you face down in the straits!"

Poole was swaying on his feet. Sutherland stood opposite him. In the slanting rays of the low sun, they cast a massive shadow against the wall.

The Scotsman composed himself and said, "There's only one way, Bill, and that's to force Parliament to see she can't grind America into the dust. That'll take time and an embargo, not beatings and burnings and riding men out on rails."

Poole snorted angrily. "The only way Parliament and American Tories'll yield is if life's made hard for them, and maybe some blood's spilled."

Sutherland cut him off. "This isn't Connecticut, Poole! No mob will scare our kind of folk into obeying you or anyone! I'll tell you this: If I hear you've begun to organize to attack anyone, I'll come for you before you do."

The Sons with Poole gasped and growled, one or two getting to their feet, anticipating a fight. But the blacksmith neither gave ground nor attacked. His mind laboring, Poole's head sank slightly. "I didn't ask you here to have it out with you, Sutherland." He stared at Owen, as though trying to fathom what the man was about. "We won't touch decent folk, and we want you on our side when the time comes."

"Don't dishonor the cause by acting in a wild and unlawful manner. I'll be at your side when the time comes." Sutherland picked up the pipe and knocked ashes from it. His hands were steady, but he was raging within.

chapter 3

VALENYA

Though he was sore at heart and longed to get home, Sutherland took time out from his canoe journey to Valenya. He put ashore a mile upstream on the same side of the river as the fort, near the fine white clapboard house Dawson Merriwether had built recently. Sunset turned the house orange, and windows were golden from the light that reflected off the river.

As an important land speculator who had been prevented by the army from buying Indian lands—regulations forbade any private purchases before new treaties were formally negotiated by the government—Merriwether had become involved in the fur trade. Though he was not a partner in the Frontier Company, he often did business with Sutherland and was known for the high quality of his Virginia tobacco, which was prized by Indians.

Walking up from where his canoe rested in withered bullrushes at the river's edge, Sutherland was met by a black female garden slave who told him Mrs. Merriwether was in the parlor, her husband asleep upstairs. Sutherland went to the front door of the house, passing through a white picket fence surrounding a good lawn that had taken root that summer. In a few years the Merriwethers would have a rambling flower garden almost as lovely as the one they had left behind in the tidewater colony. Close to the house was a proud old chestnut tree towering above the shingled roof.

Even before Sutherland knocked at the door the aging Mrs. Merriwether opened it and graciously welcomed him, though distress showed in her eyes. She had changed from her walking clothes into an elegant gown imported from France, known generally as a polonaise. Though ordinary in face, Mrs. Merriwether was always perfectly made up and very conscious of her attire. She was fashionable with vast hoops under her pleated, ruffled gown, which was dark green and had a tight bodice with several white ribbons dangling at the waist.

Removing his hat, Sutherland bowed and said, "I've come to call on Mr. Merriwether, ma'am, and to apologize for what he's suffered today. I feel in part responsible."

"Please do not blame yourself, sir," said Mrs. Merriwether, who showed Sutherland into the parlor. There, amidst the finest furnishings, a tall black house slave waited to be given instructions. The Virginia woman, however, was too distracted by the thought of what had happened that day to give any orders at all, and the man stayed motionless, as though part of the bright chamber's elegant decor. Sutherland felt uncomfortable in the slave's presence, but the man seemed oblivious of him. Mrs. Merriwether invited Sutherland to sit beside her on a brocaded settee of delicately carved walnut, which matched the chairs and a massive sideboard filled with the family's silver plate.

Touching a silk handkerchief to her lips, she said in her lilting southern voice, "I had so hoped that Mr. Merriwether and I would be free of all political harassment and conflict when we left Virginia . . . but now this! Oh, Mr. Sutherland, I don't hold you responsible, not at all, for there are others here who have grievously threatened him. My husband always has been one to stand up and speak out—" She sniffed, trying to keep back tears.

They made some small talk about Sutherland's latest trip east, and he said, "By the way, we brought some books back from Philadelphia, and I know you have quite a taste for English novelists."

"Indeed!" Mrs. Merriwether's face transformed, showing joy, and she clapped her hands. "How wonderful! It's been ages since anything modern has found me here! Mr. Sutherland, as soon as my husband is rested, we'll have you and Mrs. Sutherland for a visit, and perhaps we can forget for a little while the unhappiness of late."

Leaving the room, where the butler was still standing like a statue, they went to the front door. Sutherland kissed the woman's hand, and she curtsied like a delighted young girl.

It was almost dark as Sutherland pushed off his canoe. He paddled away, wondering how good people such as the Merriwethers could keep human beings enslaved. In the northwest there was only a small number of black slaves. Most of them were experts in the wilds, and many had Indian blood. There were free black frontiersmen, too, most of them traders or trappers. The slaves out here were more on an equal footing with their masters than the slaves of the southern colonies, because the daily hazards of the wilderness made men dependent on one another. Adventurers and traders had companions—black, white, or red—who had saved them from disaster many times.

As he thought these things, Sutherland did not notice a shadow moving outside a lighted window of Merriwether's parlor. Then it was gone, slipping quickly into gathering darkness, hurrying away as though some mission had to be completed.

In the shimmer of twilight, the big white house at Valenya seemed to float beneath the starry sky. Yellow light flickered from windows, and the sounds of children laughing could be heard on the wind, mingling with the rush of the river just a hundred yards from the front door. Owen Sutherland tied the canoe to the landing, then stood up straight and stretched out his sore muscles.

Either he had taken a few too many knocks in the riot or he was getting old. Perhaps both, he thought, bending to touch the tips of his moccasins and feeling his body respond stiffly. Sutherland was strong and lithe, but no longer a youngster with inexhaustible reserves of energy. He thought about his stepson, Jeremy Bently, now sailing to Bristol, England. That fine lad was full grown, nearly as strong as Tom Morely, and quicker on his feet than even the agile Sioux, Little Hawk. He was keener of mind than both, and would be a leader in the northwest if the charms of Europe did not keep him away.

Taking his sheathed claymore from the bobbing canoe, Sutherland thought about the young man, who was soon to study medicine at Edinburgh. That was the same university where Sutherland had studied literature and philosophy a generation ago. He contemplated with some sentiment the happy memories of those years at the university. Student inns, coffeehouses, taverns, the philosophizing and gaming, romances, dancing, and singing all came back to him, like a warm rush of blood to the head.

The chill wind of approaching winter brought him back to the present. He would not exchange this place, Ella, or the life of a free trader for anything else in the world. There had been relative peace out here these past few years, though he had fought renegades, snowstorms, and the plots of Bradford Cullen. The Frontier Company he had labored so hard to build was prospering, with a great portion of the region's peltry trade under its control. Cullen and Company was still strong, but the Boston merchant was losing ground with every passing year.

Since Indians favored Sutherland's firm for the fairness of its dealing and high quality of its goods, no other consortium of traders—save for the giant Hudson's Bay Company working far in the north—could compare with the Frontier Company. All Sutherland and Ella had dreamed of and suffered for was in their grasp. Thus, it was distressing to him that America was so close to upheaval and civil warfare.

Making his way toward the house, Sutherland saw the massive outline of seven giant stones looming from the shadows a little ways off to the right. These standing monoliths, unexplainable for their existence here in the flat, wooded country around the straits, were known to Indians as the singing stones. The name was given for the way the north wind whistled as it blew through narrow spaces between them. Sutherland had lived in sight of these stones for more than fifteen years, and it was clear proof of the respect Indians held for him that they did not drive him away from this sacred place. As an adopted Ottawa who wore a green turtle tattoo on his chest, Sutherland was even considered guardian of this site. He was indeed a guardian, but for more reasons than the presence of the Singing Stones.

Sutherland paused, removed his broad hat, and gazed at a gravesite close by. While trying to maintain peace between whites and Indians shortly after the bloody French and Indian War that ended in 1763, he had lost his Ottawa wife and unborn child to the violence. She and the babe in her womb were buried here near the stones, the grave marked by a granite marker imported from his native Scotland.

Mayla would have approved of his new wife, the former Ella Bently. If not for Mayla's heroism, Ella would have died in the massacre when Pontiac attacked Fort Detroit; it was Mayla who had warned the British of the war chief's plans to take the fort by surprise.

The sound of children came to Sutherland again, the melody of a way of life so different from that of his first, primitive years here. Mayla would not have liked such a grand house as this one he had built. She would have preferred a bark lodge like Tamano's, standing in a cove a few hundred yards down the shoreline. Sutherland's house, built in 1771, was two stories high with a chimney on either side and a steep, sloping roof in the style of the French *habitant* cottage. The roof was made of cedar shingles, not the thatch of the *habitant,* and the house was sided with clapboard run horizontally, not vertically as the French favored.

Even in this dim light Sutherland thought the place quite grand for a frontier settlement. Owen and Ella loved this home, had labored with friends and neighbors to raise it, and were always ready to consider improving or refining it one way or another. Others had followed his lead and erected new frame houses nearby, including the Greys and Tom Morely. Tom's brother, James, a year younger than Tom and a studious, sober lad, managed the company warehouse in the fort proper and lived there. But none, with the exception of the Merriwethers, had erected a home with such ambition as the Sutherlands.

The kitchen was well appointed, with a wonderfully handy set of wrought-iron cranes over the hearth to hang pots and kettles. For baking, there was a brick oven set into the chimney, and the stone sink in the kitchen was the only one of its kind in the northwest. Women came often to watch Ella pump water into it— through wooden pipes that brought the water up directly from the spring house in the basement. After being used for washing vegetables or cooking utensils, the water was released through another wooden pipe into the yard, where household ducks took great delight splashing around in it.

Valenya had an entry hall that joined the front door with the back and allowed a fresh, strong breeze to pass through the house in hot weather. On either side of the front door there were real sash windows, just brought up from Philadelphia. They were so recently installed that their raw framework, needing a first coat of paint, gave off a kind of pale glow in the light coming from inside.

In building the house, Sutherland had placed four horizontal windows upstairs, two in the front and two in the back, to light and air the children's chambers, where Sally shared space with Benjamin and Susannah. Sutherland paused to look at the roof of the house and thought dormer windows would be better up there. A new room could be walled off for Sally, who was old enough to deserve her own quarters now. Poorer folk would not have imagined so much sleeping space, but both Owen and Ella came from well-to-do families and were ever interested in the latest ideas for comfortable living.

As he strolled up the pebbled lane toward his front door, he caught the fragrance of bread baking and heard Sally playing her violin in the common room. These things gave him a sense of reassurance. Sutherland opened the door, a new one of oak recently made by Tom Morely, who had become the settlement's best cabinetmaker. As he entered he was immediately surrounded. Ella hugged him, and Sally came running, violin in hand, to exclaim that she had feared he had been hurt by loyalists. The two younger children, dressed in soft cotton nightgowns, shouted for joy, saying they had seen every bit of the riot and thought it better than the best *la crosse* match between the wildest French and Indians.

Sutherland embraced them all and walked arm in arm with Ella through the bright entry hall, which was painted off-white and had a floor of polished wide pine boards that gleamed in the light of a suspended whale-oil lamp. They went into the main room, to the right of the hall, with its massive beams and plastered walls, and Sutherland thought how good it was to be home.

He had been back only a week from Philadelphia, and much of that time was spent on company affairs over at Detroit, or in the trading house run by Jeb, Lettie, Tom, and James. Another aspect of the business—dealing with French trappers and traders— was managed by Jean Martine from his own warehouse; and up at Michilimackinac on northern Lake Michigan, the Levesques maintained a third profitable trading house.

Sutherland came with his family into the welcome light of more oil lamps and a blazing fire in a wide fieldstone hearth. The warmth flooded him as he sat in his favorite hooped-back chair, taking Susannah on his lap and telling her and Benjamin they should have been in bed an hour ago.

Sutherland faced the fireplace, which covered almost the entire outside wall of the house. It was fitted with a massive walnut mantelpiece that held a porcelain vase, silver candlesticks, and an engraved silver plate from Ella's home in England. To his left was the kitchen, part of the main common room and sharing the hearth, with a bake oven to the left of the fireplace. This was an unusually large common room, and had to be so, for often there were gatherings of many Frontier Company partners. These feasts and celebrations generally included fifty guests or more, white and Indian.

On one kitchen wall hung Ella's pots, pans, and cooking utensils. On the opposite wall, and from most of the heavy beams of the ceiling, hung bunches of dried herbs, as well as strings of sliced dried apples and peaches. Ella and Sally had been busy in the few days since returning from Philadelphia, for there was much to do before winter, and they had been gone from Valenya more than three months.

At Sutherland's right, on both sides of the window, were shelves of books: volumes of poetry, essays of Voltaire and Rousseau, the writings of Ben Franklin, and the translated work of the German philosopher Jacob Boehme. There were also books on ancient civilizations, natural science, military affairs, and politics. He had read them all, and from them drew many of the ideas incorporated in his own essays. Using the voice of a fictional Indian sage named Quill, Sutherland gave the red man's viewpoint. Quill was harshly satirical but humorous when it came to commenting on the white's bad government, and his essays were widely read in America and even in Britain.

Most of Sutherland's writing was done in the bedroom at the other side of the house. Opposite his writing desk and chair was a new four-poster bed he and Ella had brought back from Phila-delphia. On the floors of every room were bright rugs woven by Sally on her loom, which was set up in a back room behind the bedroom.

In both of these rooms were small iron stoves, a new method of heating that had come west with German Pennsylvanians. These stoves were from Philadelphia, gifts of Benjamin Franklin.

The common-room fireplace had clay tile in front of it, and inlaid inside the hearth itself were blue and white tiles in the Dutch fashion that appealed so much to Ella. Heavy andirons held an iron warming tray with a pot of herb tea—English tea and coffee were not to be drunk, as a way of defying Parliament these days.

Against the side wall of the common room was Ella's spinet, the compact, delicate instrument she had played at the fort during her stay there. Playing the spinet, with its chiming, bright sound, gratified Ella no matter what her mood. The music released her, and she had the talent to please any who listened. Ten years ago, she and a few residents of the fort had organized a chamber-music group, and it still met twice a month on Sundays to play at the homes of members. Sometimes the group gave recitals for friends, although lately political differences had hardened some hearts and it was difficult to have certain people together in the same room. Between the spinet and Sally's violin, there was never a lack of music in the Sutherland home.

Ella sat down in a rocker beside Owen, troubled to see the bruises on his face, and noticing a great rip in his shirt under the buckskin. It was a miracle Owen had not suffered worse injury, and she did not mention the minor bumps he had taken, asking only whether he wanted a meal.

"No thanks, lass; Captain Lernoult and I dined in the commandant's quarters, with much to talk about." Sutherland gave a tired grin. "I'll have a mug of mulled cider, if you please, Sal, for the good fellow favors only gin and Madeira brandy and I need a country drink."

As Sally fetched cider, Sutherland told what happened at Captain Lernoult's, and Ella was relieved the punishment was not severe. She asked about Lieutenant Davies, and as Sutherland accepted a mug from Sally, he replied, "He'll cool down; he's not a bad soldier, but too dim-witted ever to be great—he'll probably make a general one day."

Ella was uneasy at her husband's casual manner after all that had occurred, but she sighed, saying, "It seems your reputation with the army is still high, even though Henry no longer commands Detroit."

Henry Gladwin, Ella's older brother, had held the fort against the Indian uprising nearly twelve years ago. Sutherland's closest friend after Tamano, Gladwin was now retired, at home in Derbyshire, England, awaiting the arrival of Jeremy from the Bristol docks. As Ella and Owen let their minds wander over the past, speaking of Gladwin, Sally became withdrawn, her blue eyes misting. She saw in her mind the handsome face of Jeremy, whom she loved so much that she hardly noticed Tom Morely's powerful feelings for her.

Now Jeremy was away in a foreign land, in company with wealthy, sophisticated people. He soon would be hobnobbing with nobles, intellectuals, free-thinkers, rich young ladies of beauty, style, and means . . . It was all too hurtful to Sally, and she tried to mask a rising sob by drinking from her mug of cider. But she choked and began coughing so that Ella and Owen saw the tears and knew they were for Jeremy.

They changed the subject, and Ella took Owen's hand, saying, "What's to become of us? All this, I'm sure, is just the beginning of more conflict at Detroit, and it may be years before it's resolved and we can live at peace again!"

Recovering, Sally blurted, "Tom says the Liberty Boys'll want to run a few Tories out on rails!" She sat down in a chair, her face showing the worry she felt for Detroit, which until now had seen little partisan violence. "I don't want them to ride anyone out on a rail. . . ."

Benjamin spoke up. "Is that when you sit on a sharp fence rail with your legs weighted down and you get splinters in your bum, Pa? I've heard some men say it's great sport!"

Ella gave a sound of despair, and Sutherland gazed at the boy, who brushed back his dark hair, his face placid and innocent. The Scotsman said, "Riding a rail is a very painful, dangerous thing, and one can be killed by it, laddie."

Susannah, fair like her mother, rolled her eyes back and proclaimed very knowingly, "Well, it's not as bad as being tarred and feathered!"

"Yes it is, too!" Benjamin objected, and Ella tried to quiet him, but he would not hush. "Riding a rail can kill, Pa said, and a tar jacket just burns a little, isn't that right, Pa?"

Sutherland and Ella exchanged glances, sorry their children's talk should be of such terrible things. Owen said they ought to scurry to bed and not think of rails or tar, for both were evil.

Reluctantly, the children did as they were told, but at the door, Benjamin turned and said, "I won't let anyone make you ride a rail, Pa—"

"Benjamin!" Ella exclaimed. "I told you not to mention that!"

As Ella shooed him from the room, the boy cried out that he had heard someone threaten to do just that to his father, but he really would not let it happen. Soon Sutherland and Sally were left alone before the fire. They sat without speaking, listening to the pop of sparks and to the soothing sound of Ella telling the children a bedtime story upstairs. After a little while, Ella came back into the room and sat down with her own cup of cider. She asked whether Owen knew who this Hugh Meeks was.

"As soon as he landed the *Helen* the other day I learned what I needed to know. Jeb Grey found Jones in the tavern and plied him with ale until enough information came out. Jones is proud to be in Meeks's company, because Hugh Meeks is legendary among West Indies pirates. It's not often a clerk can sit at table with the likes of Cap'n Meeks and live to boast about it."

Sutherland knew much about the new master of the *Helen*. Though Jones had said nothing to Jeb about the man being sent here to harry the Frontier Company, Sutherland remarked that anyone in Cullen's pay would be obliged to do his worst against the firm.

Ella said distantly, "This was not his worst today, I'll wager."

They spoke further about Cullen, and Sutherland wondered aloud whether the man would ever be brought to trial for having financed renegade pillagers a few years earlier. Sutherland had destroyed these murderers, who had preyed viciously on the northwest fur trade, and he had gathered considerable proof that Cullen had backed them. Having brought the case to the courts in Montreal, Sutherland hoped one day Cullen would be found guilty and imprisoned.

"But the courts of every colony, including those in Boston, have collapsed with all this civil strife."

Ella said, "Ah, so many were hurt and killed because of that heartless man!"

Sutherland said wearily, "Now Cullen has fled to Boston, and he's holed up there for the winter along with the British Army. No charges have been laid against him in that city yet, but I'll bring them myself if I must!"

"Do you think," Sally asked, "that if he supports the Tories in this trouble he might gain enough influence to have the case dropped?"

Sutherland was grim at this thought. After all that he had done to overcome Cullen, the possibility that the merchant could treacherously slip free of justice pained him. He drank some cider before answering.

"These are harsh times, lass; the royal government is glad for whatever American support it can get, and a man of wealth and power such as Cullen can do much to sway a governor."

A loud booming came at the door. Someone was shouting for Owen as though the devil were at his heels. Sutherland and the women jumped up, and Benjamin and Susannah, half awake, appeared at the top of the stairs. Opening the door, Sutherland let in Tom Morely and Jeb Grey, between whom hung a limp and gruesome figure, whose legs ran with blood and whose clothes were nearly torn from his slim body.

"Merriwether!" Sutherland cried and took hold of the suffering creature, carrying him quickly to the fireplace to be laid on pillows and blankets in front of the blaze. Ella nearly fainted to see Dawson Merriwether so terribly hurt, but she worked rapidly with towels and hot water from the kettle to help clean his legs. It was Owen, however, who tended the worst wounds, which had split the man's groin and upper thighs. Ella turned away, to where Tom Morely stood, chest heaving, with Sally leaning against him in revulsion and pity.

Tom said, "The rail. Two dozen swine rode poor Mr. Merriwether on a rail, and they set fire to his house!"

"Whigs?" Ella exclaimed. "How could they—"

"We don't know who did it." Tom's eyes narrowed as Merriwether groaned in agony while Sutherland and Jeb tended him.

"It must have been Meeks!" Sally whispered, unable to look as Merriwether was turned on his side, blood puddling where he had lain.

Tom Morely shook his head sadly. "It might have been him, but if so he wasn't alone, and it took more'n just his dogs to do this. No, I'm ashamed to say there was real Liberty Boys in on it."

Tom said he had been called upon earlier that evening by a Son who had said they were going to scare a Tory and rattle his teeth a bit. Not favoring mob tactics, Tom had refused. At the last moment he had heard that Dawson Merriwether was the target, and he fetched Jeb to stop the crowd from going too far. But they had been too late. Merriwether's grand house was ablaze and could not be saved. Jeb had sent his stepson, James, to protect Mrs. Merriwether while the daring intervention of Jeb and Tom had kept Merriwether from being broken in two on the rail, for men masked in sackcloth had carried the poor fellow nearly a mile. With hands bound, his legs straddling the wood, pigs of lead were tied to his ankles to weight him down and inflict even worse pain as he bounced.

"We borrowed a Frenchman's canoe and brought him over here, thinking it was safest for him—and for us," said Jeb. "They might have waylaid us on the way back to Detroit."

"How did you get him away?" Sutherland asked, barely containing his rage as he swabbed Merriwether's wounds. "They could have thrown you on the rail instead for standing up to them."

Tom said, "Jeb took one by the hair and stuck a pistol down his throat, sackcloth mask and all. That convinced 'em their play was at an end."

"Who were they? You must know!"

"We told 'em we wouldn't ask questions and we wouldn't shoot that rascal's tongue off if they left Mr. Merriwether with us," Jeb hissed. He helped Sutherland lift the semiconscious man onto a guest bed built into an alcove at the far end of the room. "They went quick enough, though I had some trouble gettin' the pistol out of the scum's mouth. He liked the taste of black powder, I reckon."

Ella and Sally covered the quivering, feverish Merriwether with blankets and cleaned his face, which was filthy with sweat, dirt, and blood. Ella asked where Mrs. Merriwether was, and Jeb answered that he had instructed his younger son to make sure she was taken into the fort and safety.

Sutherland collected his claymore, rifle, and ammunition, preparing to go to Detroit. He intended to do what he could to organize the respectable citizens into a militia—one composing Whigs and Tories alike—to help keep the peace. Going to the window facing the river, he could see the night sky lit up where the Virginian's house burned like a beacon fire.

Ella and Owen stood together a moment as he said she should remain in the house, with doors locked and extra firearms loaded. He would be back by dawn.

Ella glanced at her drowsy children, who were shivering near the fire, too nervous to sleep. To Owen she whispered, "Do you think the Tories will come after us here because of this?"

Sutherland looked into her eyes. "I don't know who might make this an excuse to attack us in revenge. Meeks, maybe, trying to stir up things. But even without him, there'll be enough maddened Tories out there."

Just then there was a shout from the shoreline, and they opened the door to see a figure racing up from the landing. It was James Morely. The slender, dark young fellow was frantic as he dashed through the door, stumbling into the arms of Jeb, his stepfather.

"Murder!" James panted. "Murder's done!" Catching his breath, he answered the question they all asked at once. "Mrs. Merriwether! Found her in the bedroom . . . shot dead—"

There was a horrible scream. Dawson Merriwether sat up in bed, body rigid, mouth open, hands clutching at phantoms. Rushing to his side, Ella tried to quiet him and stop his wild struggling. Owen joined her, and at last the man lay back, sobbing the name of his wife and asking, "Why have they done this, Claudia? Why have they done this to you?"

chapter 4

CROSSROADS

From the start, suspicion fell on Jeb and Tom, though there was no proof they had caused the mob attack on the Merriwethers. It was Sutherland who interposed with Commandant Lernoult on their behalf, and the officer could not deny that Jeb and Tom had rescued the Virginian from the violence. There were those, however, who believed they had instigated the move against Merriwether with the intention of only scaring him and other loyalists. But when the mob had become unruly and ran amok, matters had rushed out of their control. It was then all Jeb and Tom could do, those people said, to get Merriwether to safety and make up for their terrible blunder at losing command of the Whig thugs.

Even Sutherland was discredited, particularly among newcomers to the fort who did not know him well. They suspected him of involvement, no matter what the older hands said about his good reputation. Detroit was not the tightly knit community of a decade ago, and Sutherland was no longer looked upon with unswerving respect by the entire population.

Indeed, many envied Sutherland's power, influence, and growing wealth. They suspected him of being partial to Indians in order to promote his company's trade, and accusations that would have been unheard of years ago drifted unchecked through the British populace. It was even said that Sutherland knew something about the personal treasure of the Merriwethers, none of which had been found in the house after its burning.

Hundreds of pounds sterling worth of silver plate, goblets, and jewelry, and unusual coins that had been Dawson Merriwether's prized collection were all missing. A search of the ashes turned up no sign of these valuables, the best of which had been safeguarded in the couple's bedroom, where Mrs. Merriwether's body had been found.

The house was still smoking the morning after the killing, with the stench of charred wood and burned furniture heavy in the air. Wearing workman's overalls, the tall black butler picked through the ashes, moving slowly, precisely, and with great dignity. Tears ran down his face. Nearby, a kitchen slave and two garden slaves, all women, raked what they could from the desolate ruin, all the while singing a mournful song that barely rose above the sound of wind and river. A few soldiers worked alongside them, looking for evidence that might tell who had committed the murder.

Near the charred chestnut tree, Sutherland and Captain Lernoult stood back to watch the searchers perform their dismal task. It was tough labor, and the soldiers were in shirtsleeves, though the day was chilly and dark. Haggard from a long night of piecing together the events of the crime, Lernoult sighed and turned to Sutherland. Seeing the Scotsman glaring at the vessel *Helen*, anchored in the straits just off shore, Lernoult shook his head.

"It's the Whigs to blame for this, Mr. Sutherland, not Master Meeks." His voice slow and deep, Lernoult said, "It's my conviction, however, that if any man can get to the bottom of who did this, you can."

Sutherland looked at him, then back to the ship, bobbing in a breeze that rippled across the straits. Clouds hung steely and cold overhead, as though this burning and murder had impregnated the atmosphere with the gloomy promise of a storm.

Lernoult went on, "Or do you fear exposing friends as the perpetrators of this crime, sir?"

Sutherland shook his head. "The Congress party here is not out for blood from Tories or from king's officers." His eyes fixed upon the remains of the Merriwether house, as if the ruins held an answer. "This attack was planned and begun by one who intended this result, as the theft of the Merriwether treasure proves. My friends had no part in this."

Rocking back and forth, hands on hips, Lernoult nodded. "I hope you're right; we'll soon see, for if this was the spontaneous work of a rebellious mob, then articles of the Merriwether treasure will soon be found circulating, being sold or traded by those who stole them. Otherwise, if the goods do not turn up soon, I might accept your belief that there is a single mind behind this—and he has possession of what was stolen."

Lernoult followed Sutherland's nod toward the *Helen* as the Scotsman said searching it might prove worthwhile. But the officer grunted.

"There are other places to search, where success is more likely," Lernoult said. "Besides, Meeks would be a fool to conceal so much treasure aboard his ship, knowing I'll leave nothing uncovered in my quest. No, Mr. Sutherland, Meeks is a hard man, but not a suspect as far as I'm concerned—not yet, at any rate."

Sutherland agreed that Meeks would be foolhardy to hoard the treasure on the *Helen,* if he was the mind behind the mob attack. Yet the *Helen* was soon due to depart for the East before the freeze-up, and Sutherland did not want to let the vessel slip away without its having been searched thoroughly. He looked at Lernoult in such a forthright, deliberate manner that the experienced officer knew precisely what his companion was thinking.

Lernoult grumbled, attempting to be gruff, but sounded only conciliatory. "Meeks is no suspect, but, of course . . . we have to carry out our duty and search every storehouse, cabin, lodge, barn—and ship." He glanced at Sutherland, harrumphed self-consciously, and clapped his hands at a few subordinates nearby, including the pouting Lieutenant Mark Davies.

"Muster every available man, gentlemen!" he shouted. "Divide them into squads of four with a noncommissioned officer at the head of each, and commence searching for the missing valuables. Lieutenant Davies, send delegates to the French *habitant* leaders to assure them we mean no offense by this search, and ask them to supply militia officers to accompany our search parties."

He turned to Sutherland, saying, "Yes, we'll even rake through Meeks's ship. But first, with your cooperation, I'll have a few men visit your home at Valenya—and that way no one will accuse the army of playing favorites, even with Owen Sutherland, eh?"

Sutherland nodded, a look of irony in his eyes. "At your service, Captain. I'm pleased to see the army act with such evenhandedness with a member of the Congress party."

Lernoult harrumphed again, saying, "I don't want Detroit to become another Boston, sir! No mob rule; but at the same time, no one will accuse the army of tyranny as long as I'm in command here!"

All that dreary day the search went on for Merriwether's silver and gold, with homes turned out, chicken coops and stables poked through, and trading houses investigated, their bales and bundles tediously unpacked and repacked. The irritable soldiers barely contained their resentment at this miserable task, but they were thorough. Valenya and the ship *Helen* were picked over with special care, with Captain Lernoult attending both searches, but nothing remotely incriminating was found.

The search was accepted respectfully by nearly everyone; even Hugh Meeks was obliging and fell all over himself to please Lernoult. The residents wanted justice done, further violence prevented, and the killer or killers punished. If this crime went unsolved, and the mob's leaders were not discovered, then more suffering and reprisal killing would surely follow. The emboldened mob would strike again, whether it was a Whig mob attacking other Tories, or loyalists seeking to take revenge on Congress supporters. As far as the peaceful folk at Detroit were concerned, the Whig mob and the Tory mob were equally abhorrent, for both caused pain and destruction that would echo and reecho with growing hatred and soon become unstoppable.

The next day, as a wintry wind lashed the straits, sleet turning the ground to mud and spattering on hats and oilskins, Mrs. Merriwether was laid to rest in the new cemetery outside the fort. Though the tragedy had deepened the rift between Whig and Tory, with harsh accusations hurled back and forth, hundreds from both camps attended the funeral, all sorry that an innocent woman had died this way. Each side blamed the other for forcing the conflict to such a dangerous crisis, but on this somber morning few spoke openly, and none voiced opinions too loudly.

In the midst of the mourners trudging on a path from the fort's chapel across the withered meadow was Owen Sutherland. He walked along in the funeral procession, ideas tumbling over and over as he tried to devise a way to snare the killer. He and Ella were close behind Mrs. Merriwether's family, who were preceded by the coffin in a carriage drawn by a black horse. Sutherland respected the fortitude of Dawson Merriwether, who somehow found the strength to limp, with the aid of a cane, at the side of his daughter, Matilda. He was obviously in severe agony, but this show of determination gave warning to his wife's killer that he would not rest until justice was done.

Yesterday the Virginian had been helped back across the river to stay with Matilda and her husband, Reverend Angus Lee, until his injuries healed. Fortunately, his leg and groin wounds had not crippled him permanently nor damaged his private parts beyond healing. He had been told the intervention of Jeb and Tom had prevented worse injury, but he could not recollect their coming on the scene, for he had been unconscious by then, bound upon the rail by a rope.

Matilda Merriwether Lee, veiled head hanging, was between her father and husband. Plump and haggard, dressed in black, Matilda looked far older than her thirty years. The sorrow had been almost too much to bear, and from time to time she faltered, giving way. Ella Sutherland and Sally were at hand then, coming to her elbow, to ease her along the rutted track.

Reverend Lee, careworn by the ordeal, tramped along, head bare, the drizzle misting his thick spectacles. He seemed unaware of sensation other than profound heartache. As the only Presbyterian minister at Detroit, Lee had performed the service that cold morning. Through it all, his long, angular frame had been bent, and now it remained so, as if the small prayer book he carried were a great burden. Sutherland had an eye on Lee, in case he hesitated in his step; but as they drew near to the windblown cemetery, the minister gathered himself for the final moment. With both hands he clasped the prayer book to his breast.

Holding his narrow chin high, almost defiant in pose, this native of New York Town's poorest quarter became transformed from an image of woebegone despair to one of quivering anger. Sutherland suspected the determination lighting the minister's eyes was partly caused by an inner turbulence that the fellow did not yet know how to resolve. For more than a year he had been seriously at odds with Dawson Merriwether over the differences between America and England. More than once he had preached heatedly from his pulpit that it was the sacred duty of Americans to resist Parliament's despotism and speak out against misguided government policy.

On this sad day, however, he was devastated that resistance had taken this evil turn. Never had he preached cruel violence nor expected that the leap of passions and hatreds would be so convulsive that even his own family would suffer. Reverend Lee's upraised chin was meant for all to see that he still believed in what he preached, though he loathed and condemned this brutality.

As Sutherland walked along near Ella, he heard behind him mutterings from a member of the procession—mutterings that accused Lee of having sparked vile mob criminality. Sutherland glanced back at a red-faced merchant who had said too loudly, "This is what comes of unleashing damned wild dogs! The Lord dispenses just reward for what his people do, even to his straying ministers! And this is the sorry result of calling up devils in damned folk who should be sermonized with the Golden Rule and the Ten Commandments—not browbeaten with damned political discourses that cause bloody rebellion against their betters!"

The richly garbed fellow, bowlegged and squat, did not notice Sutherland staring at him. He must have been hard of hearing, for he went on blabbing overloud about how the flock should be governed with pious words, not blasphemous tirades on natural law or inalienable rights. Ella, noticing her husband's rising anger, moved close to him, and began the beautiful new hymn, "Amazing Grace." The mourners joined in, Owen included, until the sound of wind and river were overwhelmed by the song. Soon the complaining fat man was singing as well.

The cemetery was surrounded by a white picket fence thirty yards square, and stood in the midst of an orchard of naked apple trees, clattering in the wind. The mourners crowded close to hear Lee deliver the eulogy, the Merriwether slaves in a small group at the fringe. Though many mourners were opposed to Lee's politics—including his wife, Matilda—they listened well to what he said, praying it would not ring of insurrection or rabble-rousing.

". . . Thy ways are unscrutable to Thy children, Lord," he cried out above the wind. "But we who love peace take heed that our country's course has come to a crossroads. It is for each American to choose which road we take. That our beloved wife and mother's passing might not be in vain, let us unite together against the bloodthirsty in our midst. Let us call upon our Maker to guide us through this so perilous valley of the shadow of death."

When Lee fell silent, the soft sobbing of Matilda and the black women seemed loud. Then Sutherland heard the old fellow nearby muttering that the minister even looked like a damned rebel.

That evening at Valenya, Sutherland met with Jacques Levesque and with the Ottawa Mawak, an aged chief, portly and grave. Unlike Levesque, who was dashingly gallant in his red *voyageur* waist sash and feathered red stocking cap, Mawak was the image of primitive grandeur. He wore several bright trade shirts, one over the other, and his long, greasy hair was fitted with blue and green wampum beads, a new fashion he had taken note of on a journey last year to the lower Mississippi.

Like Levesque, the paunchy Mawak was a faithful ally to Sutherland and a partner in the Frontier Company. He and the Frenchman had been on several adventures with Sutherland,

and they trusted one another with their lives. Mawak spoke passable pidgin English, which was remarkably improved by draughts of ale—and to his mind was made impeccable by strong rum. Levesque favored brandy as they sat smoking pipes—the whites in chairs, Mawak cross-legged on the floor—before a great fire. Sutherland drank ale, and Mawak's tongue soon was limbered by trade rum—well watered, for Sutherland wanted decisive talk, not the flowery orations of an Ottawa chieftain in his cups.

They had been together an hour, discussing the matter of missing treasure and the murder, when there came a knock at the door. Sutherland opened it, and in came Tamano and Little Hawk, both in buckskins, with soft linsey shirts under them to keep off the damp and cold. They had been on a mission for Sutherland and arrived without their wives; now they were hungry.

Ella and Sally came into the room, carrying plates of sliced cold turkey and strips of dried bear meat flavored with maple sugar. The food was set on a low table with a tray of French bread, bowls of olives, pickled squash, and boiled wild rice. Tamano and Little Hawk sat on the floor beside Mawak and fell to eating before any discussion began. Ella and Sally departed, and Mawak took the opportunity for a second dinner. Sutherland sat patiently with Levesque, smoking and waiting for the Indians to eat their fill. This silence was proper Indian decorum, even though the Scotsman was anxious to learn what they had discovered that day.

Beneath Sutherland's armchair lay an enormous white husky, his pale eyes lit by the fire, watching the Indians eat. This was Heera, a magnificent specimen belonging to Sutherland and trained by the expert Mawak in hauling sleds and following a scent. Though the animal gazed longingly at Mawak, attentive to every morsel the Ottawa stuffed into his mouth, nothing was offered Heera, who was perfectly disciplined. Perhaps in an Indian lodge the dog would have eaten along with his master, but Ella Sutherland had her rules, and one was that the common room be kept clean. These three Indians well knew Ella's temper when it came to such things, and in return for this delicious meal, they were as careful as any warrior could be not to spill anything on the floor.

At last, as the sound of Sally's violin drifted in from another room, Tamano and Little Hawk accepted tobacco and greeted the others formally by passing their lit pipes around.

Tamano's lean features were accentuated by the flickering light from the fire, his high forehead and large nose appearing all the more regal. As he spoke, in Ottawa, his dark eyes flashed.

"There are Indians who saw the trouble, Donoway." Tamano called Sutherland by the name the Ottawa had given him—a name that meant "fearless in the flames" because of his courage during a session of torture he had survived many years ago. "A family of Wyandots returning by canoe from attending confession in Sainte Anne's saw what happened, though there were many shadows and much heat and burning, and they recognized no one in the mob."

An eagle feather hanging at Tamano's ear slipped over his shoulder as he shook his head. "These Wyandot Hurons wanted no trouble, wanted just to get away, and they would have done so without seeing anything more had not a white man's skiff come out of the darkness, leaving the shore and making for the ship *Helen,* anchored not far away."

Tamano looked at young Little Hawk, who leaned forward, his face somber and intense—an appearance unusual for the playful, mischievous Sioux—and took up the tale, also speaking in Ottawa. "My brothers, these Wyandots are known to me. I have traded with them and my squaw has quarreled with them over religion—we are of the old faith, and they of the white man's . . ."

Little Hawk went on to say the frightened Wyandots had lain low in their canoe as the skiff passed under sail, rapidly slicing through the darkness. Its passenger—there was only one man aboard—apparently had trouble handling his craft and did not notice the canoe. So far out on the water, the light of the burning house played tricks with the eyes, so the Hurons could not identify the man at the tiller. But they were certain he belonged on the sloop, for they watched him drop sail and tie up alongside.

Little Hawk continued, "Then these Indians paddled away quickly, fearing they would be caught up in this affair, or would be blamed in some way, as Indians often are blamed for the abuse of whites by whites."

The Merriwether house had not yet been fully engulfed in flames at this time, and the mob had quickly surged away, carrying Dawson Merriwether on the rail and singing songs of mockery against Parliament and the king.

When the two braves had finished speaking, the others waited an appropriate, formal period before continuing the conversation, which went late into the night. Who the man in the skiff might be they could only guess, but Sutherland was sure it was Hugh Meeks. Now they had to prove it and have him arrested before he returned east with his ship.

* * *

As the men talked, Ella lay in bed, reading by the light of an oil lamp, waiting for Owen to come in. Sally was asleep in the loft with the children, and the German clock in the common room struck three before Ella heard her husband show the others out. He came into the bedroom, face lined with weariness. Sitting down heavily on the bed, he noticed her book, Oliver Goldsmith's *The Vicar of Wakefield*.

"Reading English novels, I see," Sutherland remarked, with a mock frown, and let the moccasins slip from his feet. "What kind of American patriot are you, then? Why don't you read American writing?"

"Because Americans can't write novels," she said, hardly looking at him, her face in the book. "They're too busy writing about politics, or half-baked natural philosophy!"

"About religion, too," Owen commented, lying back on the bed as he stared at the ceiling. "And there are a few good poets, you know. . . ."

Ella let her book fall and said, "Why don't you write me a poem? It's been years since you did, Owen. Now all your writing is Quill's essays for the people, and speeches . . . Oh, I'm too tired of it all to think or care about any of it!"

He replied that he was sick of the troubles himself. "I suppose the Sons of Liberty won't revile you for reading Oliver Goldsmith; most of them can't read anyway. Ask Sam Adams; he reads for them, and tells them what to think, too."

Ella sighed and put the book down, saying, "I can't drink English tea or coffee for fear of being unpatriotic to America; I can't import English furniture or buy English-made china, and we can't trade English-made goods anymore." She sat up, half complaining, half teasing, as she said, "But no Sam Adams committee or Congress party mob will have me give up English writings, too, husband!" Then she became quickly serious, her hand going to the braid of blond hair that fell over her shoulder and down to her breast.

She said, "Nothing can be taken lightly anymore, it seems. I tried to read tonight, but all the while I heard your voices out there, talking Ottawa, so I could barely understand a word—but I could tell that you know something about who did this terrible thing!"

Ella had known Mrs. Merriwether fairly well and was friendly with Matilda Merriwether Lee. Twelve years ago Lee had come out to Detroit on the same expedition that had taken Ella westward

on a visit to her brother, Henry Gladwin. It was then that she had
first met Owen, who had rescued her and others of their party
from being drowned in a boating mishap near Detroit. Reverend
Lee had married the Sutherlands a half year later, after the truce
was declared between Pontiac's hostiles and the British.

As Ella watched, Owen slowly prepared for bed, his thoughts
far away. She sat back, looking beautiful and soft in the lamplight,
and Sutherland wondered how Dawson Merriwether was holding
up after losing the woman he loved. Sutherland well knew the
heartache of losing a wife. He had taken cold revenge on the killer
of his Ottawa woman, and now Dawson Merriwether must be
consumed by the need to do the same.

"Do you know who it was, husband?"

Sutherland said absently, "It was Meeks."

Ella sat forward, and he told of the Wyandot family that had
witnessed someone fleeing the scene in a skiff, making for the
Helen. When she asked where the treasure might be, Sutherland
said that was what he had to find out before the ship set sail. There
was a way, he said, as he crawled under the covers and put her
novel on the floor. She moved against him, hand on his shoulder
as he said he would use Heera to explore the woods near the
Merriwether house.

"I believe the stolen valuables are buried there somewhere."
He put an arm around her and drew her close, his mind working.
After some time she commented on his distraction.

"You're so full of this dreadful affair and of the Whig cause
that there's no time left for us, for your children, or for having a
simple, happy home!" She looked away quickly, more angry than
sad, but with the world, not Owen. She did not want to distress
him at such a difficult time and was sorry to be so upset. She
threw back the blankets and sat on the edge of the bed, trying to
compose herself. After a while she asked, "What is it you want,
husband? Is it a new country, or a family? Your family needs you!
Sally especially needs you because she's been so lost since Jeremy
left, not like herself at all. And—"

She broke off, taking a deep breath and hitting the bed with
her fist. She turned to look at him. Owen lay there listening, clearly
troubled by the cares and demands that whirled through his turbulent life. Ella remembered how free and wild he had been when
first they met, how he had roved the woods in Indian leggins and
a breechcloth with bared buttocks. He had changed for her, had

given up that reckless freedom to make them a new life—domestic, prosperous, but now burdened with politics and a thousand daily chores.

Owen took her hand, and she lay down beside him, saying, "I'm sick at heart of everyone's squabbling and bickering, and now they've come to murder! Owen, we need you more than they do! We need a husband and a father, not an honored delegate to some far-off Congress, where abstract social principles and economic balderdash obsess all—" She threw herself against him but staunchly refused to cry. "Ah, Owen, my darling, I'm just not sure anymore what's right. I want us to be happy, and yet I want you to do what you must."

Ella moved back and managed to smile, but he saw a hint of tears as she said, "I suppose I'll just have to learn to share you with our country, even with the world!" She shook her head and sighed, apologizing for being selfish and jealous and petty, but he would not permit that.

"I know you're right, lass," he said, kissing her lightly. "And you know what I have to do is for our sake as well as for our country—aye, even the world." He caressed her hair, brushing it back, kissing her fingers as she touched his lips. He said, "If not for you, lass, I couldn't bear any of this; I'd be gone away west, looking for those fabulous Shining Mountains Tamano talks so glowingly about. Aye, Ella, if not for you and the children, I think I'd turn my back on the colonies and the troubles of civilization and begin again—far away, on my own."

They thought about that a moment, the oil lamp sputtering as it ran out of fuel. The house was silent, and outside the wind sang faintly through the standing stones.

Owen said, "But we have to take a stand. Now, before it's too late—or America will be nothing more than a vassal state to the lords in Parliament, looked down at, and treated like so many dogs, who—"

She kissed him roughly, silencing him, making him embrace her. Through the kiss she said, "You sound like Sam Adams of Boston! I married Owen Sutherland of Detroit!"

He pushed her back, the lamplight flickering out. "Sam Adams is a rascal and a rabble-rouser. I can't stomach that Yankee, so whenever I sound like him, shut me up just this way, because—"

Ella shut him up, and for a while, the distress of their country was put from them, if not forgotten.

* * *

Far over the Atlantic, Jeremy Bently sat on a bunk in the cabin of his ship, *Yankee*, which had been at the Bristol docks for several days now. The crossing had been rough and slow, with the ship blown off course twice and needing twelve extra days to complete the journey from Philadelphia. Since departing from his family almost six weeks ago, Jeremy had been homesick and seasick.

With him on the ship had been Frontier Company partners Mary and Peter Defries, who with their daughter and servant had gone on to the Continent to tour and arrange commercial matters. Defries was an Albany native of Dutch descent, and he had been eager to see the Netherlands of his ancestors. With them gone, Jeremy was lonely. He especially missed Sally Cooper, his childhood friend who of late seemed more like a sweetheart, though he had not expected it to turn out that way.

During the crossing Jeremy had written three long letters to Sally, and another to her in his dreary time in port waiting for a messenger to come down from his Uncle Henry Gladwin. A response to his note to Gladwin was due any day now, and Jeremy was impatient to get off the vessel and begin the carriage journey northward to the estate in Derbyshire.

For company, the young man had his pet otter, named Sniffer, who lay curled up on the bunk. Though age ten—ancient by otter standards—Sniffer was still spry and sleek. His brown fur had a healthy sheen in the light of two candles standing on a desk next to the bunk, and Jeremy wished he himself were as well kept as the otter after such a taxing crossing. The young man's side ached where an Indian slug had wounded him in October during a battle on the Ohio River, but it was not as troubling as the pain of being so completely removed from America.

Outside, the bustling port of Bristol hummed and rumbled, although it was almost midnight. Ships were being loaded by torchlight, about to set off for a perilous winter's journey to Boston. On the stone landings and wharves iron-rimmed wheels rolled and creaked, and men shouted oaths, sang songs, and labored through the night to load the vessels.

Hungry soldiers garrisoning Boston needed supplies, for many Americans refused to sell to them—and even those who were willing to sell did not do so, for fear of the Sons of Liberty. Those soldiers also needed the accoutrements of war: cannon, new uniforms, muskets, shoes, tents, and even nails and tools with which to erect decent winter barracks.

For a moment Jeremy felt sympathy for the British troops over there. They were the pawns of a stubborn government, and as the visible arm of authority, soldiers were despised by most Americans.

Jeremy had proclaimed himself an American by going ashore wearing a fine buckskin shirt, embroidered with bright colors and decorated with dyed porcupine quills. He had dressed this way not because he was a bumpkin or a newcomer to great cities, for he had spent three years as a student in Philadelphia. Rather, he had worn the buckskin as one might wear a shield with a coat of arms, or as a Scot might wear the kilt, or an Indian his best headdress. Jeremy was proud to be a frontiersman, and the buckskin shirt he wore accentuated that pride.

He had not, however, anticipated the vicious response of many landsmen, especially of the unruly dock workers. At the first insult he had taken offense and battered two men senseless. In a twinkling, he had found himself surrounded by ten others, all about to pulverize him for his insolence. Only the intervention of Americans from his vessel had prevented serious bloodshed, for he carried a hunting knife in his leggins in the manner of his stepfather and would have used it to save himself.

From then on Jeremy had run into trouble every time he left the ship—whose very name, *Yankee,* was a cause of hostility between English dock workers and the crew. He would be glad when a carriage from Derbyshire came to fetch him from this dismal harbor where everyone had an opinion on how to solve the Boston troubles, and no opinion was favorable to the colonies.

Standing up, Jeremy went to the porthole to pass the time staring at shadows, torches, the ripple of black water, and the scattered lights in windows of waterfront houses. Taverns in Bristol seethed and throbbed all night, many roisterers coming down to the docks to give a drink to friends who were working or to show off their latest doxy picked up for the night. Jeremy knew about the roughest of taverns, for he had frequented enough in Philadelphia, but the sordid, stinking atmosphere of Bristol's docks turned his stomach, and so did the growls and vulgar cries of men and women staggering up and down the cobbled streets from public house to tavern to filthy inn.

Leaning against the ship's hull, gazing through the porthole, Jeremy could not stop thinking about Sally Cooper. He sighed and stepped back from the light of the porthole, his broad and well-formed body casting a shadow on the opposite wall. The light of the candles lit Sniffer's eyes as the otter gazed up at him. Jeremy looked at his old friend, who had managed to come along on this journey only because he had sprung from the dock into the water after the *Yankee* cast off. Because of his age, Sniffer might have drowned if Jeremy had not shinnied down a line and hauled him aboard. Sniffer's company had been welcome, but Jeremy wondered how the otter would take to the Gladwin estate—and how the Gladwins would take to him.

These thoughts passed through Jeremy's mind as he said, "We'll both be out of our element here, Sniffer."

The otter blew through his snout, shook his head once, and then yawned long and slow before settling his chin on the edge of the bunk, contemplating the floor. Jeremy came to him and sat down, the youth's long legs stretching out halfway across the cabin.

"But we wanted this, eh? So we'll have to make the best of it until we can go home again and see Sally." He stroked the otter's fur, and Sniffer looked around at the mention of the name of the young woman who meant so much to both of them. Jeremy considered the pile of letters on his small desk—all written to Sally, except for two to his parents—and with each successive letter he had expressed a growing longing for the young woman.

In the past year Sally had seemed a different person, no longer a tomboy. They had never been lovers, though he knew she had been infatuated with him all these years. In the past he had never taken her seriously—but when he returned to America, he would ask her to be his wife, and they would be the happiest, best-matched couple on earth, other than his mother and Owen.

Jeremy had been careful not to ask Sally to marry him in these letters, for that would have been too much agony for both of them. He would be gone two years at least, and had no desire to be engaged by letter. There was much to do and see in Britain in that time, and he intended being free to do what he chose without feeling responsible to a fiancée.

His letters told Sally how much he missed her and asked that she never forget him. When he returned he would be a physician and would practice in the northwest, even though fees were small out there. He wanted to live in the wilderness and help build the new community taking shape at Detroit. Did she agree? he asked. Or did she prefer Fort Pitt, which was growing rapidly into a major center for commerce and settlement in the Ohio Valley?

There were many questions, much to tell of life at sea, and a cautiously worded hint that he would ask for her hand when he came back. He knew these letters would give Sally hope and inspiration. She would wait for him, but he would not twist her heart with frustrated declarations of his love.

As soon as he could, he would send these letters on a ship bearing the post to Montreal. Until then he would continue to write, including in the package a letter also for Tom Morely and one each for Little Hawk, Tamano, and Mawak.

Rising again and striding to the window, he thought what fun he would have here if all those friends were with him. They could tear apart any gang of drunken seamen, and after a week in port they would be famous across England. Jeremy's blond hair fell over his eyes, and he brushed it back, thinking he should tie it properly in a queue when his uncle's carriage arrived. Like Owen, he wore no powdered wig, as did many men of the day, and his clothes, stockings, and shoes were modest, without gaudy buckles, lace, or sequins.

In the light of the porthole, the features of his face were thrown into shadows that accentuated the fine nose and high forehead, firm lips and a dimpled chin. He looked much like his mother, though he had the blue eyes of his father and, like him, was built strongly. Jeremy's father had been an American from New England, invalided during the French and Indian wars twenty years earlier. He had died of his wounds before Ella came to the northwest with Jeremy, where she had married Owen Sutherland. Fluid of motion, Jeremy had acquired the grace and natural bearing of Sutherland. When he was in the wild, he could run tirelessly along a trail, silently, like the Indians who had taught him their ways.

He heard Sniffer move and turned to see the otter with front paws up on the desk, hind paws on the bunk, poking his black nose at a small rosewood music box. Jeremy grinned and picked up the box, which was only three inches on a side and splendidly polished from his handling during the sea voyage. Sniffer gave a snort as Jeremy wound the key.

"This makes you feel at home, too, friend." He opened the box, and it began to tinkle the melody of a French *voyageur* song well known to the people of the American northwest.

Singing the refrain softly, Jeremy sat down beside the otter, who came into his lap, listening:

> *En roulant ma boule roulant,*
> *En roulant ma boule.*

En roulant ma boule roulant
En roulant ma boule.

It was a song about a rolling ball, and about silly ducks in a homestead's pond. *Voyageurs* sang it as they paddled into the most distant reaches of the known world. It gave them spirit, companionship, and the strength to go on without ever feeling alone. As Jeremy sang the song it heartened him, and reminded him of Sally. In giving Jeremy this music box, her most prized possession, Sally expressed her love for him.

He sang, fondled Sniffer, and no longer felt alone, though he was a stranger here in the very center of the civilized world.

chapter 5

THE OLD ELM

Before dawn, leaving Ella asleep, Sutherland put Heera aboard his canoe and paddled through mist as he made for the ruins of Merriwether's house. He crossed the nine hundred yards of choppy, gray water, and then headed to where the house stood about a mile away. As he drew near the shore, he saw the rosy light of a watchman's fire. Captain Lernoult had placed a guard on the remains of the house until Merriwether could recover what was left of his possessions.

Sutherland intended telling no one why he was here, so he avoided the fire and made for a pebbly beach a little ways down-stream. As he stroked, he saw the shadowy form of the *Helen* riding at anchor a short distance off, and wondered whether by now he was too late. If Meeks had unearthed the stolen goods, he could have already stashed them on the ship, with no one the wiser. This reasoning troubled Sutherland, but he had to go on with his plan even if it failed. Time was running out, and Meeks could take the next fair wind for the East.

Heera bounded into the shallows as Sutherland hauled the canoe to shore. The wind came up, and wisps of mist whirled about like a witch's spell. In the distance, the *Helen*'s rigging creaked, a faint lantern hovering on her stern. Aboard, someone rang the bell, a muffled, clanking sound through the morning fog.

Working his way slowly along the shoreline, Sutherland found traces of a skiff having been run aground and saw where a boat hook had snagged on the branch of a maple, near the water. His Indian's sense, acquired over the years from Tamano, Mawak, and even the deceased Pontiac himself, told him much. A man in heeled shoes had stumped through here a few days ago, walking straight toward the Merriwether house. Sutherland was surprised to see how slightly the man's step indented the earth, for Meeks was a big lout and should have made deeper tracks. Perhaps the ground had been dry and hard that night? . . . Sutherland let this pass, taking note that the tree branch where the boat hook had been secured was badly scraped and mangled, as though whoever had fitted it there had done so clumsily, missing several times before getting a good hold. Meeks was nervous, perhaps, or maybe a bit drunk.

Moving like a ghost so that no watchman saw him, Sutherland turned back the way he had come. Following the return path of the man with heeled shoes, he saw the steps were clumsy now, some long, others short, some having kicked up the ground, as though the man had been staggering—perhaps laboring under the weight of silver plate and gold coin.

The trail fleeing the house went into the woods, cutting from the path that led to the skiff's landing place. Sutherland held close to the tracks, guessing he would not have to go much farther: The treasure must be hidden somewhere close. Heera ran with him, sniffing and snorting at the trail, excited by the chase, as though he knew what Sutherland knew.

Tangled bushes, thorns, and branches of pine trees slapped and tugged at Sutherland as he moved through the dim woods. The sun was no more than a cool wash of light low in the sky, and hardly penetrated the forest. Only the chirp of a startled swallow or the rattle of a woodpecker could be heard. This was one of the few places along the straits where French *habitants* had not hewn down trees to plant their fields in the usual narrow strips running up from the water. For years, this large grove had been sugar bush but now was untended and overgrown because Dawson Merriwether favored refined West Indies cane to maple sugar.

In the undergrowth it was hard to pick out the footprints, and more often than not Sutherland followed snapped branches or pine cones that did not sit quite right on their limbs. Heera, though, had a scent, and he stayed with it until they reached a mighty, spreading elm tree, where the tracks mingled and were confused, as though the man had been lost or busy with something.

Sutherland searched the ground, poking through piles of brown and yellow leaves to see whether they concealed new digging. There was none to be seen, so he followed the trail as it wound through the trees, circling and aimless; apparently the man had become lost from time to time. Sutherland came up short to find himself at the edge of the trees, where the skiff had been tied. What had happened to the treasure? Where was it buried? These last tracks showed the man was traveling light again. He had left the goods back in the woods, that was certain. But where?

Sutherland took another long look at the *Helen*, where crewmen were setting about morning tasks—repairing rigging, lines and sail, tarring the hull, and painting. The mist was rising now, and the faint scent of breakfast wafted over from the ship. With Heera panting at his side, Sutherland turned back to retrace the tracks, sure this time he would find where Meeks had buried the proof of his dirty work.

After two more hours of scouring the woods, Sutherland decided he had been wrong. There was no treasure here, even though he felt in his very marrow that there had to be. According to the tracks, Meeks had come through here only once—the night of the murder—and no one but Sutherland had been here since. If anyone had removed the goods there would be evidence that a hunter of Sutherland's skills would have found. Yet there was nothing at all hidden in the woods. Why, then, had the killer of Mrs. Merriwether come into the lonely grove in darkness? What had he done here, and where had he done it?

The morning wore on until at last Sutherland returned with the hungry Heera to his beached canoe. Disconsolate and perplexed, he let his mind work over the sparse facts. Staring at the ship, Sutherland knew Meeks would be gone soon, the valuables undoubtedly with him, and no one was likely to prove his guilt.

Sutherland sat down and fed the dog from a deerskin pouch of food he had brought with him. The Scotsman had a mind to go aboard right then and drag the swine to land; with Tamano's ingenuity and Mawak's experience, they could make him confess, for even an aging pirate could not match the Indian for devilish originality in persuasion by blade and fire.

He shook off that train of thought. Times were changing, and the rule of law must take ascendancy in the northwest. Even though a man was guilty, it could not be as it had been in the old days, when honest men took it upon themselves to mete out justice.

Before returning home, Sutherland visited Tamano's lodge and asked that a dozen good men be kept in readiness in case Meeks sailed the following morning, as Sutherland expected he would. The straits were far too dangerous to be navigated safely at night, so Meeks would have to await morning light before departing. Since there was little wind at first dawn, his vessel would be prey to twisting, treacherous crosscurrents and would have to drop downstream slowly, dragging an anchor until the wind blew well. At the right moment Sutherland would board the ship with his companions, and they would find the stolen fortune, one way or the other.

After returning to Valenya and eating his evening meal, Sutherland got up to tend the fire, tossing a massive elm log into the coals. Ella cleared the last dishes, sent the children to fetch firewood, and came back to join him. He was staring moodily into the flames as the elm spat and smoked, almost smothering the quiet fire.

After a while Ella persuaded him to tell all that had happened, in the hope some clue would suggest his next step. Sutherland did so, saying he had rooted through every moldy pile of leaves and rotting log in that old sugar bush. He paced the room, striding back and forth, talking more to himself than Ella. He was confused by the sort of tracks he had found, since they seemed too light to belong to Meeks.

"Are you sure it was Meeks?" Ella asked suddenly, then thought the question too obvious.

"Who else could it have been?" Sutherland muttered, rubbing his forehead and striding to the table for a mug of ale.

"Jones."

On board the sloop *Helen,* Farley Jones shivered with fright and cold. He sat in his dark, tiny cabin, peering out the porthole at the near shore, wishing the sun would go down. Up on deck, Hugh Meeks was stamping about, ordering his roughnecks here and there, preparing to set sail. Jones had just told Meeks his terrible secret, for that was the only way the clerk could complete his work. He needed Meeks and this ship, though it galled him to share any of the booty.

It terrified Jones to have the pirate as a partner and confidant, for the profits from selling the Merriwether valuables would be immense—good reason to murder a partner. He wished Meeks was not so damnably cool and calm! Jones longed to row ashore and fetch the sacks right away, but Meeks was cautious and favored waiting until dark. None of their dull-witted sailors would know what was what if the treasure was brought aboard disguised as something else, and none even knew Meeks had supplied the drink to inspire the mob that ransacked Merriwether's house. Looting the place afterward had been Jones's idea, told to no one.

If only that damned Virginian woman had not interfered, had

not come upon him there at the wrong moment. Fool! She should have fled the house as soon as it began to burn! Common sense told anyone that! She might have burned to death anyway—surely *would* have burned to death, even if . . . even if she had not forced him to— It was not what he had intended to happen. Jones had never killed before. It was too easy, too swift, too quickly done in anger and fear. But there had been no other way, for she had recognized him.

A chain rattled across the deck, making Jones jump, sending shivers along his arms. He gagged on a drink of stale rum and returned to the porthole. The sun was going down. It was almost time, and Meeks had better hurry.

Staring into the fire, Sutherland watched the elm log stubbornly refuse to burn. It was a long piece, with the twisty, gnarled grain that made elm so tough and ancient looking, just like that old lord of a tree in the sugar bush this morning. Sutherland thought again of the confused footprints around the tree—they belonged to Farley Jones; Ella was right there. But what had Jones done with the valuables? Sutherland wondered whether the massive, wrinkled elm trunk had opened up to swallow the treasure without a trace, like some Algonquin manitou playing tricks on white victims.

Nearby, on a stool, Ella knitted, thinking hard. She knew her man would go out again soon, perhaps rashly to attack Meeks's ship. She did not blame him, but feared what would happen if he were arrested by the authorities: imprisonment, or worse if Meeks or Jones were killed. Ella prayed Owen would get the proof in a lawful way and let Captain Lernoult take charge of the case. She knew, however, that if Meeks fled the following morning, Owen surely would chase him and the end would be decided out on Lake Erie. On the water there would be nothing to bear witness to a battle, no matter who won.

"The old elm!"

Sutherland's shout jarred Ella, and she jumped, her knitting falling to the ground.

"It's the elm!" he exclaimed, slamming his hand against his forehead. "I should have known! Oh, Mawak, you'd think me a tenderfoot fool if you knew I missed it!"

He snatched up his claymore, stuck a pistol in his belt, and threw an ammunition pouch and a gunpowder horn over his shoulder. As he grabbed a light pelt coat, he told Ella to sleep, and said he would have the proof and the valuables when he returned. "Then Lernoult can earn his officer's commission by arresting Farley Jones!" He took the Pennsylvania rifle from its place on a rack near the door and cried, "Don't worry, lass, I'm just going to climb a tree!"

Then he was out the door, and Ella ran after him. Taking down a heavy shawl from its peg, she drew it across her shoulders, going outside to see the white shadow of Heera in the gathering twilight, as the dog bounded alongside Owen. This was dangerous. *Sometimes*, she whispered to herself, *Owen is too impetuous for a man with children.*

Twilight, slow and pale, settled on the straits as Sutherland ran his canoe ashore near the Merriwether ruins. Downstream, the lamps of the *Helen* bobbed in the chop. The ship was at anchor, and there was still time for his plan to succeed—if Jones had not already fetched the valuables. His heart pounding, Sutherland dragged the canoe up on land. Then he saw what he had hoped would not yet occur: The skiff, under oars, was leaving the *Helen*, making for the sugar bush a hundred yards away. Sailing without lanterns, this was surely Jones going after the stolen goods.

Sutherland looked for the watch fire of the soldiers guarding the house, but there was none. Taking longer than he liked to run through the dim, obscure garden and around the house to the camp, he hallooed the men. But there came no answer. Heera ran this way and that, sniffing at the cold fire, digging at the rubbish pile left by the sentries. They were gone. He had wanted a witness, and the soldiers would have served that purpose well, but Sutherland was alone with only the dog.

There was no time for anything now but to get to the elm tree and take Jones prisoner, recovering the goods as well. Let Lernoult run things from there; he would have enough evidence to convict Jones, and with luck the clerk might single out Hugh Meeks as the one who had incited the mob to attack the Merriwethers.

Farley Jones could not stop his false teeth from clacking, even though he clamped shut his mouth and pressed bony fingers against his chin. Crouched in the gloomy underbrush, he was not far from the old elm tree where two days previous he had slung the bundle of stolen valuables over a high branch. Failing light made it difficult to see well, but Jones was close enough to the tree to make out the bulk of the sack. The line that held it across the branch ran on a long slant to a pine tree twenty yards behind the shivering clerk.

Back there, Hugh Meeks was untying the many knots Jones had put in the line to secure it to the evergreen, and now and again the sailor would grumble under his breath that damned landsmen's fool knots were the devil's work to undo. As Meeks toiled, Jones peered about the clearing, keeping watch in case some stray hunter or wanderer should pass by. He held a pistol in his right hand, and with the other he struggled against his chattering jaw.

"There!" Meeks grunted. "She's all ours now, matey."

He eased the line, slackening it, and moved past Jones to let the bag of silver and gold down to the forest floor. Chuckling, whistling softly to himself, Meeks made his way toward the base of the elm as Jones haltingly followed. The clerk cast nervous glances from side to side, but Meeks was confident, rubbing his hands together, his cutlass swinging casually in its scabbard behind.

"Come ahead, Farley, me man, an' let's have a look at yer ill-gotten gains!" Meeks laughed coarsely, ripping the cord from the mouth of the burlap and opening the sack eagerly. "Well, now!" He held up a gleaming silver goblet that reflected the pale light of sunset. "Not bad for a quill-pusher! Ye'll be as handy as Mr. Cullen at makin' a profit if ye keep this up, Farley, me man!"

Jones twitched, thinking he had heard a sound somewhere nearby. Meeks paid no attention, rummaging through the bag and commenting cheerfully on all he found there. Jones knelt beside Meeks, teeth still working, the pistol now pushed into his belt. When he saw the treasure, his eyes widened, glowing like lamps in their dark sockets. He let out a gasp and reached for a silver brooch studded with precious stones. Meeks guffawed and took the brooch from him, pressing it against the clerk's thin chest. It suited him, Meeks declared.

"This lot'll earn two thousand sterling in New York Town," the ship's master said, his eyes glinting as he looked sideways at Jones. "In the West Indies, them rich sugar planters'd pay twice that, an' no questions asked."

Jones was rapt, his face shining unnaturally. He did not notice his partner stand up and move back a few paces, nor did he take his attention from the silver brooch. If he had, he would have seen a dagger in the seaman's left hand, a cocked pistol in the other. The clerk was lost in thought over how well-off he had instantly become and would be for many years. He knew how to save a penny and . . .

The chill that suddenly crawled up his spine was not from the wind. He stopped short, about to stand, but a feeling of terror kept him from moving. He sensed Meeks was not at his side. Had he been a fool to trust the scoundrel? He must turn around but feared what he would meet. The blood drained from the clerk's head, and he felt about to faint.

"If you fire, you're a dead man, Meeks."

Jones quailed to hear this voice—one he knew was Owen Sutherland's—and, terrified, collapsed forward onto his face with a moan.

Meeks did not move a muscle. His pistol still bore on Jones, prostrate a few yards away. The pirate tried to locate Sutherland, but precisely where the Scotsman was he could not tell.

"Put the pistol and dagger down, Meeks; throw down your cutlass, and raise your hands." The voice seemed behind him, or was it to the left? He let the dagger drop at his feet, and with the same hand slipped the sword from its sheath, tossing it aside. "The pistol. Now, or you're flybait!"

Jones was still flat out on the ground, the bag of treasure beside him. His feet moved involuntarily, as though he were keeping time with some frantic rhythm.

Meeks said sweetly, "I fear if I drop it this here firearm will go off by accident an' shoot one of us. Let me hand it to yer gentleman-like."

Suddenly Sutherland was close behind Meeks, materializing with a soft crush of leaves and the touch of a muzzle to the sailor's head. That decided matters. Meeks uncocked the pistol, turning it upside down in his palm and holding it back for Sutherland to take.

Beginning to turn, Meeks said, "Jumpin' down from the trees with a loaded firearm in yer mitts is a chancy thing." But Sutherland's pistol poked abruptly against his temple, and he looked to the front again, licking his lips.

Sutherland stuck the sailor's pistol in his own belt, then told Meeks to stand near Farley Jones, who still lay on his belly, almost hysterical with despair. Each man was a shadowy figure now, for the night closed in rapidly, and though a glow was yet in the sky, it was hard for Sutherland to see clearly. He had to get these two to the fort, more than three miles away. He decided to march them through the woods to their skiff and have them sail to Detroit under his guard.

"Pick up the bag!" Sutherland commanded. Meeks protested that he was not as spry as he used to be and complained that the sack must weigh two hundred pounds. The Scotsman ignored him and said, "And get Jones on his feet. You have a choice: Lug the goods or take a bullet in the leg and I'll string you up by your heels until I come back with the army."

Meeks looked full of fire, and Sutherland knew he could take no chances, especially in the gathering darkness. One mistake and Meeks would turn things around, for he could break a man's back with a blow. With Sutherland's pistol trained on him, Meeks bent to help his whimpering accomplice.

Jones hardly responded as Meeks roughly hauled him to his feet. The seaman, fumbling with the clerk, was momentarily concealed from Sutherland. In a flash Jones was flung through the air like a rag doll. Sutherland stepped aside, expecting Meeks to follow. But instead of charging with bare hands, Meeks cocked and aimed the pistol taken from Jones's belt. Sutherland's own pistol swung around, but was an instant too late.

There came a blur of white, and a wild snarl. Heera was attacking. The sailor's pistol discharged. Heera howled, convulsed, and fell back, thrashing on the ground. Meeks lunged. Sutherland fired, but the bullet went wide. Meeks drove into Sutherland's chest with stunning force, and the Scotsman stumbled back, dropping the pistol. As he fell, he grappled for the seaman's throat, pulling Meeks with him. He found the throat, his strangling grip like iron, but Meeks used his weight to crash Sutherland to the ground with a bruising jar.

Sutherland lost hold of the throat. He locked his arms on his enemy's bullet head, trying to avoid the gnarled thumbs that raked for his eyes. Meeks blindly clawed and bit, tearing at Sutherland's face and bellowing. Then he was working both arms under Sutherland's back, trying to join them and squeeze the life from the Scotsman. Hardly able to breathe, Sutherland knew he was done for if the brute got a good grip on him. His own arms were crushing Meeks's skull, shaking viciously, controlling Meeks, if only for the moment.

The seaman's tough hands linked despite Sutherland's desperate efforts, and with a great roar of fury, Meeks rammed his shoulder downward against his opponent's chest. Sutherland had anticipated this, however, and at the same instant heaved mightily with his legs, going with the force of the pirate's move, jamming Meeks's face hard against the earth. With that same effort, Sutherland threw his legs high and twisted partway free, though he could not get out from under. His hands again fought for his enemy's throat, punching and smashing flesh and bone until he gripped it. Meeks's neck was thick and muscled, but Sutherland was powerful, his hands incredibly strong. At last he throttled Meeks, shouting fiercely as he shook and squeezed, hanging on as the choking pirate battled to get loose.

Employing all his strength, knowing that if he let go he would be killed, Sutherland concentrated on crushing that massive neck. Slowly he gained mastery, but Meeks was still on top. Meeks brutally kneed and punched, elbowed and battered the Scotsman with unyielding fury, but Sutherland would not let go. He felt Meeks gasping, heard him gag for breath. Seconds passed like hours. Sutherland shook, and Meeks gave way, his assault weakening slowly under the iron grip on his windpipe. The seaman tried to break away, but Sutherland deftly kicked his own legs clear and spun Meeks onto his back, slamming his head down again and again. Meeks fought for air and would not surrender, but Sutherland had him. A moment longer and Meeks would be unconscious, or dead.

Then Sutherland heard Heera snarl, and he felt the wounded dog brush against him, moving past, attacking Jones. Heera yowled in pain, and Sutherland looked up to see Jones with Meeks's dagger, about to stab the wounded dog again. Heera was snapping at Jones to prevent his escape, though the dog dragged his hindquarters, blood blackening his white coat. Jones slashed with the knife, and the husky staggered to the ground; then with ultimate effort, he sank his teeth into the desperate clerk's leg.

At that moment Meeks gave a final lunge to get free, but Sutherland grabbed him, crashing his skull three times against a rock.

"Yield!" Sutherland bellowed, anxious to go and save his injured dog. "Yield, or die!"

Sutherland heard the sickening sound of the knife striking Heera yet again, and the dog grunted but would not let go.

In his wildness, Sutherland found the power to squeeze Meeks's neck so ferociously that the sailor gave a terrible shudder and went limp. Was he done for? Sutherland could not wait to be sure. Jones wailed and stabbed again at the husky, who held fast. Screeching, raising the knife, his free hand grasping the animal's ear, Jones had the throat exposed.

Sutherland cried out, leaping across to bowl Jones over, and as Jones went down, Heera released the leg and slumped to the ground. Sutherland kicked the dagger from the clerk's hand, and Jones turned craven, begging for mercy, hands clasped before him. Heera convulsed and yowled pitiously. With a cry of anguish, Sutherland fell to his dog's side, seeing the bloody wounds and broken hip.

"Heera!" he groaned. "Ah, dog!" He forgot himself for a moment, then sensed danger. Whirling around into a crouch, he saw the glint of steel. In that same instant his claymore came out as though with a will of its own, but the tremendous force of Meeks's blow staggered Sutherland as he parried with his blade.

Meeks hacked rapidly, again and again, each time driving Sutherland down, steel clanging against steel. The wicked curved cutlass was heavier than the Scottish claymore, and Meeks beat at his opponent with all his might. Sutherland could only take the blows, the slashes, the cuts, with no chance to counterattack. In the failing light he fought by instinct, the pirate's blade more than once just a fraction from splitting his skull. He was off balance under that terrible assault, parrying desperately, countering fierce lunges with only a hairsbreadth to spare.

At his back Heera lay, dying, and then Sutherland knew Farley Jones was there, too. The clerk's shadow moved in behind. Meeks roared and struck downward. Sutherland took the full force on his sword and sank to one knee. The shadow was closing in. The cutlass thrust, and Sutherland slid just under the blade and to the left of the seaman. Jones swung some massive club, whisking just past the Scotsman's head. Meeks grunted, and the cutlass stabbed again, slicing Sutherland's buckskin shirt, cutting him, though he hardly felt it. He parried, then thrust.

Meeks defended, but gave no ground. He wheezed for breath, as though Sutherland's savage choking had hurt him seriously. The pirate swung, but now Sutherland, the better swordsman, was on his feet. The cutlass missed by inches, for Sutherland had anticipated precisely where it would go. He followed up, moving inside, hacking backhanded. Meeks yelped and fell backward, dropping his cutlass as the tip of the claymore nicked his chin. Sutherland stepped forward, Meeks at his mercy.

"Now—" he began. Too late, he knew the shadow was at his back. Jones clubbed him from behind, and Sutherland was knocked painfully to his knees.

Sutherland cut blindly at Jones, who danced about like a demon, looking for another chance. Meeks was crawling backward without a sword. Sutherland struck at him, though it took all his strength. He was close to passing out from the massive blow to his head. Jones dared to club Sutherland again and managed another solid blow. The Scotsman was reeling, battling to get to his feet.

Through the agonizing, numbing blur, Sutherland made out Meeks scrabbling on the ground for the fallen cutlass. If he got to it, Sutherland was finished. Sutherland was on his feet, swaying, like a wounded stag at bay who could hardly see either of the wolves attacking him.

Then he pretended to be done for and went limp. Meeks scurried at the cutlass, and Sutherland waited until the precise moment. Then with a ferocious yell, he stabbed at the pirate. But the violent clubbing had done its work, and the dazed Sutherland was not completely master of his weapon. Meeks was lucky, for the thrust was a fraction too slow, and he threw himself backward and rolled for his life.

Sutherland erupted with the bloodcurdling Highland battle cry, and on he came, despite the agony. He went for moving forms, hurled himself recklessly at his enemies, and the claymore was like a deadly living thing. Then, as his cries melted into the gloomy woods, Sutherland slowed to listen. There came the crashing of Meeks and Jones fleeing through the underbrush. He was alone. Almost fainting, he shifted from one foot to the other. Blood trickled down his neck, sticky and warm. His head throbbed as though it would burst.

Closing and opening his eyes, he managed to see his surroundings a bit clearer. He was nauseated and dizzy, only half conscious as he leaned back against the elm tree, searching the spinning dimness for the return of his attackers. The hiss of wind and the fading noise of men hurrying through the woods went round and round, confused with the ringing in his head. After a moment he saw the bag of valuables, left behind. He staggered forward to pursue Meeks and Jones, but his legs would not hold him, and he collapsed near the husky, fighting to remain conscious.

"Heera, lad," he muttered softly, his mind ablur, head pounding in agony. "Heera, are you still with me?"

The dog gazed back, silent and accepting of what was coming

upon him. Sutherland could hear Jones and Meeks arguing down by the skiff; there was still a chance to catch them once he regained his senses and got to the canoe. But that would mean leaving Heera behind to bleed to death.

Slowly, Sutherland got to his knees, shook off the numbness, and spoke to his dog. Heera had saved his life. Sutherland would do what he must, even though two villains escaped—for the moment. With supreme effort, he stood up, lifting the heavy dog in his arms, warm blood running down his leggins. Taking a deep breath, he walked back through the pitch-dark woods, toward the river.

Before making for the canoe, Sutherland looked at the dark mass of the *Helen* and saw the skiff already tied to its stern. The anchor chain rumbled and creaked as it was raised; sails were being set, the wind snapping and whipping the canvas with reports like gunshots across the water.

Meeks would risk the shoals at night. He had no other choice if he wanted to get away before Sutherland raised a force to follow him. Perhaps Meeks would even reach Lake Erie if he was lucky and the wind held fair for him. In that moment, though, Sutherland did not think about the ship or pursuit. He pushed his face against Heera's furry shoulder, sadness welling in him that his friend should die because of such swine as Meeks and Jones.

Heera whined once, trying to lick Sutherland's face, then gave up, allowing himself to be carried to the waiting canoe. Downstream the ship was leaning with the wind, cutting sharply into the middle of the wide river, in full flight for the open lake. By morning, Meeks would be through the lower narrows, soon to be swallowed up by the vast reaches of Lake Erie.

Sutherland laid Heera in the canoe, glanced once downriver, and saw that the *Helen*'s running lights were masked now so she would not be seen and hailed by the watch at Fort Detroit. Gathering his strength, he hurried back to the elm tree for the treasure, then returned to the canoe. By now the ship was out of sight, around the leftward-curling bend. He quickly tore up part of the burlap sack to use as bandages to stanch the flow of blood from his husky, then he pushed off from shore, paddling as rapidly as he could for Valenya.

Sutherland would assemble men to follow Meeks in the hope that a contrary wind or shoal water delayed escape, but he would ask no man to hazard the dangers of Lake Erie now that winter was fast descending. His immediate concern, though, was for his dog. Ella was a remarkable healer, and if anyone could keep Heera alive, it was she. Yet the dog was slipping away fast. His eyes were closed as he lay motionless in the bottom of the canoe.

Paddling rapidly, Sutherland spoke to Heera of old times, using words of encouragement. He sang a *voyageur* song of the trail, and in the dimness a glint told that the animal's eyes were open again. That gave Sutherland hope.

In the common room at Valenya, Ella and Sally labored over the unconscious Heera. Lying on a cowhide cushioned by beaver skins underneath, Heera was kept warm beside the roaring fire. Ella and Sally swabbed clean the bullet wound and stitched the slashes on the dog's neck, while Benjamin and Susannah fetched water and rags. They also brought a bowl of warm milk and honey, a treat the children always secretly gave Heera out in the milking shed to spoil him. They had hoped it would rouse him to drink, but he did not stir. Benjamin whimpered, fighting back tears, and Susannah's lower lip trembled every time she looked at the blood-smeared dog.

Sally washed the caked blood from Heera's coat, and Ella tried to set the dog's right hindquarter, which had been broken by the bullet meant for Owen. The lead had gone right through, but the bone was cracked, high on the dog's rear leg. Ella sewed gut into the lips of the wound, closing the gash; then she bound up the leg against Heera's body, fitting a crude splint that held the limb from moving.

Owen and the men—except for Jeb Grey and James Morely, who carried the treasure directly to Captain Lernoult at the fort—had taken canoes in pursuit of the ship. Ella knew her husband was in danger, but she kept her attention on Heera, whose chance of surviving such damage was slim.

Hour after hour they worked on the dog, who lay motionless, unconscious throughout. The younger children, exhausted from misery and lack of sleep, curled up on the floor nearby. The pan of milk and honey—cold and untouched—stood between them as they slept. Just before dawn, with the lamps turned down, Ella and Sally had done all they could and wearily sat back in chairs before the dying fire. Sally poured them lukewarm tea from a pot by the hearth, and they drank in silence, their aprons bloody and wet. Heera lay so still that Ella went to him to see whether he was breathing.

"He's with us yet," she said, stroking the animal's ear, which did not move in response. "I would that Tom and Owen come back soon; I don't like them on the river at night."

Returning to her chair, relaxing now, Ella thought of Tom Morely. Tommy was a fine, strapping fellow, honest and brave. But he could not win Sally's hand, though he tried hard and was cheerful enough about it all, acknowledging that Sally pined for Jeremy. Tom admitted he was not a scholar like Jeremy; he tried to please Sally and to understand her interest in literature and music, but unlike Jeremy he was lost in those worlds. Ella looked at Sally, who leaned back with eyes closed, the fire's glow warm and red on her face. When Sally first came to the Sutherlands she had been fleeing from imprisonment with the Ottawa, a tribe that had murdered her entire family during Pontiac's uprising. Owen and Ella had wanted to adopt Sally, but she rejected their suggestion—gently—because even then she loved Jeremy and did not want to be his sister. It had seemed puppy love then, but the relationship had deepened. In January Jeremy would attend Edinburgh University to continue studying medicine, and perhaps his budding romance with Sally would end by then. Yet he had spent three years at the Academy in Philadelphia and had not found another girl to love, nor had Sally cooled toward him.

Ella had always imagined Sally and Jeremy to be more brother and sister than possible husband and wife, and she still found it hard to think they might marry. In her heart she believed her son would return to the northwest one day, but he would be greatly changed. As wonderful a woman as Sally Cooper was, it would be surprising if the two of them ever married, for Ella well knew the excitement and heady pleasure of upper-class life in Britain, having been born to it herself. Her passion for Owen and the love of the northwest had made a frontier woman out of her, but somewhere within were fond memories of civilization, art, culture, music . . . all the charms of the Old World that she knew could captivate a young idealist like Jeremy.

She hoped those charms would not hold him in Britain—not for her own sake, nor even for Sally's sake, but because it was best that Jeremy shape his own life without entanglements. Ella wanted her son to take the best of Britain and transplant it to America, to the northwest, where future civilization could make a better world if the right people cultivated it properly. *Dr. Jeremy Bently*. That sounded so good to Ella, who dozed off as the fire was dying.

Gray light brightened the eastern sky behind the house, filtering through the kitchen windows and into the common room. Ella sat up and rubbed her face, then looked at the dog, who as before was barely alive. She tossed wood into the fire, awakening Sally.

"I was dreaming," Sally said, then peered sorrowfully at Heera before kneeling down to him.

Ella stoked the fire and asked, "Dreaming about what? Jeremy?"

Sally glanced at Ella, surprised that her thoughts were so transparent. She gave a soft laugh and caressed Heera's shoulder.

"Yes," she replied. "About Jeremy . . . and me. I hope he writes soon so I get a letter with the spring post! He will write, won't he? He said he would! If he doesn't—"

Ella smiled and stood up, ready to wash and make breakfast. "I'm sure he will, Sally; he won't forget us so soon."

Sally closed her eyes, as though wishing she could go back to her pleasant dream. "We had ten children—or was it twelve? Never mind, they were all beautiful, except for one strange thing . . ."

Ella went to the kitchen and took the heated water from above the fire, pouring some into the stone sink. She busied herself washing hands and face, and as she did so asked Sally, "What was so strange about the children in your dream?"

Sally sat back on her heels, a little annoyed and perturbed. "They all were boys, all with brown, curly hair, and none of them acted like proper doctor's sons!"

Scrubbing her fingernails with a small bristle brush, Ella turned and called out. "Sounds like Tom Morely's little ones!" She meant that as a teasing joke, but Sally saw no humor in it.

chapter 6

YOUNG WOMEN

By early afternoon, Sutherland returned, unable to overtake the *Helen*, which had escaped to open water. There was no way to catch Meeks and Jones now, for the weather had turned foul and a storm threatened to break that evening. Erie was a deadly place when a winter squall blew in, and Sutherland would not gamble the lives of his friends in the pursuit. After dismissing his men, he paddled across the choppy river to Detroit and explained to Captain Lernoult all that had happened.

Exhausted, angry at having lost Meeks and Jones, Sutherland did not tarry long at the commandant's office, particularly when the surly Lieutenant Davies began to suggest that Sutherland's story might be false. It took all Sutherland's willpower to keep from flattening the lieutenant, who had implied that the Scotsman was involved in the crime and now was laying the blame elsewhere. Only the presence of Lernoult had cooled Sutherland, for the commandant did not doubt what the Scotsman told him.

As he canoed back to Valenya, Sutherland thought of Lernoult's statement that all the evidence pointed to Meeks and Jones as the culprits. Lernoult had said the treasure would be returned to Dawson Merriwether, and a thorough investigation would be made to prove beyond doubt who killed Mrs. Merriwether.

"Detroit's people will know you had nothing to do with this," Lernoult had said. Yet Sutherland knew there would be a few, like Davies, who preferred to think all Whigs were capable of such viciousness. Lernoult trusted him and would hold him blameless in the Merriwether affair, but there would be doubt in the minds of some for as long as the conflict raged between Whig and Tory.

Shaking off these gloomy thoughts, Sutherland returned to Valenya. He strode to the house, where he joined Ella, Sally, and the

75

children in the common room. Immediately he went to the injured
dog lying before the fire.

A look at the wounds and bandages told him Ella had done all
she could. Heera was no longer losing blood but was terribly weak
and obviously might not survive. Sutherland felt as though a great
burden bore him down. There was no other dog like Heera. Benjamin and Susannah were on the floor, the girl reading nursery
rhymes with feeling, hoping Heera would wake up to listen. Benjamin, extremely sad, lay on his tummy, hands folded beneath his
chin.

Needing to walk outdoors with Ella, Sutherland said to them,
"Stay with Sally and watch over Heera, children, while your mother
and I go for a stroll along the river."

Benjamin murmured, "What if Heera dies?"

But Susannah, blond pigtails flapping as she shook her head,
cried out, "Heera won't . . . he can't . . . he won't! Don't say such
things, you—you boy!"

With that she threw aside her book and lay next to the huge
white dog, kissing his head and caressing him. Benjamin's mouth
quivered, and he tried not to show his desolation. At that moment,
Owen thought he noticed something. He let out a faint whistle,
the three dropping notes he always used to call Heera. The dog's
ear twitched. Benjamin gasped, and Susannah squealed, hugging
the animal close. Sutherland whistled once more, this time a little
louder. Heera's eyes opened despite Susannah's smothering embrace.

Astonished, Benjamin got to his knees, and his sister fell back
against Sally as they all gazed at the dog. Heera was making a
soft whining sound. Sutherland spoke his name, and Heera lifted
his head slightly when Ella knelt beside him.

Susannah pushed the bowl of milk and honey toward the dog,
and Heera sniffed it, a kind of inspiration lighting his eyes. Weakly,
he licked at the bowl, then rolled onto his belly to lap hungrily at
it. The children were babbling in joy.

"He'll live! Heera will live!" Benjamin exclaimed, then dashed
into the kitchen to fumble with the honey jar and a jug of milk.
Grinning, Sutherland came to the husky, who raised his milky
face to lick his master's hand.

"Yes," Owen said, winking to the children, "he'll live. The
milk-and-honey cure has done it again." He nuzzled the dog, and
Ella stroked the animal's head, tears in her eyes.

"Good Heera," Ella said, and Owen put his arm around her,

grateful for all she had done. Then she drew her husband to his feet, saying they should take that walk now.

Owen agreed. Ella had exhausted herself with this ordeal, and his own nerves were taut; both needed air and each other's company. Sally exclaimed that she was going to run to tell the Greys and Morelys the good news and flew out of the house. Benjamin stamped happily back into the room, a jar of honey in one hand, milk in the other. Heera might have drowned in affection and sweet milk that afternoon if Sutherland had not warned his children to let the dog rest.

Relieved, and as content as he could feel considering the escape of Meeks and Jones, Sutherland went with Ella to the door. Leaving the younger children with the dog, they threw on hooded capes and stepped outside into a misty rain and a wind that was brisk and invigorating.

Fog obscured the far bank of the straits, enclosing the Sutherlands, and they were grateful for the solitude. Taking Owen's arm as they walked slowly along the beach, Ella said nothing until he commented that Hugh Meeks was a remarkable seaman for having sailed through the narrows at night and reaching the lake before dawn.

Ella said, "He'll never come back to Detroit after the authorities learn about him, and neither will that miserable murderer, Jones!"

"Aye, but that won't do justice for the death of poor Mrs. Merriwether." He tossed a pebble into the rough water. "Getting them into a courtroom will be as hard as bringing Bradford Cullen to a reckoning."

Ella added that with Cullen safe in Boston, Meeks and Jones would surely make for that city to rejoin him and be protected from prosecution—at least until the civil strife in the colonies was resolved.

They walked some moments without speaking, the wind picking up, blowing through their clothes and their hair. Sutherland asked Ella if she wanted to go with him when he attended the second Congress in Philadelphia that spring.

Ella shook her head, and with a voice that wavered slightly, she said, "If we both go, I fear we might lose what we have built here." Turning to look at the house, where smoke drifted low and cloudy from a chimney, she said, "Meeks is not the only one who would see Valenya destroyed and folk such as us driven out forever."

Sutherland knew she was right. If they went east together, the empty house would be a target for Tory mobs, and the Frontier Company would be weaker for the absence of both of them. Word would pass quickly through the Detroit community that he was returning to Philadelphia, and there would be some who would think this a chance to destroy Valenya.

"Our kind are not wanted here these days," he said, "but I'm sure that once we come to terms with Parliament, things will settle down again. Just keep to yourself and to our friends when I'm gone."

After an hour, Ella and Owen Sutherland wandered back toward the house, passing the standing stones, stoic and grand in the windy rain. The couple was unmindful of the bad weather, glad for this quiet time, because too often they had been apart and too soon it would again be so.

As they went hand in hand along the beach, they came to the canoe racks, where a birchbark boat was propped upside down on slender poles. Here they heard a voice, and looking closely saw Sally and Tom sitting under the large master canoe, sheltered from the rain. Tom's head rested on a supporting pole of the rack, and Sally was leaning forward, reading to him from one of the many pamphlets widely circulated in America to express one or another political viewpoint.

In the midst of the rising storm it was a pretty picture to see these young folk absorb themselves in what sounded to Owen like poetry. Moving closer, Ella and he listened unobserved, for Sally was intent on her pamphlet, and Tom had his eyes closed.

> Along thy fields, which late in beauty shone,
> With lowing herds and grassy vesture fair,
> The insulting tents of barbarous troops are strown,
> And bloody standards stain the peaceful air.

Smiling, Sutherland told Ella this was a popular poem by John Turnbull, an American opponent of British policies in beleaguered Boston.

"It's titled 'An Elegy on the Times,'" he said, whispering, so Sally would not be disturbed. "It's about the occupation of Boston by the army, and it's a glittering, bombastic piece."

Ella could not help but giggle, saying "Not bombastic enough to keep Tommy awake . . . see?"

Indeed, Tom's head was drooping, though Sally did not notice. Voice rising with emotion, she recited verse after verse—and there

were sixty-eight of them! Ella and Owen lingered nearby, enjoying
the sight and Sally's impassioned reading.

> In vain we hope from ministerial pride
> A hand to save us, or a heart to bless:
> 'Tis strength, our own, must stem the rushing tide,
> 'Tis our own virtue must *command success*.

Sally put her all into the last two words, and that stirred Tom,
who awoke, pretending to clear his throat. He forced himself to
listen. No scholar, Tom was interested in Sally, not in high-blown
patriotic elegies. He admired, but he did not comprehend, her
intellect. The rest of her he loved, though Sally was the only
person who seemed not to know it. As Jeremy Bently's friend,
Tom had not pressed his suit too forcefully on her, knowing how
Sally missed Jeremy so.

Yet, though he was not disloyal to his absent friend, Tom did
not give up trying to turn Sally's head his way. He hoped she
would see how much he loved her and would in time forget her
feelings for Jeremy. Tom was even willing to endure this poetry
for Sally, and that was considerable proof of his love for her.

Owen said, "It's difficult to be young these days."

"At least these two are both on the same side politically, and
so are their families."

"No Romeo and Juliet, they," Sutherland said. "What will
become of them, and of Jeremy? Sally loves the lad, not Tom,
but when Jeremy comes back, he won't be the same."

"She knows that." Ella leaned against her husband, the rain
heavy on her cape and hood, but she did not mind. With a stifled
laugh, she said, "See there—Tom is slipping away again."

Tom's head nodded once, twice, and then he was asleep. Sally
was completely lost in the passion of her poem:

> So must we sink? and at the stern command,
> That bears the terror of a tyrant's word,
> Bend the weak knee and raise the suppliant hand;
> The scorned, dependent vassals of a lord?

Sutherland hissed, "Never!" Ella poked him to be still. Sally's
words were tossed about by the rising wind, and the canoe was
like a restless creature on its wobbly rack, rattling and shifting
with the gusts. The wind howled through the standing stones, and

the Sutherlands drew their wet cloaks closer about themselves. It was amazing that Sally was so determined to go on reading, though her pamphlet fluttered as if about to blow away.

Sutherland noticed the canoe above her head was not lashed tightly enough, and he was about to advance and secure it. But Ella touched his arm so he would not interrupt.

"Let's go home," Ella said. "We're not needed here."

"But the lashing—" Owen began to protest as Ella tugged at him, insisting the youngsters be left to their dreams—waking and sleeping dreams, for Tom was in a deep slumber, never mind wind or Sally's oration.

Just then, the wind rudely buffeted the canoe above them. The rack yielded and the whole affair collapsed, covering both her and Tom. Before the Sutherlands reached her, Sally struggled out from under the canoe, holding on to the pamphlet, the gale blowing her skirt about. When she saw Tom's legs sticking out unmoving from beneath the craft, she yelled in fright.

Joined by the Sutherlands, Sally leaped to yank the heavy canoe aside, and there lay Tom—as he had been earlier—fast asleep. Sally did not realize this and thought him stunned. She threw her arms about him, shaking him until he awoke with a start.

"Tommy, Tommy! Oh, you poor thing!" she exclaimed. The Sutherlands tried not to laugh as Sally mothered him.

"It looks bad," Owen said grimly. "Just lie there, Tom, laddie, and come to your senses!"

"Is that you, Mr. Sutherland?" The young man was embarrassed that Sally was embracing him in sight of others. At the same time, he marveled that she actually had her arms around him. "Come to my what?"

Ella leaned down. "Don't move, Tom! That canoe gave you a nasty bump, I'll warrant. Yes, I can feel it here on the back of your head. Feel it Sally, dear?"

"What?" Tom exclaimed, but he easily gave in as Sally's hand went behind his neck, searching for the lump. "Oh. Yes . . . the bump on my noggin. Yes, there it be, Sal. Yes, that's better. Yes . . ."

Sally tried to soothe him, her eyes wide, face closer to Tom's than it had been since the night a year earlier when he had kissed her once, unexpectedly. To her it had been a surprisingly pleasing kiss, though they had not repeated it. Now she was sure she felt a terrible bump on her friend's head and rubbed it gently. He began to close his eyes.

Sutherland said, "Quite an ending to quite a poem, eh, Tom?"

"Poem? What poem? Oh . . . yes, Mr. Turnbuckle's poem. Yes, the, ah, 'Elderly in These Climes.' Yes, sir, a real danged poetical poem it is! Won't you finish reading it, Sal?"

With that, Sally sat back, giving a melancholy sigh. "There is no more," she said, almost to herself. "And that's not the title." Tom never understood poetry, or anything else that had to do with things more sublime than cabinetmaking or fur trading. She loved him like a brother, but wished he were more sensitive, like Jeremy.

Sutherland sensed Sally's disappointment with Tom and said quickly, "The rest of the poem, as you must know, Tom, wasn't published in every pamphlet printed; and I have to admit, you're right. The remaining part not published is every bit as exciting and . . . ah, bombastic as this was." Surprised that Tom should know there was more to the original Turnbull poem, Sally looked from her foster father to her friend and back. "And that original title you just mentioned, Tom, was discarded by the author just before the work went to press, though I see you hadn't heard— which is understandable, being far out here at Detroit."

Sutherland told the young man the correct title, and Tom repeated it carefully, nodding to Sally, who stared a bit sideways at him. She was even more amazed.

The Sutherlands bade good-day to Tom and told Sally to bring him in for supper. Then they departed, leaving Tom confused but a bit more prepared for Sally when she asked how he had come to be so schooled in modern literature.

"Shucks," he said, rubbing the back of his skull. "A fella can't always allow himself to be ignorant of such things—you always say that yourself, girl! And besides . . ." He took her hand and put it behind his head. "Besides, anything that pleases you must be worth followin', so I been keepin' up on things, includin' Mr. Turnbuckle!"

Sally smiled wistfully. Tom was lovable, though he was still not as swift as Jeremy Bently. For all Tom's massive build and utter fearlessness, he was the gentlest, kindest man she knew. Impetuously, she kissed him on the forehead, and he held her from moving away. With a giggle she pulled back, the wind whirling her wet hair. Smiling, she said it was time to go.

He said, "That kiss made me feel a whole lot better, an' I do believe one more would be the powerfullest cure an' make me fit as a new fiddle!"

She laughed, then remembered that remarkably sweet kiss they had shared. She could not make sense of it. Why was Tom here when she did not love him? Why was Jeremy far across the sea, though she loved him more fiercely with every passing day? Why had Jeremy's kiss not been quite like that brief touch of Tom's lips last spring?

Tom was grinning. Sally scolded him for a malingerer and said he could kiss his girlfriends in the fort if he wanted to. It was true that many young women were in love with Tom, though he took none but Sally seriously.

"There's nobody else here to cure me right now!" he said and gave a long groan. "'Tis you, Sal, the only one can show this poor boy mercy, lest he—"

All of a sudden, the wind again pounded the canoe, which leaned precariously on the remains of the rack. Everything collapsed, with Tom beneath it. Sally yelped and scrambled under the canoe, fearing he was really hurt badly. This time he was ready for her. As she poked her head under the overturned canoe, his lips met hers.

Again, the kiss was perfect. At first, Sally could not draw away. When she did, her face was flushed, and she was short of breath. Tom got to his knees beside her, neither of them feeling the rainstorm.

He said, "Nice kiss, wasn't it?"

She took a deep breath. "Who taught you to kiss like that? Those Indian girls, or the French?"

Tom chuckled and reached for her, but she stood up, shivering from cold and confusion. He got to his feet, giving his cloak to supplement her own. They walked back to the house, and Sally realized to her surprise that she really wanted an answer to that question. Probably it was the French girls, she thought, though some of the Indians were wanton enough to have schooled Tom in anything he fancied to learn.

Dismayed, she felt what might have been described as jealousy. If it had been Jeremy and not Tom, she was sure it would most certainly be moody jealousy, but jealousy it could not be. She did not love Tom Morely—not the way she loved Jeremy—and she never would.

In Bristol, Jeremy was on deck just after sunrise, looking down at laborers moving goods from ship to warehouse, dock to wagon. Barrels rumbled over cobblestones, men steering them deftly and recklessly on their way. It was a miracle that none of those endless streams of hogsheads and barrels collided. Workers rolling barrels, pushing handcarts, hauling bales or sacks, scurried like ants from a broken anthill, and there was scarcely room on the wharf for a pedestrian to move.

Now and again a carriage drawn by fine horses would clatter and clop into the street near Jeremy's ship, carrying a merchant prince with his accountant, or sometimes his entire, well-dressed family. The carriage would pass among the swirling laborers as a canoe cuts through water lilies, no one daring to block the horses of someone who employed them. Jeremy felt pity for these Bristol dockhands, who would never know the kind of freedom he possessed in the American wilderness. The struggle to survive in this city was more merciless and more fierce than life in the northwest, for all the forest's hazards and difficulties.

Just how would he endure this country if the rest of it was like Bristol, swarming with dirty, poor folk rooting about in filth and breaking their backs for a pittance? The land he came from was sparkling, fresh, bursting with promise. To Jeremy, Philadelphia had been a paradise of intellectuality, prosperity, culture, and modest good manners. But this first impression of Mother England was a dismal one indeed, and homesickness welled in him even more sharply.

At his side, Sniffer put his paws on the railing to examine what it was that took up his master's attention. At that moment, another coach came into the waterfront street, finding it difficult to pass, for this time the laborers were slow to move aside. Heavy barrels lumbered close to the legs of the pair of nervous horses, and the animals shied, obliging the driver to use his utmost skill to prevent mishap or injury to his team.

From the first it was apparent to Jeremy that this coach was not the property of a merchant or a shipowner; if it had been, the men would never have been so insolent. To the envious workers, this smart, sky-blue coach of some landed gentleman had no place at the docks, and they made the most of harassing it, though subtly enough so that none could be pointed to as an intentional troublemaker.

Jeremy laughed to himself, seeing a spirit of defiance among these English laborers. He was glad they were more than mere docile beasts of burden for the wealthy and could express resentment in some small way. As the coach drew near to the wharf of the *Yankee*, a young man thrust his powdered head out a window and began to belabor workers who had backed a cart of cotton bales into the narrow roadway between buildings and dock. The three men pushing the cart made as though they understood nothing, chattering and joking among themselves in such a comical way that before long two hundred pairs of eyes were watching the scene, delighting in the frustrating of a petty nobleman.

The man in the powdered wig urged his driver on, but as he did so, a bale of cotton was tipped from the cart by an unseen hand. It thudded to the cobblestones near the horses, causing them to rear in harness and wrench the carriage sideways toward the slimy water. At that, the man inside sprang out to confront the workers, all of them burly and mean-faced. About Jeremy's age, the nobleman wore a dark-blue frock coat, and his white wig gleamed like a beacon in the miserable surroundings.

Jeremy took some interest in this scene, seeing the nobleman might be in danger. As the gentleman commanded the rude carters to move away their freight, more and more workmen gathered around to watch and laugh. It would take nothing for some low dog to flit a blade into the man's back just for the sport of it, and by the look of the crowd, that might happen.

Jeremy touched the tomahawk hanging at his belt beneath the hunting shirt. He told Sniffer to stay where he was, and strolled down the gangplank, unaware the otter was scampering along behind. A few men from his ship called out that Jeremy should avoid this trouble, but he waved them off. Why he was going down there he did not really know, except that he liked the courage and the looks of the man from the carriage, and the odds seemed unfair.

The stink of briny water, urine, sweat, and tobacco mingled with coal smoke and the acrid smell of ship's tar. The crowd was loudly mocking the nobleman, who stayed quite calm. The horses whickered, trying to back away, and though the driver wanted to jump down beside his passenger to help, he dared not lest the team take fright and panic.

At the end of the gangplank, Jeremy leaped upon a long, high pile of timbers meant for ship's masts, giving himself easier access to the scene of the argument. In a moment, he was standing above the nobleman and carters, and Sniffer crawled unseen into a space between two timbers. The workmen with the cotton bales were pretending idiocy, babbling and drooling, apologizing and rubbing their heads; one of them even feigned a fit, falling upon the ground, kicking and shrieking, to the hilarity of the others. By now the

man from the carriage was trembling with rage. Although he carried a sword under his coat, he had made no movement toward
it; Jeremy knew that to do so would mean serious bloodshed. He
hoped the city watch had been alerted and would arrive before
matters got out of hand.

Then Jeremy understood why this fellow was so cautiously
restrained. Through the window of the carriage he saw a young
woman, lovely of face, with dark eyes that shone from beneath
the brim of her plumed hat. Those eyes gazed at Jeremy, as though
imploring him to help. That made him uneasy, for there seemed
little he could do. Jumping down among the mob at this moment
would be foolish, for enough of them disliked him as it was. To
stick his nose into this affair would mean a certain riot, which
might result in the woman's escort and Jeremy both being killed.
Better to await the watch.

Jeremy looked at the woman, then at the nobleman and dockhands, and back to the woman again. She was very beautiful. At
that moment a beefy carter with a green kerchief tied over his head
leaned toward the gentleman. Pretending deafness, he purposely
tried to step on the nobleman's polished shoe.

The man in blue, however, was no fool. Jeremy sensed he had
been through tight spots before, for he cleverly let the other's foot
come down, took the weight of it on his own, and with a quick
movement of his leg, sent the lout sprawling. The mob hooted
and roared, some cheering on the nobleman, but the friends of the
dock worker were angry at such humiliation. The trouble had
brewed strongly enough. If the watch or some merchant with
authority did not arrive quickly, blood would certainly be shed.

The man in the green kerchief got to his feet, murder in his
eye, and clenched his great fists. The nobleman touched the hilt
of his sword. A few clubs appeared. Onlookers quieted, as though
all caught their breath simultaneously. The girl again looked out
the window, saw what was happening, and again begged Jeremy
with her frightened eyes.

The horses sprang in harness. Some men backed off. There
was a shout of warning, and the leader of the carters showed a
short knife as he moved forward. The sword had still not left the
nobleman's scabbard, but in the hush, his voice rang out, "Take
another step, knave, and I'll run you through!"

The bully grinned, showing a toothless mouth. He looked from
side to side, then—as Jeremy knew he would—made his move.

No one saw quite how it happened, but in the next twinkling, the knife was struck from the man's hand, and the nobleman's sword-point was an inch from his eye.

The worker hesitated, but his followers were serious now; the nobleman was as good as dead. A quick look from one to the other, and the carters tensed to attack. Then someone shouted in surprise, and a crashing rumble turned every face toward the great pile of masts. It was as though the timbers had come alive, rolling ponderously down into the mob, forcing the men to leap aside. The jostling dock workers crashed into one another, knocking each other down in their haste to escape as twenty enormous timbers jolted into them. The carters were driven back to the building walls in their fright, though no one was hurt seriously.

The collapse of the mast pile had been more intimidating than dangerous. The horses and carriage were far enough away to escape damage, but the noise and surprise had worked well to break up the mob for the moment. Jeremy threw aside the pole he had used as a lever to start the avalanche and, calling to his own crewmen running down from the *Yankee*, jumped from the timbers to join the startled nobleman.

Soon there was a tight knot of men protecting the carriage, as Jeremy's Americans came to him. The surly dock workers re-grouped, but in the distance they heard the whistle of the watch. Quickly, the wharf and street were cleared as men ran back to work. The cart and bales of cotton were removed by the culprits who had begun the harassment, and all was as innocently noisy and as congested as before.

The handsome nobleman sheathed his sword and gave a deep, sweeping bow to Jeremy, who answered less dramatically, though with politeness. In his hunting smock, simple homespun breeches, and dark stockings, Jeremy was a marked contrast to the splendor of the other man. His sailors, rough and smeared with dirt, tar, grease, and sweat, seemed shy in the presence of the Englishman in blue, who thanked them for their aid and gave one a purse of gold crowns for their pleasure. Then he turned to Jeremy.

"Good sir, I am at your service." He bowed again, though less deeply. "Richard Weston of Derbyshire."

"Derbyshire!" Jeremy exclaimed, then remembered his manners and introduced himself.

"Master Bently!" Weston cried out with a laugh and gripped Jeremy's hand. "You are the one that brought me to this hellion's

den! I'm sent by your uncle, Colonel Gladwin, to fetch you away
to Stubbing!"

Weston laughed again and stepped back, hands on hips, to look
Jeremy over. The young frontiersman grinned at this coincidence,
thinking he soon would see his uncle again after more than ten
years. He examined Richard Weston as closely as he himself was
examined. Weston was not very tall, but was strong, lean, and
lithe, like a panther. His radiant blue eyes and delicate features
told nothing of the man's courage, which was obviously great.

Abruptly, Jeremy thought of the lovely woman in the carriage
and turned to see her gazing down at him, her lips parted in
amazement. She wore a striking hat,. plumed with ostrich and
circled with a brown satin band that matched her brown riding
jacket. She wore no gloves, and her hands were fine and perfectly
attended to in a way that Jeremy had never seen before, even
among the belles of Philadelphia. They looked at each other—
she openly and without self-consciousness, he carefully, lest his
fascination with her beauty annoy her escort.

Weston stepped to the carriage, saying, "Miss Penelope Graves,
allow me to present the object of our quest: the frontier physician
himself, Master Jeremy Bently!"

Jeremy said he was no doctor yet, but had only begun his study.
As he spoke he found it hard to take his eyes from the woman.
She was, he now knew, the daughter of the British merchant
Raymond Graves, a close friend of Henry Gladwin's and a leading
partner in the Frontier Company.

His voice a bit tight, Jeremy said, "I have the greatest admiration for your father, Miss Graves; when he came to the northwest
a few years ago we became fast friends, and he talked often about
you, though he did not, ah . . . Well, I mean to say he spoke of
you as though you were a child, not a—a beautiful woman."

Weston laughed warmly, and Penelope smiled. She said, "Papa
always will consider me a child, though I'm old enough to give
him grandchildren."

Weston said, "And saucy enough to tell him so! Master Bently,
when you're ready, we can carry you northward to your uncle,
whom I serve as aide-de-camp—though our camp is an English
estate, and I spend more time in London attending to his duties
than at Stubbing."

Weston explained that Henry Gladwin was deputy adjutant
quartermaster, responsible for matters of supplies and finances for

the British Army's North American establishment. As his civilian assistant, Weston traveled between the Stubbing estate in Derbyshire and the offices of the British Army at Whitehall in London, where the Gladwins owned a town house.

Jeremy was confounded when Penelope remarked, "Richard would have it no other way, for he has a bevy of true loves in London, and only a handful in Stubbing—if one does not count the dairymaids."

Weston chuckled. "As I remarked, Master Bently, Miss Graves, my dearest cousin, is saucy!"

"Your cousin?" Jeremy exclaimed, more loudly than intended. So she was not his sweetheart. Though he did not admit it to himself quite yet, he was glad for that.

Penelope laughed, "Did you think I was Richard's doxy then?"

Jeremy looked from Richard to Penelope, then said, "Saucy, you are indeed, Miss Graves—as your father once confessed to me, but I'd forgotten."

"And you are blunt, as all Americans are!" she replied, a glint of good humor in her dark eyes. "It's a quaint fault I find quite charming in you colonials."

Weston, in a stage whisper, said to Jeremy, "Have a care, my friend, for Penny is set on marrying the first Yankee who'll have her—"

That got Weston a smart clip on the shoulder from Penelope's parasol, though she was giggling. In their sport they had forgotten about the gawking seamen of Jeremy's ship, and when Penelope heard them laugh, she blushed and pulled back inside the coach, closing the leather curtain. Jeremy dismissed his men, and told Weston he would have his trunk brought down to the coach in ten minutes. After he changed into more civilized clothes, he would return, he said.

But on hearing that, Penelope threw back the curtain and declared, "Leave on your woodsman's smock! It's also quaint, and it will remind Colonel Gladwin of the romantic frontier!"

Jeremy laughed lightly at that. "Uncle Henry would be better reminded of his command at Detroit if I came to him with blood on the shirt and my scalp lifted."

Penelope gasped, her face turning pale. Richard Weston winked at Jeremy, then went to the driver to have the coach moved closer to the ship in case the ruffians came back for more after the half-dozen constables of the watch departed.

Jeremy walked past the jumbled mast timbers, making for the

gangplank, when he heard Penelope cry out. He spun to see her leap from the coach, her billowing gown sailing behind her as she rushed toward him. She came on, running very unladylike, but stopped short, leaving Jeremy astonished and confused. She was bending down to the masts, as if searching through them for something, clucking her tongue and murmuring sympathetically.

Jeremy came to her and heaved back a timber so she could better get at whatever it was she was after.

"There! Got you, little one!" she cooed, and stood up, her arms full with a brown, furry bundle that licked at her face and snorted.

"Sniffer!" Jeremy shouted, fearing the otter had been crushed by the rolling timbers. "Give him here! He's mine! Oh, Sniffer, what have I done to you!"

Penelope handed the otter over, saying, "He's not hurt, but it seems he got trapped in there; I saw him struggling to get out. So this is Sniffer!" She laughed in her attractive way and tickled the otter under the chin. "I heard more about Sniffer from Papa than I did about Master Bently and all the red Indians combined!"

Jeremy recalled how Raymond Graves had taken to Sniffer and spoiled him shamelessly. It was as though the otter remembered something, too, for he sprang back into Penelope's arms, sniffing and nuzzling so that she laughed for joy and hugged him. Jeremy grinned, relieved the otter had not been injured. They looked to be a good pair, Penelope and Sniffer; watching them, Jeremy knew the otter, at least, would make the most of life in Britain.

It was strange, but Penelope reminded Jeremy of Sally. Though this Englishwoman was far more refined, educated, and sophisticated, she had that same exuberant, happy quality that made Sally so wonderful to be with. For all her genteel bearing, Penelope Graves was genuine and appealing, and Jeremy sensed the next two years could be special. He was almost over his homesickness.

chapter 7

CONSTANT BILLY

On a rainy Sunday evening the Sutherland family made
the most of a quiet time in the common room. Ella sat at her spinet
playing Couperin and songs by Handel, while Owen was seated
on the sofa, where he read once more the letter Ben Franklin had
sent him from London. Sally sat with Susannah at one end of the
trestle table, sewing clothes for the Dutch terra-cotta doll they had
purchased in Philadelphia, and Benjamin occupied the other end,
struggling with schoolwork.

The sound of beautiful music filled the room, which was warm
from the crackling hearth. There was plenty of light from whale-
oil lamps, and the rain pattering down outside was a comforting
sound as Sutherland reread the paragraph in Franklin's letter that
warned of England's unwillingness to compromise with the stand
of Congress.

The statesman urged Sutherland to attend the Congress when
it met that coming spring, saying someone must voice the opinion
of those who lived in the great northwest, "which is the future
inheritance of all our people."

Sutherland stopped reading as he heard Ella brightly play a
song from *The Beggar's Opera,* an old favorite musical play that
portrayed life in Britain. The songs were clever and funny, mocking politicians and sympathizing with thieves and robbers; the
opera was a voice of the downtrodden, depicting them as spirited
and strong, in spite of bad rulers and oppressive laws.

Sally sang while Ella played, and Sutherland sat back to listen,
smiling contentedly. Susannah fussed as she tried a new dress on
her doll, and Benjamin's tongue poked out the corner of his mouth
as he labored over mathematics. Susannah learned womanly ways
from her mother and Sally and was also quick to grasp the same
subjects Benjamin studied. However, Benjamin went three times

a week to Reverend Lee's school in the fort, while Susannah was taught at home by Ella.

Ella was changing the tune to a sentimental ballad, titled "Constant Billy," about a girl whose true love will never come back again. Sally found it difficult to sing, though Ella and Owen, who now joined in, were in full voice, apparently unaware of her sensitivity.

> Oh, my Billy, my constant Billy,
> When will I see my Billy again?
> When the fishes fly over the mountains,
> That's when I'll see my Billy again.

Though the song had long been familiar to Sally, it seemed to have more poignancy than ever before because of her feelings for Jeremy. Hard as she tried to prevent it, she felt like crying. She abruptly turned away to sew again, and Owen realized she was sad. He cleared his throat, and Ella stopped playing, but Benjamin kept singing away until his father asked him to choose another song.

Ella said, "What about you, Sally? What'll we sing?"

Sally just shook her head, not looking around, and the Sutherlands exchanged glances. She was always a joy, full of light whenever she entered a room, and that made her sadness even more oppressive.

After a while, Ella went to put the younger children to bed, and Sally packed away her fabric and sewing materials. Sutherland was now trying to read an essay in the *Pennsylvania Gazette* but was hard put to concentrate, because he sensed Sally had something important to say. She fussed around the table, not departing for her own bed, yet apparently unable to speak. Sutherland laid down his paper, then spoke gently. "What is it, lass? Will you tell me?"

Sally looked up, her lips working slightly, eyes wet. She sniffed and sighed, saying she was just being silly. "I never thought a song could mean so much, Owen." She wiped her nose, feeling foolish. Sutherland noticed Ella at the bottom of the stairs, but he made a slight motion with one hand, and she turned and walked into her bedroom.

Sally sat down heavily in the chair, looking at her hands clasped in her lap. She said she longed to be cheerful, but it was so difficult. "How can I just ignore that he's so far away? I know I must, but how?"

Sutherland sat in a chair beside her. Putting a hand on her shoulder, he said, "There's only one way, and that's to go on the way you always have—making the most of life, being young and happy. Hey, lassie, there's a hundred lads out there who would be proud to have you on their arm, and grand ones, too, like Tom Morely."

Sally shook that off. "Tom's just a friend. You know that, and so does he."

"Still, you can have good fun with friends! So you must or you'll be old too soon, just as too many young folk are old these days." He became serious. "Sally, our world is not what it was; we're in dangerous times that require us to make the most of every hour." He squeezed Sally's shoulder. "Live for today, Sal! There's no other way."

Sally gazed at him with her large, shining eyes and smiled. Taking a long breath, she again looked at her hands. "Owen, may I ask a very personal question? One that's been haunting me of late, because I feel perhaps my situation might be similar to what yours was years ago."

In the bedroom, Ella tried not to listen, for she anticipated Sally's question.

"Owen, how did you possibly overcome the . . . the awful—I mean, how did you go on when your first wife died?"

Sutherland maintained his calm, but the question played upon a nerve and upon tragic memories. Sally saw this immediately and felt terrible that she had been so unfeeling.

Before he could reply, she groaned and got up. "Oh, I'm sorry! I'm such a selfish fool! I'm truly sorry, Owen!" She stumbled away, running to her weaving room, unable to stop crying.

Ella came into the room and sat with her husband, a hand on his arm. He was thinking, but not about the past; rather, how to cheer up Sally once and for all.

"You know," Ella said, "perhaps we could talk to our friends, asking them to help; if Sally gets so busy with them, she'll forget all this sadness."

Sutherland agreed to ask everyone to show how much they loved Sally. He and Ella considered the list of friends, including Levesque, who had rescued her from the Indians; Mawak, who had taught her to be an expert with sled dogs; Tamano and his family; Little Hawk; Jean Martine; the Greys; the Morely men; and so on.

Sutherland said with enthusiasm, "And I'll get a perfect present for her: some maple-sugar candy! She loves it, and our warehouse has some shaped in the form of a heart."

That encouraged them both. Ella went to soothe Sally, and to say that the question about Owen's loss was quite understandable. She told Sally that Owen had done precisely what he had suggested, and that was live every hour to its fullest, no matter what.

Two days later came the send-off of the canoe brigade, which was heading to the northern villages to trade for Indian pelts. The work of supplying and outfitting the canoemen had been done, and in a gray, wintry dawn they prepared to take leave of Detroit. After a candlelight service in the fort's Church of Sainte Anne—patron saint of *voyageurs*—Levesque oversaw the loading of thirty canoes. It was a reflection upon the uneasy, disorganized time at Detroit that this flotilla was departing for the north country so late in the season. Their journey would be hazardous, and they sent prayers to the saint asking for mild weather and favorable winds.

Sutherland's belated return to Detroit as well as the difficulty in procuring trade goods—because of the embargo—had delayed the departure. Most of what was loaded into the forty-foot canoes of the north had been shipped that autumn to Detroit by Peter Defries. This Frontier Company partner, who made his headquarters in Albany and who was now traveling in Europe, was also secretly acquiring guns and ammunition for the rebels. With British trade goods spurned by the company, Defries had had the devil's own time accumulating enough American-made wares to outfit the canoemen, but he had managed to do it before he sailed. Sutherland stood near the landing, grateful for the tenacity and genius of his friend.

All other trading firms in the northwest were owned by one or two principals, unlike the Frontier Company, which was made up of several leading partners and scores of minor partners. There were no employees in the Frontier Company, for every member— including these French and half-breed *voyageurs*—owned shares in the profits. In these times of intense competition, self-reliance, and racial hatreds, no one but Owen Sutherland could have formed such a company. It was his remarkable influence among red and white, French, Briton, and American that had achieved it despite the intrigues and attacks of Bradford Cullen, and despite the economic hardship that had befallen British America after the French and Indian War.

Now Sutherland faced his greatest challenge. It was one thing to match courage and strength against flesh-and-blood renegades, but it was something else to reject the firm's prime source of trade goods and its sole market, for the sake of a political ideal. But by refusing to buy British goods, Sutherland had done precisely that. Because of this stand, he, Defries, and other partners in the firm would be hard pressed to find goods to trade, and they would also have difficulty finding markets for the pelts.

Though some of his partners had angrily quit to operate on their own or in the employ of others—partially because they feared the government would rescind Sutherland's license to trade—Sutherland stood fast, praying the struggle would end in favor of the colonies by springtime.

As he stood in the wind, his frock coat flapping, head uncovered, Sutherland counted himself lucky to have the loyalty of Levesque and the *voyageurs*. The host of sleek canoes, pregnant with the goods Defries had managed to secure, lay deep in the water so that only their slim gunwales and curved prow and stern showed. Some carried four thousand pounds, including their men, and before this journey was done many would have traveled seven hundred miles into the interior. These boisterous canoemen could make eighty miles a day if their pride or lives required it.

A hundred scarlet stocking caps dotted the shadows of early morning, and French voices rose in song as one by one the canoes pushed off. The embarkation always thrilled Sutherland, who had spent many good years with these men, and he loved them for their courage, strength, and unfailing spirit. In Jacques Levesque's canoe, floating near the landing, was his lovely Angélique, respected as one of the most knowledgeable traders in the country. She sat with their three young children, who were half awake under blankets in the middle of the canoe. They would winter together at their permanent home in Fort Michilimackinac, located at the juncture of the Huron and Michigan lakes, where the company had a major trading house.

From behind, Sutherland heard a shout, and he turned to see Ella, Sally, and his two children come out of the fort. With them were Jean Martine and Jacques Levesque, whose dark, handsome face spoke of worry and doubt. Martine went to bid farewell to Angélique—his daughter—and Levesque approached to shake Sutherland's hand.

"For the first time in my life," Levesque said, his face drawn and shadowed in a way Sutherland had never seen before, "I wonder whether my furs will have a market in the spring."

Sutherland nodded. "They'll have a market, *mon ami*, even if I have to portage them to the Mississippi and peddle them on my back to the Spaniards."

Levesque gave a dry, curt laugh, saying, "Until your colonies permit trade with England, you refuse to send pelts over the water to London?" Sutherland nodded his head slowly, saying nothing.

The Frenchman continued, "For now I am with you in this, Owen. But if the squabble between you *Anglais* threatens to ruin the fur trade and our company, and if Americans try to bully us French, then I will leave you."

Sutherland gripped the man's hand and replied, "I would ask no one to stay because of friendship alone; but I do what must be done. Until the spring, my friend, *bon voyage,* and may the Old Woman Wind blow softly."

There was no more to be said. Levesque strode down to the water and climbed aboard the canoe. Without men like him there could be no Frontier Company, and no fur trade at all. If the trade stopped, Indians would be without the essentials of life, for their very existence hung on the slender thread of manufactured goods, powder, and hunting rifles for which they paid with pelts. If the trade shut down, whole nations of Indians would starve.

Sutherland regretted also that his faithful English supplier and partner, Raymond Graves, would suffer along with the company if Parliament and Congress were not soon reconciled. During Sutherland's trip to Philadelphia he would be compelled to establish commercial contacts with wealthy American merchants there; the Frontier Company must somehow find suppliers in America who would take his pelts in exchange for trade goods.

"It's a beautiful sight," Ella said, interrupting his reverie, as she and the children waved to the canoes shooting upstream, red paddles flashing in the water. "Sometimes I wish we could go with them and not come back until this tug-of-war with Parliament is over."

Sutherland agreed. It would be good to go northward, away from all the turmoil; but someone had to stand up for America, even if it meant the risk of utter defeat. If things went wrong, all he had built would suddenly be swept away.

A few hours later the Sutherlands were climbing into their long master canoe, tied up at the fort's landing. They were greeted by Mawak as Sutherland was on the dock untying the line. Mawak gravely addressed Sally, who looked up from where she knelt in the canoe, then came onto the dock at the Ottawa's request.

Standing straight and solemn, wearing a high-crowned hat with a peacock feather and sewn wampum beads, Mawak gave a short speech in which he called upon the sun to shine in Sally's heart.

"Open your eyes to what is good and true; let the wind blow away the tears," he said, hand floating as though on a breeze before Sally's surprised face. "And to open your heart, this Injun presents gift sure to make you happy." He grinned and handed over a small package, then grasped Sally by the shoulders. She smiled at him and said her thanks. Mawak then strode proudly back to the fort.

Sally returned to the canoe, smiling. "This is the second present I've received today—Jacques Levesque gave me a wonderful maple-sugar heart." She giggled as they all looked at her; fumbling with Mawak's package, she confessed she had eaten the sugar all by herself.

Sutherland laughed, saying, "Well, that's all right. You can share with us, for Ella and I bought you one, too!"

The children squealed as Ella gave Sally a fist-sized chunk of maple sugar decorated with a bow of red ribbon. Then Sally opened Mawak's package to find it was also a maple-sugar heart. Apparently Sutherland's invitation to cheer up Sally had been well understood, and Sally's friends all knew how much she loved maple sugar.

As they laughed over the coincidence, Tamano and Lela appeared on the wooden landing and called to Sally.

The Chippewa's pretty wife knelt and handed a wrapped parcel to Sally, saying, "We think of you when we at trading house this morning! You like it!"

Sure enough, it was another maple-sugar heart. Seeing that Sally now had three, Tamano insisted that he sample some. He and Lela sat down on the dock, legs dangling, and soon all were munching maple sugar, passing the time of day and enjoying themselves. Now that the canoe brigade was on its way and winter close, there would be a time of rest, because soon they would be snowbound and the straits frozen solid.

"Hey, Sally!" Tom Morely now stood on the landing, looking down at her, a small package in his hands. "Glad I caught you before you left!"

They all laughed as Sally said, "If it's a heart of sugar, just open it up, sit, and share it!"

"So that's where them hearts all went!" Tom declared. "I meant to buy you one this morning, but I was too late. So . . ." He knelt and handed Sally the carefully wrapped box. She took it eagerly, enthusiastic at all this attention.

She now realized that some plan had been cooked up, yet she had in no way anticipated Tom's gift. It was a hair barrette of beautifully carved hickory polished to a fine luster and designed with skillful simplicity.

Tom said a bit shyly, "I did it in the cabinet shop this morning after I saw the sugar hearts were gone." He grinned in his infectious way.

Sally marveled at how exquisite the barrette was, then with Ella's help placed it in her long hair. Lela and Ella admired Tom's craftsmanship, and Sutherland remarked that he ought to make a few more to please all his many sweethearts.

Sally glanced at Owen a little sharply at first, then pretended to be nonchalant. Tom chuckled and stood up, saying, "Won't ever make but one of these. It's special, Sal."

Sally smiled and looked around at her friends and family. Her melancholy had been swept away. Tossing a piece of maple sugar to Tom, she then blew him a kiss.

As Sutherland cast off the line, he whistled in admiration. "Well, Tom," he said with a wink, "you've finally won her heart . . . or a piece of it, anyway."

Sally blushed, and Tom stood back as Tamano helped Sutherland swing down into the stern of the canoe. The Chippewa gave the craft a shove with his foot, and the Sutherlands were on their way back home to Valenya. Tom and the Indians waved, and Sally waved back, touching her hair. She was delighted with such affection, and Tom's unexpected gift was indeed something wonderful.

As the canoe drew away, Sutherland observed her gazing back at the landing and Tom. He smiled to himself, then gave a shout to Benjamin to put away the sweets and start using his paddle. With Ella paddling in the bow, they swiftly crossed the river, singing all the way. The songs were from *The Beggar's Opera*, but only the funny ones; no one sang at all of "Constant Billy."

The journey by coach to Derbyshire was the strangest four days of Jeremy's life. Even the magnificence of Philadelphia and the grandeur of the ocean after the wilds of Detroit had not prepared him for the stark contrasts: teeming cities, coal-mine-blasted hillsides, beautiful country lanes, smoky smelting furnaces, tranquil valleys and rivers, and throbbing factories. By British standards, it was a long way to Stubbing—more than a hundred miles—and the frequent changes in scenery, people, and atmosphere astonished and awed Jeremy.

Their route north from Bristol took them first through the limestone Cotswold Hills, which rose steeply from the Severn estuary to the west, then sloped gradually eastward, green and grassy even in early December. Flock after flock of sheep crowded the stage track, or were chased by shepherd dogs into the limestone walls of circular folds. Jeremy had never imagined so many sheep in all the world, let alone in one small part of England. Up and down the vales, his carriage spun through the land many Americans called home, though they had never been there.

At the outset Jeremy was quiet, engrossed in the passing world— a world that had bridges five centuries old, and buildings from an age before America was even discovered. With Sniffer contented in the company of Penelope, lavished with sweets and caresses, Jeremy gave his full attention to the countryside. Richard slept through much of the journey, untroubled by the constant jarring of the carriage and frequent stops to rest the horses.

By the time they ran down from the Cotswold Hills, following the pretty banks of the River Avon, Jeremy had begun putting question after question to his companions. They indulged his curiosity, pleased with his interest in their land.

They passed the first night in a country inn and by the second day were in the beautiful Vale of Evesham, where the Avon flowed between the Cotswolds to the south and wooded uplands to the north. Here Jeremy observed new canal locks in the river, where boats were let down to the lower water levels approaching the Severn estuary. It thrilled him to see such engineering innovations as this canal, and he was excited to be so near the home of William Shakespeare at Stratford-on-Avon. Again his English friends took pleasure at his enthusiasm.

They traveled much of the distance by a barge on one of the newly dug canals leading through country known as the Midlands. Hilly and well-watered, the region was thick with ironworks and textile mills. As they journeyed, Jeremy understood what America must mean for these centers of production: America was the inexhaustible source of raw materials such as indigo, cotton, flax, beaver pelts, cowhide, and timber. These were processed here and transformed, much of it shipped back to America for sale as finished goods. No wonder the colonies were forbidden to make hats, cloth, ironware, and a host of other items, for if they did, Britain would lose its greatest overseas market. Three million colonists and uncounted thousands of Indians consumed vast quantities of British goods, and Parliament was determined to keep things that way as long as possible.

It was a sunny day, unusual here for December, Jeremy was told, but near cities the sky was grimy and lowering and stank of the sour smell of coal. Philadelphia burned mostly wood, but England's fires and furnaces fed on coal, which was plentiful and near the surface. Furthermore, the mighty English forests were nearly all gone, devoured by rampant industrial growth that had hurled England into the forefront of world manufacturing and trade.

It was shocking for Jeremy whenever their carriage swung out of a pretty woodland—always owned by a duke or earl and protected for his play—and came into view of a brawny city. The most astonishing sight of all was Birmingham, which not long ago had been a sleepy market town. It was late one afternoon when the carriage sped around the eastern side of the smoky town, and Jeremy asked a thousand questions about the people, spires, chimneys, domes, and bridges, all of which Richard answered cheerfully while Penelope napped with Sniffer in her lap.

"Do you see that street there, on this side of the river?" Richard asked, indicating with his glove a raw, half-built row of brick houses at the edge of a withered hayfield. "Well, that was meadow just this spring, and I grazed my horse where that gent's privy stands! Yes, Jeremy, 'tis a marvelous age of industry and progress we live in. Green today, brick-red tomorrow! My friend, you are in the very center of the world's most dynamic nation, the cradle and the stronghold of the mightiest, most industrious people on earth."

Jeremy murmured that it was indeed so.

Richard declared, with a slap on the knee, "You Americans are fortunate to be our cousins and benefit from what we've built. Why, if it were not for the protection of the British Empire and the Royal Navy, the helpless American colonies would be dominated by France or Spain, perhaps even by some German count or a petty rajah! You could never send a merchant ship even across the bay without some foreign privateer making her his prize. . . ."

Richard went on at length like this as the dreary city of Birmingham drifted past a mile to the west. Jeremy could not disagree with Richard's description of America's reliance on the Empire, nor could he object when Britain's overwhelming military might

was brought up. Richard was eloquent about his country because
he loved it, not because he meant to brag or to belittle America.
He seldom said a word against the colonies, despite the quarrel
between them and the mother country.

That night they slept in another modest inn, a good distance
from a noisy factory. In the morning, they climbed aboard again
under the gaze of gaunt, sleepy-eyed children from an industrial
village. Their sad appearance wrenched Jeremy's heart. More than
once he asked Richard how so many people could go hungry in
the greatest country on earth. Richard said, with sympathy, that
England was not perfect, but there were many of the upper class
who were trying to improve the lot of the poor by increasing charity
and making better laws.

"We are growing so fast here," Richard said, pensively looking
out the window at a little girl waving to the coach. Her face was
filthy, clothes torn, toes showing through her shoes, though the
weather was rapidly turning cold. "Our country cannot keep up
with itself and its needs, and there are those of us who care nothing
for the welfare of these people—only for machines and manufactured wares."

He went on to explain that government management of American affairs had deteriorated because of a lack of stable leadership
in Parliament. As a result, America had grown away from England,
and what the two peoples shared in common was not enough to
keep the colonies contentedly subordinate to England.

Jeremy replied, "We do not consider ourselves as subordinate
to England, but as British subjects who deserve to be represented
in Parliament."

Shaking his head, Weston said, "Great cities like Birmingham,
Coventry, and Bristol have hundreds of thousands of people who
are not represented in Parliament because our system has not been
modified to accommodate sudden growth and changing population;
but *they* do not cry out for liberty, or rights, or oppose taxation—"

"They're not Americans," Jeremy said, watching Penelope stir
and open her eyes; she was very, very beautiful.

Richard said, a bit harshly, "Nor are they rebels against the
crown! They're not foolish enough to put their heads on the block
for the sake of saving a few pennies in taxes."

"Americans feel there's more to it than that," Jeremy answered.
"We're not to be treated like Russian serfs, and we're not the same
as the poor of English cities. We'll stand up for our rights if we're
forced to."

Penelope's voice was soft, but the apprehension she felt came through as she said, "Will you outrage Parliament and tweak the nose of the army for those rights you speak of?"

Jeremy nodded. "If pushed to it, America will fight."

Richard was about to speak, but Penelope interrupted, "And you, Jeremy, would you fight us, too?"

He felt a twinge to look into her eyes and contemplate the possibility of war with her and Richard. Still, Jeremy believed in what he said. "If the right men lead America, I would follow them anywhere, against anyone, as long as I agreed with the cause."

He sat back, the sun slanting through the leather curtains, falling on Penelope's pretty hands, which lay upon the sleeping otter. For a fleeting instant Jeremy longed to reach over and take those hands, squeeze them, and tell Penelope not to worry. There were too many cool heads on both sides of the Atlantic for civil war to break out in America. As he looked away through the crack between the curtains, she leaned to him and gripped his own hand warmly.

"I pray," she said, "that no one will cause your country to go to war with us."

Arriving in Derbyshire, Jeremy felt as though he had just come home. Nothing was spared to make him happy, and his dignified Uncle Henry, now in his middle forties, was even more imposing a figure than he remembered from ten years ago, when Gladwin commanded British troops at Fort Detroit. Gladwin met the carriage, his garb modest but exquisitely refined, and from the start he and Jeremy renewed their close friendship.

"Do you still know how to use a foil?" Gladwin asked, clapping Jeremy's shoulders and stepping back to admire his nephew's remarkably strong and well-formed physique. "By the looks of you, I should have said tomahawk—Tamano's been making you into a brave, I'll warrant! Go on, prove me right or wrong—how does an Indian move on a hunting trail?"

Jeremy leaned forward, his figure becoming bent, like some creature of prey, and he took a swift few steps that way, to his uncle's approving laughter.

"You've got it in your blood, Jeremy, just like Owen! I never could really take to that country, Englishman that I am."

"Indian ways are my ways, sir," Jeremy said, grinning. "But I've not neglected the swordsmanship you taught me."

Shorter than Jeremy, Gladwin was fit and slender, but with a deep chest that was disarmingly powerful for all his cultured clothes and powdered wig. Gladwin's legs, in silk hose and breeches, were also sturdy, recalling younger days when he had fought in the wilderness, marched with Rogers' Rangers, and battled French and Indians in the most bloody engagements of the last war. He had been an officer in the handpicked 80th Light Infantry, forest fighters who beat the enemy at their own game.

Jeremy found it difficult to imagine Henry Gladwin in rugged Fort Detroit, for his uncle was too comfortably dressed, too cheerful and well nourished to fit the mold of the undaunted commander who had endured siege, terror, and isolation for nearly half a year at the edge of civilization.

Then the young man realized his uncle must be thinking similar thoughts about him, for he, too, had changed and now aspired to be a physician. A moment passed in this exchange of inspections, and without speaking they suddenly embraced, Gladwin's face showing profound emotion.

From inside the mansion—a great stone affair with massive exterior beams, a red slate roof, and more gables than any Philadelphia residence—came a petite, pretty woman, ten years younger than Henry. Jeremy's aunt, Frances Gladwin, was introduced by her husband, who said she had canceled a week's worth of sittings with the artist Romney in order to be on hand for Jeremy's arrival.

Mrs. Gladwin smiled at Jeremy and, freeing one hand from a fur muff, took hold of his, saying, "It's wonderful you've come at last! Henry has told me so much about you, and I can see his hopes that you would become a fine man have not been disappointed!"

Jeremy truly felt reborn after the desolate sea journey and the initial strangeness of England. As he gazed at the kindly Frances Gladwin, he realized there was a very good side to England, one that few Americans ever experienced. His aunt was the picture of modesty in a dark green sacque dress without hoops and tied at the waist with a white band. Her hair was gathered under a silk turban that trailed down her back, and she gave the distinct impression of one who is full of energy and the joy of life.

With his uncle and aunt on either arm, Jeremy approached the mansion. On the steps of the house he turned to look over the broad grassy lawns, perfectly cared for and bordered with shrubs and shaped hedges.

"So this is England!" he said softly, more to himself than to his uncle or aunt, and they smiled at each other.

Henry Gladwin said, "Derbyshire, my boy; but I'll warrant you've already seen that there are other places not so beautiful, nor so tranquil as our little corner of this country."

Jeremy saw what seemed to be a shadow pass over his uncle's strong face. The eyes became distant, his thin mouth even more compressed.

Frances Gladwin patted Jeremy's arm. "In all the years Henry was away, he never imagined the industrial changes that have come upon us, even though it was he and his soldiers who won the Empire for us—the Empire that consumes what we manufacture in those hideous cities!"

"'Tis true enough, dearest," Gladwin said, letting his sadness depart. "I've been home these ten years, but still I can't get used to the blight on our land, the manufacturers, the upstart merchants who would be knights, the commoners who would be lords by rising on the ash piles of their ironworks and the bones of—"

"No politics!" Mrs. Gladwin declared. "Please, Henry?"

At that moment, Penelope came up the steps, Sniffer a bundle of fur in her hands. Gladwin said, "Thank our Maker that England yet possesses the beauty of our winsome Penny to outshine—"

Sniffer sprang into Gladwin's arms, causing his wife to shriek in fright and stagger back a few paces. A footman came to the rescue, shoe off and held high to smash this beast from his master's chest. But Gladwin was laughing aloud and cuddled his old friend close.

"Still alive, are you?" Gladwin received a happy lick from Sniffer, and he called to his reluctant wife to make the animal's acquaintance. "I thought this fellow'd be someone's gloves by now! Hah! Don't snort at me; I was only joking!"

With Gladwin carrying the otter, and Richard Weston following at a polite distance, Jeremy entered the house, his aunt on one arm, Penelope on the other. He could scent the aroma of dinner, and in a chamber beyond the entrance hall he saw maids setting silver on a white tablecloth. The estate at Derbyshire seemed the most beautiful place on earth, and Jeremy Bently felt fortunate to be here.

chapter **8**

LOYALTY

In a paneled waiting room, richly furnished with brocaded mahogany chairs and Persian carpets, Farley Jones sat alone and downcast. Too terrified to hope, too melancholy even to sit up straight, he hunched over, elbows on knees, face in hands. He was in a wing-backed chair next to a desk where a secretary should have been, but the secretary had been sent away from the office as soon as Jones and Hugh Meeks had entered.

They had come here to the center of Montreal directly from the docks, where a hired boat had taken them after their flight from Detroit. In an adjacent room, Bradford Cullen was being told the bad news about their Detroit setback.

Jones sat like a creature almost without life. His wrists bore the cord marks where Hugh Meeks had bound him after they passed Fort Niagara on the way to Montreal. How Meeks had guessed he intended to flee rather than face Cullen's rage Jones could not tell, but Meeks was cunning and knew the hearts of murderers. Only when they walked the streets of Montreal had Meeks taken off the bonds, and by now it was too late to get away. Jones could never escape from this city, where Bradford Cullen had allies and killers enough to run him to ground.

Farley Jones was a beaten, doomed man. What Meeks and Cullen were saying on the other side of double oaken doors surely would seal the clerk's fate. It was only with the utmost restraint that Meeks had not slit his throat and tossed him overboard during their flight across Lake Erie. Jones knew by now that Meeks had kept him alive to blame him for their bungled affair in Detroit. Bradford Cullen would not spare the life of even Hugh Meeks if his wrath got the better of him, and having Jones for a sacrifice might save the seaman's neck.

Jones sighed and rubbed his sore wrists. He swallowed hard, and for the first time in many, many years, tried to pray.

Behind the polished doors, Meeks sat on the edge of his chair, his usual fierceness now only a latent fire in his eyes. Looking almost humble in a weathered brown frock coat, and needing a shave, Meeks was in the presence of a man as cruel and ruthless as he, but far more powerful.

To see Meeks and Cullen together in the same room, one would have thought the pirate the real arch-villain, capable of anything. Seated behind the broad mahogany desk, Bradford Cullen seemed no more than just another wealthy merchant, repulsively fat, pompous, and physically a coward. He was dressed in the very best green broadcloth and a silk blouse, neither of which could disguise his swollen, misshapen body. Cullen—who was in his seventies—resembled an old toad in thick spectacles as he listened to Meeks make excuses. With his massive head framed by the chairback, his curled wig made him seem even more short and squat. But though Cullen was ugly, with beady eyes and a sickly, pale face, and though his clothes and possessions might seem more than he deserved, he had made himself what he was by ruthless cunning and boldness. Cullen shrewdly manipulated a hundred wealthy men, and as many politicians. A thousand lesser folk from Canada to Georgia and even abroad made their living by serving him and his agents.

Whoever underestimated Bradford Cullen was on dangerous ground. Those who trusted him eventually paid for their ignorance, and those who fought him seldom won. Only Owen Sutherland had battled Cullen and Company and triumphed, and Cullen would never forget that defeat. By skill and courage the Frontier Company had beaten him in the northwest fur trade, and Cullen had lost a small fortune. His hired killers had been slain, his fur company rendered almost impotent because of the hated Sutherland's brilliance. Cullen had even been forced to flee from Montreal back to Boston to avoid prosecution by Sutherland for being the backer of outlaw raiders. He had sworn revenge on Sutherland, even if it took the rest of his life to achieve it.

This was the first time in almost a year that Cullen had been back in Montreal. He had come in secrecy, arriving by ship and slipping ashore at night, and had taken up lodgings at these offices that still belonged to his firm. He had left his aging wife and unmarried daughter at their palatial home in Charlestown, outside

Boston, in order to arrange critical affairs in Montreal. For two weeks he had not left this stuffy, hot building, all the while negotiating pacts with loyalist merchants and power brokers to oppose the possible rising of Whigs in Lower Canada. Ultimately his aim was regaining control of the lucrative northwest fur trade that passed through Montreal, heading over the sea to Britain. To that end Cullen had been winning the support of many who viewed him as a favored member of the Tory party in Boston.

This very night he had intended sailing with the tide for Boston, but the awkward arrival of Meeks and Jones and news of their incompetence at Detroit had delayed him. As Cullen listened to Meeks talk, he raged to think that both Tories and Whigs at Detroit knew his own agent had committed a senseless murder. Word of this would eventually reach Montreal, and for as long as the murder was connected to Cullen and Company, even unscrupulous associates in the city might hold off from joining him. Popular emotions must be considered these days, if they could not be controlled, and Cullen was furious that his plans to unite Montreal loyalists under himself had been jeopardized by such a stupid act of greed at the wrong time.

Meeks tried to salvage his own reputation by saying he had successfully agitated against Whigs and the Frontier Company at Detroit, and had secretly instigated the Sons of Liberty to attack Dawson Merriwether. Though the seaman's own men were the masked leaders of the assault, Meeks swore he had not slain the loyalist's wife.

"Believe me, Mr. Cullen, sir, I didn't no way have nothin' to do with the killin' of that woman!" In the face of Cullen's cold, murderous rage, even the indomitable Meeks felt his mouth dry up and his hands sweat. Though the pirate feared no man, he was very anxious to please his master, because he believed serving Cullen would lead him to limitless wealth and power. Meeks had reason enough to dread Cullen's wrath, reason enough to be humble and apologetic, even though he had the strength to crack the fat man's neck with a snap of the wrist.

Doing his best to shift the guilt for embarrassing Cullen at Detroit, Meeks cursed foully and declared, "'Twas that damned poxy clerk! Swine! He set Sutherland onto us, and it was by sheer smart thinkin' that I got us both away, by thunder!"

As Meeks spoke, it was as though the pirate acted out a speech he had rehearsed during the three weeks of travel to Montreal. He told not only of the murder but of Sutherland's flat refusal to accept Cullen's offer of an alliance. His hands moved clumsily, and he tried to grin at the right places, clucking his tongue and shaking his head in profound earnestness as he told of his own worthy behavior on the company's behalf.

None of Meeks's gestures or hearty talk changed the terrible, foul look that took over Cullen's face. Grinding his teeth, slowly tapping the table with pudgy fingers, the merchant listened, scheming what he must do about this unexpected interference with his plans.

Meeks ended with, "Ye may lay to it, sir, this old sea dog kept a bad situation from gettin' worse! If not for me, old Farley out there'd be in the clink, spillin' the beans about our company and about the mischief we played 'em rebels, and—"

"It won't do."

"What's that, sir?" Meeks cocked his head slightly, as if to hear better. A muscle twitched below one eye.

"It won't do," Cullen said, his voice breathy and high, a wheezing sound that came through his nose, for his thin lips barely moved.

"No, sir, it won't!" Meeks blustered, slapping his hat on a knee. "We done messed up—"

"Mr. Meeks." Cullen leaned back in the chair, which creaked under his weight. He controlled the fury. "You should have killed Sutherland when you fought him. That's what I hired you to do."

"Sir, I . . . it was too dark, sir; he got away, and we had little enough time to get ourselves downriver afore—"

Cullen laughed, his anger turning to scorn that rang out in a slow, mirthless chuckle that could be heard by the frantic Jones out in the waiting room. Meeks stirred, leaning forward, for his fierce pride had been goaded. In that sudden confrontation, the pirate was dangerous, even to Cullen, but the merchant saw the blaze in the man's eyes and the clenched fists. Allowing his mocking laughter to die, Cullen again took the offensive.

"You've failed me, Mr. Meeks, but think it no shame to have been unable to kill Owen Sutherland. You're not the first, you see." As Meeks steamed, Cullen took paper and pen from where they lay on the desk. "I'll give you one more opportunity to prove your worth." He wrote something and signed his name with a small flourish. "Here's my note for quite a generous sum. It will fit out a vessel, which you are to take immediately to England, and then to the Netherlands, if need be."

Cullen told the astonished Meeks that he was to sail for England

and find out all he could about Peter Defries and Jeremy Bently. The merchant suspected the Frontier Company was attempting to buy war material in Europe for the Whigs of America. As a pirate and smuggler himself, Meeks, more than anyone, could discover whether Sutherland's company was engaging in illegal trade.

"Do your work well, Mr. Meeks, and you'll be forgiven for your incompetence at Detroit—and rewarded handsomely for success." Cullen shoved the document and another paper across the desk. The shipmaster was dumbfounded to read how much he would profit as a spy for Cullen and Company. "There also are the names of influential acquaintances overseas who will cooperate with you when it comes time to have Sutherland's people arrested. Tell them what you learn!" He leaned back and peered through small, glittering eyes. "Mark me, man: I want firm proof that Sutherland's people are traitors, rebels, enemies of the king, and I want that proof within a half year. Any later than that and I'll be unable to make good use of it, for affairs between the Whigs and General Gage in Boston will have gone too far by then."

Cullen casually dismissed Meeks, who rose briskly and saluted, beaming with gratitude and ambition. "What about Jones, sir? He's waiting—"

Cullen waved a hand and gave a noise of disgust. "Prove to me you can at least kill *him*." He motioned to the door. "Take him around back, to the stable or somewhere—but mind you, no blood! And no body!"

Meeks shrugged his shoulders to loosen them. "My pleasure, Mr. Cullen," he grinned. "Won't be sight nor sound!"

He went to the door, but hesitated when Cullen called his name. The merchant was deep in thought, a soft hand to his lower lip; then he slowly wagged a finger.

"No, not quite yet. No."

"Sir?"

Cullen was chuckling as he said, "Don't kill him at all. Send him in. I have a use for the imbecile. Sorry to disappoint you, my man. Send him in, and tell him not to worry, because it sickens me when he's so green with worry. Then his teeth rattle— Off you go, my man. I'll expect a report from you with our company's first vessel to Boston from London this spring."

A moment later, in came a shivering Farley Jones, walking as though asleep, his feet barely off the floor as he shuffled toward Cullen, who indicated the chair Meeks had used. Jones sat down, and appeared drawn close about himself—arms tight against his body, legs together, eyes extremely large in his sallow face. The wooden false teeth clicked with amazing speed.

Cullen sighed. Shoving a decanter of brandy and a glass toward the man who had been his clerk for nearly ten years, he said, "Get some heat into your blood, Farley. Don't worry, don't worry." Jones tried to pour a drink, but he trembled so that he splattered brandy on the vast mahogany desk. As if expecting Cullen to shout at him, he cringed visibly, but the merchant simply laughed slowly, with pitying contempt.

"Farley," he began with another long sigh, "you have much to make amends for, and I intend to give you the opportunity."

Jones gaped and began to babble his gratitude until Cullen shut him up with a curt knock on the desk top, saying, "You'll go to Albany this winter and will serve me as an observer in that den of Whig iniquity. Using your knowledge of the trade, make the rounds of every warehouse and find out about every ship that comes or goes. I'll expect you to keep a weather eye out for any activity of the Frontier Company."

"Oh, Mr. Cullen, Mr. Cullen, you're too good to me!" Jones might have fallen to his knees had Cullen not looked away in disgust. "I won't fail you, sir! Thank you, sir! I won't fail you, sir!"

Cullen wrote out a voucher for Jones to draw cash from a merchant house in Albany that did some business with his company. He made no response to the simpering obeisance paid by the quaking clerk. Those clicking teeth did annoy him, though.

"I want to know everything—everything—about the Whigs and Sutherland: who's in power in Albany and who'll be in power. Do not let it be known you're still my agent, for I'll announce it that you've been fired and have run off somewhere. And get out of Montreal quickly, before you're arrested for doing in that Detroit woman! Albany's under a different provincial jurisdiction, so they won't bother you there." Saying this, Cullen's face changed briefly, taking on a glossy malice. "If you are arrested or otherwise throw my company into further public disrepute, you'll die, whether you're in or out of jail. Understand?"

Jones understood, only too well. He took the voucher and skittered backward out the room, knowing he was lucky to be alive. The miserable fellow was supremely thankful to have another chance to serve Bradford Cullen, to whom he owed everything.

* * *

As guest of honor at the Gladwin estate, Jeremy had complete freedom of the fine manor house and lush gardens. He enjoyed strolling on paths that were hedged into a maze, around gazebos and pools, and past flower beds. A few days after his arrival, a reception was held in his honor, and there he met a host of relations, childhood friends of his mother, curious neighbors, all eager to meet the American scholar who had befriended and fought Indians.

Sniffer, as usual, was the center of attention; Jeremy was grateful for that, because there was entirely too much activity, talk, and debate about British-American relations to suit him. More than once he slipped away in company with Richard or Penelope to escape the flock of chattering visitors, and as the days passed, these three became fast friends.

Penelope's father, Raymond Graves, was away on a sea voyage to India, but her vivacious mother, Rebecca, more than made up for her husband's absence by treating Jeremy like a member of her own family. Pert and graying, Mrs. Graves was shorter than Penelope and not as rashly spontaneous; but she had a bright way about her that suggested Penelope's character, and she was an attractive woman who obviously had been the girl's tutor in feminine ways.

Rebecca Graves and Richard Weston were the best of comrades, or at least it seemed so to Jeremy, for the older woman often dragged Richard away on some errand, leaving Penelope and the American newcomer alone. This occurred whether Jeremy was at the Gladwin residence or at the Graves estate a mile away, and after a while, Penelope seemed almost embarrassed when it happened with such regularity.

Penelope was unfailingly kind to him, always cleverly diverting the conversation whenever someone pressed for his opinion on world affairs. She knew well how to brush off talk of civil unrest in America, or how to exhibit the profoundest boredom at such discussions. The only time Penelope ever annoyed Jeremy was when other young women were on hand—and there were always many, it seemed. Too often she managed to insist to Jeremy that one thing or another needed doing. Then—much like her mother with Richard—she would excuse them from their company and politely leave the most interesting and delightful women with someone else.

Though Jeremy's thoughts frequently dwelt upon Sally Cooper, he was fascinated by Englishwomen and wanted to meet more of

them. Penelope's frequent pruning of such meetings was a bother
to him, but always she managed to overcome his annoyance. He
found her company enough.

When they were alone, they talked about each other's lives and
countries. It was apparent that Penelope was no spoiled, aloof
daughter of wealthy parents, because she told him of her earnest
desire to help the poor however she could. Her most interesting
notion was to found and teach in a school for children of factory
workers in the new neighborhoods of Birmingham, where these
families were crowded into row houses, and there was much crime,
ignorance, and sickness.

Jeremy thought that was an admirable idea, although Penelope's
parents apparently were not so sure. They had not yet given a
direct answer when she asked them about beginning such an undertaking. Her parents were kind, generous folk but preferred their
only daughter to help the poor from a distance, not as a teacher
in the classroom, which was a scandalous idea for an upper-class
lady in that day and age.

In their many conversations Penelope asked Jeremy much about
America and the wilderness, which seemed too enormous for her
to comprehend. She even wanted to know everything about Sally
Cooper when the matter of his close friend came up. Jeremy teased
Penelope with the comment that he had not known the English
were so much like Americans, ever prying into personal affairs of
people they hardly knew.

They were in the Gladwin garden, leaning against the wall of
a small stone bridge over a stream where Sniffer paddled lazily
in the water. Penelope was lovely in a yellow walking dress, a
scarlet serge cape thrown over her shoulders against the cold, and
a yellow bonnet covering all but the long auburn curls that hung
in rolls over her breast. Jeremy wore a dark blue coat with no
collar, and under it a ruffled beige shirt and a beige waistcoat with
matching breeches and stockings. These clothes had been gifts
from his Uncle Henry and Aunt Frances. On his head, however,
was a warm, red *voyageur*'s stocking cap brought from America.

"The English are not as prying as Americans," Penelope objected. "Why, I've heard that a traveler in America can't pass a
thousand yards down the lane without being asked a hundred
questions about his destination, his home, his religion, his tailor,
his profession, his latest meal, and his political beliefs."

Looking down into the crystal, shallow water, Jeremy smiled
as he said, "That's true, but Americans don't ask about sweet-

hearts, the way English women do." Penelope blushed and half turned her back on him.

The sky was gray, the color of a winter storm, and if Jeremy had been at Detroit, he would have been ready for snow. In this strange land, however, the weather had tricked him time and again: raining when he thought it would snow, turning sunny when it should have poured. He had given up trying to prepare for changing weather, for it changed too frequently. Anyway, much time was spent indoors, as would certainly be the case in two weeks when he traveled north to Edinburgh to begin his studies. He missed the outdoor life, his body feeling too stiff and sluggish after weeks at sea and two more weeks here in England.

As Penelope thought of an appropriate response to Jeremy's teasing, he had the urge to do something physical. When she turned to face him again, he was standing on his hands on the wall of the bridge. Gasping, Penelope cried for him to be careful. Then she laughed as he walked on his hands along the wall.

"Show-off!" she told him. "That's not proper behavior in the company of a lady—unless you mean to impress her."

Jeremy slowly let himself down, his face red, breath short from exertion. It felt good. "Who would I want to impress, then?"

"Me," she replied, pretending to be coy, and coming close enough that he could smell her perfume. "And I am impressed."

Jeremy shrugged. "If you knew my friends Little Hawk or Tom Morely and saw them do that and more on galloping horses, *then* you'd be impressed!"

She showed her amazement, repeating, "On galloping horses? Really? Do all Americans learn such marvelous things?"

"Well, it's not all that difficult, really. You just have to know the horse, and you can't be afraid."

"Can *you* do it?" Her eyes were wide. "On a galloping horse?"

"Only to impress English ladies, you know." He folded his arms, looking serious. "Otherwise, we backcountry Americans consider such exhibitions more or less dull. We prefer wrestling grizzly bears, or swimming up the Niagara waterfalls, or shooting the left eye out of mosquitoes—or at least speechifying about such bodaciousness."

"Can you really do it? Can you? On a horse? Galloping?"

A little while later, they had taken two thoroughbred mounts from the stable, riding out of the estate and into the nearby forest toward a high meadow two miles off. Jeremy was uncomfortable in the small English saddle, preferring to ride bareback, but his high-strung animal might have taken fright at that. Riding side-saddle, the wind blowing her hair, Penelope trotted along beside him, a glow of happiness on her face. In front of her clung Sniffer, one paw clutching her coat, another hooked to the saddle. He was nervous, but willing enough to try this new experience.

The trees gave way to a grassy meadow, recently mowed and dotted with stacks of hay. Jeremy thought his horse too skittish and wished he had a wild Indian pony or a Canadian horse with its shaggy coat and long tail. How this thoroughbred would respond when Jeremy did his tricks was a question there was only one way to answer.

Penelope stopped at the edge of the trees, and Jeremy tossed her his red cap. His handsome horse was eager to run, and with a whoop he let him go. Never before had he been on such a fast animal. Indian ponies and French horses were nothing compared to this one, who put his ears back and thundered over the field, the ground a furious blur beneath. Wind poured against Jeremy as he brought the horse around, amazed that he was already three hundred yards away from Penelope, though he had only begun to gallop.

Just a suggestion of doubt crept through Jeremy's bones as he felt the horse behave uncertainly. But then a horse was a horse, he said to himself, directing his animal on a course across Pene-lope's field of view. Leaning into the animal's stride, he put pressure with his hands on the base of the neck, letting his weight move forward and gradually bringing up his legs. His full weight was on his hands, the wild-eyed horse blowing but not breaking stride. Jeremy's legs rose until they pointed high above his head. Over the pounding of hooves, he heard Penelope shriek with de-light, and he felt exhilarated.

His mount was steady, racing along, the grass whizzing by, and Jeremy knew the horse could be controlled. He let his legs down, turned the animal, and galloped back across Penelope's view. Reassured, he performed Little Hawk's trick of lying down at the side of the mount's neck, hidden from the girl. From that position he pretended to fire a bow, holding on with only his legs. This redoubled Penelope's amazement and glee.

On the next pass, Jeremy stood up, holding the reins with one hand, and saluted before letting himself drop into the saddle to turn for another run. Penelope was ecstatic. The world was Jeremy's just then, and he imagined himself in the meadow above Detroit, vying with the Sioux or Tom for the day's honors as Sally judged them.

This time he knew Penelope would be astounded, for Little Hawk's favorite and most dangerous trick was next. Although Jeremy had not quite learned the art of hanging under the animal's belly, he thought he could do it well enough, for his confidence was high, rising with the sight of Penelope's joyful face.

Galloping across the field, he howled like a Santee Sioux, then let his body drop to one side, again out of sight of the girl. This was the moment. Holding onto the saddle girth, he swung himself under the horse, so that the sharp hooves flashed just inches from his body. But it was too much for a gentleman's horse. Jeremy had just taken his delicate position when the animal rebelled and broke away. The thoroughbred bucked and bounded in long leaps, kicking his hind legs high, trying to dislodge the creature clinging to his belly.

Jeremy could not swing up again. The force of the jumps and bucks was stunning, and it was impossible to hold on for long. The leaps jarred him, and he clutched desperately to the saddle leathers, his legs gripping the sides of the horse. With every return to earth Jeremy suffered a vicious pounding that knocked the wind from him and bruised his chest. Blinded by dirt and sweat, he could barely see where they were heading, but he anticipated the worst, for the terrified animal was completely out of control.

A hedgerow of thorns was closing fast. Hooves whisked past his skull. His arms and legs ached, and his face and throat were thick with dust. The hedgerow was much too high for the horse to leap, and the sharp branches and broken limbs would scrape Jeremy from the horse like a caterpillar from a leaf. That, he realized with dismay, was just what his mount intended. He must let go. Battered like an old rag doll, he had no other choice. There was nothing else for it but to drop off and hope he survived the trampling. To live, he would have to be very lucky. It was now or never—

In the next instant, just about to release his grip, he saw the legs of another galloping horse come alongside his own. With a fierce whinny and much snorting, his panicked animal veered away from the hedgerow, being brought under control by Penelope. Jeremy held on, coughing up dirt, until his mount stamped to a halt, lathered and frightened. Jeremy's legs fell to the ground, but his hands clung to the leathers, too stiff to let go. Then Penelope was at his side, helping him get free, and Sniffer licked his face in sympathy.

Through a dusty mist, Jeremy saw her kneeling over him, the scarlet *voyageur's* hat still tucked into her bodice. Her eyes were wide, her face pale with worry. Pride was injured more than body, and Jeremy came to his senses, sitting up and moving his bloodless fingers to bring them back to life. He looked at Penelope, then at his hands, then back at her, seeing that enchanting, teasing humor in her eyes.

She asked, "Do American horses kick as high as that?"

"Much higher," he replied, spitting grit from his teeth and stroking Sniffer. "Are you impressed?"

"Very," she giggled, covering her mouth with the stocking cap. "What do you call that last trick?"

"Biting the dust." His face was expressionless, but he was trying not to laugh. "I'm a little out of practice."

"Really? I thought you managed to bite quite a lot of dust!" She giggled again, and he broke down, laughing heartily as he took his cap and jammed it onto his head. Penelope asked if she could see that last trick once again.

"Can't," he said, getting up painfully. "Got to meet with Uncle Henry for tea in an hour. Anyway, you're already impressed enough for one day, aren't you?"

"Very," she said again, taking his arm intimately and walking with him toward the waiting horses.

She felt light on his elbow, yet firm and soft. It was wonderful to have Penelope's company. She took some of the pain from missing Sally. He had not yet sent off Sally's letters, for too much had happened since arriving in England, and merchant ships to Montreal were few and far between this season.

In his spacious, airy room, Jeremy leisurely changed into clean clothes, putting on the best-quality Holland linen shirt, a black silk cravat, and a pair of breeches that were full enough to be comfortable, yet stylishly close-fitting at the seat and thighs. Before leaving the room, he noticed a new wig on the stand near the dressing table and smiled to himself. This was the third attempt by Frances Gladwin to persuade her nephew to wear a wig, as any gentleman should. It was a simple, plaited queue, expensively made of human hair, already powdered in case he decided to put it on in private, without the fussy attendance of the usual man-servant.

The first wig Mrs. Gladwin had left discreetly on the stand had been a massive periwig that would have overmatched a bear's skull. When Jeremy had avoided mentioning its presence in his room, Mrs. Gladwin had tried again, making certain the second wig to materialize in his quarters was more modest. She chose a full Ramilies, with only one queue, but magnificently curled and sporting a scarlet bow at the back.

Like the second, this third attempt made no headway with Jeremy's taste. He would wear no wig at all, and was among the very few young men of the day beginning to object to a fashion that had reigned for more than a century. Aunt Frances would be disappointed that he was so set against proper dress, but Penelope Graves had never even hinted he ought to wear a wig. Penelope's silence on the matter was some reassurance that he was not a complete freak in British society, and that perhaps others of his generation were seeing his point. To him, wigs were hot, cumbersome, affected, and much too powdery, causing him to sneeze whenever a nearby wearer turned his or her head.

Shortly, Gladwin greeted Jeremy in the library. The officer was dressed in a beige satin damask banyan, a wealthy man's house robe that reached to the floor and was gathered at the waist by a drawstring. In the informal manner of the day, Gladwin's head was swathed in a purple turban, as he took some respite from his own wig.

Coffee and biscuits were brought in on silver plates, and china cups of exquisite design were offered by a servant, who afterward departed without a sound. As Jeremy sipped his coffee, he marveled at this heady new life in Derbyshire and could not deny he relished it a great deal.

Gladwin opened the conversation with the usual politeness, but Jeremy sensed something serious was on his uncle's mind. His guess was proven true when Gladwin laid his cup on the table and stared closely at the young man before saying, "Do you support America's Congress?"

Jeremy sipped some coffee, affecting nonchalance at a very touchy subject. He thought a moment, then replied, "Yes, sir. Though I reject the violent behavior of some who back Congress, on the whole I believe in the cause of liberty Congress represents."

Hardly waiting for Jeremy to finish, Gladwin said, "What if that course were set upon total independence?"

"Sir?" Jeremy could not believe Congress had any such intentions. "Why should Congress seek independence? We're all British! We all benefit from the Empire! We simply demand to be treated as free British subjects, and Congress is our best means of assuring that."

"My question, my boy, is whether you would support the Continental Congress if independence from England were its aim."

Regaining composure, Jeremy almost began to laugh at the absurd notion of the American colonies breaking away from Mother England. On the serious side, any such attempt would mean a terrible war, brother against brother. After a weighty moment of silence, Jeremy spoke up. "I would only say, Uncle Henry, that most Americans feel as I do; we simply want our rights, and the only way we would move toward independence is if we were pushed to it with no other choice."

Gladwin's eyes, full of brooding anger, fixed upon Jeremy and held him a moment. "Pushed to it, you say," Gladwin murmured; then he threw himself from the chair, and in a swish of the banyan, strode across the room to peer, unseeing, out the window to the garden. "Pushed to it. . . . Yes, that may very well be what will happen."

He swung around, the look of a warrior in his face. "The powers that rule in England have taken all they will take or can take politically from American Whigs. Therefore, General Gage has been told—I should say it has been made obliquely clear to him that for the sake of his career he must nip this revolutionary bud before it blossoms, and do it soon!"

His warlike fierceness changed to frustration and anger. "That means, my lad, that we will see the army undertake some provoking campaign in Massachusetts this spring—a campaign with the clear objective of drawing American Whig militia into a battle!"

Jeremy stood up, the shock of what he was hearing making it difficult to speak. "Sir . . . that will bring on war!"

"War!" Gladwin said and sat down heavily, head in hands. "Yes, that will mean war, and the environs of Boston will be the first battlefield. Oh, these foolish, foolish ministers, who think Americans will be whipped to obedience like curs. But they don't know Americans, don't know them at all."

"There must be compromise!" Jeremy cried. "We're all the same people! I can see that now, though I would never have known it had I not come to England!" He began to walk the floor, mind awhirl.

Sighing, Gladwin sat back in his chair, head tipped backward. "Compromise? Sons of Liberty want no compromise; they want independence. Gage wants no compromise, for like the government, he wants to destroy resistance to our domination of the colonies. Anyone in England or the colonies bent on compromise will be swept aside by war."

Then Gladwin gazed at Jeremy, bringing the frontiersman's pacing to a halt. The old soldier said, "Jeremy, Parliament has asked me to return to America—to command an army, if the insurrection worsens."

Jeremy could say nothing. To think of his uncle making war against Americans was too terrible to contemplate.

Then Gladwin penetrated his nephew's very soul with a look that only a professional soldier could give. He asked, "Where do you stand, Jeremy? If we fight, will you support Congress or Parliament?"

Jeremy sat down, hands on his knees, sweat prickling his scalp. The wound in his side, from the bullet he had taken in battle a few months ago, ached, though it was fully healed by now. He could taste the gunpowder, hear the cries of wounded, smell the blood. . . .

"Last summer, that question would have been simple to answer, Uncle; but now that I have seen England, met its people, read and spoken and listened . . . Last summer I would have taken a rifle and marched to Boston to fight for the minutemen; now that choice is not so clear."

Jeremy wanted to rush away, to think, to consider his future, his loyalty, his dreams. Composing himself as best he could, he asked that his uncle excuse him for a while. "You deserve an honest answer to your question, sir, but I must have time to think."

Gladwin understood and nodded. Jeremy opened the door partway, then paused before leaving. With much restraint, he said, "If war comes, I will fight for those who have the best interests of my country at heart."

Leaving the room quickly, he encountered Penelope and his aunt in the broad hallway. They obviously had heard his last statement and were distressed, though they tried to conceal it. Awkwardly, Jeremy excused himself and hurried from the house, striding into the damp cold and through the garden, his thoughts raging.

Shortly, while he leaned over the stream, standing on the stone bridge, Penelope came to him, Sniffer toddling behind. He turned away from her, too upset to speak. Saying nothing, she laid a warm red cloak over his shoulders, then walked on to leave him alone.

When Penelope was a little ways off, with Sniffer still following beside her, Jeremy looked up. He meant to say something but could not find the words. She must have sensed his feelings, for she stopped and looked back at him, her beautiful eyes shining with sadness. Before going, Penelope gave him the slightest smile that said she comprehended and respected his turbulent emotions. He watched her go, and as she disappeared from view, the violence within him subsided.

Perhaps, he thought, Gage would resist political pressure to provoke a battle. Perhaps Sam Adams would not have the power to rouse the mob to further insults upon the government and military in Boston. Perhaps... It was no use. There undoubtedly would be fighting and killing, but where he would stand was not clear at all. How could he fight his uncle, or Richard Weston? And especially, how could he declare himself the enemy of Penelope Graves? That last, he knew, was impossible, and he would never do it.

chapter 9

WINTER FESTIVAL

On a fine Saturday morning early in January, all Detroit was busy with preparations for a winter festival four miles upriver at *le grand marais,* or great marsh. The swamps were flooded and frozen thick, perfect for skating, ice fishing, and ponycart racing, and the settlement's young men had completed their annual work on longhouses built in the middle of birch and maple woods that stood deep in snow.

For a while, the hostilities of party and politics were put aside by longtime residents of the fort and settlement. Though newcomers were unused to the carefree attitude of Detroit's people, they were persuaded to join in the cheerful mood that prevailed almost everywhere. The arrangements for the festival were nearly ready, the organizing committee had done its work well, as usual, and after normal affairs of business and home had been tended to, folk would be free to enjoy the weekend's fun.

In the Morely-Grey storehouse on rue Saint Jacques, Owen Sutherland was busy at the company ledger, while Jeb and Lettie Grey and James Morely took inventory. Ella and her children were at Bill Poole's smithy to select some ironware for her kitchen. Soon they all would take horses and sleighs up to the marsh. Other than James, who was unusually withdrawn this morning, most young folk had gone ahead. Sally was already on her way to fetch Tom Morely at the boatyard, where he was working on some cabinetry in the master's cabin of a new sloop being built.

The Morely-Grey storehouse was quiet save for the sounds from outside of soldiers shoveling the streets clear, and the steady buzz of excited people departing for the party at the marsh. Now and again they heard a shouting *habitant* gallop his sleigh through the street, yelling at pedestrians to get out of the way. No one became angry, for all the French drove like madmen, but they were skillful and seldom crashed.

Sutherland sat at the far end of the large warehouse, which was built of rough, squared timbers, with plastered walls and plank ceiling and floor. Shelves along the walls were densely packed with colorful merchandise that was being sorted and counted by the Greys and James. The Frontier Company did most of its local business from this shop, serving two thousand whites and five times that many Indians from the straits. There was also another warehouse for the Frontier Company. Much of the goods for distant trading and the *voyageur* supplies were kept a few streets away at Jean Martine's building. Being French, Jean had good links to boatmen and *habitants*, knowing them and their needs.

In the center of the Morely-Grey warehouse were two long aisles of bags, crates, and bales, all open for buyers to inspect. Arranged neatly on the floor were sacks of twisted tobacco and tobacco bricks, bags of cloves, raisins, Indian rice, Carolina rice, and several grades of wheat and corn flour. Side by side stood barrels of salt and sugar, pork grease, and tallow, and there was one choice keg of costly bear grease that Indians loved so much, along with several of salt beef and salt pork for the British-Americans. Also in these aisles were stacks of various quality cotton shirts, breeches, blankets, blanket coats, capes, and stockings. Grouped together were iron and copper kettles, brass cookware, brooms, shovels, farm tools, household items, lanterns, and large crockery.

The shelves were filled with ladies' and children's clothes, an assortment of hats and jewelry, vermilion paint for Indians, medicines, sewing needs, playing cards, hunting knives, pipes, Dutch looking glasses—everything from purgatives to boxes of combs. The colonial, Indian, Briton, soldier, adventurer, scientist, or French *habitant* could find his heart's desire here, whether it was wampum beads, writing paper, recent books, ink, fishing gear, string, or a new rifle.

These last were on display along with pistols in a locked wall rack. Nearby were the rammers, worms, flints, leather patching, powder horns, and selections of ball that each weapon required. Company gunpowder was locked up in a stone magazine that had been built by the French regime a hundred yards down the street in a corner of the graveyard next to the timber-built Church of Sainte Anne. Powder was generally ordered from the Frontier Company ahead of time, and the buyer picked it up at the magazine, accompanied by a representative of the trading firm.

Strong drink was kept in a back room of the Morely-Grey storehouse, behind the counter at which Sutherland sat working on one of the heavy ledgers. On this counter there was always a small keg of good rum, diluted to popular taste, tapped and ready, with a mug or two handy for customers. Everything contributed to a mingling, pleasant fragrance, and although the great hearth at the center of one wall was empty, an iron stove in the middle of the room made the place cozy and warm.

Usually on Saturdays the Frontier Company warehouse was thronged with customers carrying freshly cured pelts, maple sugar, British sterling, or even Spanish pieces of eight. The currency most used in the northwest was that of New York colony, for it was stable, dependable, and plentiful. Yet it was not unusual for company goods to be sold for Hudson Bay Company brass trading coins, which bore the image of the king on one side and the beaver on the other—heads and tails.

It was different from the usual Saturday, however, and it was not only because of the excitement preceding the winter carnival that this storehouse was quiet. The Whig leanings of Sutherland and his partners had lost them many customers, but matters had indeed worsened beyond that: Yesterday the military had formally announced that it would no longer purchase supplies or equipment from the Frontier Company. Captain Lernoult had been put under pressure from his superiors in Montreal. They had sent an unusual express by dogsled ordering a stop to all trade between the Frontier Company and Fort Detroit's garrison and the handful of smaller dependency posts that were supplied through it. That was why Sutherland was here; for he had to plan for next year's shipments.

It appeared that orders had come through the governor's office, directly aimed at Sutherland's firm. He had been singled out as an example of the army's unwillingness to deal with active supporters of Congress and the trade embargo. Sutherland estimated that business transactions worth at least fifteen thousand pounds sterling would be lost to the Frontier Company, a terrible blow.

Further complicating the loss was the intensification of hostility toward the company throughout the community. The Congress party had been thrown into disrepute with the killing of Merriwether's wife and the destruction of the merchant's home. As a result, few were willing to align themselves with Sutherland, even if they agreed with the acts of Congress. Soldiers were told not to shop here, and many *habitants* were reluctant to patronize the company for fear of being accused of opposing the king. Even Indians were unsure of what to do about Sutherland's firm, now that the army shunned it. Most stayed away, though they privately did some business with the partnership.

It was fortunate that Sutherland's winter traders were already out with trade goods and supplies. Had they known the Frontier Company was being marked for punishment, some might have avoided working with Sutherland until it was clear which was the stronger side—Whig or Tory.

In spite of the bad news, Sutherland's family and friends were resolved to enjoy the weekend celebrations, and they had enough friends on their side to assure them the pleasure that always reigned at the *grand marais* festivals. As he completed his tedious book-work, goose quill in hand and a pot of ink nearby, Sutherland hardly noticed the voices of Lettie and James rising in argument. Sutherland was submerged in his work, having made a space on the counter by pushing aside the small scales, fabric shears, jars of sweets, and a pile of Whig pamphlets recently published in Boston and Philadelphia that extolled the virtues of the Congress and the trade embargo. His own essays in favor of Congress were printed in all of them.

The heated conversation at the front of the warehouse soon became loud enough that Sutherland looked up in astonishment as James declared, "To blazes with the embargo and with politics, Ma! I'm sick of it, and I say it isn't worth us going under! The next thing you know we won't be able to sell the army any Indian presents, and that'll be another ten thousand sterling we'll lose!"

James whirled and stamped along the aisle between cookware and barrels as he left his startled mother and stepfather behind. Dressed in a soft leather waistcoat, loose shirt, and breeches, James was unpretentious and sincere. He had curly black hair and a refined, attractive face, appealing to girls who liked the quiet, shy type. He passed Sutherland at the counter without speaking. Suth-erland watched him storm into the rear apartment, where he had lived alone ever since his mother, stepfather, and brother Tom moved across the river last year. James slammed the door, and his parents came slowly to the counter.

Both Lettie and Jeb were sad, for they had worried that some-thing like this might happen. Their relationship with James had been worsening with every setback the company suffered. James was the most serious of all the partners, and unlike the headstrong, reckless Tom, he loved his work as clerk and manager of the warehouse.

James was a brilliant manager and had a keen eye for a good trade. An important ingredient in the company's ideal combination of wit, courage, brawn, and experience, he was excellent and honest in every capacity. He had educated himself well, but unlike

Jeremy, preferred to go into the trade rather than study further.

As Lettie and Jeb approached, Sutherland drew rum from the keg for himself and the big Jerseyman; for Lettie he poured a mug of dark Bristol beer, foaming and strong. The three friends toasted silently.

Lettie spoke first, wiping suds from her long upper lip. "I'm afraid Jimmy won't follow us no more; he wants to be neutral. . . ." Her voice trembled, and she sighed. Jeb was visibly angry as he brought chairs for both of them, and they sat down across the counter from Sutherland. Trying not to weep, Lettie took a shaking breath and said, "Mark thee, Owen, it ain't that Jimmy be willin' to crawl to the army—"

Jeb slapped his knee, unable to speak at all just then. He had raised Lettie's sons as his own for almost ten years, and they meant much to him. It hurt to have one oppose him at such a critical time.

"I know, Lettie," Sutherland said, putting his mug on the counter and closing the ledger. "We all have our convictions, and I'm afraid James has convictions different from ours. I'm sorry for that."

Just then the apartment door opened, and out came James, his eyes red as he asked Owen for rum. James normally drank nothing stronger than beer, and Lettie watched anxiously as he forced down a burning swig that was more than he should have taken. Managing not to cough, he prepared to make his speech.

"There's no point in my going on with the company if you won't cooperate with the authorities, Owen." Sutherland listened, and Jeb leaned forward, head bowed, as though ashamed. "We've got no future here now, and all our work will be for nothing if we keep on going head-to-head with Tories, with Parliament, with the army, with other traders! We can't survive this way no matter how hard we work—especially if we lose thousands of pounds sterling in army contracts, and if we refuse to sell our pelts to British agents! I don't give a tinker's damn about politics; it's clear business sense. And my sense tells me our company's days are numbered unless we change!"

Lettie protested, "Don't give up like that, son! We'll bring Parliament to its knees afore long, and they'll change governments. Don't thee see? They'll have to be sensible, them that takes power in Britain, then we'll be top of the pile again! That's good business sense too, ain't it?"

"That's foolish speculation in something we can't control!" James yelled, slamming down the mug so that the rum spilled over his hand and onto the counter. Sutherland gave him a rag, and he hastily wiped up the counter as he spoke. "The Tories in Parliament will be thrown out in disgrace if they even suggest giving in to the colonies! Tories can't back down now after all the trouble we've made. They'll force us against the wall first, and make us surrender all our rights, or else take up arms!"

"You're dead on, there!" Jeb said with a snarl and stood up. "But we ain't gonna surrender our rights! And the company ain't gonna lick any boots just because British lords are tightening the noose! No! We got to rip that noose off our throats, and do it quick!"

Lettie came between her husband and son, for they had argued like this before. Her husband suspected the boy was cowardly, yet even though Jeb loomed over his stepson, James did not give way.

James said coldly, "Pa, the only noose is the one we're putting on ourselves because we want to change the order of things— things that don't need changing at all except that radicals have convinced you and everyone else that Parliament wants to keep us under their thumbs!"

"And so they do!" Jeb shouted, clenching his fists.

"If so, then it's a damned profitable thumb for us!" James shouted back.

"If you were any kind of man at all," Jeb blared, "you'd know when a bully's got his knee in your back, and you'd do something about it!"

James threw aside the rag, squaring his shoulders to Jeb. "I know a bully when I see one! Keep your own damned knee out of my back—"

Sutherland shouted and sprang across the counter, grabbing big Jeb by the shirt and lifting him off the ground as he tried to get at the boy. Lettie pushed James back, but her son did not want to fight, though he was no coward. His heart was nearly broken by having his mother caught between him and Jeb, and seeing his beloved company suffer.

Tears streamed down Lettie's face as she shook her younger son by the shoulders. "Won't thee give us a chance to prove we're right? Why must thee speak out against me and thy pa so?"

"He's not my pa!" James exclaimed, shaking with emotion. "My pa'd be no Liberty Boy if he were alive!"

The room became instantly hushed. What James had said seemed to hang in the air, as though the very walls of the family warehouse had caught those harsh words and would not let them pass beyond into the world, where they did not belong.

Sutherland knew James had spoken without thinking, without meaning to hurt Jeb and Lettie so. Sutherland wished the lad would take back what he had said, admit that he did not mean it, but James stood fast, stubborn and unrelenting.

Jeb had calmed by now, disappointment replacing blind rage. Lettie looked at her son with a mixture of surprise and sorrow.

Sutherland released Jeb, who stepped back, head hanging. The Scotsman said, "Gentlemen, let this pass." Words alone could do little, could neither change James's opposition nor relieve the company's distress, but words were all he had just then. "It'll take time to come through this. Think! Think of all we mean to each other, all we've been through! Don't be so hasty, James, or so hard on us, for we're following the only just course, and we believe it's for everyone's sake."

Lettie sobbed, "Have faith, son! Thy pa had faith in what we done, and we come through, just as we'll come through this. . . ." But she saw James was closed to her words, and she turned away to put her head against a cabinet and weep. Jeb had tears in his eyes, and James stared helplessly, almost desperately, at his parents. The cheerful noise from the street grew louder as a squad of soldiers went past, shouting and laughing as they hauled a load of firewood on ox-drawn sleds. Their hard work done, there was nothing ahead but celebrating for two days.

Sutherland said, "Shake hands now. Jeb? James? Shake hands now, for Lettie's sake!"

They did so, but could hardly look at each other. James went to his apartment, but before he closed the door, he said, "I'm going away this spring. I'm going to Montreal." He looked at Sutherland. "I'm selling out my interest in the company, Owen; I won't be back, at least not as a partner."

"No!" Lettie cried. "Don't be rash, son! Please!"

"Give it thought, James," Sutherland said. "Give careful thought before you do this."

James glanced at Jeb and his mother, then said, "I will; I'll give it until April." Then he closed the door, leaving the atmosphere muted, save for Lettie's soft crying. In the streets Frenchmen were singing as one sleigh after the other dashed by, bells tinkling, voices sounding through the empty warehouse like an echo of times long past.

Sally Cooper walked along the river's edge to fetch Tom from his work at the boatyard a few hundred yards from the fort's water gate. The building of a ship always fascinated Sally, and she admired the trim vessel as she approached.

To be named *Felicity,* the schooner was fifty-five feet long and sixteen feet across at the beam, the widest part in the center of the deck. She was well on her way to completion, with the sleek hull already sealed, blackened with pitch and tar most of the way up to her gunwales. Workmen in small groups were leaving for the festival, carrying tools over their shoulders or in heavy leather satchels. As Sally passed, carpenters, shipwrights, riggers, and smiths greeted her, touching their hats and nodding good-day.

She knew most of them, and one young lad teased her, saying Tom was lurking in the cabin, waiting for her. She should take care, he said, for Tom had installed a lock that only he could open. In high spirits, Sally bantered back at them. When one asked for a dance that afternoon, she told him to write to her secretary. He jibed back that Tom Morely needed no written request, so why should he?

Sally climbed a ladder set against the hull, keeping the plum-colored greatcoat close against her legs. Other men were passing by on their way to the fort, and she waved to them, feeling pretty and fresh. Dressed warmly in fur leggins and hat, she was eager for the fun soon to come at *le grand marais.* It was a cloudy day, not very cold, just right for the outing, even if there was a flurry of snow.

On the deck, Sally was confronted with piles of coiled rigging, stacked lumber, unstepped masts, two brass swivel guns lying unmounted, and several buckets of nails, pitch, and the caulking material called oakum. She could see from the good workmanship that the *Felicity* would be an excellent vessel.

Tom had taken this cabinetmaking contract partly because he was not the kind to winter with traders in the north, nor was he enthusiastic about clerking in the warehouse. Also, he was paid well as a journeyman cabinetmaker, being among the best at the fort. But more meaningful than the pay alone was a love for his work. As Sally came clumsily along the crowded, unpainted deck, stepping over spars and cordage and lumber, she called to Tom, but got no answer. Undoubtedly he was absorbed in his work.

As she reached the low cabin door opening she heard the rasp of a file. No door was hung as yet, so Tom could not have had any lock. Sally realized his friends were well aware he had a soft spot in his heart for her, and that was why they were so waggish. Entering the dim cabin she saw Tom intently shaping a carved shell decoration on a built-in blanket chest. She stood watching this tall, strong fellow delicately form the design, sleeves rolled up, his large hands as agile and sensitive as a musician's.

She had seldom seen him work at cabinetry before, though she had been impressed with the furniture and chests he had made as gifts for friends and family. Somehow Sally had thought of Tom more as a fur trader whose diversion was woodworking; but now, seeing him almost caress the wood as he gave it shape and beauty, she could tell he loved this most.

Tom stepped back to get a better perspective and bumped Sally. She put her hands over his eyes. Sally was tall, but had to stand on her tiptoes to reach him. At first he gave a grunt, as though annoyed, then said, "Don't tell me—Mawak!" He took her hands and said, "No . . . too soft for Mawak." He kissed them. Sally tried to pull away, but he kept hold and said, "Fawn Eyes!"

He whirled, lifting Sally off the ground with a laugh, and pressed her hard against the wall. When they were face to face, Tom seemed as amused as he was surprised. He grinned impishly.

"You ain't Fawn Eyes . . ."

Sally was annoyed. "Who's Fawn Eyes? And put me down!"

Tom blushed a bit, keeping his body against hers as he answered, "Not you, I guess. I'm more glad it's you, Sal."

"Who's Fawn Eyes, I asked?" She struggled until he set her down.

"Hey," he said eagerly, sweeping his arms at the cabin, "how do you like it?"

The small room was fully paneled, with handsome molding. Soon it would be stained and varnished, he said.

"It looks really lovely," Sally replied, running her hand over the cabinet door, which was perfectly joined and skillfully designed. "Where did you get the idea for this? It's so beautiful, Tom."

He said he had been reading British books on furniture making, and Sally was impressed. Then she came back to her subject and asked who Fawn Eyes was.

Rolling down his shirtsleeves, Tom said it was getting cold. "Let's go to the warehouse and have some hot cider afore we head for the party!"

"You won't tell me who she is?" Sally did not really know why she was so angry. Tom was not her sweetheart, even though he wanted to be. This Fawn Eyes should mean nothing to her.

The playful look on his handsome face left it, and he became earnest. "Sal, you know how I feel about you." He began to put his arms about her, but she stiffened and looked down at the wood shavings and sawdust on the floor. He sighed and put on his heavy coat, which had been draped over a sawhorse.

"Sal," he said. "When the time comes that you care for me the way I care for you . . ." He went to her and took her hands. She looked up at him and did not pull away.

"What then?" she asked.

"Then it won't matter who Fawn Eyes is, because there won't be any more like Fawn Eyes. Only you."

Sally shook her head a little, saying, "Does she matter so?" Tom kissed her softly, and again she felt that wonderful fire within at the wonderful touch of his lips.

He put an arm over her shoulder and said, "If Jeremy don't send you a long letter by springtime, then nothing will hold me back from telling you how much I love you, Sal."

"Nothing's holding you back anyway," she said with a smile. "Except maybe Fawn Eyes!"

He spun her out of the cabin, and they hurried from the ship, both cheerful and looking forward to a day of skating and dancing and feasting. Tom wanted them to enter the marathon dancing that night, but she suggested he take Fawn Eyes instead. Ignoring her, he said tomorrow there would be ponycart races down the ice of the Rouge River, and it would be a wonderful weekend of shooting contests, footraces, and eating delicious broiled trout just taken from under the ice.

Laughing and running through snow back to the fort, Tom and Sally were the best of friends, if not lovers. He respected Sally's intention to wait for Jeremy, but had not given up hope that she might one day love him. He had felt those kisses, too, and even Fawn Eyes could not thrill him the way Sally did.

The party at *le grand marais* went on all day, and there were more than two thousand people. Old folks sat on chairs around blazing bonfires, while younger ones skated, skimming under branches, through thickets, and over frozen logs. There was barrel jumping, figure skating, sprints, and long-distance races. The Indians won the races, as usual, for they were incredibly fast skaters, and Tamano was the best at the endurance.

Though he had lost his former blinding speed, Tamano knew how to pace himself in the winding eight-mile course that began at the fort and twisted through swamp and woods. During the race, hundreds of skaters shot along the riverbank, past crowds of cheering spectators who drank mulled cider or hot chocolate. At the marsh the competitors dashed around a tall mast, where a whaleboat had gone down in shoal water during a storm that fall, then returned for the finish at the fort.

With one hundred yards to go, Tamano came first, his iron skates a blur at the final sprint. Little Hawk, his lean and quick protégé, challenged him, but failed by a very narrow margin to take the lead in the last few yards. Laughing and near to collapsing, these two embraced after crossing the finish line, where a cannon was fired from the fort's blockhouse in the victor's honor. Tamano's Ottawa wife, Lela, and their twin boy and girl ran to him. Unlike their elders, the five-year-old children wore white man's clothes. Under her blanket coat, pretty Catherine had a long brown dress of calico, with a short, French-style jacket of blue serge, and her hair was tucked under a white mob cap. David, who was a stout little fellow, wore breeches and an undyed linen shirt gathered at the waist by a scarlet sash, like a French *voyageur*. Although Tamano and Lela were more comfortable in the traditional clothes of their people, they encouraged their children to take on white habits.

Little Hawk's squaw, the Chippewa White Dove, and their two small boys congratulated him, proud of his own showing. Tamano rubbed Little Hawk's head and snatched away his fur cap, saying in Chippewa, a tongue the Sioux brave knew well, "You let an old man win! Admit it!"

Still panting for breath, Little Hawk could not speak and hung over his pudgy wife's shoulders. Shaking his head and grinning, Little Hawk flashed sign language that told everyone who understood, "If I cannot breathe, I cannot win!"

Sutherland translated for Ella as they approached the Indians, their own two children in tow. These close friends helped Tamano try on the fine pair of snowshoes he had won as first prize. They were wonderful *racquets*, worth as much as an excellent rifle. Other distance skaters were skimming over the line, shouting compliments to Tamano. Among them was Tom Morely, out of breath, and Sally caught him as he slumped in exhaustion. After Tom recovered, the couple skated away with the Indians to clamber aboard waiting sleighs for the trip to the great marsh and the remainder of the day's activities and feasting.

Sutherland and Ella were arm in arm, a flock of skating, falling children rushing around them as they followed Tom and Sally.

The Sutherlands observed the young couple, also arm in arm, and then looked at each other. Without having to speak, they knew there was far more to this relationship than Sally realized. They felt sympathy for Tom Morely, who was honorably trying not to take advantage of the absent Jeremy.

Ella said, "Tom knows he has to give the girl time to make a rational decision about whom she really loves."

Sutherland nodded, for his wife had spoken his own mind. "Still, she better hurry or she'll lose him, too."

They all drove sleighs to the marsh, where fires roared at both ends of a forty-foot shelter, and a spitted ox roasted slowly over one. At the other mouth of the longhouse sat several Indian children, listening to Matilda Merriwether Lee talk enthusiastically about the Bible and Christianity. The children were wrapped in blankets and fur, seated on logs and folding chairs, and Matilda stood before them, telling the tale of Adam and Eve in the Garden of Eden. Each child had a cup of cider, given by Matilda as an extra incentive to listen politely as she went about her missionary work. Since the tragic death of her mother, Matilda had taken fervently to spreading the gospel, and to children in particular. She and Reverend Lee had none of their own.

Sutherland and Ella were passing this scene on their way to the shooting contest he had entered. His fine Pennsylvania rifle—a gift from Benjamin Franklin—was under his arm in a case and wrapped in a blanket to protect it from the cold. As their children skated around, the Sutherlands paused to listen to Matilda, who appeared inspired at having so large an audience. Mawak, the aged Ottawa medicine man, was on hand, garbed in a bright trade shirt worn over a pelt coat. He sat on a log near the fire, listening gravely. There also were Tamano's and Little Hawk's families; and the portly Canadian partner, Jean Martine, placidly smoked a pipe as he listened with amusement.

Matilda wore the finest mink coat and hat, with matching boots and leggins, so that only her rosy face showed through the furs. Her gloved hands moved in flowing circles and arcs as she told how God created Paradise and Adam. When she explained how Eve sprang from Adam's rib bone, it set the children to looking around at one another and at their parents, who were kind enough to say nothing. Old Mawak, too, seemed startled to hear that woman had been made of a man's rib.

". . . and then the serpent spoke to Eve," said Matilda in her sweet voice, though she tried to be very ominous as the first woman was persuaded to eat of the Tree of Knowledge. Mawak leaned forward a little, wondering whether he had ever heard this particular version before. Indians told their own tales of creation in many different ways, and none knew greater variety than Mawak. It was very interesting and he found himself drinking the cider down quickly so it would not distract him from listening. Not even the children were more attentive than Mawak.

The hot, crackling fire, distant fiddle music, and the shouts of skaters and sleigh riders were a fine background for Matilda's eloquence. Nearby, a thickly bundled Reverend Lee stood with Ella and Owen. He was thinner and more frail than ever—understandably, because his marriage to Matilda was in difficulty. His persistent support of the Congress party was setting Matilda increasingly against him. Though they loved each other, they were seldom seen together in public these days except at services and were thought to be suffering from hopeless melancholy.

Lee continued giving Sunday sermons in an unused barrack, but most Presbyterians in the settlement found it hard to come to his chapel, and it was said the army soon would ask him to find other facilities. There was little talk anymore of building him a new church, though the Sutherlands and a few others promised to help him in this. Matilda had finally persuaded Lee to keep politics out of his sermons, but references to fire and brimstone too often sounded like guarded descriptions of Parliamentary devils and loyalist Judases. Lee was looking better today, however, because Matilda was happy. It was a relief to the Sutherlands that they were enjoying themselves.

"How wonderful it is to see my wife out and around again!" Lee said to Owen and Ella. His thin, nasal voice was soft but had a quality of resilient strength to it that told he was recovering from his family's tragedy. "My wife hasn't seemed so vigorous since the . . . Ah, but then human nature can be wonderfully adaptable, even in the worst of circumstances."

Sutherland touched the minister's shoulder, saying, "We all have to go on, Angus, and I'm sure Matilda will find her own reasons to go on."

Momentarily, Lee's eyes closed as he said, "So I pray, Owen; so I pray, every day of my life."

Matilda came to a resting place in her talk; the first man and woman were cast out of Paradise, and the children seemed to have absorbed quite enough for a while. Mawak, on the other hand, had thoughts of his own on the subject of creation. Being a member of Lee's Indian choir, he considered himself a true Christian who had the added good fortune of being a medicine man of the Ottawa, well versed in the lore of his people. He wanted to share his own wisdom with so knowledgeable a white woman, and he rose, doffing his feathered fur hat with a flourish.

Matilda was more familiar with well-behaved Indian children than with a proud but disheveled Ottawa medicine man, and she stepped back as Mawak came forward. He tried to keep her from getting too close to the fire, but his hand on her elbow was a trifle too much for Matilda. She shuddered slightly, dusting off the spot where he had touched her.

Reverend Lee was uneasy. He offered to take her away, speaking kindly to Mawak, but the old Indian held his forefinger in the air and said, "This Injun think preacher lady tell helluva good tale, and you young 'uns around here listen close, hear?"

Unsure what to say, the prim Matilda nodded once with a forced smile and thanked him. Though Lee tried, he could not pry his wife away, for she wanted to go on with her story to the children as soon as they were ready for more hot cider. But Lee knew that once Mawak had the floor, he would not easily relinquish it.

"Tell helluva good tale," Mawak said again. "Tale so good, it make Mawak think of true Injun story about white bear."

He half closed his eyes and began to ruminate, recalling an Ottawa legend in which a young Indian sees a great white bear in a vision. The children were immediately entranced, but Matilda was impatient to tell about Cain and Abel. Their conflict actually was intended to be the most important part of her talk, for it illustrated the tragedy of strife between brothers, such as that developing in America. She longed to interrupt, but let Mawak have his moment.

"This here white bear come up to Injun and sit close beside him; bear think, scratchin' nose"—Mawak ponderously did the same—"scratchin' ear, then sayin': 'Injun boy, it time to tell true about Great Spirit, maker of heaven and earth. Listen close, Injun boy; open ears, open heart, 'cause this here white bear been up in heaven a while back, and me and Great Spirit had some heap big words together—'"

"See here, Mawak," Matilda said sharply, though trying to be polite and almost touching his greasy shirt. "I do wish you'd not distract the little ones from the Word of God."

Mawak was surprised to be interrupted. He came back, as from a dream. "This Injun ain't finished yet, preacher lady. Hold on to your horses. Now, this white bear was sayin'—"

Matilda was flustered. "That's just it, Mawak! Bears can't talk! We all know that! Not even white ones, and I think you've been quite rude to interrupt my story."

Reverend Lee was embarrassed and tried to pacify Matilda, but she ignored him and beckoned to the children, who sat up and gave her their attention once more. Mawak, meanwhile, was dumbstruck. Just as Matilda began to speak, he interrupted in his heavy, languid way.

"Preacher lady . . . preacher lady."

"What is it now? Can't you see—"

"Why bears no can talk?"

Exasperated, Matilda shook herself and muttered to Reverend Lee, "How on earth you ever got mixed up with creatures like this, I'll never know! Please tell him to be still!"

Lee wanted to be gentle and said, "Mawak, everyone knows animals don't really talk—though you're spinning a nice yarn. We call them fables, and we know that whenever animals talk in stories they're meant merely as an amusement, and they're not true at all."

Mawak nodded slowly, rubbing his large chin with thick, bony fingers. Then he raised a hand and said, "Ain't true, you say? What about talkin' serpent in Paradise? Christian snakes talk? Injun bears talk, too."

He beamed at his logic, and the children laughed, chattering among themselves, then cried for Mawak to go on with his story. This he did, with great solemnity and deliberation. Dejected, Matilda demanded Lee take her back to the fort immediately. He tried to soothe her, but it was no use.

"If you care at all for me," she whined as Mawak droned on nearby, "you'll take me away from this place, take me away from these people!"

She ran off, slipping and sliding on the ice, and Lee hurried close behind, trying to help her. The Sutherlands watched them struggle up a flight of wooden steps built into the bank. Then the Lees got into a sleigh, whose driver was for hire to make the trip back and forth to the fort.

"It's a shame," Ella said. "Though it's ten years she's been out here, I don't think she belongs anymore."

"She might get over it," Owen said as they walked toward a clearing a hundred yards off through dense pine trees, where men were beginning to practice target shooting.

"She'll only get over it if Angus becomes a Tory like her father; but that's something he'll never do. I worry for Matilda."

Ella was right. Though Lee's sermons had toned down, it was rumored that a petition was being circulated to ask his church elders back east to remove him for being a political firebrand.

"If he were in Massachusetts," Sutherland said, watching the sleigh with the Lees depart for the fort, "his pews would be full, and they'd have built him a new church long ago."

The minister's fate and their own were on their minds as the Sutherlands walked away from the bonfire at the longhouse, where Mawak continued to tell his story. Neither wanted to think the worst, however, for today was to be fun. Both were absolutely determined to make the most of it. They were walking along a narrow, curving corridor in the pine trees, and abruptly had the same idea: They began to race, laughing and tugging at each other like children. They barged between pines, trying to be the first to reach the next bonfire.

Suddenly Ella took a shortcut through a thick stand of balsam fir, leaving Owen on the winding track. She thought she would easily win, but there was a loud crashing nearby, and as she ducked under a branch he was there, just ahead of her. She grabbed at his arm to hold him back, and they wrestled, falling into the snow, laughing and struggling like young lovers. Then Owen kissed her, and Ella felt weak, happy, and wonderfully blessed. She gazed at him and they smiled. He was about to kiss her again, and she closed her eyes—only to have an icy handful of snow rubbed in her face. Squealing in surprise, Ella reached for her own snow, but then Owen did kiss her, so passionately, so warmly, that she lay back and held him close, both of them feeling unexpectedly at peace.

With the sound of merry people on every side, Ella and Owen Sutherland lay alone, contented, behind the sheltering pine trees. Whatever was ahead did not matter just then.

chapter 10

GOOD COMPANY

The winter of 1774–1775 held the northwest in a cruel grip that year. Even though the festival at *le grand marais* had been a social success, it was not long before hard feelings returned between loyalists and Congress party people. Because the work of the fur trade would not really begin until the canoe brigades returned that spring, there was plenty of time for discussion, meetings, and debate. The Sons of Liberty were at one pole of the conflict, and Dawson Merriwether's Tories were at the other.

Sutherland lost more and more friends and was unwelcome in homes where once he had been honored. It was a sad time, a time of disillusionment for many whose friends, neighbors, and family chose sides that opposed their own.

It was a blessing that the young were able to enjoy the wintertime. Sally and Tom took pleasure in skating together for hours, and Benjamin was fast becoming skillful at the Scottish game of shinty, played with a small ball, goals, and sticks with a crook at one end. Though normally played on a field, the children of the northwest played it often on ice, skating rather than running.

Although James Morely was not as fast or powerful as his brother and the Sioux Little Hawk, he was athletic and wiry, and on the ice he was a master at shinty. James had taken Benjamin under his wing and had taught the boy to be a deadly scorer, making the most of Benjamin's speed and intelligence, which was far superior to that of most ten-year-olds. He held his own even against Tom, who was also a good player. Sutherland and Ella enjoyed watching the boys and young men playing shinty, and they liked the way Benjamin was so fearless, yet also smart.

One Sunday afternoon Sally and the Greys stood with the Sutherlands watching a game in the shipyard cove near the fort. The settlement had organized several teams, each putting fifteen persons on the ice, and this was a match between two of the best. Benjamin did very well, scoring often and leading his side to victory.

At the game's end, the boy skated happily off the ice toward his friends and family. He wore a thick vest and breeches, but was otherwise lightly clad. James Morely skated alongside him and patted his back in congratulations.

Tom, who was on the losing team, came off at the same time, tapping his brother's curved stick with his own and saying, "You should be the one who's congratulated, little brother. You taught Ben how to win!"

James smiled at that, his gladness cheering up everyone else, for they all had been troubled at his decision to go to Montreal. Since his argument with Jeb in the warehouse, he had not changed his mind. Sutherland, too, admired the young man, wishing there were something he could say to persuade James to remain with them.

Shaking the fellow's hand, Sutherland said, "Benjamin's fortunate to have you show him so much, James; he talks about you as if you were the wisest man alive."

James grinned at the compliment and tousled Benjamin's dark hair. "A good pupil makes a wise master. But he'll soon be the master, and I his pupil!"

Benjamin piped up, "Only if you stay with us!"

James gave the boy a smile and said, "You'd better hurry and learn all you can before winter's done. There now, I've given you a goal, and see if achieving it doesn't make you the best shinty player hereabouts before the ice is out!"

Most players and their relations were drifting off to the fort or to cabins for an early dinner, and the Frontier Company's major partners had planned to dine together at the Morely-Grey warehouse that day. The cove was empty except for them.

Sutherland said, "I wish you'd teach Benjamin as much about clerking and running our warehouse when I'm away in the colonies."

Benjamin lit up, bouncing around in excitement. "Would you, James? Would you? I'm old enough now, and I can do more than just count pelts—"

James's face fell. He touched Benjamin's shoulder to stop him jumping up and down. To Owen he said, "I'll be going east with you on the *Trader,* and then . . ." He glanced at his family and at Jeb in particular, saying, "But until I go, I'll do whatever I can to give Benjamin a good start in the company."

Benjamin protested. "You can't leave the company!"

Susannah shushed him. "You were told not to mention that to James! It makes everybody sad."

"You can't!" Benjamin cried, shaking his younger sister off. "It's not right."

Suddenly Tom Morely scooped Benjamin onto his shoulders and gave a shout. "Come on, everybody; Ma's got a prodigious feed in the oven at the trading house! Come on, little brother, Sally, Susannah! Let's eat!"

As Tom strode away with him, Benjamin stared back, eyes fixed on James, who followed beside Sally. James did not look at the boy. He and Sally were last in line, with the Sutherlands and Greys walking ahead with Tom.

Sally put her arm in James's and smiled at him. He smiled back, but it was a half-hearted one. She cared about James, having been brought up along with him and Tom over the past ten years. Compared to Tom and Jeremy, James was most like a brother to her, and the inner pain he had been enduring touched her also.

They said nothing for a while as they tramped through frozen snow toward the fort. The sky was dark, promising a snowstorm that night.

Sally spoke first. "You won't really go, will you? I mean, this trouble will pass eventually, and we'll weather it just as we've weathered other things."

"Sal," he said, his skates cracking through the crust on the snow. "Sal, I don't have things to keep me here, the way you have your family, and Tom has you."

"What? Tom has—"

James smiled, this time with real humor. "Don't deny it, but that's not what I'm talking about. What I'm saying is that a man has to stand by his beliefs, and my beliefs in all this aren't the same as Owen's or Jeb's or Tom's. I'm a free man, and I'm British. The company's going rebel, but I won't go with it, even though I love you all. Somebody has to keep his head if there's to be any hope for us."

Feeling depressed, Sally could make no worthwhile reply.

James became more serious and said, "In Montreal there's a new trading group being formed, calling themselves Northwesters. They're good men—you know them: McGill, Henry, Pond, Blondeau, the Frobisher brothers."

Indeed, Sally knew them as leading free traders who had usually formed loose partnerships for a season or two, but never lasting companies such as the Frontier Company.

"Well," said James, "they're forming a company based on our own partnership principle, with all having a share in the profits. I might join them."

Sally was astonished, and asked whether James had told Sutherland.

"I intend to soon, but first I have to make up my own mind about the future."

"But, James, you already have a partnership in the best and strongest company on the frontier! Why start again with others?"

They were entering the fort, which was quiet except for some of their own people, who were playfully scampering about on the way to the Morely-Grey warehouse.

James said, "Because, Sally, the Northwesters are loyal to the king, and I told you, I don't like what Congress is trying to do. I think they're after total independence one day soon."

Sally felt very sad as she said, "We'll miss you if you go when we need you so much!"

James had a deep hurt. "I've promised Ma to wait until spring to decide—I have to admit, I'm not absolutely sure yet."

Sally hugged his arm. "Good!"

He said, "Let's not talk of it anymore; we've had a good day, and I've enjoyed myself so much that it's really hard to think of going."

Sally squeezed his arm again. Then, seeing Tom at the warehouse porch where he let Benjamin down to remove their skates, Sally changed the subject. "James, who's Fawn Eyes?"

He was startled at the question and seemed to know something, for he said, "Why do you ask me that? Tom's the one who— No, I'll say nothing!" He grinned that boyish, cheerful smile that made him so well liked by everyone. "Now, Tom's standing there thinking I'm trying to charm you away with me to Montreal! Let's hurry. I'm hungry!"

Tom was watching them as they ran, his dark eyes fixed on Sally. Soon they were all in comfortable wooden clogs, and Sally put her hands on the arms of both brothers as they entered the Morely-Grey warehouse. A long trestle table was covered by a linen cloth, set with silver and china. Chairs and benches were all around, candles and oil lamps lit the room, and there was a cheerful racket of excited children and good conversation.

After helping serve the enormous meal of trout, roast beef,

squash, rice, and pickled vegetables, Sally sat down at the laden table. She was glad when Tom came to her, shooing Susannah over one chair to be beside her. Tom was not as educated as James, nor as worldly as Jeremy, but he looked at her in a way that set her spine to tingling and made her heart beat a little faster.

Jeb said grace over the long, well-laid table, the hushed families seated by candlelight around it. Sally bowed her head, meaning to listen to the prayer, but she found herself thinking about Jeremy so far across the sea. She missed him as much as ever and wondered what he would say in his first letter. She hoped he would ask her to wait for him—as he had not asked her to when he had left. No matter what she felt for Tom Morely, Sally was sure her heart belonged to Jeremy, even though he was in a different land and might come back as someone she did not know.

Jeremy had been in Edinburgh nine weeks and the city was wonderful: bustling, cosmopolitan, friendly, with everything a young scholar could ask for. He had friends among fellow students, and the landlady of his rented room on Princes Street was like a loving grandmother to him. He had a striking view out the window of his row house, looking northwest to the massive outcrop called Arthur's Seat, which rose eight hundred feet above the city. To the right he looked at Edinburgh Castle frowning down from its hill. There he could always find a diversion when books became oppressive. Even in winter one heard bagpipes skirl from Castle Rock, and Jeremy spent many hours strolling and thinking up there.

Yet he had never before felt so alone in the world, burdened by the weight of his difficult studies and by the dangerous political unrest in America. Further, he felt an outsider here in Scotland's grandest city. Though he liked and admired the British, there were times when their smug self-righteousness annoyed him. More than once he considered roaring from the window at the top of his lungs, just to see what those fine and proper ladies and gentlemen promenading on the street below would do. He suspected they would do nothing, either out of sophisticated self-restraint, or because they understood that struggling young scholars like him now and again needed to scream madly from their windows out of frustration.

But in all the English-speaking world he could not have been in a more desirable or bountiful city for scholarship. For example, it was here in 1768 that the new *Encyclopaedia Britannica* had been published; and in James's Court, not far from Jeremy's room,

lived David Hume, one of the greatest philosophers of the day;
James Boswell and Dr. Samuel Johnson had met in Edinburgh,
debating, composing diaries and prose; and a number of leading
Scots poets dwelt in the city. Side by side with artists and writers
were avant-garde scientists, physicians, inventors, and architects
who worked, wrote, and taught so prolifically that few other cities
in Europe could compare with the collective genius of Edinburgh.

From the start, Jeremy longed to be a part of this flowering
intellectual heritage. He was glad to be here, though he despised
the odors from reeking sewers and the stench that settled on the
city when a sea mist drifted up the Firth of Forth to mingle with
Edinburgh's smoke.

Studying medicine, he was in company with promising, gifted
young men from England, Scotland, Ireland, France, Germany,
Poland, Russia, and the Low Countries. There were even two
other Americans—sons of wealthy New York Tories, and more
British than the British, but Jeremy could take them well enough.

Had he been more familiar with the city, he might have had
an easier time of it in those first weeks. As it was, everything was
new to him, and the close friends he had made in Derbyshire were
too far off to be of any comfort. Even faithful Sniffer was back
in Derbyshire, being cared for by Penelope Graves, who had come
to adore the mischievous otter. Old Sniffer was better off in her
hands, for Jeremy's own were overfull with work, and he needed
to give his total attention to studies.

In the middle of February, on a snowy, gusting afternoon, he
sat by the glowing coal fire in his room, thinking whether or not
to go to the nearby public house for the usual meal of beer, mush,
and sausage. He was not very hungry, but he needed to get out,
to refresh himself before going on with a long night's study of
zoology. An enormous book on the subject lay open on his desk,
four others sat in a pile at his feet, and sheaves of paper with dense
notes were scattered about the room. On his cot were piles of
books concerning botany, herbal studies, homeopathy, biological
science, Greek philosophy, mathematics, Bacon's and Newton's
work, and several important monographs by learned physicians
that had been read recently before the Royal Society of London.
These monographs had yet to be read by Jeremy Bently, and that
pressing, tedious chore was too long overdue.

Among other things tumbling through his tired mind was the
question of whether he should apprentice himself to a surgeon soon
to learn that skill as well as medicine. Also nagging him were the

letters to home and Sally, tucked in his traveling chest and yet to be mailed. Perhaps he would send them off with Peter Defries once the Albany Dutchman came back from the Continent and the *Yankee* left dry dock in Bristol. Just the thought of hearty Peter and his family made Jeremy grin. How were they doing in this foreign world? Had they made it to the Netherlands as Defries had sworn he would? Jeremy wondered whether they could put up for long with the pompous formalities and pretentious attitudes of many in the British merchant class—a class fast rising to power in the world and taking on nobility's trappings, if not the code of honor.

Then there was Penelope Graves. Jeremy could not be sure what she meant to him. He delighted in her company, and there was something about her that very much appealed to him in a way Sally never had. Yet she was not Sally. She had none of Sally's physical strength and recklessness. She was not as headstrong and audacious as Sally, though Penelope could be impudent enough when it suited her.

There was a knock at the door. The gentle voice of Mrs. Shaw, the elderly landlady, asked whether Jeremy was prepared to receive some company.

"Quite a lot of company for your chamber, sir." She laughed and said something to whoever was out on the landing. "Quite rowdy company, too, though pleasant enough, I daresay, sir."

Before Jeremy could even open the door, and as he was still throwing on the red-flannel student gown that every young man wore at the university, there was a loud stamping and halooing outside, and the unmistakable voice of Peter Defries rang through the house.

Jeremy whooped for joy, and Peter thundered into the room. He tried to lift Jeremy from the ground, met resistance, doubled his efforts, and found himself in a bear hug almost as powerful as his own. These two were the same height, though Peter was huge in the shoulders and chest, and Jeremy was more athletically proportioned. As the men tussled, Mary Defries and her daughter, Jeanette were scolding Peter, the girl yanking at her father's coattails, insisting he act more civilized. The landlady went downstairs chuckling as Peter let go of Jeremy and peered around the room as though revolted that it was so small and overstuffed.

Jeremy greeted Mary and Jeanette with an outpouring of affection that told he had been without intimate friends or family for much too long. Mary was pretty as ever, looking radiant from her exciting travels to the Continent. Like her husband and daughter, she was dressed for the cold, wearing a heavy frock coat of brown serge, with brown hood and gloves, and her skirt was protected from the snow by a wet "safeguard" of heavy linen that was suspended from her waist.

Eleven-year-old Jeanette Marie, prim and rosy, was as dark of hair as her mother and father were blond. She was Mary's child by a Scottish soldier who had been killed in Pontiac's Rebellion, but for all the tenderness she was given by Peter, she might have been his own blood. Peter and Mary, who were in their early thirties, had no other children.

Jeanette's eyes were blue like Mary's and Peter's, her skin fair; she wore clothes that imitated her mother's, though they were even more spotless and more carefully protected from the slightest soiling. Jeanette was an extremely intelligent child, cautious and polite, the opposite of her father, who was carefree and rash. But she adored him, though she was ever busy trying to make him a gentleman.

Jeremy picked up Jeanette and raised her to the ceiling. She squealed, giggling and squirming. Like Sally, Jeanette had a tremendous crush on Jeremy, though she was bright enough to know it was only a fantasy.

"So!" Jeremy cried and spun around with her. "You're the proper Dutch lady now, are you? Where's your windmill and wooden shoes, then? And why don't you have one of those funny white caps with wings on them?"

Jeanette kicked a little as he put her down, declaring, "In Amsterdam and Leyden they don't wear funny caps! The Holland Dutch are even more elegant than Albany Dutch patroons, and just as elegant as Dutch New Yorkers."

Finishing his inspection of the room, Peter grumbled, "What in the name of Jehosaphat're you doin' in this cramped little hole, boy? Hibernatin'?"

Mary elbowed him. "You don't need much space to study, Peter. Sometimes the less the better, for then you don't have to waste time enjoying the comforts of where you live." She glanced around at the sloppy room, the small fire, and the bed piled with books. "It is a bit tiny, though, isn't it, Jeremy?"

Jeremy insisted it was enough, and suggested they take a look at the excellent view outside the window. "By the way, I was about to have dinner. Shall we all go together? You'll see where doctors-to-be are fed, and you'll see why the sight and smell of blood bothers them not at all."

"Hold on!" Peter declared, his meaty hands up to stop them. "We got the best lodgin's in the city, 'cept for what the Duke of Edinburgh and a few of his cronies've cornered! We're dinin' there, and your university associates will have to miss your company for once."

He glanced sideways at Mary, and pretended to whisper, "'Fore you know it they'd all gather round our table and expect to be fed like so many hungry puppies!"

Jeanette insisted, "Let Jeremy make the choice, Papa. He's our guest."

"I'll give in, Peter! Take me to the finest dining place in Edinburgh, in Scotland, in all Britain, if you choose!"

"We've been to all those places," Mary declared. "It's been a wonderful trip! London is marvelous, but I suppose medical students don't get much chance to visit Vauxhall Gardens or Ranelagh or Covent Garden."

Just then Jeremy remembered his letters to Sally, and he handed them over, asking they be sent as soon as possible. Then he went behind a screen, changing into clean clothes, and as he dressed, Peter and Mary told of their adventures through the Netherlands, France, and England. They had made many an acquaintance who would gladly do business with the Frontier Company, if the colonial embargo of British goods went on much longer. There were ample markets to sell pelts in Amsterdam, and manufactured goods for trading to the colonists and Indians were plentiful there.

Jeremy pushed on a hat, and they crowded downstairs, bidding good-bye to Mrs. Shaw, who stood at her door and beamed to see the young man in company with good friends. Jeremy inquired after their black servant, Emmy, and they told him she had taken ill and was being cared for at their lodgings. Then the subject was once more about politics.

As they went through a light snow toward the waiting carriage, Jeremy said, "The colonial embargo surely won't go on for long!" He lifted Jeanette into the door as the coachman held it open. "After all, we're all one family—"

Jeremy stopped short. In the carriage, wrapped snugly in a beaverskin cover, and wearing a dark hood that contrasted with her shining face, sat Penelope Graves. Jeanette began to titter and covered her face. Jeremy sprang aboard to embrace Penelope.

"I hope you don't mind," Penelope said, as though she had been uncertain of his reaction. "The Defrieses stopped at Derbyshire, wanting to know where to find you so they could visit you before they went back to America, so, I thought I might be of some help. I wanted to see you ... to see that you were all right, I mean."

Jeremy turned to Peter and Mary, who were sitting opposite with Jeanette, leaning against one another, a pleasant look on their faces. He grinned at them for their little surprise. Then he said to Penelope, "You'll have to share my company with Jeanette, you know."

"She knows," Jeanette said, jumping across and planting herself between them and tugging Jeremy's arm under her own. "Miss Graves already asked if I'd mind, and I said you're nice, but much too old for me."

Penelope said Sniffer was at home with Richard Weston, who had become another favorite companion to the otter. Jeremy sensed Penelope wanted to see him without any distractions, and that suited him fine.

Jeanette snuggled against Jeremy, who put his arm over her shoulders and felt Penelope touch his hand for just an instant. A moment later, the coachman closed the door, the horses blew and snorted, the driver cracked his whip, and the carriage lurched away. They sat contentedly observing one another or looking out the windows at the serenity of a city in wintertime. Jeremy and Penelope often glanced at each other. Between them, pretty Jeanette let her legs, covered by the beaver skins, swing back and forth with the rhythm of the coach.

Peter disturbed the mood by addressing Jeremy. "As I was sayin', the embargo'll go on, I tell you—"

Mary broke in, "No politics, Peter! Not today."

"All right," he said, pushing his hat back on his head. "All right, but after we eat I'm gonna tell the lad about London politics, and how nobody here gives a hoot about America except to make a dollar by skinnin' our hides—"

Mary took Peter's hand and squeezed, and he relented. Penelope seemed very troubled, Jeremy noticed. There was something in the air, something on the minds of his friends that said matters between America and England were even worse. But Jeremy did not want to think about such things at all just then. He wanted company, laughter, good cheer, and a brief escape from the toils and worries of his daily life. The others knew this, too, and did their best to make the day a special occasion for him.

Though Peter did not say it outright during the course of the lavish meal, he hinted that it might be some time before he and Jeremy saw each other again. Peter suggested that England might not welcome him back ever again.

While the women, at one end of the table, talked about Christmas traditions in foreign countries, Peter leaned over to Jeremy and whispered, "I'm bringin' a few Hollandish things home to Albany that the king's harbor masters and customs men won't like if they find out about 'em."

The candles set on the table flickered light over silver and linen, illuminating the remains of an apple tart, and sparkling through half-full wineglasses. Jeremy concentrated on these things, reluctant to know how his friend and his family's company might be conspiring at treason. He said nothing, but Defries went on, "The Dutch've sold me some saltpeter and sulphur in barrels— several hundred of 'em. . . ."

Saltpeter and sulphur, mixed with charcoal, was gunpowder, a scarce commodity in America. It was badly needed by local militia, who were hard pressed to supply themselves since Parliament recently had shut down shipments of gunpowder and arms to the colonies. Jeremy was agitated, but still he said nothing.

Pleased with himself, Defries chuckled, "And some brass— cylinders, like, with holes bored in 'em—say about ten."

Cannon barrels.

"You know, Jeremy, there ain't nobody like Holland Dutchmen when it comes to makin' fine muskets and rifles—"

"Stop," Jeremy whispered. "Say no more, Peter! I don't want to hear about it . . . I can't hear about it now! You're talking about armed rebellion—"

"I am," Defries said coldly, his face suddenly grim and drawn in the candlelight. "I hadn't known you were so taken with this here country that it would change your heart altogether, Jeremy." Defries looked at Penelope as he spoke; she was joking with Mary, paying no attention.

Jeremy shook his head. "It's not that. I just want to see a peaceful solution! If you smuggle over arms and ammunition, our hotheads will get bolder, and there'll be no stopping them from shooting down whoever stands up to them."

Defries took a sip of wine, then said, "You're in an ivory tower here, lad; and I suppose if I was studyin' in college, and if a sweet young English thing was soft on me, I'd find it difficult to make a choice in this. No, I don't blame you."

Jeremy sat back, surprised at Peter's comment about Penelope. But he held his peace, for by now the three females were aware of the hushed conversation, though they could not hear it. Mary insisted the men be more sociable and asked Peter to tell them of the New Year's celebration in Holland.

"Yes, yes," Defries said, clearing his throat. "I was just tellin' the lad they got excellent fireworks in Holland. Really give a bang! Terrible expensive, but I'll wager they'll find a ready market for fireworks in America these days!"

Later, the Defrieses retired to their lodgings, giving Jeremy and Penelope the freedom of a crisp winter evening in the city. The wind had died down, and Edinburgh seemed to be in repose, except for back streets, where taverns and public houses were full of merrymakers. In company with Penelope, Jeremy found it easy to let Peter's munitions smuggling slip from his mind. They left their coach and driver at the tranquil base of Arthur's Seat and took a stroll up the steep path, where new snow had been scraped clear by an ox and wagon trailing a snowplow. It was an exhilarating night. The moon, almost full, hung above the deep blue crest of the snow-covered hill.

As they walked, Penelope gave him her arm, and he asked whether her parents had replied to her idea of establishing a school in Birmingham where poor children might be taught fundamentals of reading, writing, and arithmetic.

"Their silence is as much an answer as 'no' would be," she said. "They've put me off by saying it would cost too much to fund a building, school, and staff. But I'm not giving up yet, for there are others of means and position who'll support me—and when they do, Mother and Papa will surely grant their consent."

"Won't they simply forbid you to do it?"

"No, because I'll have lord this and lady that as my sponsors, so you see it won't be just one stubborn Englishwoman filled with idealism. Someone has to help our poor people, and I intend to try!"

They walked a little further up the hill and came to a flat place, where they turned and looked eastward over Edinburgh. Across the firth, the lights of ships in the harbor twinkled against the black water, and distant towns were sparkling clusters scattered here and there on shore.

Jeremy said, "In Detroit there's real need for schools like the one you're planning, and no one would think you too good to teach. You'd be welcome and could do so much."

"That sounds like where I should be! Perhaps after the school in Birmingham's begun I'll go to America and start another at your Detroit—do the children of factory workers there speak English or French?"

Jeremy chuckled. "There are no factories, other than a sawmill or smithy, but in a few years there'll be enough children to warrant an even larger school than they have now."

He told her about Reverend Angus Lee, his own schoolmaster. Lee was a good teacher of boys and he might be open-minded enough to accept a schoolmistress for the girls.

"On the other hand we have an old Ottawa medicine man named Mawak who doesn't think much of white education for men and women," Jeremy said, thinking fondly of his tutor in Indian ways. "He'd rather teach our boys how to be real men, hunting, fishing, and making war; he'd say all the women should be good squaws, sleeping with honored guests, cleaning game, chewing deer hide until it's soft enough for her husband's moccasins."

Penelope was dismayed until Jeremy said many French and Indians at the straits would send their daughters to Penelope's school if they were convinced it would improve chances of rising in British-American society.

Penelope and he imagined a small white schoolhouse overlooking the straits, perhaps near Valenya—a place she had heard all about and thought must be a heaven on earth. Jeremy did not try to persuade her otherwise, although he wanted to be nowhere else just then than Edinburgh.

"I like this city," he said, "even if it's not home."

Penelope moved against his shoulder and said, "I think you're the sort who'd like being anywhere. I mean, you know how to make the best of things no matter where you are—England, Scotland, or even the wilds of America."

He put an arm around her waist. Just below them, on the winding path beyond drifts of bluish snow, the carriage waited. From here the two side lamps shimmered like eyes watching them, but they seemed quite alone. This was the best Jeremy had felt since coming to Scotland.

Penelope asked, a little forced, "Are the Scottish lassies as charming and winsome as your Sal at home?"

"What? Scottish lassies? Hah! With all my studies, I've not a moment to myself to meet a lass, though I doubt there's few anywhere who could compare with—" He found himself gazing down into Penelope's eyes. "With Sally." In those eyes he saw a question. Peter's earlier comment about Penelope being in love with him came to mind. Now Jeremy knew it was true. Penelope did not look away. He could almost hear her heart beating. Or was it his own?

He said, "Few can compare; but I would say, if it suits you, that you are . . . that you mean much to me—"

There was a sudden shout, and a dozen boys on sleds came hurtling down the steep slope, howling and shrieking, tumbling and sprawling right and left. The gang whirled past in a chorus of merriment that set Penelope and Jeremy to laughing. His arm was close about her, and she turned to him, smiling. He knew then it was his own heart pounding, and he kissed her. Penelope's eyes closed. She shuddered, as though holding something in. She did not kiss him back, but let him kiss her and put a hand on his cheek. As he drew his face from hers, she opened her eyes.

"Perhaps . . ." she whispered. "Perhaps in time you'll think I—" She touched his lips with her fingers. "It suits me, Jeremy, that I mean something to you."

He shook his head a little. "Penelope, words can't express what I want to say. It's not that you aren't—"

Unexpectedly, she kissed him. He enclosed her in both arms, and her hands went behind his head. With the sound of the children playing, and the shining silence of the city far below, they embraced as though they had found each other for the first time. He kissed her cheeks, her hair, her lips, and she trembled all over, whispering his name so softly that he could barely hear.

"Penelope," he said. "It's all new, all—" They kissed.

After a little while, a time that was too brief, a bell tolled ten, and they had to go. Penelope, who was staying in the same building as Peter and Mary, would return to England with them in two days. Jeremy had so much studying to do that he would be hard pressed to see her in that short period. As they stood there he wanted only to hold on and not let her go.

Penelope said, "I love you, Jeremy." Her hands were on his shoulders, her body pressed close to his so that her cape fell over his arms. "I'm not asking anything in return, not now, not yet, but I can't help but tell you that I love you. Do you think me a fool?"

He gave her a squeeze and smiled. "Penelope, I think you're wonderful. But with me things are not all so simple—"

"Let's not force anything, Jeremy." She pulled away and took his hand to lead him back down the slope.

He caught her and pulled her back to him, kissing her until she yielded and crushed against him as hard as she could. For a moment longer they stood together, her head on his shoulder.

He took a deep breath and said, "We both need time, Penelope; time to think, time to see things as they really are." He eased her back until their eyes met and held. "I'm not sure what I feel, Penelope, but if I know what love is, then . . . then I truly love you."

She sought the meaning behind those words, her eyes again intense, questioning. "Am I—?" She gave a little laugh of irony. "Am I like so many women I've heard of, who fall in love, who are loved for a little while, and then lose their lover to the world, lose him to another way of life?"

"Not yet."

"Not yet?" She sighed, a shaking release of emotion, and said, "No. Not yet; you won't do that, will you?"

He moved away in confusion and passion and tried to be light, saying, "If you'll swear never to love me and leave me, then I'll swear the same!"

She smiled, despite herself, and kissed him. "It'll do neither of us any good if we dally here in idle talk of love, and then you fail to pass your exams because you're frostbitten!" She began again to lead him to the carriage. Soon they were running, her hand in his. They slid the last twenty yards to the coach, Jeremy howling and startling the horse. The animal pawed and snorted and awoke the coachman, who was bundled up in the driver's box.

When the carriage stopped in front of Jeremy's lodgings, they made plans to see each other at least twice tomorrow, before Penelope and the Defrieses departed. As he left the coach, he kissed her, so tenderly that it took her breath away. When he drew back, she said, "If you keep on so, I'll be unable to resist you, even if you tell me you're leaving for America on the next ship!"

He opened the door and jumped out, and as he closed it said through the window, "I'm staying here until I'm a doctor. America won't see me until then, so I won't leave you before 1777!"

They parted, the coach clattered away down the quiet street, and Jeremy watched until it went around the corner, leaving him alone again. Before turning to his front door, he thought about the package of letters he had given Peter that afternoon, including the homesick missives to Sally Cooper. He still had strong feelings for Sally, but he needed to reconsider them before she read those letters and thought he was willing to marry her.

Snow began to fall, and he shoved his hands in the large pockets of his frock coat. Tomorrow he would get those letters back, revise them, then return them to Peter with some of the more passionate lines to Sally recast or omitted. It was not that he did not care very much for her, but time and distance change a person, and he wanted to step back and see just how he was changing before he committed himself to her. He could yet taste Penelope's kiss. She was so wonderful! A rush of joy surged through him, and he took the row-house steps four at a time.

A passing night watchman, swinging a lantern, called out, "Eleven of the clock, and all's well . . . 'cept for young university lads what ain't abed at a decent hour!"

Jeremy unlocked the door and waved at the bent, old fellow, who nodded and waved back, saying loudly, "When they bound up steps like that, it ain't because they've been inspired by books! Have a care, laddie! Love can always wait, but your professors won't! Good night to you! Eleven of the clock, and all's well!"

The next morning, Peter asked Jeremy to breakfast with him alone at a public house known as the Anchor Tavern, a good place, frequented by intellectuals. At first Jeremy had suggested they dine conveniently at Mrs. Shaw's, but Defries had refused, saying he wanted to talk in private.

The Anchor was comfortably appointed, clean and well lighted from several windows facing the street. The floor was covered with an inch of fresh sawdust, and everywhere one looked the walls were decorated with seafaring woodcuts, naval symbols, and oil paintings of ships. There were unlit candles on the dozen or so tables scattered about, and at least eight scholars pored over books while they ate breakfast. Defries, robust and seeming to glow in the sunlight falling through the windows, was out of place among these haggard, concentrating students.

Sitting in a booth, Jeremy and he passed the first course in general conversation, and it was not until Peter had eaten his fill that he became businesslike. Over a third cup of tea, after the other dishes had been cleared, he came rapidly to the point. In a low voice, he said some of the Frontier Company's partners had agreed to do all they could to support the cause of liberty and the Congress in the developing struggle.

"There's only one thing Parliament will understand, Jeremy, and that's hot lead! You've met them that's in power, and it's clear they aim to hold on to power by grinding America into the mud—and I ain't gonna sit back and let it happen!"

Jeremy objected. "For one thing, I haven't met so many of the people in power, except for the guests at Uncle Henry's estate—"

"Lord Dartmouth, Lord Falmouth, Lord Bigmouth, Lord—"

Jeremy waved that off, growing annoyed, and Peter gave in a bit, saying, "All right, they ain't all tyrants; but them that're decent ain't tryin' to stop what's happenin' to us at home, are they?"

Jeremy thought Peter was missing the main point. "How are your smuggled guns and powder going to change things over there except get innocent folk killed? It's in provincial assemblies that Americans have to make their weight felt—not by wielding guns!"

Peter shook his head ponderously and sighed. "Look, Jeremy, if Parliament knows Americans got the wherewithal and the will to fight if the ministers turn the screws any tighter, then they'll think twice about turnin' 'em; that's only common sense!"

"They won't back off at threats any more than you would! They'll fight you if you hold a gun to their heads—"

"Not to their heads; just up on the table, where everyone can see it good."

"It's dead wrong!" Jeremy declared, loudly enough that a few scholars reading over porridge looked up in annoyance. More carefully, he said, "The colonies can't win by force of arms. They haven't a chance. It's not only madness to try, but it's damned cruel to the folk who'll follow glory-seeking leaders into rebellion—and that's what it is: rebellion, pure and simple! Peter, in the name of God, think rationally! You're challenging the whole Empire, and you're gambling that the Empire won't fight. Well, it will fight, and the people who follow you will pay in blood that'll be on your hands!"

Defries was pale, his jowls working, and he took a deep breath. He had feared Jeremy might not be fully behind the Whig cause in America, and he had pressed the lad far enough to make sure. A certain sadness came into his eyes. Jeremy saw it and felt miserable. Reaching across the table to take his friend's hand, Jeremy said he was sorry, but he meant every word he had said.

"I know." Defries's voice was hoarse. "I just hope whatever happens at home this spring will be short-lived, and that it'll all be over before you come back."

Jeremy wanted to appeal to Defries, to say he must not risk his neck in such a wild act of treason, but his friend was already on his feet, calling for the tavern keeper to square the account. Defries said they would meet him at their lodgings in the morning before they returned to Bristol and the *Yankee*'s dry dock. Jeremy nodded and looked down at his empty cup. A moment later they exchanged a brief handshake, and it pained Jeremy that they were being torn apart.

He watched Defries go toward the glass door, then looked down at a heavy book on zoology that lay on the table, but he had no desire at all to open it. At the last minute he remembered the letters for Sally and called to Peter, who was about to close the door.

"Don't worry about them," Peter said, putting on his hat. "I sent them out with the post this morning, and my agent at Bristol will soon have them on their way to the West Indies, then up to Savannah, and from there up to Philadelphia and Pitt and Detroit."

And Detroit. And Sally. Helpless, Jeremy sat down heavily as Peter left. The letters were gone. His expressions of devotion from an age ago were on their way, and there was nothing he could do to stop them—nothing to do but to write another letter explaining to Sally about Penelope.

Today he and Penelope would be together, and that sent a thrill through him. Even the dismal conversation with Peter could not overcome his excitement. He only wished he had been able to prevent those letters from ever leaving Britain.

The following evening Jeremy was back at his studies, sealed up in his room and certain there would be no other surprise visitors to interrupt him between now and exams in April. He had welcomed the visit, yet these past two days had stirred a storm of emotions that still had not subsided.

Rising from his desk, where an oil lamp flickered over open books, he gazed out the window at the winter's dusk of southern Scotland. The sky was a rich hue of purple and blue velvets, and the stars hung above the city's rooftops like miniature crystal torches. This was a magical world, a world that seemed as unreal as the faint light from the stars.

Leaning on the windowsill, his forehead against the cold glass, he closed his eyes. What was real? His love for Penelope, or his memory of Sally?

Penelope Graves left him breathless, contented, desiring nothing else from life but the warmth of her in his arms. Holding

Penelope close, Jeremy found it hard to contemplate anything else at all, not even the cause of liberty that his own family at that very moment was pursuing so passionately, so perilously.

Yet, for all Penelope's love, and his love for her, they had parted last night uncommitted. He was responsible first for those letters to Sally, whom he would not hurt. Penelope understood when he told her everything, and it seemed she loved him all the more, though she ached so that he felt it, too. They had parted sharing an intimacy that went beyond embraces or words, but there was no promise given or received.

On the sill was the little polished rosewood music box Sally had given him to remember her by. That life all seemed so long, long ago. He picked up the box and opened it. Only the last few notes of the *voyageur* song tinkled slowly and then stopped. It needed rewinding, but he did not do it. Closing the lid with a click that seemed strangely loud, he replaced the music box on the sill. That old song would do no good just then, for it was too beautiful, too haunting, and made him sad as it had never done before.

PART TWO

Rebel and Loyalist

chapter 11

OLD FRIENDS

In mid-March the ice began to give way at Detroit, and each night when the wind came up, the straits boomed and grumbled as cracks opened and floes shifted. With the advent of spring, Owen and Ella felt strangely uneasy, expectant of trouble as never before. They both sensed something ominous building in their country, though they avoided speaking of it, trying their best to be cheerful and to prepare for the arrival of the pelt harvest.

Then, happily, they had visitors who distracted their gloomy minds and brought back warm, exciting memories of the past in the northwest. Trudging out of a snowstorm, Mel Webster and his new Indian wife arrived without warning at Valenya. Responding to the yipping and howling of Heera outside, Ella opened the door and cried out with delight as a tall, lean fellow appeared, shaking snow from his fur hat and kicking ice from his rabbitskin boots. Behind him was a young squaw, as tall as he and pleasant of face, who was swathed in a beautiful gray trade blanket and carried the two pairs of snowshoes she and her husband had just removed.

Heera bounded in the door, jumping up on Mel, who laughed and let the dog lick the frost from his scraggly blond whiskers. Ella called Owen and Sally, and welcomed Mel with a great hug. Fair-haired, stooped, and in his middle thirties, Mel had friendly blue eyes and an easy smile. Laughing, he threw off his coat and hat and gave them to Sally, who also embraced him. Then he shook hands with Owen, who was astonished to learn they had crossed the dangerous ice from Fort Detroit in this snowstorm.

"Wasn't much for Hickory, here," Mel said in his slow, drawling way, and indicated the woman, who was shaking hands with Ella. "This is my wife, an Oneida, and she's uncanny at crossing water, frozen or half frozen, deep or shallow, in storm or in flood!

And traveling in the woods she never gets lost, even at night. Hickory, these are the Sutherlands."

Quieting Heera, Owen greeted the tall woman, who spoke a soft, clear English obviously learned at one of the many mission schools in the Iroquois country to the east. The Oneida were one of the powerful Six Nations, called collectively People of the Longhouse, or Iroquois League by whites.

"It is an honor and pleasure to meet Donoway of the Ottawa and family," Hickory said, curtsying a bit stiffly, but well enough. "Singing Bow has told me much about you and the love he has for you."

The woman used the Indian name for Mel Webster: Singing Bow, given because he entertained them with his wonderful fiddle playing. In all the northwest, no one could outshine Mel on the fiddle, and he was known from Philadelphia to the Mississippi. A native of New York, Mel had come to the northwest several years ago in search of buried Indian treasure. Finding adventure and danger in company with Owen Sutherland, he had forgone the hunt for treasure in favor of living with the Indians. In the past few years he had learned much from them and also had taught what he could of white culture, husbandry, manufacturing, book-learning, and language.

Loved by the tribes, Mel was regarded by them as something of a kindred spirit and medicine man. At the same time, he was welcome in his wanderings at white frontier communities, and scores of families gladly opened their cabin doors to him. Everywhere Mel went he left something good, whether it was a song, news of the outside world, lessons in planting fruit trees, working metals, or even in manufacturing gunpowder. To the Sutherlands, it was obvious that his new wife adored him, and it was no wonder, because Mel's genius and many skills were a marvel to all he visited.

"Hickory's the best guide a man could have," Mel told his friends as he warmed his raw hands before the fire. "She's a compass, sextant, dowser, bloodhound, and magnet for wherever you're headed, all in one!"

The squaw smiled, an innocent sweetness in her face, which was plain but appealing. She had high cheekbones, a wide brow, and dark, shining eyes. Ella thought Hickory looked very dignified, dressed in a long gown of linsey that was elaborately embroidered and hung down over warm woolen leggins. One of the most re-markable things about her was the unusual thickness of her forearms, which were complemented by strong, sinewy hands. Her obvious physical power was a contrast to her kindly disposition and modest demeanor. Though he was the same size as his wife, beside her Mel looked thinner and more frail.

Taking note of Ella observing Hickory, Mel said, "She's also the finest axman I've ever seen! Yes, I mean it! She'll put your average woodsman to shame, and has more than once."

Hickory smiled demurely as Mel said that was how she had earned her name, which in full was "hickory splitter who is stronger than a white lumberjack."

"Hickory, for short," Mel said, beaming.

Standing with an armful of furs and boots, Sally declared, "You'll have to tell us how you met, but first I'll get rid of these and put on some tea and some food. Wait with the details, Mel; I don't want to miss anything!"

As Sally hurried into the hallway, Ella called to her to see whether the children were still awake, for they would be excited to see Mel again.

After Sally replied that Benjamin and Susannah were already in their beds and fast asleep, Ella asked Mel how long it had been since they last saw him. "You don't look like a medicine man, though that's what we've heard you'd become."

Mel laughed quietly as they all sat down around the blazing hearth. "It's been only four months since we were in Philadelphia to see Jeremy off, but so much has happened that it seems ten years."

Momentarily, Mel's face became gloomy, firelight playing about its creases and shadows as his thoughts drifted. Ella and Owen agreed that much had changed since Mel and Owen helped bring an uneasy peace to the Ohio Valley last autumn. They had managed to prevent the wholesale destruction of villages in the heart of Shawnee and Delaware lands by prevailing on a Virginia militia army to call off its campaign. Though the Virginians at first had dared defy their royal governor's order to withdraw, they had finally agreed rather than risk being named rebels and arrested for treason.

Before that war, Mel had alternated between traveling among the northwestern Indians and teaching geography and languages at the renowned Philadelphia Academy. No other white, except for Owen Sutherland, knew as much about the red men of the northwest and about their current difficulties caused by colonial unrest. These two friends had much to talk about, particularly concerning the uncertain stand of the Iroquois League in the colonial unrest. Mel had lived among the Oneida for two months and in that time had also become acquainted with the other members of the league: Seneca, Mohawk, Onondaga, Cayuga, and Tuscarora.

Ella looked at Mel, who was thinking intensely, Hickory sitting by his side. "What will the Iroquois do if civil war comes to America, Mel? Will they stay neutral?"

Mel, who was a neutral himself, answered slowly, deliberately. "The Six Nations are convinced civil war will soon erupt among the whites. They believe they'll have to choose one side or the other in order to protect their land and their own future," he said. "Unfortunately, most believe their enemy is Congress; they're sure the king will protect them from Whigs and Congress."

Mel said the fierce Seneca and Mohawk were definitely in favor of the king, especially because they were Anglicans, members of the royal family's own faith. Onondaga and Cayuga probably also would stand with the king, leaving only Hickory's Oneida and the weak Tuscarora—converts of Boston Puritans—to support the Whigs.

Sutherland stood up and went to the mantelpiece, leaning over the fire. "The Indians had better choose the right side—the side that wins. But no matter who Indians fight for, settlers will pay for it, Whig or Tory."

That brought silence to the room, except for the sounds of Sally bustling in the kitchen and the voice of the wind. In the distance, they heard whistling as gusts blew through the Singing Stones; it was an eerie wail that seemed to Sutherland more desolate and mournful than he had ever heard before.

Ella was somber, and Hickory stared at the floor, where firelight flickered over it, casting moving shadows that took on life. Mel and Sutherland fell into deep thought, and even Heera, lying under a chair, seemed pensive. Then Sally joined them from the kitchen, unaware of the conversation.

"Will you give me some violin lessons, Mel?" she asked brightly, laying out a rich tray of food and drink on the low settle that stood in the midst of them. "I've missed those lessons so, and I want you to teach me some waltz tunes."

Mel laughed and slapped his knee. "How can I refuse my best student?" The dark mood vanished, everyone stirring and shaking off the dourness. Even the wind and the standing stones lost their haunting quality as Sally broke the spell.

Mel and Sally spoke of music as she poured cider into mugs, then sat down beside Hickory. The Sutherlands, too, changed the subject, turning the talk to Mel's travels. Sally and Hickory took an immediate liking to each other, though few words passed between them. After a little while, Sally asked to hear how the Oneida squaw and Mel had met.

Blushing, and filled with wonder, Hickory said, "Husband fly like a bird to me! Like a bird to me! Really, he can fly, he can fly! Not so far yet, but . . . really, really, he can fly!"

Amused and at the same time bewildered, Sutherland wanted an explanation. Indians always spoke in metaphors, but Hickory seemed, strangely enough, to be making a statement of fact.

He asked Mel, "Were you borne to her on the wings of Cupid, old friend, or upon his fleet arrow?"

Mel smiled to indulge Sutherland's humor, but he arrested everyone's attention by saying pointedly, "Hickory speaks the truth. I am learning to fly."

They knew Mel was an avid inventor and scientist who gobbled up everything there was to learn about modern developments and natural philosophy. Laughing, Ella mentioned this and added, "We hardly thought of you as a magician, too. Just how far can you fly? Did you flap across the straits tonight with Hickory on your back?"

Mel again smiled indulgently, as though he knew something they did not. As he munched on a roll and marmalade, he dug into his pack and drew out a worn leather case with some folded diagrams inside. Showing them to his friends, with Hickory looking on proudly, he said, "That is how I fly."

Sutherland turned the paper one way, then the other, until Mel showed him the proper way to view the pen-and-ink drawings.

"Looks like a tiny figure suspended from a mushroom, or perhaps a floating handkerchief. . . ." Sutherland said.

Ella said her illustration looked like a wooden bird, very awkward, and with the body of a man. Sally's was a series of circles with a fire burning under them and notations that included "hot air," "ballast," and "fire grate," but made no sense at all to her.

They looked at Mel, and his face was tinged with mischief and wit. "Those are levitation machines, my friends." They were struck dumb. "At this very moment, someone, somewhere, is experimenting with one sort or the other, and before we are very long in the tooth, someone will have successfully levitated one. Perhaps it will be me!"

Mouth hanging open, Sally asked, "Hickory said you *already* have flown. . . ."

Mel took a drink of tea, shrugged, and said, "In a manner of speaking, though it was mostly straight down from the top of a tree."

Hickory said, "Fly like a flying squirrel, like a squirrel, right into the village, right over the council house, over the council house, right—" She giggled and covered her mouth.

"Into her father's lodge," Mel said. "Through the roof, and crash, down into Hickory's bed! Love at first sight! Well, the old man was more amazed than he was angry, but he insisted I marry the girl right on the spot, more or less. As it turned out, we suited each other, though she tends to repeat herself a bit too much. We're happy; but her father's the local medicine man, and he couldn't put up with another medicine man like me flying to and fro from one side of the village to another, always threatening to either sail away and abandon his daughter, or misjudge things and mess up his roof again!"

Hickory said, "Father told us to stop flying, to stop flying, but my husband is a great man, a great man, and we have gone away from my home so he can go on with his work."

Mel said wherever they went over the course of the past few weeks they were ordered out because of his reckless experiments with wooden wings, kites, and other contraptions that had not as yet been given names. White settlers as well as Indians were so superstitious that Mel was fast losing his reputation as a dependable doctor and educator. He was becoming regarded more as a madman, if not a sinner against natural law.

Mel explained that the attempt to "levitate," as it was called, had captured the imagination and talents of many brilliant men of their time, though mostly in Europe, not America. He brought them up to date on experiments, failures, deeds of courage, of foolhardiness, and of ambitious desperation. No one noticed Benjamin and Susannah in nightgowns, concealed near the door. They might have been listening to a wizard's spell.

As he talked, Mel waxed ever more eloquent about the lore of flight, and they were soon absorbed in tales of Persian kings borne on flying carpets lifted by eagles, legends in the Bible and Chinese writings concerning flying chariots; the story of Icarus, who plummeted to the earth after his waxen wings failed when he flew too close to the sun. Mel became more passionate, his voice a whisper, and he spoke of historical figures who believed man one day would learn to fly.

"Leonardo da Vinci, back in the fourteen hundreds, sketched flying machines just like these I've shown you; Giovanni Danti constructed wings that would have been perfected had he not been so badly hurt in a crash; and the Frenchmen Besnier and de Bacqueville had some success, though there's been no breakthrough as yet.

"Yes, there've been many attempts, some successful, some not; I've copied all I could read and tried nearly all, tested them all in the past half year until I believe none will work . . . none but the latest invention! An invention that has not yet been brought from the drawing board into reality, but it *will* work!"

Mel held up the diagram with the circles and fire, and explained that if someone could manufacture the correct fabric, shape it, and fill it with hot air, one could fly.

"It's already been done on a small scale. But a balloon has never been fabricated large enough to carry a man aloft, and I want to be the first to do it! Look, it works like this. . . ."

Mel took out a silk handkerchief, shaped it into half a sphere, and held it over the fire.

"Your hands!" Ella warned, but Mel was so engrossed in his performance that he seemed oblivious of the heat and pain.

The light cloth flitted upward two feet, and Mel caught it before it fell back into the flames, a look of triumph on his face. The cry of amazement from Benjamin caught Owen's attention, and the two children were called into the room and permitted to stay. They sat entranced near the fire.

"You see!" Mel declared. "If it were contained, the heat would make a more enclosed form rise until it reached a height of . . . of . . ."

"To the stars themselves, themselves!" Hickory said, rapt and admiring. "Singing Bow will one day walk with the gods, with the gods among the stars!"

That brought Mel back to earth, and he shrugged again, a bit sheepishly, saying he would be happy only to fly with the eagles— at least at first.

Sutherland said he had heard even Benjamin Franklin was an avid follower of the development of this novel science.

"And that," said Mel, "is why I've come all this way through the wilderness to see you, Owen! You are a friend of Franklin's, and I wish to have a letter of introduction to him. I'll go to Europe if I must to meet him, and that, too, would be glorious, for over there he could introduce me to a dozen geniuses, scores of believers who know it is man's destiny to rule the clouds, the—"

"Stars," Hickory said, eyes wide, mouth full of raisin cake and beer. "Stars."

Sutherland was dubious about man's ruling even the sea but was impressed with Mel's intelligence and vision. He had never thought much about flying before, but the more Mel talked, the more fantastically possible it really seemed, if only one could assemble the right mechanical device.

He said, "As it turns out, Mel, I received a letter from Dr. Franklin in November, saying he was returning to Philadelphia from London for the Continental Congress this spring. I plan to go there myself then. Would you like to go along?"

Hardly had Sutherland spoken these words when Mel and Hickory were on their feet, hugging each other, shaking his hand. Hickory, too, had high regard for Benjamin Franklin, who was known throughout the world as the leading scientist and natural philosopher of the day. Franklin's protection of helpless Indians during a rampage of Pennsylvania backwoodsmen in 1764 had made his name honored among the tribes. To Hickory, they might have been talking about King George instead of about a persistent colonial gadfly who pestered Parliament for the sake of American rights.

The actual planning of the trip that night left Ella somewhat melancholy. As the others talked downstairs, she put the children to bed, and knew the parting was nearly upon them. She must stay behind, separated from her man for at least half a year. It was far too long, but she would endure it for him and for the sake of the Frontier Company. And for their beloved Valenya. The house had never felt more like home than it did on this wintry night. Ella kissed the children and blew out the candle.

Just after the ice had left the straits in mid-April, the winter traders and trappers returned to Detroit in a massive flotilla of four hundred brightly painted canoes. In order to come in together for a spectacular procession, winterers had met up on Lake Saint Clair, and there groomed themselves, put on their best, and had a long night of celebration before arriving home as heroes.

The day was warm and windy, bursting with spring. Freshly turned *habitant* fields ran up from the water's edge in narrow strips between budding maple groves, apple orchards, and fallow land where cattle and horses grazed. Combined with the blue sky and windswept water, it was a perfect setting for the jubilant canoemen, who descended the straits like a host of migrating water creatures, scarlet hats and paddles glowing in the sun like fire on the rushing water.

Everyone at Fort Detroit and in the settlement along the river hurried to view this annual, unforgettable sight of spring. Waving handkerchiefs and blankets, whites and Indians collected by the thousands, as would spectators at a London parade, to welcome home family and friends.

Wives and sweethearts called out to their men, children looked for fathers and brothers, and parents nervously sought some sign that their sons had survived the rigors of another winter in the wild. The community at Detroit had been expecting the arrival of the gleeful, singing *voyageurs* at any time; every house had been cleaned and polished, tables were set with food, beds had been newly made, and garments that had been sewn or woven over the winter were laid out, waiting to be found.

The Sutherlands came to the landing at Valenya, having been interrupted while in a company meeting. With them were Mel and Hickory, the Greys, Tamano, Little Hawk, and the Morely men. The many youngsters howled and waved, screeching in delight when a thousand *voyageur* flintlocks were fired simultaneously into the air in the *feu de joie,* the "fire of joy." Again and again the canoemen fired the traditional salute of the *voyageurs*' homecoming, and Ella and Owen felt a surge of happiness that only a resident of a northwestern fur post could know at such a time. For half an hour they shouted and waved at passing friends and partners, seeing Jacques and Angélique lead the company's brigade toward the Detroit storehouses across the river.

Ella's pleasure mingled with the depressing knowledge that the time of Owen's departure was at hand. Once the furs were counted and baled and loaded into the hold of the company's ship, which was due to arrive from the East any day now, her husband would be on his way. How Ella longed to go with him! Not only did she delight in the company of her husband on such journeys, but she loved Albany and Philadelphia.

Yet it was unreasonable even to consider going, for she had accepted the task of staying at Valenya throughout this uncertain time. She would not show weakness now by asking Owen to take her, though her heart was wrung in that happy moment. Last autumn in Philadelphia seemed so very long ago. As Mel had remarked, it might have been ten years for all that had changed in Ella's world.

As Owen waved his broad-brimmed hat to the last passing *voyageurs*, Ella felt a chill and turned to look at the home they had built with their own hands. How she loved it! Shivering, she ran her hands along her arms, though she wore a woolen vest and warm linen blouse, and it was not cold. Valenya, shining in the morning sunlight, looked proud and beautiful. It would be lonely with Owen away.

The *voyageurs* were all past now, and the Sutherlands soon would cross over to the fort to meet their people. Except for the Sutherlands, Sally, and Tom, the others took canoes immediately, anxious to renew friendships among the traders and boatmen. Ella and Owen strolled arm in arm toward the house, watching the children race ahead, laughing and teasing. Sally and Tom were near the door, looking at sprouting daffodils, Tom observing Sally more than the flowers.

Ella and Owen paused a moment, watching everything, finding words too painful, like gaps in their silence where something precious slipped through and was wasted. It was easier not to speak. Their touch was more meaningful, and for the moment expressed all that needed to be said between them.

It was a spectacular harvest of pelts that spring, and Detroit found new life welcoming home its *voyageurs* and traders. No company had done as well as Sutherland's firm, which could realize a profit of twenty thousand pounds sterling from a total quantity of furs worth thirty thousand.

Though for Sutherland this was a time of parting, of making plans and saying farewell to family and friends, most residents of the straits were enjoying endless homecoming celebrations that went on for a week among the French *habitants* and half-breed *métis*. Even the divided British settlers and traders took on a more cheerful air. Spring was a time of hope and rebuilding, and these first days of April were full of work, bounty, and the natural exuberance that comes in those weeks just after winter.

By now, Sutherland had heard from James Morely about the plans for a new partnership among Montreal merchants and traders. If it was successful, the proposed North West Company would be serious competition because the principals were among the boldest and sharpest trading men in Canada and the northwest. Yet Sutherland was not worried, because the Frontier Company was so well established that only catastrophe could dislodge it. Even the civil turmoil of the day would have to be far more serious before the company would lose so much ground that anyone—Cullen or the North West Company—could easily overtake it.

Now that there had been a glorious pelt harvest beyond anyone's wildest hopes, Sutherland knew the Frontier Company would continue to lead the way. Of course it was critical he sell the pelts for a good profit, and that was why he intended taking them himself to Albany. He would make certain that a sizable financial return was received for the partnership.

A few nights after the canoes returned, a party was held at the Morely-Grey trading house in honor of the *voyageurs*. It was a cold evening, and the fieldstone hearth in the warehouse blazed, illuminating a long plank table set with pitchers of ale and punch, sparkling decanters of wines from Quebec and Madeira, and pewter dishes of delicacies from abroad. They also had roast duck, pork, fish, and pudding aplenty. The room was fragrant with the heady scent of food, punch, perfume, and balsam pine that decked the walls. Shelves of goods were curtained by sailcloth, and everything else had been removed from the floor to make room for dancing.

In better days there might have been five hundred revelers at a Frontier Company celebration, but the civil strife and factional hostility kept many from coming. The Sutherlands and ninety friends enjoyed themselves anyway, "jigging off" their troubles to the music of Jean Martine's concertina and a band of fiddlers, including Mel Webster. It was a raucous, uninhibited party, just like the old days when folks were more carefree and nothing could get them down.

They did French cotillions, English line dances, and reels and jigs from Scotland, Ireland, Quebec, and Virginia. The trading house floor fairly shuddered to the beat of music. Shoes and moccasins, bare feet and wooden clogs all banged and clumped in time. Mingling with the laughing and singing were the clink of glasses and the shrieks of jovial Indians who did their own version of the reels and jigs. It was a grand party, and all the more so because folk let themselves go for the first time in the long year since serious trouble had come between America and England.

Between dances, Ella and Owen watched the children, white and red alike. The little ones raced around the hall, between the legs of musicians, around resting dancers, under tables, all of them eating sweets and drinking fruit punch until they were pleasantly sated and spent. Eventually they gathered near the hearth, where a tipsy Mawak held forth, seated in a rocking chair and telling them story after story about the manitous and nature spirits he had known and outwitted.

As the music began again, Ella asked, "How can they understand him, Owen? He's speaking more in Ottawa than English, yet it seems to me too much in English for the Indian children to follow."

Sutherland hied her away to the floor, saying, "They've all heard his stories so many times that they know the yarn he's spinning, no matter what tongue half of it's in!"

The trading house thundered with happiness and music, and when some French beaux began to cry out for the waltz, the joyfulness rose to a crescendo. Abandoning the floor to the young folk, who had a passion for this new dance that was sweeping the western world, the older couples gathered along the walls to applaud and sing.

The waltz, or German dance, as many called it, was the rage of the younger generation, and these Frenchmen recently had learned the step-slide-step in Montreal. Though a more proper gathering would be scandalized by a couple embracing as they danced, the jubilant folk of the Frontier Company cared nothing for propriety when it stood between them and a light heart.

The outrageously heady waltz was said to be the epitome of an age when young people in Europe and America cried out for freedom and fulfillment. Sutherland thought about this as he and Ella watched couple after couple attempt the waltz, some successful, others clumsy.

Sutherland leaned over to Ella and translated a line from Goethe's new novel, *The Sorrows of Young Werther,* which he had just read in the German: "'Never have I moved so lightly. I was no longer a human being. To hold the most adorable creature in one's arms and fly around with her like the wind, so that everything around us fades away.'"

Ellas's eyes shone as he translated the philosopher's description of this passionate, floating dance. "Let's do it!" she whispered. Then they were out with the other boldest couples, uncertain and awkward at first. By watching the Frenchmen, they found the time and the sense of the waltz—imperfectly, but buoyantly enough.

Sally was startled to find a ruddy French *voyageur,* a bit older than she, bowing deeply, inviting her onto the floor. She had never tried the waltz, but in a moment, she was the most enthusiastic dancer of all.

Laughing and spinning, they skimmed around past the spectators, her partner and she radiant with the intoxication of the dance. Then Sally caught sight of the only gloomy face in the house. Tom Morely was glaring at Sally's partner in a way that dismayed her, but she tried to ignore him, determined to have fun.

Twice more around the floor, and Sally saw Tom once again. This time she missed her step and lost the rhythm, because a voluptuous Chippewa girl, fairly drunk, was standing right in front of him. The squaw was facing Tom so closely and pressing so seductively against him that Sally's mouth dropped open. At first, Tom's eyes were held on Sally, who kept dancing. But after a moment, he could not help paying attention to the pretty young Chippewa. Apparently at her suggestion, they, too, began to waltz. It was completely impossible for them, but that did not matter as they flew around the floor, the Indian girl giggling and flirting with Tom, who obviously enjoyed it.

Sally began to lose interest in the waltz, and when her French partner asked what was the matter, she nodded at the Chippewa girl and wanted to know her name.

"Aha!" the fellow replied with a soft whistle. "That is a lusty one. I had heard she was after Tom; she is called Fawn Eyes."

Sally staggered to a halt. Feeling hot and dizzy, she excused herself to sit down a while. Her partner left her at a chair and went off to dance again. Soon, Sally felt more angry than dizzy and made up her mind to fetch Tom and dance with him herself.

But when she saw him across the room, he was going out the door with the Chippewa girl, and they vanished before Sally could take a step. Feeling miserable, she drifted to a window. Oblivious of sound and happiness, she gazed through the thick, frosted glass, and made out the dark figures of Tom and Fawn Eyes running away down rue Saint Jacques.

At that moment, Ella and Owen came dancing past and made an abrupt halt near Sally. Owen called, "Hey, lassie, this is the dance of your times! Grab a lad and teach us how to do it!"

Sally looked around at them, trying to smile. They noticed her confusion, suspected why, and Ella gave Owen a subtle push toward her.

"Teach Owen the way, Sally, before all my toes are crushed!"

With that, Ella took hold of Jean Martine, concertina and all, and whirled him giddily away, leaving Sally and Owen alone. Sutherland bowed to the young woman, held out his hands in the reverse, and Sally promptly corrected him. Then she laughed, tried to forget about Tommy and the wench with the doe's eyes, and resumed her part in the merrymaking. After the waltz, Owen left her with James Morely, who agreed to be her next student, and went to find Ella.

As another waltz began, the Sutherlands went to fetch refreshment. They found chairs in a corner, and took in the hall and people. Enjoying the occasion thoroughly, Ella held her husband's hand as they sat back, happy and tired.

Lettie waddled through the dancers toward them, her face gleeful, red, and soaked with sweat. She clapped her pudgy hand on Sutherland's shoulder and cried above the music, "My Jimmy's changed his mind! He'll stay with us! Ain't it a joy?"

Ella and Owen were delighted to hear that, and looked across the room to see James and Jeb drinking rum and talking warmly, the older man's arm over his stepson's shoulder.

Ella squeezed Lettie's arm and kissed her cheek, saying, "Better days are on their way! This spring we'll all start anew, and after a long, cold winter, our folk'll be less eager to fight each other; they'll want to work! That's what I like most about spring-time—"

There came a loud crash, and rocks flew through the windows on all sides. Men shouted, women grabbed for screaming children. Ella found Benjamin on the floor, blood streaming from his head, but he was conscious. The doors were thrown open as Sutherland led a charge outside, a poker from the fire in his hand. But in the icy, dark night, there was no one to be seen, for the vandals had fled. From the distance came a mocking cry. "Dance, rebels! Do yer practice for the gallows tree!" High-pitched laughter followed, and a few lanterns appeared at doors farther down rue Saint Jacques as residents came out to see what was going on.

Standing in the chill, Sutherland and the others lost their mood for the party. The men returned to the hall and gathered up their distressed families. A few, like Benjamin Sutherland, had cuts and bruises from stones or flying glass, though none was serious.

Later, when the trading house was empty, Sutherland stood with Ella near the hearth. The Greys and the Morely men had gone to their beds, and Sally had taken the children to a back room, where cots were prepared for them. The debris from the stones had been cleaned up, the windows covered with oilskin or old blankets. The fire was low and Sutherland poked it, thinking how his company could come through this crisis.

There was a serious question about whether the Frontier Company could go on as it had, growing and prospering. If civil war broke out, he thought it could not. At least not if he followed the course of the Congress party.

If Sutherland were loyal to Parliament, the whole strength of the British Army and Royal Navy would protect and support him. Also, the furriers of London would lavish attention upon him and the company, for other American trade would surely come to a standstill if there were a full-scale rebellion in the colonies. But if he continued his stand with Congress, he risked losing all. What would happen to the Frontier Company, to Valenya, and to the families of rebellious partners? If war came, he might be forced to abandon Detroit, his home, and the company, taking his family with him.

He told Ella those thoughts, and she agreed. If they did not shun Congress and matters deteriorated further, they risked imprisonment or perhaps attack by a Tory mob. He said they might all have to leave Detroit until the trouble passed; then they would return to begin again.

"Begin again..." Ella tried to fight back tears that would not yield. "Oh, Owen, beginning again... after so much time and so much work? It seems impossible!"

Stroking her hair, he whispered, "Not impossible; nothing is impossible, and together we can do anything. Perhaps even make a new country."

chapter 12

PARTING

The first ship to arrive from the East was the Frontier Company's smart sloop, named *Trader*. The vessel brought the latest news, none of it good. In the past, a supply ship reaching Detroit was an occasion for celebration and for devouring any word of the outside world, including the latest inventions, fashions, cultural tastes, writings, and music. But this year the arrival of *Trader* caused profound disappointment.

Events in the East were even more grim and depressing than before winter. In a counteroffensive against the colonial embargo of British goods, Parliament had decreed that no direct trade whatsoever would be allowed between American ports and foreign countries. All vessels had to touch in Britain first to be unloaded. That was a dire blow, for direct commerce with Madeira and Africa was critical to colonial prosperity, and the great expense involved in rerouting ships reduced profits drastically. Just as serious was a declaration that closed the rich North Atlantic fishing grounds to New England fishermen, guaranteeing economic disaster to one of the most important industries in the northern colonies.

Word came, also, that an incensed Massachusetts was racing to establish a strong provincial militia army founded on its well-trained minutemen and other volunteers, and every effort was being made to accumulate stores of arms and gunpowder. During the winter, bold New England militiamen had swooped down on a fort in Portsmouth, New Hampshire. These Yankees had overpowered guards and spirited government stores of ammunition away to where other war material had been collected.

On the morning of Owen's departure, Sutherland and Ella watched the final cargo being loaded into the sleek black *Trader*, which had rakish trim picked out in white and red. They were surrounded

172

by dozens of laborers loading bales of fur, bags of Indian rice, and piles of bound buffalo robes. Sutherland touched his wife's arm and said, "The time is nearly upon us, lass. Are you sure you won't go with me?" Ella did not reply, but suggested they walk along the beach with the children. Sally trailed behind with Benjamin and Susannah, unusually long-faced, in her charge. Ahead, Heera lapped the water. He was healed from his wounds and as strong as ever.

Sutherland was dressed in an elegant russet broadcloth frock coat, with matching smallclothes and a linen cravat. He wore no hat nor wig, but looked every bit the wealthy merchant who had the empire of international commerce at his feet. Beside him, Ella, too, wore her best clothes. Despite her heavy heart she was incredibly beautiful in a yellow sacque dress with ruffled sleeves, open in the front with a white petticoat showing. Her hair was arranged in a modest pompadour, with curls tied by a yellow bow at the nape of her neck. She carried a wide straw hat, always her preference over the caps and bonnets most women wore.

Ella was the image of the prosperous merchant's wife, except for one thing: She walked barefoot along the beach. Sutherland always liked to see her this way. He let Ella walk a little ahead, aware that the answer to his question was that she would stay.

They heard a shout and turned to see Dawson Merriwether hobbling along the beach after them, cane in hand. Owen called to the youngsters to go ahead, for he sensed the Virginian had something serious on his mind. Otherwise, Merriwether would not allow himself to be seen in the presence of so staunch a rebel as Sutherland. The Scotsman saw he had recovered from the injuries of riding the rail, though he was not as spry as before.

Ella spoke first. "It's been too long since we've seen you, Mr. Merriwether."

Merriwether greeted Ella with a touch to his hat.

Sutherland said, "If you'll do us the honor, perhaps you will join us—"

Waving a hand impatiently, Merriwether interrupted, "No, no. This isn't a social call, more's the pity. I'd like to speak to you in private, Mr. Sutherland, if your wife will kindly excuse my rudeness."

Ella nodded, bidding him good-day, and went to where the children and Sally were up along the beach, playing with Heera. Merriwether guided Sutherland toward a small fishing boat that lay upside down on the riverbank.

As he walked, the Virginian said, "'Tis merely a few words—words of good sense, if I might say so—that I wish to leave with you before you make this lamentable journey to Philadelphia and to those"—his voice hissed—"those rebellious Congress party scoundrels!"

Reaching the overturned rowboat, Merriwether rested against it, and Sutherland waited to hear what he had to say. Merriwether removed his hat, pondered it a moment, then looked up at Sutherland. The man's cold eyes glinted as he spoke in a voice quavering with anger and remorse. "For the love of God, Owen, and for the love of our country, turn back from this misguided obsession of yours before it's too late! Too late for all of us!"

Sutherland made no reply.

"Owen, what you are about to do will damn you, will damn your company, and what's more will imperil the lives of your family and friends! Owen, hear me when I say there are loyal men at Detroit who fear you, and your presence is all that prevents them from brutally attacking Congress lovers here; but if you leave, then not even the British Army will be able to stay their hand!"

Sutherland's nerves tingled at the thought of a loyalist mob on the loose. To him and his family, beautiful Valenya seemed like a living being—a being now in deadly danger. More important than the house, though, was the safety of his family and friends.

"Hear me, Owen, as one who agrees with your principles and your opposition to Parliament's buffoonery. Hear me as one who wants liberty in America as much as you. What your Congress is about will cause the direst calamity and disaster! It can only end with the utter defeat and subjugation of America for a hundred years to come.

"Think, Owen, what Parliament did to Scotland, to your clans after the failure of the '45 rising! Think of the slaughter, the executions, the exiles!"

"Speak not of that, sir!" Sutherland's blood boiled at the memory of a downtrodden Scotland after the defeat of Bonnie Prince Charlie in 1745. "This is not Scotland! And if truth be told, I am more than a Scot! I'm an American first! And in part, my stand has been taken because of what Parliament did to Scotland; I will not let that kind of oppression happen here!"

"But the army—"

Sutherland lost his temper. "Three thousand miles of ocean separate Britain from us!" He strode up and down, active and vigorous while poor Merriwether seemed bent and crippled by all that had befallen him. "Only a fool, or a hopeless, heartless tyrant, would presume to send any army against America and expect it to beat us down!"

"That's just it!" Merriwether, too, stood up, though pained by the effort. "They *are* fools in Parliament, fools or wily foxes who will stop at nothing to subjugate us! But I tell you these wicked Congress delegates are just as bad: Debtors! Liars! Unscrupulous rabble-rousers, most of them! They're godless men who'll intoxicate the rabble with high notions, and when the time is ripe, they'll clamp chains on that same rabble just as neatly as Parliament has clamped chains on us!"

"No!" Sutherland declared, a fury erupting from him. "There will never be chains on me—nor on you, if I know you, sir! But these matters are out of my hands. It's all gone too far already to be stopped!"

He came toward the downcast Merriwether, whose head was bowed. "Don't you see?" Sutherland asked, placing a hand on his shoulder. "Congress already rules us, not the king, not Parliament. I go to Philadelphia for the very reasons you've suggested: I go to be sure no one tries to shackle us or tries to slice the northwest up as a pride of lions would devour their catch.

"At the same time," Sutherland said, "I believe the moment has come for a united colonial government to rule America in partnership with Parliament. Our future will be decided in Philadelphia, not London; I pray that Parliament will see that, accept it, and come to terms with it. Otherwise . . . otherwise there will be war."

Merriwether was composed and looked stronger than before, as if he had said and done all he could.

"Very well," he began, still looking at the ground. "I respect your motives, sir, but there are others who say you are a treasonous Son of Liberty, eager to start fighting, in fact determined to get in the first blow for total independence. Believe me, your pilgrimage to that godforsaken Congress will fortify such suspicions."

Taking a trembling breath, Merriwether continued. "I will do what I can to temper their madness, but I . . ." He broke off and bade Sutherland a safe journey, then struggled away, cane clicking on the stones of the beach. Sutherland watched in silence as the merchant left. Then at the last minute, Merriwether turned to call out, "God help you, Sutherland! God help us all!"

Saddened, Sutherland rejoined Ella and tried to shake off the melancholy. Sally had run ahead with the children, amusing them by splashing water on Heera and chasing him around. Owen reached for her hand, and she abruptly threw herself roughly against his chest. She wept, trying not to, but unable to stop. Owen held Ella close, not caring that there were a hundred pairs of eyes on the nearby dock and around the fort's water gate.

Finally, he said, "We have two hours before the *Trader* sails; let's go to the old mill."

Ella nodded, wiping her eyes and managing to smile. Sutherland called to Sally, and she herded Benjamin and Susannah along to join their parents. Susannah, always able to communicate with her mother without words, took Ella's hand and walked close to her. Benjamin leaped upon Owen's back, and his father raced along the water's edge with him, now and again threatening to tumble into the river and causing the boy to scream in delight.

Heera loped off, and Sally walked with Ella, neither of them saying much, both feeling low. Sally was melancholy, remembering her own good-bye to Jeremy Bently at this old mill, which stood below the fort in a clump of trees near the river. The mill was three stories high, with a rickety wheel on the pond side. It had no roof, but there were the remains of crossed sails, which long ago had caught the wind to power the works when the stream was frozen. The mill had been abandoned twenty years earlier when competing mills were built nearer the fort and put the *habitant* owner out of business.

They sat in grass by the clear millpond, a small pool isolated from the vast straits that led southward and away to the rest of the world. Sally offered to take the children and leave Ella and Owen alone, but they wanted her with them. He said with a wink, "Besides, if Ella and I are alone, she'll start crying."

That got him a smile from Ella, who said, "I've wept already, and I'm done with tears. Let's make this farewell one to remember as a time when we were happy together."

Benjamin was racing about, arms spread wide, imitating Mel's descriptions of attempts to fly. He flapped his wings, now and again crowing like a rooster and fluttering around.

"Silly boy," said Susannah, brushing back a wisp of hair. At age eight, she looked very much like Ella. She said with considerable gravity, "He should cry like an eagle, not cockadoodledoo like a rooster!"

Owen lay back, the sun warm on his face. Sally was tossing sticks into the placid water, remembering how she and Jeremy used to come here when they were children. Just like Benjamin, they had pretended to be what they were not.

"I'd like to fly if it could be done," Susannah suddenly announced as she plucked a buttercup and held it under her mother's chin. "If I could, I'd fly to Edinburgh and see Jeremy right now."

"Take me?" Sally asked with a smile.

"I would, but then I'd have to take Tom Morely, too, or he'd never forgive me!" She waved her arms like elegant wings, slowly and gracefully.

Owen looked over at Ella; then they both turned to Sally, who was blushing slightly at the mention of Tom Morely.

Susannah said, "Lots of boys want to marry Sal, but she likes Tom the best! 'Cept for Jeremy."

Sutherland asked, "What will you do, Sally, if Tom speaks his mind to you and demands an answer one way or the other?"

Ella cut in, "That's not fair, Owen. Let the girl take her time about this; she's young enough."

Sally was smiling contentedly. "Tom won't say any such thing, because he knows my heart belongs to Jeremy."

Owen took a blade of grass between his teeth and said, "Were it I, I'd make you decide, for or against me, once and for all."

Sally became a bit more serious. "When Jeremy comes back, I intend to marry him."

Owen sat up, also serious. "Lassie, that young man hasn't even sent a letter to you, to any of us. He's far away, in another world, and you can't set your heart on a dream!"

Sally said, "He'll write, I just know it. He'll tell me all that's happened to him, all that's on his mind, and he'll ask me to wait for him."

"And if he doesn't?" It was Ella who asked that question, and she surprised herself with the bluntness of it.

"He will." Sally said softly; then as though trying to convince herself, "You'll see."

A little while later, Owen said to Ella, "We can still change our plans, lass; you can all come with me."

Ella said she would not leave Valenya. "There will be much to do, husband; you'll need me here, and if I can help you, send word."

"But if there's any danger at all, I want you to go to Montreal." He took her hand. "If I find things eastward to be a threat to you out here, I'll come for you or send word to meet me in Montreal. If there's trouble, the safest way to travel will be by ship. Promise me you'll go if there's any threat of trouble."

She promised, adding, "Come back quickly, husband! We need you here."

Sally moved away, joining Susannah and Heera at the pond's edge. Benjamin went along, curious about what they were so busy watching.

Sutherland was feeling more uneasy as the moment of farewell approached. "Listen, Ella, we can hire someone else to stay at Valenya, to protect it, and the company will manage—"

She kissed him quickly. "It's time for you to go!"

Susannah called them to come see an enormous bullfrog she had cornered. Benjamin yelled that he had caught it first, and Sally held Heera back from trampling it in curiosity.

"Come on, then," he said, pulling Ella up. "I won't see a Detroit bullfrog for a long time to come!" As Ella stood, he held her against him and said, "This is the last time we'll ever be apart."

Ella nodded, tears coming again, but she was able to smile at him. Arm in arm, they went toward the children and dog.

Jeremy arrived back in Derbyshire after four months of study in Edinburgh, and as he dismounted from the coach at the door of his uncle's mansion, he felt as though he were coming home. The weeks he had spent here in December and January had been among the most enjoyable of his life.

It was mid-May, and the estate was in full bloom. Willows hung soft and green above the stream, lawns were freshly mowed, and thousands of flowers nodded in the sunlight. A black West Indian gardener waved as Jeremy alighted, and a maid and butler rushed out the door to welcome him as though he were the son of their master. Jeremy was well dressed in a gray frock coat, with high, glossy boots, soft tan breeches, and a new-fashion hat with a narrow brim and high, tapering crown. His long hair was neatly clubbed at the nape of his neck and tied with a black silk ribbon.

To his surprise, out of the mansion came Penelope Graves, who rushed into his arms in a swirl of petticoats. He hugged her, then they held each other off and took a long, long look. Penelope wore beige ruffles and lace, her hair was dressed close to her head, modest and very pretty.

She said, "My, but you're the image of an Edinburgh physician!"

"Not yet," he said with a smile. "If the next term is as difficult as this past, I might do better as a fur trader than as a candidate for medicine!"

He embraced her again, and she insisted he would make a great success as a doctor. Out the front door came Richard Weston, and Jeremy was astonished to see him in the glittering scarlet, white, and gold of an ensign in the Seventh Welsh Fusiliers. Jeremy whistled in admiration as his friend walked casually down the steps, looking spectacularly handsome and well aware of it.

Jeremy walked to one side, hands on hips, nodding slowly. They came face to face, and he touched the silver officer's gorget—the crescent symbol of rank that hung from the neck—saying, as though to himself, "The Indians always prized taking one of these. They'd rather have a gorget than a scalp, and these shiny things made officers easy to spot in battle. This'll make a fine target, Richard."

"New England provincials can't shoot straight, no matter what those Yankees claim," Weston chuckled, glancing at his cousin Penelope, who abruptly had become serious.

Jeremy looked at him, saying, "Provincials? What do you mean?"

Just then, Sniffer waddled from the house, struggling to get into Jeremy's arms. Jeremy gave the chubby creature a hug, glad to see him again. Then Henry and Frances Gladwin came to the door, both wearing comfortable morning clothes—she in a lacy blue mobcap, gown, and shawl, and he in his banyan and turban—and their welcome distracted Jeremy from the question he had put to Richard. Sniffer squirmed to be set down, and pranced inside, quite at home and seemingly reigning here. After the greetings were done they all trooped into the manor house, and Jeremy looked over his shoulder to ask Richard again what he had meant.

Richard said, "I'm going to America to join the fusiliers and put down the insurrection in Massachusetts."

Jeremy stopped short, though Mrs. Gladwin and Penelope were on his arms. He looked at Richard and then at Henry Gladwin, who was rubbing the side of his nose, gazing at the polished floor.

"Insurrection?" Jeremy asked, annoyed. "You mean the government's sending soldiers over there to stop a few rioters in Massachusetts Bay? That's absurd! There are ten thousand troops in America already! Four thousand in Boston!"

Gladwin said softly, "Let's discuss this inside, my boy." He motioned for Jeremy and Richard to enter the library, and his aunt told them to come to the parlor for coffee soon. Jeremy went to the room, glancing once at Penelope as she walked off with Mrs. Gladwin, thinking how lovely she was, and how good it was to be with her again. Then the seriousness of what his friend and uncle were about to discuss came over him, and he felt oppressed, his stock too tight, his heart beating too fast.

They sat around a large table, and Gladwin quickly explained that the New England colonies were now in full rebellion.

"Less than a month ago, General Gage had half his command shot to pieces when he marched out to confiscate provincial supply dumps in Lexington and Concord—remember, I had told you to expect some aggressive act by Gage this spring."

Gladwin went on to explain that Gage was bottled up in Boston, having built a strong redoubt across the peninsula to prevent a full-scale attack by the enormous force of militia calling itself the Army of New England that had assembled to fight the troops.

"People here at home know little about this as yet, and the news is only just now trickling in." Gladwin looked exceedingly grim and tired. "It appears twenty thousand of your countrymen dare to bear arms against the king, and your Continental Congress has agreed to take charge of the New England militias."

Richard leaned forward, saying with a sneer, "They call the rabble the Continental Army or the Grand American Army! Hah! Ridiculous, foolhardy, and—"

"Brave," Jeremy said, feeling as though someone else had used his voice. He was dismayed and agitated to hear how colonial difficulties had erupted into armed rebellion, but he admired the courage of the New Englanders. "How will Parliament deal with twenty thousand Americans in arms when there are no more than thirty-five thousand soldiers in the entire British Empire?"

Richard chuckled at that. "My dear fellow, one British soldier is worth a hundred provincial rabble! Gage simply mismanaged the entire Lexington and Concord affair; he kept withdrawing while those Yankee cowards took potshots from cover. If I were in command, those traitorous rebels would have been knocked on their empty heads, run to ground, given a taste of the bayonet . . ."

As Weston went on, Gladwin looked at Jeremy, both of them deeply distressed. Richard ended his speech by saying he would be in Canada in a few weeks, and from there the British Army eventually would mount an invasion of rebellious New England from the rear.

He said, "General Gage might save his reputation by attacking westward from Boston; then the rebels will be caught in a pincers movement—God help the poor scum!"

"Don't use that language in my presence when you're talking about Americans!" Jeremy's face was red, his jaw set.

Richard sat back, surprised, and tried to lighten the mood. "Quite, quite, Jeremy. I forget you have a few friends in the rebel camp, and I must admit they might not all be scum, though their unmanly behavior in shooting our troops from behind trees in Massachusetts suggests otherwise. But please take no personal offense; I was merely speaking of American rebels in general."

Gladwin said, "Don't underestimate Americans in battle, Richard, or you'll pay the price—just as a few French generals did in the last war."

For Jeremy's sake Richard tried not to smile at that; instead he tapped impatiently on the polished table.

Gladwin spoke again. "Furthermore, Richard, don't expect enough British regiments to be assembled in Canada before next spring, or even a twelvemonth from now; at the moment there are fewer than five hundred regulars in Lower Canada, not enough to march through rebel New England and join Gage."

Richard thought about that for a moment, and asked, "How many will we need then, to cut off New England? Fifteen hundred? Two thousand?"

Without hesitation, Gladwin said, "Ten thousand regulars with cannon, and another ten thousand loyalist American militia."

Richard was astounded, and his mouth dropped open. He repeated Gladwin's words, once more repressing an urge to laugh; but when his disbelief passed, he obviously was thinking seriously about the old soldier's judgment. He said most high-ranking officers estimated that no more than two thousand regulars combined with Gage's force in Boston could secure the Saint Lawrence Valley, the Hudson Valley, and even New York Town.

"My dear General Gladwin, surely you don't believe ignorant farmers and shopkeepers will stand up for long against king's troops! Please, sir, that goes against all logic, and all the reports of our leading statesmen—"

Jeremy interrupted, "Uncle Henry, how can the rebels supply themselves with powder and ball, with weapons? They have no standing army, no commissaries to support a military force, not even a means of uniting their colonial militias under one commander. I have to agree with Richard in this—the rebels can't sustain a prolonged war."

Gladwin looked even more serious and glanced at Richard as though they shared some secret that embarrassed them. Then he said, "My boy, your friend Peter Defries has had some thoughts along those very same lines; I regret to tell you that he's a wanted man, accused of high treason, and when he's caught, he'll be hanged."

Jeremy sat back in his chair, stunned. So Peter's smuggling was far more serious than he had imagined. Gladwin said informers had reported Defries to be combing Europe for arms, ammunition, and gunpowder. Jeremy had known from Peter's hints that some military stores might be sent to America, but that he should be after a large quantity was startling.

Gladwin said Defries and his family were believed to be back in the Netherlands, but when they returned to England they would be arrested promptly. The ship *Yankee* was out of dry dock and had vanished, much to the embarrassment of British military authorities, who were searching the entire coast for her at that very moment.

Weston said, "It's believed your smuggler friend will try to fill the ship with disguised military stores, but we'll catch him before he gets away with it—the entire Royal Navy will hound him if ever he gets out to sea."

Jeremy rose and went to the large window, where warm spring sunlight poured in, bathing the elegant room as though it were part of some dream. At any moment he might awaken to find himself again a boy at Detroit, in bed under a skin blanket, listening to distant Indian drums beating out the war dance. Those had been frightening days, but these were fast becoming worse. His loved ones were undoubtedly on the side of the rebels—Peter's movements abroad and with the company ship proved that. But where did Jeremy himself stand in all this? He knew only that he was against civil war.

Perhaps there was some mistake about Defries. He turned to face his uncle and friend, who became gloomy when Jeremy asked, "Might the government's agents have been wrong?"

Gladwin replied, "We have it on excellent authority from a trusted loyalist, an experienced American seaman who is employed by a certain Boston merchant faithful to the king." He shook his head, saying, "I'm afraid it's true, Jeremy; Peter's doom is sealed."

"Not until he's caught," Jeremy said to himself.

"What's that?" Richard pressed, having heard Jeremy speak. "Do you think a smuggler can get past the entire British Navy? That's right, the entire navy will be after him! He's no ordinary smuggler, for Captain Meeks told us your friend has leading rebels in America ready to buy—"

"Richard!" Gladwin was annoyed at Weston's slip, revealing the name of the spy who had informed on Defries. "Say no more about this confidential matter."

Jeremy waved that off, saying, "I know no one named Meeks, though I'll warrant the Boston merchant you speak of is one Bradford Cullen!"

Weston and Gladwin tried to remain unmoved, but Jeremy was convinced he had guessed correctly.

"It doesn't matter now who has proven himself loyal," Gladwin said. "The affair is out of my hands, and there's nothing I can do to save Peter—more's the pity, for I respect the man."

Though Jeremy controlled his bitterness and sorrow, he could not help saying, "Uncle Henry, it matters very much whom the government chooses for friends, don't you see? It's the likes of Cullen my countrymen despise, because he's a robber and bloodsucker, and it's he who represents British authority!"

Though this was all new to Weston, Gladwin understood, for during his years in the service he had seen corrupt merchants gouge the military. Suppliers to the army in America sold their goods at enormous profit, and sometimes refused to sell if no payment was to be had, even when troops were starving. Whole armies had surrendered, too weak and sick to fight the French simply because iron-willed merchants had hoarded essential food and stores— more than once heartlessly stockpiled in the very forts that fell to the enemy. Gladwin knew Cullen and his kind only too well. But making war dictated alliances. At the moment the king needed whomever he could find in the colonies to match the growing power of the rebels.

During coffee, Penelope took note of Jeremy's heavy heart and suggested they stroll to the stone bridge to let Sniffer have a swim. She tossed a light cape over her shoulders and picked up the sleepy otter. With a smile, she gave Sniffer over to Jeremy.

At once Jeremy changed his mood, glad to have his old friend in his arms again. How Sniffer had aged in the past half year! The otter's eyes appeared somewhat glazed, and he was lethargic, though affectionate enough to his master.

They went out into the bright sunshine, making their way slowly along the meandering garden path. Two men nearby were planting cherry trees, and others were mowing or raking cut grass that filled the air with its fragrance. Penelope spoke enthusiastically about Gladwin's garden, which grew wild in some places, unlike the

cultured French gardens where the trees were all shaped into mounds
and walls and squares. She asked if he could see in a tree the pair
of cardinals brought from America, but Jeremy said nothing. Penelope showed him new flower beds, shrubs, and pink dogwood
flourishing in a grove not far from the stone bridge. He hardly
replied, a hand automatically caressing the slumbering otter in his
arms.

Thinking his mind must be on his studies, Penelope asked about
them. He said they were going well, and it seemed he would finish
everything within one year instead of two. Penelope cried out that
this was wonderful news and hugged him, awakening Sniffer, who
snorted and jumped lazily to the ground. Though Penelope congratulated him, Jeremy still could not shake off his piercing dismay
at what was going on at home, thinking perhaps he should return
to America immediately.

Seeing how absorbed he was, Penelope did not press any further. Sniffer plodded at her side as she walked along in silence,
her long gown swishing as she went. Neither she nor Jeremy spoke
until they passed the willows and arrived at the little bridge over
the stream. Here Sniffer splashed about stiffly in the water, and
Jeremy leaned over the side of the bridge to watch, thinking about
the past and the future. He closed his eyes as a spring breeze
soothed him. Penelope leaned against his shoulder, her arm pressing his, not very insistent, but firmly enough to get his attention.

Still Jeremy did not respond. Once more his mind was on the
letters he had sent Sally. In the past few weeks he had come to
the conclusion that he owed Sally something now that she must
have read those emotional letters. In them he had hinted strongly
at a future together, and he could not deceive her. He had tender
feelings for her, but they were not the same as what he felt for
Penelope. He must tell Sally that he loved another.

This heartache had caused him much difficulty ever since Penelope's visit to Edinburgh. That, combined with the news of chaos
in America and the wild risks taken by Peter Defries, left Jeremy
at a loss for what to do. He gazed down at Sniffer, who was
content in his stream, floating on his back under the bridge. Penelope was laughing and tossing pebbles around the otter, dis-
tracting and confusing him as though minnows were impudently
scooting past.

Jeremy turned and leaned against the stone wall to look at
Penelope. She stopped playing with Sniffer and gazed at him.
"Oh!" she said with a start, and from inside her short cape took

out a letter. "In all the excitement I almost forgot to give this to you."

"It's from Peter and Mary!" Jeremy exclaimed, hurriedly breaking the seal.

"It came by messenger with another letter for me, and I've had it a week or more, waiting for you to come back; in the accompanying letter Peter asked me to tell no one about this, nor to send it by the public post to you."

Penelope was a little strained, though obviously trying to be lighthearted. She knew something. Jeremy began to read to himself, realizing Peter had dictated the letter to Mary, since his ability with the pen was limited.

> ...I can't speak for anyone else, Jeremy, but for my family, we wish you well and hope that one day you will see the justice of our cause. You have your own life to live and honor to keep as you see fit, and so do we. It is our sincere prayer that we will always meet as friends, never as enemies.

Peter wrote that he would convey word to everyone in America that Jeremy was doing fine and had settled in well, "though perhaps *too well* as a Britisher for my taste."

Then, as he ended this letter of farewell, Peter revealed something that caused Jeremy to stagger and read the sentence three times over: "To my regret, the vessel carrying your letters home was lost in a gale, and all your writings are swallowed up in the sea. . . ."

Penelope felt the tremendous rush of emotion that erupted in him. She touched his arm lightly, and he took her hand, squeezing it harder than he meant to. Absently, he folded the letter and tucked it in his coat, then turned to Penelope, who took his hand in both of hers. He was looking at her in a way that made her heart leap, and before she knew it, he was kissing her. She threw her arms around him, and he lifted her feet off the ground, forcing the breath from her in a squeal of happiness.

She kissed Jeremy again and whispered, "Did Jeanette ask you to kiss me good-bye, then?"

Jeremy shook his head. Now he must compose a letter to Sally that would express his changing sentiments and his undeniable love for Penelope Graves.

Suddenly it occurred to him that this letter from Peter had been

sent from somewhere in England. He released Penelope, dug the
letter from his coat, and turned it over and over, trying to find
some hint of where Peter might be. He asked Penelope about it,
and she said she knew a way to find out. Grabbing Jeremy by the
hand, she dragged him through the garden, old Sniffer shaking
off water and struggling to keep up. They ran until they reached
the small cottage of a kitchen maid, who had the day off, and
Penelope called "Muriel!" then rapped loudly on the door.

From within came a sluggish, tired voice, as though Muriel
had just awoken. The door opened, and a pretty though sleepy
maid appeared. At the sight of Penelope, Muriel gasped and began
apologizing for the slovenly condition of her house, but Penelope
shushed her.

"Never mind all that, dear!" Penelope declared. "Just answer
a question or two, if you please."

The agitated woman composed herself, and when Penelope
began to ask about the young messenger who had been there the
other day, she flustered, and a gleam came into her eyes.

"Aye, ma'am, he was a nice one," she replied. Penelope asked
whether she knew him very well, and Muriel said, "Ah, no, ma'am,
he didn't even stay the night . . . not the whole night through, I
mean."

Penelope was on Defries's track, for Muriel said the messenger
came from Gloucester. Jeremy wanted a more precise answer.

Brushing back her hair, and letting her tongue flit across her
delicate lips, Muriel said slowly, "Well, now, he did say if ever
I was in them parts to come visit him at the inn called Sign of the
Bull." She giggled and winked to Penelope. "Must've been his
own sign, ma'am, for bull he was, indeed, I'll say!"

The *Yankee* must be in a harbor at the mouth of the Severn
River, since this messenger had told Muriel he normally worked
on the docks near Gloucester, where the American had hired him
to deliver the letter to Derbyshire.

Soon, Jeremy was readying a mount at the stable. He and
Penelope were alone in a dim stall as he tightened the girth on the
saddle. Rebel or not, Peter must know the government was after
him, and he had to get away immediately. Jeremy was not about
to let Peter hang without trying to save him. He put aside the grim
consequences of aiding a rebel.

To Penelope, Jeremy said, "Tell my uncle I was called away
on urgent business, and that— Look, tell him you don't know
why I've gone or where!" Then he took her roughly in his arms,

almost hurting her. "Penelope, don't become mixed up at all in this affair."

"I already am," she said, moving against him, and his hold on her became a warm embrace. "I know you must go to warn Peter and Mary about something, though I don't know precisely what; I suspect it has something to do with the troubles in America."

He nodded. "It's dangerous, Penelope. You must not know any more than you already do."

"And you?" She put her hands behind his head and drew his face down to hers. "It's dangerous for you! Let me come with you—"

"Impossible!" He wanted to pull away, but the scent of her, the beauty of her, kept him close.

She said, "I know Gloucester well, for I've spent summers there with my family. I can be of help—"

"No! The authorities might already be involved." He released her, but she stepped forward and kept him from mounting the horse.

Holding his arm, she said, "There is no Sign of the Bull tavern in Gloucester!" Jeremy hesitated, anger rising in him. "Muriel was wrong, but I know the place she means—it's on the waterfront, alongside another score of taverns just like it."

"Well?"

"Take me with you!"

"No! What would your family say?"

She became unexpectedly glib, smiling as she said, "The Gladwins expect me to leave here for Birmingham this afternoon, by my coach; I'm due to meet with a lady who intends to help found a school for the education of poor children. . . ."

She said the plot was simple: She and Jeremy would depart together for Birmingham by her coach, and there hire another carriage to reach Gloucester, which was a day's journey farther. Jeremy said her parents would object to their traveling alone without a chaperone.

"They expect I'll be met by someone in Birmingham, where I'm to stay a few days." She giggled. "Mother and Papa will ask nothing at all about my visit, because by now they absolutely detest the idea of a young lady teaching science and history and mathematics!"

Her parents hoped Penelope would lose interest in this scandalous dabbling in matters that young women of her class should remain well above. They wanted her to be a lady of leisure and of dignity, not a struggling teacher trying to educate others to be both wise and modern. But they knew it would be best if she were allowed to indulge herself and then tire of the notion.

"Ted the coachman is a friend to me, and he won't mind at all if we lodge him in a comfortable inn with a small pouch of silver."

Jeremy slowly shook his head and smiled. "You're quite good at conspiring. Perhaps you'll be prime minister one day."

"An awful bore!" She was in his arms again. "I've been conspiring to be alone with you." Her words were soft, and he held her close. "It was all just an imaginary plot, a dream, until now—"

She kissed him urgently, and passion flooded through him. How wonderful she was!

As she laid her head against his chest, he whispered, "Marry me."

Unsure whether he really had said that, Penelope dared not look up at him until he lifted her chin and kissed her.

He said, "I love you, Penelope, and if you'll marry me, I'll take you to the most beautiful country in the world."

Penelope was trembling. Her hand went to his cheek, and he took it, kissing her palm. "Nothing would make me happier, my darling. Nothing!"

chapter **13**

YANKEE

Within the hour Jeremy and Penelope bade a casual farewell to everyone at Derbyshire, Jeremy saying he would go to Birmingham on business. He added that he would see to it Penelope did not yet commit herself to becoming a teacher. As the coach drew away from the Gladwin estate, they sat properly opposite each other, waving to their friends. But as soon as they were out of sight, Penelope sprang across into Jeremy's arms, laughing and kissing, and he enfolded her, forgetful of their worries.

At their insistence, the coachman hurried the two-horse team along, and was kept so busy driving narrow country lanes that he hardly noticed the leather curtains drawn closed for most of the journey to Birmingham. Inside, the seat was not nearly long enough nor wide enough for them to lie in embrace, and with every bump and lurch of the coach they were near to falling onto the floor. They lay back, teasing, caressing, and occasionally grabbing the seat to keep from being hurled off.

For the rest of the day Jeremy hardly thought about all the bad news he had heard, for Penelope was close in his arms. He had never felt this way before. In the past, physical passions were easily sated in occasional trysts, but he had never known such a complete attraction for anyone. The childish kisses he had shared with Sally Cooper and the playful, carefree romps with willing girls at Detroit and Philadelphia were nothing compared to the happiness he felt with Penelope in that jostling coach. He wished their ride could end in some peaceful meadow, where no one would disturb them and the rumor of war was not to be heard.

After stopping overnight outside Birmingham—each sleeping in separate rooms in a dignified country inn—they went on the next day in a hired two-wheeled gig that Jeremy drove. Ted, the coachman, was told to wait for them at the inn, to enjoy himself with some silver they gave him, and to expect their return the day after next. He may have suspected something was amiss but did not ask why they went into the city without him. He was content enough to take some time off, and there was a pretty serving wench and a new billiard table for amusement.

Jeremy and Penelope followed the highway through the Cotswolds, traveling on canal barges where possible, and making good time in perfect weather. Following the sparkling Severn River through country that was hilly to the south and forested in the north, Jeremy and Penelope appeared to be newlyweds on a honeymoon. More than once they were asked whether they had just married, and always they replied in an obscure way that earned either congratulations or a sly wink of understanding. They did not care. Jeremy became determined and thoughtful now, aware he might become embroiled in Peter's danger.

Penelope, who had not been told all the particulars of Peter's involvement in smuggling, took note of the intense grimness that came over Jeremy as they rode through villages approaching Gloucester. They were still following the twisting Severn River, which grew wider as it neared the estuary. Peter's ship could find many safe harbors here—harbors that were closed to approaching vessels whenever the tide was out. The region was a smuggler's sanctuary.

The *Yankee* could not put in at a Dutch or French coastal city to fetch cargo because British regulations forbade all direct commerce between Americans and foreign ports. European harbors were patrolled by British warships even more tightly than was the Severn estuary. Jeremy presumed Peter had hired fishing boats to carry the goods to England—a common smuggling strategy—and then had the arms carted overland to Gloucester.

It was late in the afternoon when they arrived at Gloucester's outskirts. The country was lovely, its rugged beauty enhanced by the orange sun going down, casting shadows across low pastures and woods.

On the busy waterfront they found the tavern known as the Laughing Bull, which Muriel had meant. In return for a few shillings, two men staying at this rundown place told Jeremy of a road leading along the southern bank of the river. It would take him to one of the many lonely coves best known to smugglers. Though they refused to say the *Yankee* was anchored there, it was obvious Jeremy was in luck.

Excited, Jeremy touched his hat to the villagers and began to return to Penelope, waiting out in the coach. At the last moment, one of the men broke off from guzzling ale to say gruffly, "Word o' warnin' to yer, guv."

Jeremy stopped.

"Customs gents was in, askin' for the selfsame tub."

Jeremy froze. Fear rushed through him. The man saw his shock and said, "Didn't think ye was no customs man.... Listen, they went back to fetch some troops and maybe warn the revenue cutters, so ye got a bit of time left—though not much, I'll wager!"

Someone else said with a guffaw, "Hurry up, lad, an' if ye get to yer American mates in time, ye'll have a chance to prove just how smart colonial tars be! They'll have to run for it right quick. if they ain't sailed by now!"

Jeremy hardly heard this last. He dashed from the inn, leaped aboard the carriage, and urged the horse down the road. He told Penelope nothing as they raced through flocks of sheep, scattering the farm animals, whirling along the highway. The river was opening on their right, where the blazing orange sun was almost behind the hills and lit the water like molten fire.

Following the directions, Jeremy turned the galloping horse down a village street, startling a long funeral procession, whose members shouted insults and shook fists from the cloud of dust behind the gig. When they came to a country inn, Jeremy reined in his horse, and as he held the animal, stamping and blowing, Penelope asked what was the matter.

He said brusquely, "Come on; you'll lodge here for now." He kicked the brake forward and sprang from his seat. Lifting out Penelope's bag, he prepared to take her down.

"No!" she declared.

"Don't be a fool!" He held out his arms.

"I'm going with you! And don't call me a fool! Not if you want to marry me!"

The fat innkeeper stood at the door, rubbing a glass in his apron, enjoying the bickering between young gentry folk.

In a hushed voice, Jeremy said, "It's too dangerous, Penelope! I won't have you mixed up in this! Come down now, or—"

With that, she snatched the reins and clicked the horse on its way. Jeremy shouted, and she yelled out that he had better run if he wanted to come along. Snatching up her portmanteau, he dashed down the road, losing his hat, and the innkeeper laughed heartily.

Penelope slowed enough for Jeremy to jump aboard, and then she declared, "Don't tell me what I'm not supposed to do! Just direct me! I'll show you how to drive!"

He felt like throwing his arms around her, she was so incredibly perfect. With a laugh, he shook his head, then told her to swing off the main road and head down a rutted path that went toward the water. Indeed, she was an excellent driver, more than able to master the narrow lane as Jeremy looked about for the ship.

On the way they pounded around a curve and came up behind a dozen marching Redcoats with a captain at their head. The soldiers cursed as Penelope nearly ran them over, strewing men and muskets right and left as the gig thundered past. Jeremy was sure they were heading for Defries. Penelope held alternately on to her hat or to the seat of the bucking carriage as Jeremy urged her to go even faster.

Trees and bushes were a blur as they sped along a low stretch of road. When they rose to higher ground, Jeremy saw the masts of a sloop, less than two hundred yards away in a sheltered cove formed by a jutting spit of land. Jeremy whistled and took the reins, standing up to drive as though this were a French *calèche* in a race at Detroit. Penelope grabbed for the seat, making not a sound, though Jeremy risked a disastrous crash.

Water glinted through the trees to the right. Just before they were about to turn that way into the *Yankee*'s cove, Penelope gave a shout and pointed at a British cutter sweeping down from the north. Its naval standard, a red field with the Union Jack in the upper corner, snapped proudly at its stern ensign staff, signifying its intent to engage an enemy. The ship moved to block the mouth of the cove before the *Yankee* could escape.

Jeremy's cart was on high ground, and he could see both ships, with the long spit of headland standing between them. Soon the cutter would swing around the point, about a mile off from where the *Yankee* rode at anchor in the sheltered cove.

Jeremy forced the horse down an impossible slope, nearly tipping over the gig. Driving through bracken and long grass, they made for the beach near the ship. On the beach, which was straight ahead, were a few barrels and bales. Several skiffs plied the hundred yards between ship and beach, manned by laborers who earned good pay from smugglers and were not concerned with whom they were helping by their work.

Jeremy's heart pounded. He could see Peter on deck, Mary at his side. Jeanette and Emmy, the elderly black servant woman, were nearby. When Jeremy reined in the horse and jumped down from the gig, the workmen on shore became nervous and hurried off, not knowing who he might be. But at a cheerful bellow of recognition from Defries, they went on with their labors. Everyone was amazed, however, when Jeremy stripped off his frock coat, boots, breeches, and shirt, and, almost naked, dived into the water, swimming madly toward the ship.

Reaching the *Yankee*, he climbed up netting hung down for the workmen and was pulled aboard by Peter, who sensed trouble was brewing.

"There! Around the headland!" Jeremy panted, water dripping from him as he pointed to the end of the peninsula. "British cutter coming for you! You've got to go! Fast!"

He was exhausted from his wild rush, and Mary threw her cloak over his shoulders. Jeanette ran to hug him, heedless of how wet he was. Peter wasted no time. Grabbing a speaking trumpet, he called to his captain and crew; before Jeremy had finished telling Defries he was a wanted man, the anchor cable was cut by an ax and men were at the oars of the ship's jolly boat, hauling the ship into the deep water of the channel so that she could set sail and flee.

Jeanette had no idea of the peril. Emmy, her nurse, was already trying to persuade her to come below as Peter had just commanded, but the child was excited to have Jeremy aboard.

"I was feeling so sad to leave England, thinking you weren't coming," Jeanette said, laughing and taking his hand. "But if you'd just told Papa to wait a moment, you could've come over in a boat, and you wouldn't be so wet."

Jeremy wanted to say something natural, something easy to the child, but he was driven by fear for her and the others. Mary looked at him, an unspoken question in her lovely blue eyes. He knew she was wondering if he was going to America with them, and he shook his head. Mary bit her lip, turning away. Peter again cried for the women to go below.

The ship was alive with scurrying seamen, the crash of line and tackle, the crack of canvas sail being unfurled. Sailors in the rigging were shouting as they prepared the ship for escape, and someone sang out:

"A Yankee ship came down the river!"

The others joined loudly in the chorus:

"Blow, boys, blow!"

The lead roared,

"And all her sails they shone like silver!"

"Blow, my bully boys, blow!"

The ship shuddered as the sails filled and flapped. Jeremy heard Jeanette protesting to Emmy that she wanted to stay near Jeremy now that he was finally with them. Her eyes full of tears, Emmy gazed at the young man, and they touched hands, for they had known each other a long time. Emmy turned away, leading Jeanette to the cabin. Something stuck in Jeremy's throat, and then Mary came to him, taking his hands.

"Better tell Peter now," she said. She, too, fought back tears. "Tell him quick, Jeremy, so he'll not have time to think about it!" Then she kissed him, said farewell, and hurried to the cabin, closing the door behind her.

Slowly, Jeremy took off Mary's cloak and held it uselessly. He felt a growing ache take hold of him. He was torn: A man in the topmast shouted, "Sail ho! Revenue cutter! Ten guns!"

There she was, coming around the point under full sail, her gunports open. She was ready for a fight, and the *Yankee* was now cut off from escape.

Peter turned to Jeremy and declared, "Better wave good-bye to your friend on the beach, lad! Them navy boys might send a boat ashore to trouble her—" Peering through the spyglass, Defries saw to his astonishment that it was Penelope Graves in the lonely carriage. The beach was deserted, save for her carriage and the few bales and boxes left behind after the workmen ashore fled.

Peter faced Jeremy squarely, looking him in the eye. Though the big, blond fellow had no idea what it all meant, he knew Penelope was in serious danger. He gave the speaking trumpet to Jeremy.

"Hurry her away from there, before it's too late." Then he shouted to the shipmaster, who was on the quarterdeck near the helmsman, "Show these limeys what she's made of, Cap'n! Let them Jack Tars out there have a lesson in sailin'!"

Defries tossed a pouch of silver coins to the foreman of the frightened workmen, who were clambering over the side to their boats below. Then he clapped a hand on Jeremy, telling him to get dry clothes down in his own cabin.

"Good to have you with us again, son!" He gave a hearty laugh and embraced Jeremy. "Thought you might have gone for a king's man!"

Jeremy stood back as the ship swayed and swung out under the power of the oarsmen in the boat. Crewmen were running out cannon, carrying kegs of powder and boxes of shot and ball. He looked at Penelope, standing in the carriage on shore, then observed the ominous approach of the cutter. Defries took a brace of loaded pistols from a brawny mate and stuck one in his belt. The ship bustled with men working, singing, and shouting defiance at the navy, even though each knew this might be his last hour on earth.

Jeremy again looked shoreward. Penelope waited in the carriage, holding her nervous horse as she gazed across the water at the departing ship. This moment was so unexpected that nothing remotely like it would ever have entered his mind when he labored over his books at Edinburgh. The beach and Penelope were drawing slowly away. She was dwindling, the British cutter growing larger. Jeremy would always fight to protect his friends, to defend his country, but the question of who was right and who was wrong was not at all clear in his mind. Was Peter's fight his?

Yet one thing he knew very well: He loved the woman on shore, and she loved him. Above all else, that love shone like a beacon and made more sense than all the theories, debates, or conflicting policies of king or Congress.

The wind came up, blowing out to sea, a good sign for the *Yankee*. The ship surged forward as though made for the wind. Cold and wet, Jeremy turned to Defries, who held the second pistol out to him. There was no emotion in Defries's face, even when Jeremy did not take the weapon.

"I'm staying in England, Peter."

Defries did not appear surprised. He shoved the pistol into his belt and offered his hand, which Jeremy firmly gripped. "Take the dinghy ashore, then." He surrounded Jeremy with his long, powerful arms, and whispered, "Godspeed!"

Jeremy declined the offer of the rowboat. He went to the railing, taking a long look at the warship waiting beyond the cove. Nodding at Defries, and with overwhelming emotion in his voice, he said, "Show them how a Yankee can fly! God be with you!" Then he dived overboard, surfaced, and did not look back at the ship. Swimming strongly for the beach, he had never felt such terror in his heart, though it was not for himself. It would be almost impossible for Defries to escape the stronger gunnery of the cutter.

Stumbling out of the water and up onto the sand, Jeremy was met by Penelope, who hugged him fiercely. She was as frightened as he. They watched the *Yankee* sail out of the cove, directly for the cutter. From where they stood, they could see the British ship swing broadside and drop anchors fore and aft, making an effective barrier between the cove and the wide estuary. Five cannon were aimed at the American sloop, but the *Yankee* kept on sailing, a strong wind speeding her along. Jeremy was no seaman but knew enough to tell that the wind behind the *Yankee* was the only advantage she had. To keep from being blown out of position, the British ship had chosen to ride at anchor. If the *Yankee* skirted the cutter, she would risk running aground. Furthermore, the naval commander counted on the threat of his heavy guns to stop Defries, making him come about and be boarded without a fight.

As he quickly dressed, throwing his frock coat over a shaking Penelope, Jeremy said to her, "That cutter thinks Peter'll just roll over and surrender! He won't! Look, the *Yankee*'s going to run past, guns or not!"

Run right at the cutter seemed a more correct description, for the American sloop bore down on the anchored cutter, the full force of the wind in the *Yankee*'s billowing sails. She was heading right into the other ship's broadside. It was a tremendous gamble for Defries, but he had no other choice, for fleeing too soon to one side or the other of the cutter might strand him on a bar or earn a destructive barrage of cannon fire.

Coming straight at the cutter this way, Defries made a small, difficult target and had the advantage of confusing the cutter's master for as long as possible. No sensible smuggler would dare to escape in such a situation; but Defries had a cause and a country.

"Now he'll have to move either port or starboard, and he'll be fired on," Jeremy said quietly as Penelope gripped his arm. "His only hope is that the commander won't believe he'd try it, won't believe he'd have the insolence not to surrender! Look, they're only two hundred yards apart now!"

From the beach they heard the voice of the cutter's master calling shrilly through a speaking trumpet for the *Yankee* to haul wind and lower sail in preparation for boarding. The sloop kept bearing down on the cutter at astonishing speed. The naval commander shouted a warning to Defries that he would fire if not obeyed.

Like a bird flying over the water, the *Yankee* was less than a hundred yards from the guns of the cutter. Jeremy and Penelope were transfixed, ready for the crash of cannon that would shatter the *Yankee* and leave her helpless.

Then, at the very moment when the cutter was surely about to release a broadside, the *Yankee* heeled wildly over, as if to come about and surrender. But in this swift maneuver she actually picked up speed, racing toward the cutter's bow. These American seamen coordinated their magnificent skills to heel once more, this time to starboard, so that the five cannon on the *Yankee*'s port side came up out of the water. At the same instant, the gunports were suddenly opened, catching the cutter's cannon crew by surprise. The *Yankee*'s broadside blistered the cutter, scattering gunners and raking the deck so that no one could fire back.

Jeremy howled in amazement as the *Yankee* left the anchored cutter smoking and splintered. All the angry British sailors could do in reply was to fire a couple of small swivels from the quarterdeck, doing no damage at all. On board the cutter, all was chaos as seamen tried to retake their posts and gun stations. They cleared away debris and wounded, hauled up anchors, and swung through the rigging to set sail and pursue the fleeing sloop, which was borne on a strong breeze, heading for the open sea.

Though Jeremy opposed Peter's rebels, he could not help but whoop for joy to see Defries get away. It was still many miles out of the estuary and thousands more across a sea ruled by British ships, but Defries had the advantage of speed and maneuverability, and if he were as lucky as he was brave, he would be home within four weeks.

Just then Penelope saw the squad of Redcoats, two hundred yards off, clambering down the path the carriage had made through the bracken. She and Jeremy leaped aboard the gig and began their own desperate flight. Jeremy saw a road at the far end of the beach and made for it, crying to Penelope that she must keep low.

The soldiers scrambled rapidly, trying to cut them off on the beach. Jeremy howled at the horse, whipping him to gallop through the treacherous, soggy sand, and the gig swayed and slid along the water's edge. The Redcoats shouted for them to halt in the name of the king. Penelope hugged close to Jeremy. There followed the sharp pop of musketry, and bullets struck the coach. One grazed the neck of the horse, who surged in his traces, panicking until Jeremy fought with the reins to keep his head forward.

Charging along, Jeremy saw the Redcoat captain come running across his path, pistol aimed, sword held high. Jeremy swerved the horse, surprising the officer, who slipped and slid on the sand as he struggled to get out of the way. At the last moment, he presented the pistol. He fired, and Penelope gasped and lurched against Jeremy, who cried her name but dared not stop to help.

Keeping the horse under control, Jeremy bolted past the soldiers, toward the far end of the beach. As he drove, he tried frantically to get some response from Penelope, who was heavy against his shoulder, her head almost covered by his coat that she still wore. Then the Redcoats were left far behind, and he reached the road. As soon as he could, Jeremy stopped the gig. Desperate with fear, he grabbed Penelope by the shoulders, and she opened her eyes. There was no sign of blood, but she seemed to have been hit by the officer's bullet.

"Penelope," he groaned, "what have I done to you?"

"Jeremy . . ." Penelope got a breath and sat up straight, one hand on her forehead. She had been badly shaken, the wind knocked out of her; but amazingly she seemed otherwise unhurt. Jeremy was sure she had been shot and nervously searched his coat. Then he saw the small hole, where the bullet had torn through the fabric. It must have struck Penelope! Fearing she had been wounded, but because of shock did not yet feel the pain, he threw open the coat and examined her side. At last he found the bullet.

From inside the pocket of his coat, he took Sally's rosewood music box, which had been split by the slug. Still lodged in the box, the bullet had smashed the workings. Its song would never play again.

Two hours later, they were riding easily along a country lane, traveling to Birmingham and then Derbyshire. Since fleeing the smuggler's cove, they had hardly spoken, and all the while Penelope had held the ruined music box in her lap.

After some time in thought, she asked, "Are you sorry not to be with Peter and your family in all this?"

"No," Jeremy said quietly, "because I'm no rebel. But I intend to go home soon to see to it that my family doesn't get caught up in this any further." He sighed heavily. "Yet I fear it may be too late. . . ."

chapter **14**

VALLEY OF THE MOHAWK

When it sailed from Detroit, the ship *Trader* carried prime pelts worth thirty thousand pounds sterling, but there was nowhere, as yet, to market them. In that rapid journey across Lake Erie, Sutherland considered what he would do if merchants in Albany or Philadelphia were unable to buy his goods. Then he discarded such thoughts, for the others in the company trusted him to succeed. This was the most valuable load of furs ever harvested by the Frontier Company, and ironically the British market had never been so desperate to buy. Sutherland, however, would not sell to Britain, and that was final.

He was risking all his company had acquired in the chance that new buyers would be found in the colonies rather than in England. Undoubtedly no easy political solution would be reached between Parliament and Congress, and it might even take another year before the trade embargo achieved what it was meant to: the recognition by the British that America was no longer to be taken for granted as some docile vassal state overflowing with tribute for British overlords.

Sutherland thought about Peter Defries, who had sailed to Europe on the other company ship, *Yankee*. He wondered if the Dutchman had found European merchants with whom the Frontier Company could clandestinely trade in West Indies ports. Sutherland also hoped that the dangerous part of Defries's mission— acquiring desperately needed munitions to strengthen the hand of Congress—had succeeded and that by now Defries would be safely back in the East.

The journey to Albany was seven hundred miles, requiring the transshipping of the pelts at Niagara, where they were placed in flatboats—bateaux, these were called—to be sailed or rowed to Oswego on the southern shore of Lake Ontario.

At the Lake Erie landing, near the post named Fort Erie, which stood just above the falls, Sutherland saw the ship of Hugh Meeks. The *Helen* was up on the ways, out of the water, as though forgotten by her owner, Bradford Cullen. As his men portaged the goods down to Lake Ontario, Sutherland asked residents about Meeks and Farley Jones. Those two had departed quickly after arriving at Fort Erie last year, leaving only a skeleton crew to watch over the ship. Bradford Cullen had not sent a new master to take the *Helen* back into the northwest, and it was obvious that Cullen and Company would do poorly this trading season.

Perhaps Cullen was making such a profit selling supplies to the British Army in Boston that the fur trade was unimportant now. Or it might be that he feared the risk of putting a ship and trade goods on the lakes if serious fighting was expected to break out. Being close to British headquarters in Boston, Cullen was surely able to learn much that western traders could never know concerning military intentions this spring.

Hearing from soldiers that the Iroquois were restless in the valley of the Mohawk, Sutherland bought some trade goods at Fort Oswego in case he needed presents to pacify Indians who disliked Whigs. He was glad to have Mel and Hickory along, for they were well known among the Iroquois and could do much to assure safe passage down to Albany.

From Oswego, the convoy went up the Onondaga River, into Oneida Lake, and then up Wood Creek. This route had several difficult portages, with swamps and rapids. Sutherland, in company with Mel and Hickory, stayed with the goods the entire way, directing a convoy of two canoes and three large bateaux. The craft were handled by fifteen strong men of good voice and bold disposition, including the blacksmith Bill Poole, the stubborn Son of Liberty, who had hired on to work his way back to Albany. From there Poole would go home to Connecticut for a visit to his family. During the trip Sutherland and Poole grew to respect and like each other, though they still disagreed on the need for mob action to enforce the trade embargo and intimidate Tories.

It was late May when they arrived at Fort Stanwix, a post at the end of a swampy, mile-long portage between Wood Creek and the headwaters of the Mohawk River. The beautiful Mohawk flowed from west to east, serving as a busy corridor between the valley of the Hudson and the northwestern interior. Fort Stanwix, built at the start of the French and Indian War nearly twenty years earlier, commanded this key portage known as the Oneida Carrying

Place, after the Iroquois tribe that dwelt in the region. Sutherland had passed Stanwix many times in his travels, and each time he saw it, he marveled at how a government fort could be allowed to deteriorate so.

Though Stanwix was an important post in the colonies, guarding one of the best routes to the interior from the East, it was too weak and rundown to be defended even against a dozen imaginative attackers. In its center stood a modest blockhouse of logs, surrounded by a square of earthworks one hundred yards around. The earthworks were at the mercy of rain and wind, and badly needed repair. Upon these eroding works were rotting pickets, some falling down; between the pickets, a few Oneida children chased their hoops, infuriating a Redcoat sentry walking his beat nearby. As the soldier shooed the youngsters out of the fort, Hickory began to yell a greeting, and the children recognized her.

Mel and his squaw were soon welcomed by several families of Oneida who lived in cabins nearby. The Indian men had been fishing in the muddy edges of the Mohawk, which was a few hundred feet wide here. Seeing their friends, the fishermen came excitedly toward them, their catch hanging from poles, nets over their shoulders. It was a happy reunion for Mel and his wife, who received fish as presents and gave some trinkets in return. As Sutherland looked on, he thought how easy it would be for a few more Oneida warriors to join with the men of these families and take Stanwix from the handful of soldiers in the garrison.

Sutherland bade his men lay their bateaux along the riverbank in preparation for caulking and other minor repairs. Using the best boats and canoes for shelter, the expedition put gear, goods, and bales of pelts underneath and fell out along the portage trail from Wood Creek. The forest was dense around the clearing, which was a mile or so across, with Stanwix in the center, north of the river. They would camp here tonight and tomorrow set off for the final one hundred and twenty miles down the Mohawk to Albany.

The arrival of the trading party attracted considerable attention among the Indians and a few white families dwelling nearby. As Sutherland waited for someone from the fort to meet him outside the main gate, he looked the soldiers over. They were mostly men of the New York provincial independent companies. Regulars in drab buff uniforms, these men were not the brilliant, spit-and-polish soldiers of the British Army, though they had been battle-tested against the French and Indians and had proved their worth since being formed in 1755.

Mixed with these twenty York troops was a squad of six Red-coat regulars. Mel told Sutherland they were under the command of a young British lieutenant. Looking at the unshaven, bored soldiers of both king and province, Sutherland could not help but mark the sharp contrast between them and the Oneidas. The Indians were well-off, comfortable in their modest houses that were surrounded by neat vegetable gardens, woodsheds, pigsties, and a barn or two. Compared with the orderly Oneida homes, Stanwix was a dreary, shabby place that spoke eloquently of the army's stingy budget and lack of concern for its troops.

Sutherland was hailed from the fort's western sally port, and turned to see a York corporal in company with two Redcoat privates making their way toward the expedition. For all the simplicity of his uniform, the Yorker was trim and clean, holding himself in a dignified military manner that made him appear more impressive than the stiff Redcoat privates in their scarlet.

Corporal Gavin Duff presented himself courteously to Sutherland while the Redcoats strolled along the lines of weary pack-men. As Duff inspected Sutherland's papers—trading license, bills of lading, and receipts for duty paid—the two privates checked the bateaux, canoes, and packs to see that everything was in order and no smuggled goods were in sight. There was no doubt that smuggled goods—as usual—were somewhere present in the cargo, but in exchange for several twists of tobacco and a jug of hard cider, the sentries paid little mind to the few packages that had no bills of lading or stamped duty receipts. These belonged to the packmen, who made a small profit by carrying out their own pelts to trade in the East.

Corporal Duff routinely handed back Sutherland's documents, accepting a pouch of tobacco, and asked about news to the west. Then, as Sutherland folded away his papers in a leather carrying case, Duff asked whether he might be the same man who wrote the political essays under the pseudonym Quill.

Sutherland looked closely at the soldier, who was about twenty, ruddy, and robust, with blond hair showing under a secondhand wig, and friendly blue eyes. Sutherland said he was the very same, and expected some verbal abuse or rudeness on the part of a professional soldier, who might object to Quill's radical leanings. But Duff showed only uneasiness, saying Sutherland had better take care in future dealings with regular troops and customs officials. The Scotsman asked why, and Duff glanced toward the two Redcoat sentries, who were busy inspecting packs.

Duff took Sutherland aside and whispered, "There's spite between your kind and mine, ever since the battles at Lexington and Concord; there's a poison that might get you thrown into the clink if you give anyone the least occasion—"

"Hold on, Corporal," Sutherland said, not understanding. "I'm obeying the law! What's this about Lexington and Concord?"

Astonished that Sutherland had not yet heard the news sweeping through the colonies, and perhaps all the world by now, Duff gave a rapid explanation of the bitter fight between Gage's handpicked troops and Massachusetts militia a few weeks previous. Duff spoke quickly and enthusiastically, his voice inadvertently rising until it rang out loudly enough to be heard by Sutherland's startled packmen. Bill Poole and the others howled in glee, slapping their hands and springing up to do a jig of triumph. Though Duff's Redcoats were annoyed, the corporal clearly favored the colonial militia.

"Them minutemen whipped the tar outa them grenadiers," Duff chuckled. "Kicked them all the way back to Boston, cutting them to ribbons, the bloodybacks."

In Sutherland's whirling mind the incredible importance of Duff's words struck home. What should he do about his family back at Detroit? Would they be in danger if the fighting spread beyond New England? Would they be persecuted, driven out, or even arrested if loyalists in the northwest decided to consolidate their strength and ruin Congress supporters?

A host of thoughts assaulted him. Unexpected decisions must be made. Should he immediately go back to Detroit? Would he be the focus of loyalist attacks if he went home? Perhaps Ella would be safer if he were not at Detroit until the conflict in New England ran its course. But if fighting began throughout the colonies and became a general uprising, then he must find a way to have Ella and the children secretly spirited down to Montreal.

Since Canada and its French majority were no more than lukewarm at best to rebellion and to Congress, Montreal would surely be safe until Parliament and the American Whigs came to terms. Sutherland did not believe the fighting could become so widespread that it would rage out of control before Parliament at last gave in to American demands for equality in the Empire.

Then there was this fortune in furs—a fortune that represented the worldly possession of dozens of Frontier Company families who had entrusted him with its safety. In Albany he might find a ready buyer, but to get there he must take the pelts through the valley of the Mohawk, where there was such a strong and warlike

Tory faction that he might run into trouble.

No matter what he did, it must be done immediately, for there was no time to be lost. There was as yet no fighting in the Mohawk Valley, but soon there might be, and then his convoy would be in real danger.

He knew he must go forward to Albany. Ella and the others would have to fend for themselves until he either returned or found a safe way to get them out of the northwest. But as for going down to Philadelphia for the Congress, he was not so sure anymore. His family came first.

Suddenly, the excited chattering of the packmen stopped. Grinning, Duff went on in glowing terms to describe the triumph of the colonies against nearly two thousand British soldiers who had been sent out to destroy or capture provincial war supplies at Concord. Then Duff sensed the tension in the air and paused, looking around. On the rampart above him stood a British officer, whose face showed fury to hear Duff's cheerful narrative. To Sutherland's surprise, the officer was Lieutenant Mark Davies, the same soldier he had tangled with during the Detroit riot, and whom Lernoult had reassigned.

At first Davies said nothing. The very ugliness of his expression, the vindictiveness, flowed like a torrent toward Sutherland and Duff. As the ranking officer at miserable little Stanwix, Davies reigned supreme. The startled corporal snapped to attention.

"Bloodybacks, eh, Duff?" Davies said languidly, the anger seeming to leave him, replaced with a kind of gloating irony. "Corporal Duff will soon know what it means to be called 'bloodyback'! He will at once turn over command of the guard to Sergeant Matthews, hand over his weapons, and consider himself under arrest! Sergeant Matthews!"

With that, a Redcoat, somber and nervous, came running from inside the fort to stand beside Duff, who looked sick. Sutherland knew there was nothing he could say to Davies to stay the lash.

As Davies descended the rampart at the other side of the wall, Sutherland motioned to his own men to maintain discipline. In particular, he gave a warning glance to Bill Poole, whose manner was sullen, calculating. Poole knew a change had come to the world—a change that meant Lieutenant Davies was not as all-powerful as he had been before the battles in Massachusetts.

The blacksmith's eyes gleamed with insolence and confidence, but he smiled at Sutherland, teeth showing white through his beard, as though promising restraint in the face of the officer's arrogance.

Davies and the remaining three Redcoats came out of the fort, but no York troops were with him.

"Well, well, Scotsman, we're together again," Davies said, strolling casually forward, hands clasped behind his back. "And at such an opportune moment—I mean at a moment when we'll have the chance to discuss the fascinating turn of events in Massachusetts Bay."

Davies looked down the line of packers, lying by the bales of fur and the overturned bateaux. A few Oneidas had drifted near to watch, and with them were Mel and Hickory, solemnly listening.

Sutherland responded, "I'm anxious to hear all the news myself, Lieutenant." He called to his men to make camp in a clearing near the stream.

"Not so fast!" Davies snapped, his voice cracking as he lost some composure. "Keep your men where they are until I give the command! This is king's property, and I'll say who camps, who stays, who goes, and who . . . who—"

"Kisses your arse?" Sutherland was smiling, a disarmingly winning smile that enraged the officer, who had expected obeisance, not defiance.

Davies motioned to his Redcoats, and as though it had been rehearsed, they surrounded him and Sutherland, musket butts grounded, but bayonets fixed.

Davies stepped close to Sutherland. "Yes!" he hissed, his breath unpleasant, his watery eyes bloodshot. "And before I'm done with you and your scurvy rabble—"

Abruptly Sutherland spoke past Davies, addressing his men, who were on their feet, ready. "Hold your ground lads, but if this pimp makes the wrong move, take him prisoner or kill him, no matter what happens to me."

"*Sutherland!*" Davies shrieked. "You're a damned rebel, and I'll see you hanged for this!" He began to stamp, his dingy wig flopping, his fists raised.

Again speaking past the officer, Sutherland said, "Put the bateaux in the water, lads! We'll camp downriver, where the air's a bit better."

Davies whipped out his sword. The worried, outnumbered Redcoats obeyed his shout to bring bayonets to bear, but Sutherland moved like a panther, his own claymore flicking out. He knocked Davies's weapon to the ground with a dull, metallic thud, then sprang out of the ring of nervous Redcoats and called on his men to join him.

Davies was helpless. Though he had a garrison, he knew he could only depend on the six Redcoats. That fact was borne out by the presence of Corporal Duff standing at the fort's gate, with several other provincial troops. Duff looked less like a prisoner than a ringleader, though all the Yorkers in the fort were clearly not on his side. Bewildered, humiliated by Sutherland a second time, Davies was at a loss for what to do. His Redcoats were outnumbered by Sutherland's followers, and the provincials under his command might disobey, for they apparently despised his severity and domination. Duff and his friends had not yet mutinied against their commander, but Davies could see that might happen if he pushed the fray further.

Sutherland spoke. "I'm truly sorry this has happened, Lieutenant, for I want to hear about what occurred in Massachusetts; but I'll wait until I reach Albany, where I have friends who'll tell me everything. We're leaving, and don't try to stop us."

Davies realized it was one thing to harry and delay Sutherland in the official capacity as commander of this fort; but it was another thing entirely to spill blood. Sutherland had friends in high places—yes, even in the British Army—and that was reason enough to intimidate the officer.

Quivering with uncontrollable fury, he cried out, "Go, and be damned! But I'll send a full report of this to General Gage, and he'll know you for a rebel who drew a sword on a king's officer! You'll be marked for arrest, Sutherland, and if I have anything to do with it, you'll be hanged."

"Have a care, Lieutenant, that it's not you General Gage chooses to discipline," Sutherland replied as his snickering men lugged boats and gear toward the Mohawk. Even the Oneidas found the scene amusing.

With that, Davies whirled away. Finding Duff and the others at the gate, he pointed at him and roared, "Take that man away! Put him in irons! He'll have a hundred lashes for his insubordination, and anyone else with his attitude will pay the same! Take him away! Take him, damn your eyes!"

For just a moment, no longer than it takes to breathe once, the Yorkers hesitated. The pause was so brief that civilians might not have noticed it, but for soldiers to show the slightest reluctance at the command of an officer was a serious, foreboding thing. Davies sensed it, too, and in that same instant was not sure what to do.

"Take him, you provincial curs!" he screamed, face as red as his coat. "Take him or I'll have you all drummed out for rebels with a thousand lashes each to remind you of your sins!"

That worked. Duff took the first step to withdraw, not wishing to bring punishment on his friends. The corporal went back into the fort, and several provincial troops showed their support for Davies by falling into step behind the prisoner as part of the guard detail. Sutherland watched all this, sorry for the young man, and seeing how even professional soldiers were divided in their political sympathies.

In the past, more than half the men recruited for British regiments serving in North America came from the colonies. Most regular soldiers had roots or families in America. They were forced by their profession to put down civil disturbances, while their hearts often were in sympathy with the Whig cause. It was apparent that the eight independent companies of New York had a good share of Whigs, and here at lonely Fort Stanwix, Lieutenant Davies was in a precarious position.

Sutherland watched the officer storm back to the fort, shouting commands, sending men scurrying right and left. He had not even picked up his sword, and his scabbard was conspicuously empty. Then, just before entering the gate, Davies stopped short, seeing a party of Indians approach from the southwest. Sutherland recognized them as Senecas, apparently back from the hunt, for they were laden down with partridge, a doe, and a few swans. Leading this group of nine armed young men was an enormous warrior, much taller than Sutherland, with a long face both grave and ugly.

Lieutenant Davies glanced over his shoulder at Sutherland, quickly commanded one of his men to fetch the fallen sword, and straightened his uniform coat. The Seneca band approached slowly, feathered heads high, conscious that every eye was upon them. There was no more warlike, feared race of Indians in all America, and these haughty warriors were the best of their generation. They were fine specimens, strong and regal in bearing, but their leader was by far the most imposing. He was tattooed from forehead to belly, his barrel chest bared. Unlike his companions, who were dressed in white-man's breeches and shirts decorated with beads and dyed porcupine quills, he wore the old-fashioned short buckskin kilt of his forefathers. At the gate this fierce warrior threw down the doe he was carrying as though it weighed nothing and raised his right hand to Davies.

The lieutenant quickly sheathed the sword just handed to him by a soldier and returned the salute.

"How, Manoth!" Davies cried, casting a gloating look at Sutherland. "How and welcome, brother, war chief of the Turtle Clan, scourge of our king's enemies!" Actually chuckling, Davies went to the big Seneca and embraced him, the Indian's bear grease liberally staining his scarlet uniform. Sutherland knew that such familiarity with an Indian was unusual for a British officer; Davies was making a point very clearly.

Leading the Indian party into Stanwix, the officer ordered the gates shut behind him, leaving Sutherland and the packers wondering what was being said. Then Hickory came to Sutherland's side and spoke in a breathless, trembling voice.

"Manoth, that Seneca, longs to be a leading war chief! He hates the Whigs and has promised to eat the heart of any who defile the name of King George, our Great White Father across the sea."

Hickory looked at Sutherland, as though expecting some reply, but the Scotsman simply nodded once and turned to his men.

"We'll post watch tonight, lads," he said to them. "Consider yourselves in enemy territory until we reach Albany."

Poole threw his head back, guffawing as he said, "If this were my expedition, Owen, I'd capture Stanwix and the Mohawk Valley for Congress and kick Davies all the way to the sea."

Sutherland looked at him a moment, then replied, "If this were your expedition, son, you wouldn't get out of this valley alive."

Poole laughed once more, though a bit hollowly.

Speaking to Mel, who was fidgeting nearby, Hickory said, "I am afraid, husband." She waved a hand at the clearing, where the Oneida had been gathered to welcome their expedition. It was empty. "We are alone."

Later that day, Sutherland's group made camp at a pretty glade on the north bank of the Mohawk. It was a fine afternoon, sunny and fresh, and he gave the men the rest of the time off to fish or hunt. These upper reaches of the river were fairly remote from the settled lower districts of German Flats, Stone Arabia, and Cherry Valley, which was a country thick with Whigs and radicals. As Sutherland rested in the shade of an overturned bateau, he considered the meaning of all Duff and Davies had told him.

Anxious to learn what he could about the fighting, he decided to have Mel and Hickory take a canoe several miles downstream to the Oneida village of Oriska. There they could learn from the Indians or nearby white settlers what had happened in Massachusetts. Mel was the best choice for this mission because of his command of Indian tongues as well as his ability to speak German. Many settlers along this stretch of the Mohawk were Palatine Germans who spoke only the old language.

Farther downstream Sir William Johnson, the late British Superintendent of Indian Affairs for the northern districts, had brought thousands of Catholic Scots and Irish over to populate vast holdings he had received as gifts from the Mohawk. In the decade since the French and Indian War, Sir William had become a prince in this country and a representative of the mighty Iroquois Six Nations. He had guided and advised them in everything, and when he died last year, he had been succeeded as superintendent by his able nephew, Guy Johnson, who lived downriver to the east, among Mohawks and loyal white followers.

As Sutherland relaxed, smoking a pipe, he pondered what Guy Johnson and his loyalists would do in response to the eastern uprising. A solid Tory, Johnson opposed the Whigs, as was natural for a man whose authority, title, and salary came from Parliament. He had the ability to sway the Iroquois and thus was a powerful man in these worsening difficulties.

If Johnson became reckless and tried to enlist the Iroquois as fighters, then Sutherland's efforts of years ago would be returning to haunt him. Sutherland once had taken Johnson under his wing and taught him about the Illinois Indians. Returning a favor to Sir William, Sutherland had thoroughly instructed Guy Johnson, helping him become a worthy assistant to his uncle.

Though relations between white and Indian on the eastern frontiers were shaky these days, it was certain the majority of the two thousand Iroquois warriors would heed the command of Guy Johnson. As administrator of essential government supplies sent regularly to the Indians, and as their trusted spokesman in colonial councils, he was something of a god to most Iroquois.

Only Hickory's Oneidas, influenced by New England missionaries, and a few Tuscaroras, who were more like whites than Indians, might recoil if Guy Johnson called on them to take the warpath against American rebels. But the Oneidas and Tuscaroras together had only two hundred fighting men, and without a Whig army to support them, they would be outnumbered and compelled to ally with Johnson's loyal Indians and Tories or be destroyed.

While these thoughts went through Sutherland's mind, the sun began to go down, reddening the sky and leaving the forest cool, ruffled by a springtime breeze. In the camp evening fires were stoked, and men came in with game or fish. As cooks prepared supper, there was much talk and eager speculation over what had happened in the East, though no one knew the real gravity of the Lexington and Concord fights. It was not until Mel and Hickory returned at nightfall that it became clear civil war truly had begun.

Mel and his squaw had stopped at a German tavern a few miles downstream, where they had conversed with white travelers and the innkeeper, and with some Onondaga Indians returning from Albany. The news was grim: Massachusetts was supported by all New England, and an army of twenty thousand militiamen was besieging Gage in Boston.

Before the campfire, while eating roasted pigeon, Mel told what he knew. "Tomorrow we'll be in the thick of it; everybody to the eastward is yammering about war, though most hope it never comes out here.

"Some are boasting they're king's men, others are claiming to be neutral; but the ones who favor Congress are afraid to talk too much for fear of Guy Johnson's people, who are canvassing door to door, demanding that everyone sign a loyalty oath or risk jail."

Mel looked around at the other men, who were listening intently as they ate. Most of Sutherland's party were Whigs, but others were opposed to taking up arms in rebellion. Yet there were no arguments, no fights, because to get through Johnson's country they had to stick together. Mel said bands of armed loyal Highlanders were enforcing the signing of the loyalty oath, and they might make trouble for the convoy.

When Mel was finished with his tale, Sutherland said, "See to your weapons tonight, lads. Your first duty is to get to Albany with the pelts; then you can choose what you want to do about this affair."

He looked at each one, silently asking whether they would remain faithful to him for the remaining few days of travel.

"Any man who wants out," Sutherland continued, "can go now, with my promissory note for payment to be redeemed at the company office in Albany."

No one moved. Even the less radical were the kind who kept their word, and though it was dangerous, they would stand by Sutherland just as they had been prepared to stand by him at Stanwix.

This formality done, Sutherland began to plan their movements to best avoid Tory settlements. Suddenly there was a loud noise in the bushes, as of several men running. Among the packmen, rifles and hatchets came out as Corporal Gavin Duff came stumbling from the trees, winded and in agony. Three provincial soldiers were at his side.

Duff collapsed to his knees, sweating and fevered, unable to speak. One of Duff's men, a private, helped his friend to the ground, saying, "Not on his back! Keep the poor bastard off his back, Mr. Sutherland!"

Duff was eased onto a blanket that covered some soft balsam branches laid out for a mattress. The packmen clustered around the soldiers, who were tired and very agitated.

Sutherland asked, "You've deserted?"

The private furtively glanced at the packmen, and nodded. "At dark we left the fort, twelve of us in three groups, all goin' a different way. One of us was even a Redcoat! I'm goin' home, sir! I'm joinin' the New England army! After what I seed of poor Duff's beatin', I hates British officers, and I means to fight 'em till they're out of New York once and for all!"

As Hickory bent over Duff, removing his bloodstained coat, Sutherland took a long look at the lash marks. At least a hundred crisscrossed the corporal's back, through raw flesh to the very bone. This was the way of the army, brutal and heartless.

The packmen went into an uproar, calling for the deserters to join them on the journey to Albany and to fight anyone who tried to stop them. When Sutherland raised his hands for silence, they all turned to him. "You're welcome with us, gentlemen," he said. "The use of the lash is an unwarranted degree of discipline. But if you mean to be soldiers fighting for liberty, don't delude yourselves about the need for discipline."

This created confusion and angry muttering. Bill Poole voiced their thoughts when he asked, "You mean we'll have to bare our backs for the New England army, too? Hah! That's just what we're fightin', and I sure as hell won't let no officer lay the cat on me, Owen!"

Sutherland's appearance was suddenly so fierce that the chorus of approval following Poole's remarks died down immediately. The Scotsman said, "If you won't obey, you won't make soldiers, and you'll be useless to Congress—worse than useless to America."

He looked around at them, seeing their faces angry or resentful, though a few who had been in the army knew exactly what he meant.

"If there's to be war," Sutherland said, watching Hickory swab Duff's wounds, "then it may last for years. If there's to be an

American army capable of taking on the lobsterbacks, it'll need discipline, self-sacrifice, and respect for commanders, whether you elect them yourselves or they're placed at your head by some general you don't know—maybe even by a general from another colony!"

They guffawed and cursed at the idea of a leader coming from a place other than their own home colonies, and their loud declarations that no one would lead them without their consent left Sutherland sullen.

Just then Duff came to. A frantic look was in his eyes, and with great effort he rasped, "Sutherland, you got to get away, tonight . . ." He coughed, grimaced in pain, and nearly fainted.

Sutherland knelt at his side and asked what he meant. Duff managed to lean on one elbow, motioning for Mel to wait before administering a cup of water mixed with brown laudanum paste to quiet the hideous pain.

"Davies . . ." Duff fought the agony, his eyes going out of focus. "Davies has sent an express to Guy Johnson, asking for a force of loyal settlers to cut you off and arrest you for a rebel! Mr. Sutherland, if they catch you in the valley, you'll be tried for treason!"

Duff groaned, and Mel moved in to administer the bitter and dark opium tincture. Knowing what the drink was, the soldier downed it in a few gulps, desperate to have his hurt relieved. The drug would soon make him fall asleep, but until it did, he spoke on.

"Whigs would help us, sir, but they ain't formed up in militia companies as yet. Nobody wants to make a move that would bring on all-out fighting in the valley. . . . If it starts now, it'd be the ruin of the Whig settlers, for sure." He became woozy, and lay on his side, his voice weakening as he said, "Don't let your men start anything, Mr. Sutherland . . . not yet, or there'll be hell to pay, and we'll lose the valley . . . to Tories . . . before we can . . ." He passed out.

Sutherland left Hickory and Mel to tend to Duff, and the men began to talk in hushed tones among themselves. Sutherland knew full well the meaning of the corporal's warning. If a loyalist militia was strong enough to keep the rebels from forming their own companies, then Johnson's people would win the Mohawk Valley for the crown. All Johnson needed was for some Whigs to begin shooting, and the loyalists would attack, snuffing out the rebellion here before it even caught fire. So far the Whigs were law-abiding, but one premature move to oppose Johnson would offer a legal excuse to arrest all suspected Whig sympathizers before they could form a body of fighting men. Certainly a battle with Sutherland's party would be just that excuse.

The Yorker private with Duff came to Sutherland, fear in his expression as he said, "Lieutenant Davies called on some Senecas to help run us down, sir, and I think they'll be used to block you as well."

Another deserter said nervously, "If the Injuns join Johnson and run loose in the valley, there won't be a Whig farmhouse from here to Schenectady left standing—not unless our boys have time to collect into a militia! Good Lord, Mr. Sutherland, folk'll be in a bad way if you start a fight with Injuns on your way through to Albany!"

Yet Sutherland and his men might have no other choice but to fight. No one would take the pelts from him, and no one would throw him in prison without a struggle.

He promptly set his men in motion, breaking camp, launching the canoes and bateaux. With the guidance of a deserter they began making their way down the Mohawk River through darkness, hoping they would avoid Johnson's loyalists. Sutherland wanted to keep from firing the first shot, but if they were intercepted, they would battle all the way to Albany if they must. It did not matter whether Johnson's loyalist force was made up of Senecas, or Sutherland's own kinsmen, Scottish Highlanders.

chapter 15

LITTLE FALLS

That same night, word of the fighting around Boston reached Ella while she was at home with the children, putting them to bed. After heating the sheets by rubbing a bedwarmer full of hot coals over them, she heard a loud knocking at the door, and Heera began to bark. She quickly tucked in Benjamin and Susannah, then hurried downstairs, the bedwarmer held before her on a long pole. Sally let in Jeb Grey, Lettie, and Tom Morely, all of them showing strain and worry.

Lettie took the bedwarmer from Ella and said with fear in her voice, "The killin's begun, love! Thy man's walkin' straight into a hornet's nest! Oh, Ella, I be sorry to sound so—so alarmist, but you got to know things're gettin' bad!"

Jeb put his arm around Ella, who had been struck hard by the horror of what she had heard. They all went into the common room, where a small fire was cheerfully crackling in the hearth. Candles and an oil lamp burned on the trestle table, where Sally had laid her sewing, including one of Tom's best shirts. The girl and Tom sat down next to each other at the table as the older folk also took chairs to discuss what must be done.

Ella listened, head in hands, to what Jeb could tell about the uprising, but no one knew yet whether it would spread beyond New England.

"There's rumors," he said, "that delegates to Congress'll be arrested wherever Tories or soldiers can catch 'em. Lots of folk are sittin' tight to see who'll take charge of government affairs where they live. The Whigs got hold of some counties, while the Tories got others. No more killin', so far, 'cept what's gone on in Massachusetts Bay."

"And out here?" Ella asked, longing to be six hundred miles away with her husband. "Where do the Sons stand tonight?"

Jeb replied, "They're being very quiet."

Tom said, "Already a few've been arrested by Captain Lernoult for talking too loud against the army and Parliament when they were drinking at the Brave Wolfe."

"You must all be very careful!" Ella insisted, holding the hands of Jeb and Lettie; Sally did the same to Tom, who put his other hand on hers. "Say nothing in public one way or the other, or the Tories will have you jailed. . . ." Her thoughts suddenly flew away as she wondered what was happening to Owen just then. Did he know? Was he in danger? Indeed they were all in danger now, at least until some peaceful means of solving differences was agreed upon. Surely King George and Parliament must realize colonists were willing to die for what they believed. The king had to call off the soldiers now!

Jeb said, "I wish Owen were here; he could keep things calm, and enough Tories would accept him as a Whig representative."

"Yes," Lettie agreed. "Thy man's absence is a sore loss for us at Detroit, Ella; the Tories got the upper hand, and they'll keep it, even if it means jailing every knave what forgets to remember the king's birthday."

"June fourth," said a small voice from the doorway. It was Benjamin, who stood wide awake alongside his sister. Having heard all that had been said, the children began to ask questions about the troubles, questions that touched too close to the awful truth of slaughter and bloody civil war. Ella found it impossible to keep the truth from them, or to redirect their curiosity. She had to tell of the killing, of the danger of speaking too freely to Tories. She warned them to be silent about her family's stand when they were at the fort and not to talk about politics.

"And be sure not to tell anyone what we or our partners are doing, or who we're doing it with! Understand?"

Susannah and Benjamin nodded, though they really did not grasp the weight of what Ella was saying. Even though the Frontier Company as a firm would take no official stand in politics, some partners would do all they could to support the New England militia fighters against the Parliamentary army in Boston. Ella and her friends intended to send goods and provisions secretly to rebels on the frontier, who would be challenged by loyalists for control of the backcountry.

This had been agreed to before Owen departed. Although some partners, such as the Indians and French, would carry on their own business as usual, without taking sides in the conflict, others, including the Sutherlands, Morelys, Greys, and Defrieses, would be united against the British. Secretly at first, and then openly as the Whigs gained power, these partners in the Frontier Company would be with the rebels in arms. There was much to be done clandestinely for the cause, and if Captain Lernoult got wind of what Ella and her friends were about, they would be arrested or driven from their homes.

After sending the children to bed, they made detailed plans. When they finished, the house was dead quiet, teacups and beer mugs standing cold or empty on the table. The clock chimed twelve. In that hushed moment, with the last chime fading away, Ella found herself gazing around the comfortable room.

It was so peaceful, completely removed from the outer world, that she never wanted to leave it. It seemed a haven, where they were safe as long as they did not leave. Ella feared what would befall her and these friends if they departed.

Through that long night Sutherland's convoy poled or paddled slowly downstream, careful not to run aground or become caught in unexpected rapids. There was a moon, and that was good, but a strong breeze chilled their bones. As hour after hour passed, Sutherland wondered what they would encounter when the sun rose. His instincts told him to make for shore before first light, then reconnoiter the riverbank ahead with the best men he had. Unfortunately, none of his packers were wilderness scouts, and the provincial soldiers with him were of little use as spies in the woods.

Struggling against agony, Gavin Duff recovered from the laudanum and sat in the snub-nosed prow of Sutherland's bateau. Duff knew the river well, having been posted to forts Stanwix and Oswego during the past six years. His wife and child dwelt in Kinderhook, on the other side of Albany, and often he had made the journey by water, even traveling in darkness to avoid losing precious time on leave. Sutherland asked Duff for advice, and the corporal replied in a tight, gasping voice, summoning all his strength to speak, despite the awful pain he suffered.

"'Tis my counsel, sir, that we keep to the river all tomorrow and through another night, if your men be up to it." He grunted, shifting his weight on the seat to relieve some discomfort.

Duff said they might outrun Lieutenant Davies's express before he reached Johnson Hall, the stronghold of the local Tories, forty miles away on the north side of the river. Duff's voice was so soft that the sound of water rippling past almost drowned it out.

"Davies won't expect us to fly so fast, and his patrols'll look for us upstream afore they learn we've gone downriver all night and given him the slip." He paused to take a swig of rum, and Sutherland's mind wandered back to Detroit, to Ella, to what might happen at Valenya when word of open rebellion arrived there. Then he returned to business at hand and listened to Duff.

"After Johnson Hall it's still forty miles to the Hudson River, and fifteen more to Albany, but it's a country controlled by Whigs, and the loyalists haven't the strength to do a thing there!"

They went on slowly, one bateau after the other, Mel's canoe in the lead flitting here and there to sound for depth or to warn Sutherland about obstacles, shoal water, or rifts. About three o'clock they passed a rapid, not as swift or brawling as north-country white water, but taxing enough for weary men trying to maintain strict silence while wading at the edge of the stream, hauling the flatboats by rope. Everything went smoothly enough, save for a man or two stepping into a pothole and going under. Fortunately, no one was lost, and the party continued as before.

The land on both sides of the river began rising, the sky being shut out as hills blackened the horizon and loomed ever higher over the travelers. It was as though they descended a long flume, into the heart of the earth, hemmed in by the dark riverbanks that were split by the glint of moonlight on water. Now and again they saw a cabin window as a far-off spot of yellow, and occasionally a campfire could be seen on the northern ridge, to the left, above the river.

The Mohawk began to swing from south to east, around steep hills. The water on the north side was so filled with rocks that they had to cross the stream and follow the southern shore. As the boatmen poled quietly through the bubbling shallows, keeping boats from grounding, Sutherland saw a lantern moving through the darkness, toward the river. He felt for his loaded rifle, instincts warning him that the convoy had been discovered. This lantern meant someone might be setting them up for ambush.

The anxious whispering of Poole and Duff mingled with the sound of the river, and above it came a cry from shore, in a husky, sing-song voice.

"Meester Sutherland, that you, sir? This Joe Onayote, Oneida headman! Pull to shore, if you please!"

From Mel's canoe hovering nearby, Hickory gave a shout and replied in her own language. Then to Sutherland she said, "It's

my uncle, my uncle! It's Joe Onayote, sachem of my people!"
She babbled cheerfully back and forth to the shadowy figure with
the lantern, and Sutherland called for his men to put ashore.

They drew into a cove overhung by massive willows and alders,
and before long more lanterns were lit, shielded by the thicket of
trees along the bank from any spies who might be across the river.
This southern shore of the Mohawk was populated by Whig farmers, while the northern bank down to the Caughnawaga near Johns-
town was mainly Tory.

In the muted light of lanterns, Sutherland met a lean, bent old
Indian who was treated with considerable respect by Hickory and
Mel. Joe Onayote's English was good, though tinged by a German
accent learned from his white neighbors. After Sutherland formally
greeted him with a pouch of tobacco, they sat down together to
hear what he had to say. With Onayote were three other elderly
Oneida warriors, who partook of the smoke and sat on their haunches
as Onayote told why he had stopped Sutherland's convoy.

"You don't get by Ta-la-que-ga," said Onayote, his long arms
moving in the darkness as he spoke, so that the blanket over his
shoulders seemed to form wings. "Davies send Seneca down there
to wait for you, to make trouble, to rub you out."

Listening along with Sutherland, Mel, and Hickory was Corporal Duff. The boatmen were resting on the bank, eating and
drinking and having a smoke before setting off again. Onayote
said twenty-five Senecas under the warrior named Manoth—the
giant they had seen with Davies at Stanwix—had hurried through
the woods that night and were positioned at a carrying place, called
Ta-la-que-ga, or "the place of many bushes," where they would
prevent Sutherland's passing.

Duff said softly, "That's called Little Falls by us, and it's about
seven miles ahead; we got to take the boats out there and haul
them over the King's Road to the lower stretch, but to do that we
got to hire carts from a Scotch miller named McAllister."

"Scotch bastard," Onayote muttered, without rancor, as though
this were the usual Oneida name for the loyalist followers of Guy
Johnson. "More Scotch bastards coming upriver," Onayote went
on, in a grating, throaty voice. "Guy Johnson bring his people up
for meeting with Injuns at Stanwix. He got three hundred men and
families comin' up King's Road, and they telling Injuns rebel army
coming soon, coming to arrest loyal folk. Manoth hold you fast
if Davies tell him so." Onayote moved his arms, enfolding an
imaginary captive and saying, "Johnson like to have what you got

in boats, Meester Sutherland. His people plenty mad to leave valley—them Tories outnumbered, got to go sooner or later—Johnson like to take your furs to Montreal, I'm thinking."

There was a silence as Sutherland thought what he must do next. Duff said, "Even if Manoth wasn't waiting for us, McAllister at Little Falls won't give you carts if Guy Johnson or Lieutenant Davies has told him not to. That means we can't get around the falls in less than two days, because the climb's too steep, and we'll have to carry everything bale by bale, boat by boat. . . ."

Onayote said, "You smarter to stay with Oneida till Johnson and Scotch bastards pass by, have council and go away to Oswego; you safe with us—we hide you good."

Hickory said rapidly, "My uncle's village is not far away, not far! We'll be better off there than meeting Manoth again!"

It might have been prudent to leave the river and wait until the Tory refugees and their Indian allies left the valley, but Sutherland was short of time. He had to get to Albany, sell the furs, then rush to Philadelphia before returning to Detroit to fetch Ella and the children.

He asked Onayote, "How long do I have to wait, honored sachem?"

Onayote slowly shook his head. "Johnson people and Injuns like to talk, drink, smoke, talk some more. . . . Maybe two week, maybe three."

That settled it. Sutherland thanked Onayote for his warning, then said, "We're going now, and we'll get past the falls before Johnson's people come up, Manoth or no."

"Manoth *verdammt* bad dog!" Onayote declared, grumbling. "Like to be warrior chief, like to prove worthy of Johnson's praise! Manoth bad dog. He don't like who Davies don't like, and I hear tonight Davies don't like you."

With that, Sutherland thanked Onayote and rose. He called to his men to get back in their boats, and then said to Onayote, "I'll do all I can to prevent bloodshed, because I know the Tories are looking for an excuse to start arresting Whigs in the valley; but I might have to forget my scruples if I'm to get through."

Though not knowing what Sutherland meant, Onayote glanced fondly at his niece, Hickory, and said, "This old Injun go along a little ways . . . maybe far as Schenectady, eh?" He tugged the blanket closer about his shoulders and stood up. "I like to help a Scotchman who isn't a bastard son of a bitch, and I like to see my Hickory safe on her journey."

Sutherland agreed gladly, thinking the Oneida might have a role to play in the plan taking form in his mind. Soon they were back in the boats, poling or paddling downstream toward Little Falls. They drifted without lights, and soon the lantern of the other Oneidas who had stayed behind was only a tiny spot against the dark mass of shoreline. The convoy was floating into morning light, soft, blue, and lustrous behind the hills. A sheen of mist rose on the water, full of mosquitoes and black flies that became ever more pesky until a breeze came up and blew most away, taking the mist as well.

It was not long before Sutherland put his plan into effect. Working in the dim light, he emptied a keg of undiluted rum into a wooden tub placed in the center of the boat. His men licked their lips and passed joking comments around until they saw Sutherland open a pound wad of chewing tobacco, black and oily. Breaking it up, he dropped it into the liquor, and protests and cries of dismay followed. Sutherland simply chuckled and asked where the powdered ginger had been stashed. The ginger was in another bateau, so he asked Mel, who was close by in a canoe, to paddle over to the boat that had it. Before Mel pushed off, Sutherland said, "Toss me your tin of laudanum, laddie; don't wórry, I'll buy you a new one in Albany!"

Taken aback, Mel said, "All of it? There's twelve ounces of opium tincture in there, Owen!"

"Perhaps I won't need it all," Sutherland replied softly, catching the tin as Mel threw it over. "Only as much as it'll take to persuade Manoth and his warriors to let us pass the falls in peace."

In the first hour after sunrise, Manoth's Senecas hung sleepily about a makeshift camp beside the river. They were on the north bank, a few yards above where the water began to foam, plunging and crashing its way to the drop called Little Falls.

A cold spray drifted up from the river, soaking blankets and robes, laying a fine wet haze on leaves and trees and on the grist mill owned by Angus McAllister, the Scottish loyalist. The mill stood hard by the water, its raceway cutting out from the turbulent river, directing a strong current toward the waterwheel that powered the mill's machinery. Made of planks, with a fieldstone foundation, the mill was like a squat, sturdy creature huddling on the edge of the rapids. It was a neat, well-kept building, painted red and trimmed in white.

The Indians were camped near a barn a little above the mill,

close to a cow pasture beside the King's Road. This east-west road
ran along the north side of the river. Here it climbed over rocky
outcrops before descending steeply toward the stretch of riverbank
below the falls. Looming over the mill and Indian camp were
soaring cliffs on both sides of the river, and the roar of the falls
echoed steadily through the chasm. Looking downstream from here
one could see the massive lump of rock called Moss Island, around
which the river split as it dropped swiftly to the placid, deep water
below. The island was uninhabited, for to try to reach it would
be foolhardy. Few boats could cross that pounding rift, and any
making the attempt would likely be swept away to be obliterated
in the waterfall.

Thus, Manoth and his ally Lieutenant Davies had chosen a
good place to stop Sutherland's convoy. The only way past the
falls was over the King's Road, Duff had told Sutherland, and
carts and draft animals were required for bateaux. Even if these
were available—and McAllister would refuse a Whig's request to
hire them—the chilled and hungry Senecas who had hurried here
last night would prevent Sutherland's boats being portaged.

From within the small whitewashed cottage attached to the mill
there came a shout and the jangle of a meal bell. The door was
thrown open and out strode the short, wiry McAllister, carrying
a large black iron pot of steaming porridge. Behind him came his
eight-year-old son and slightly younger daughter, both carrying
pails of milk, wooden bowls, and spoons for the warriors who
could use them. Last through the door was Mrs. McAllister, short
and thin like her husband, wearing a spotless white mobcap and
apron.

Seeing food, the Indians gave a chorus of approval and crowded
around a plank table, where the bowls clattered as the porridge
was served out. The daughter ladled milk into each serving, and
Mrs. McAllister frugally dealt each a dash of salt in the Scottish
way of eating oats.

The miller stood back to watch, motioning his family back into
the cottage. Indians were unpredictable at best, and he wanted his
wife and children kept out of the way. McAllister was about fifty
and had married late in life before emigrating to America. His
gray hair was clubbed severely, and he wore a leather waistcoat
and linen shirt with the sleeves rolled up. Crossing his arms, he
watched the Senecas poke at the hot gruel, sniff it, lap at the milk,
then begin to turn sour, disappointed faces toward one another.

McAllister cheerfully shouted, "Eat up, gentlemen! Porridge

is the best thing in the morning! I'll bring ye a pot of tea out directly, and we've some biscuits on hand if ye like!"

He realized the warriors were not inclined to favor this sticky, tasteless Scottish dish, but he did not care. McAllister knew what was good for them, for he ate boiled oats every day and credited oats for his good health, strong body, and ability to work hard, morning to night.

"Go on, then!" he cried, as a stern uncle might speak to children. "If ye're about to take on a Scot, ye best have a Scot's breakfast to give ye're the courage."

At that, Manoth swung to glare at him. The Seneca's eyes were afire, showing black resentment. His painted face was contorted, and the other warriors stood back to observe their leader, who strode slowly toward McAllister. The Scot did not flinch, standing with legs apart, arms still folded, and a look of calm defiance about him. Manoth stopped close to the loyalist, towering over him.

McAllister's wife was at the door, hand to her mouth. Her husband looked up at the warrior, clenched his teeth, then said, "Lieutenant Davies gave me no requisition to feed ye, big fella! My family and I've given this out of friendship, and also because we agree with thwarting rebels whenever we can."

Manoth stared, hands on hips. McAllister put his hands on his own hips and stood like a miniature of the Seneca, though dressed in civilized clothes.

After a moment, the Indian spoke, slowly and ponderously, "Warrior no eat damned horse food, papoose food!"

McAllister's face turned red. He began to quiver, barely able to keep his hands from becoming fists.

"Papoose food, is it?" He pointed fiercely at the steaming porridge on the table. "That 'papoose food,' my trusty Seneca warrior, is the daily victuals of the finest soldiers in the world! That 'horse food' is what Scottish Highlanders have eaten before every battle, before Stirling, Bannockburn, Fontenoy, yes, even before the battles against yer former beloved French allies, when Scots showed whites and Indians how to die like men at Ticonderoga!"

Raging now, McAllister stamped to the porridge, stuck in a wooden spoon, and brought up a gummy, scalding dollop, saying, "Porridge oats, ye redskins, is what Owen Sutherland ate afore the Battle of Bushy Run, when he and his few Highlanders broke the back of Pontiac's ill-conceived rising! Yes, and he left a wind-row of dead Seneca behind in his counterattack!"

Manoth took one step, which put him inches from the miller, hand on his tomahawk. There Manoth froze, madness welling at the hated memory of Bushy Run, when the best Indian fighters were chopped to pieces by Black Watch Highlanders guided by Owen Sutherland. Manoth himself had fought there, and in the end he had fled from Sutherland's desperate counterattack that had prevented a certain Indian victory.

Manoth had taken all he could, and McAllister knew enough to shut up. The Indian gained some self-control, saying loudly, "Davies pay for breakfast! Seneca take whole cow! Make feast! Make war feast!" He released a guttural laugh and looked about at his men, who were nodding and uttering agreement at his plans. To McAllister, he said, "Davies pay! Seneca now eat cow."

McAllister rose to his full height, which was approximately equal with Manoth's chest. "I dinna crawl to white Whig or Tory Indian, my friend! I'll sell ye a cow, but only if Lieutenant Davies pays first, sterling, and the price I—"

Everyone stopped abruptly. Over the pounding river a fiddle could be heard playing a Scottish dance tune, and from the distance came a hearty sound of voices singing along. Music and song rang around the shadows of the gorge, and the Indians looked from one to the other, as though hearing evil spirits.

McAllister cried, "It's Sutherland! They're here!"

The warriors leaped about in confusion, snatching up weapons, hurriedly painting their faces, taking one last glance into hand mirrors to satisfy themselves that they were disguised enough and ugly enough not to be recognized by the ghosts of those they killed.

The Highlander shouted, "Now remember, Manoth, ye promised there'd be no blood spilled unless Sutherland tries to pass! Davies will be here in a few hours with Guy Johnson, and they'll arrest these rebels legally!"

Manoth looked surly at that, but knew the little man was right. Few in the valley wanted civil war to begin, and most hoped that violence would be kept out if possible.

Making appropriate motions with his hands, the Seneca grunted, "If Donoway push Manoth, Manoth push back. Harder!" Then he grinned, showing yellow teeth, some of them filed to a point.

McAllister said, "I'll do the talking! Davies and Johnson both want Sutherland under arrest, not dead! He's got too many powerful friends, and if they should all come to take revenge on the Seneca—"

Manoth waved him away and called to his men. Some hurried down to the riverbank, where a wooden landing pointed out over the water. They stood in array, forming a crescent from the landing, up a little slope, and back to the King's Road. At Manoth's instruction other warriors drifted into the trees, some climbing up as sharpshooters, a number concealing themselves in bushes. Manoth had twenty-five fighters, but after he readied himself for Sutherland, only a dozen were in view.

McAllister took his dark-blue hat and coat from his wife, who had fear in her eyes as she told him in a trembling voice to be careful.

Tugging on his frock coat, he said, "There's duty to be done, Jane. King's duty! I've got more in common with the Senecas than with Sutherland, more's the pity!"

He took a gnarled hickory cane from her and flourished it, telling her to go back into the cottage and stay there with the children. Then they both paused to listen to the singing, which was much closer now and very spirited.

She said softly, "That's a Highland tune, Angus. Oh, it gives me the chills to hear it here, especially to hear it from—"

"Go in the house, woman!" McAllister insisted, pointing the cane at the door. "Bide inside and dinna come out till I tell ye!"

She touched his arm, and he gave up his severity, patting her hand kindly. She went inside, and he turned toward the singing, which was so surprisingly jolly. McAllister had expected that Sutherland might have been warned by some Whig spy about Davies being on the lookout for him. Sutherland must not be the experienced former soldier McAllister thought he was, for he should have known about the Senecas waiting here and not be hallooing himself in as though he were on some gentleman's picnic.

Well, that was not McAllister's problem. He was no soldier, just an honest king's man who would refuse to hire carts to rebels. He would, of course, do all he humanly could to keep these Senecas from starting a fight. He glanced back at his pretty mill and cottage. If it became a battlefield, he had much to lose.

chapter **16**

MANOTH

Standing in the first bateau, Sutherland called out to his men, "Now, lads, let's have a round of 'The New Deserter'!"

I am a young farmer and Johnny's my name...

His men joined in, even feeble Duff, who was wearing a brown blanket, still suffering from his lashes. Each bateau drew close to the one before, and as they steered or rowed the men sang out the fanciful ballad of a young soldier who deserts time and again, only to be caught, forgiven, and sent back unpunished to the ranks. At last, he is caught again and sentenced to death; but he is pardoned and finally set free from the army by a sympathetic commander.

The convoy was just a hundred yards from McAllister's now, and as Sutherland sang loudly he marked the Indians on shore, noting those hidden among leaves and branches. On the landing Manoth stood out, and Sutherland knew immediately this warrior would be happiest if there was a fight. Sutherland would oblige him if need be, but to engage concealed Indians meant certain destruction.

"All right, lads!" he cried out, his voice echoing from the stone cliffs. "Let's give 'em a northwestern fire of joy! But don't plug any of 'em!"

At that, the men raised muskets and pistols high, pointing them in the air, and fired an echoing salute to the Senecas and Mc-Allister. It was custom for the Indians to reply in kind to such courtesy, and a few raised their weapons without thinking, but Manoth roared a command, and they stopped before answering the fusillade. The Senecas were confused that these Whigs would be coming so friendly and so politely to their camp when Whigs hated Senecas and the feeling was mutual.

In Mel's canoe sat the Oneida Joe Onayote, wrapped in a new trade blanket of bright blue with white stripes. Joe was nervous, but he grinned rigidly toward shore, where he recognized some of the Senecas, foremost among them Manoth. Joe knew Sutherland's plan, and agreed it was unfortunately one of the lowest of low tricks often played on Indians by unscrupulous fur traders. Yet if it saved lives, he would support it.

Raising his right hand, palm forward, Joe called to the Senecas in their own tongue, introducing Sutherland as Donoway of the Ottawa, and also Mel Webster as the famous Singing Bow. Hearing how important their quarry was, the younger Seneca looked even more confused, for they had been told by Davies to expect ordinary Whig traders. The Indians glanced uncomfortably around at Manoth and McAllister, who stood near each other on the landing.

Before Sutherland's bateau could come against the dock, McAllister waved his cane and shouted, "Ye're not welcome here, Sutherland, so turn around and head back upstream to yer German friends! I'm saying this to ye only out of common blood, man! Ye're a Scot, and so am I, and that's why I warn ye dinna come ashore! If ye do, I canna be responsible for the consequences!"

Sutherland said with a grin, "Good-day to you, Mr. McAllister. How, noble Manoth, scourge of his enemies, pretender to the war chieftainship of the Seneca and of all the People of the Longhouse, right hand of King George the Third, captain of the loyal Indians, rightful heir of the title 'Great Oyster Shell,' who protects the Six Nations in war against their enemies—"

As he climbed from his bateau, Sutherland went on with this exaggerated but warmhearted greeting to the Seneca until Manoth's foul expression changed to one of suspicious contempt. He enjoyed well enough being addressed in a manner he considered befitting his rank in the warrior class, but he never before heard any greeting so complimentary. The other Senecas became more restless.

Hickory joined Sutherland, who went on with his speech as she translated for the benefit of all the Indians. But soon they were distracted from watching their leader by the remarkable industry of Sutherland's boatmen, who were dragging craft ashore, quickly setting up plank tables as though for a trade session, and unpacking all sorts of gear. The Senecas marveled at the sight of new mirrors, gleaming knives, trade blankets of pure white and brilliant scarlet, women's yarn stockings and frilled blouses in colors that would appeal to any Indian wife, mother, or fiancée. There was even a case of men's ruffled shirts being opened by a humming boatman who laughed and joked with his friends as though these Indians were laden with pelts to trade, not weapons.

Not all Sutherland's men were as casual and cool as this one, however. Those who had dealt with dangerous Indians before knew their only hope lay in confidence, bravado, and generosity. Others who were not traders, such as Bill Poole, were tense, extremely anxious, watching for some hint that Manoth's men would treacherously strike.

Poole sweated as he helped overturn a flatboat and lay it in the sunshine. He looked out of the corner of his eye and clenched his fists unconsciously as a young warrior nearby toyed with a scalping knife. A warning glance from Mel Webster steadied his hot temper.

Poole whispered to Mel, "This ain't my style, friend! If it were up to me I'd lay into these red devils and take my chances afore they jump us."

"It's not up to you," Mel said, tuning his fiddle, maintaining a cheerful appearance, and starting up another tune, this one a hornpipe. "Give us a dance, Bill! Come on, they'll think it's a war dance, and that'll spook 'em!"

Poole could not help but chuckle. He glanced about the clearing, saw Sutherland deep in conversation with the grumpy McAllister, and caught Manoth's dark eyes staring right at him. In the trees, other Indians were shifting uneasily, guns at the ready, waiting for some signal from their leader. These Indians, also, were fascinated by all that was being unloaded from bales of trade goods and boxes of clothes.

Mel again called for a hornpipe, and with a sudden whoop, Poole threw aside his wool cap and began jigging in time, winning the applause of friends and earning the rapt attention of the Senecas.

Sutherland just then was answering McAllister's demand to know what was going on. "A trade fair, of course! We heard that two thousand of Johnson's people and Indian companions are descending on your homestead, and we mean to be here when they come! A Scot knows when to make a penny, eh, McAllister? You'll be paid a fair commission, of course. Now, we'll start with these Senecas! Hey, Manoth, look here, you're in luck!"

With Hickory translating loudly enough for all the Indians to hear, Sutherland said it was Frontier Company policy to lavish the first-comers to a trade fair with gifts in order to stimulate further trade later on and to convince later arrivals of his firm's good faith and openhandedness. Though Manoth hardly believed Sutherland, the other Indians, especially the young ones, elbowed one another, eyes greedily fixed on the sparkling goods being displayed.

Sutherland called out, "And as we begin our acquaintance, friends, we'll have a toast to King George!" He beckoned for the wooden tub of liquor to be placed in the center of the clearing, where a small council fire had ceremoniously been built and lit. When Sutherland brought forth the alcohol, McAllister went into a rage.

"That's against the law, Sutherland!" He stamped toward the tub, which had a ladle and ample mugs around it. "Ye'll be arrested for serving them liquor, for debauching redskins!"

"Dinna trouble yourself, laddie!" Sutherland proclaimed gently. "It's only a dram or two apiece, so your hoose winna be burnt doon by drunken Indians! And look here, I've a wee drop for ourselves!"

Sutherland slipped a flask of the finest Scotch whiskey into the startled miller's hands. McAllister hesitated, glancing over his shoulder to where his curious, worried wife was still standing in the doorway.

"Aye, well noo . . ." the man said, absently, turning away from his woman and uncorking the bottle; he took a sniff, his nose twitched, and his eyes widened. "Man . . . that's the real thing! I havena passed a drop of this over my lips in—"

Then, with supreme inner fortitude, he shoved the whiskey back to Sutherland, declaring, "No, no! Ye'll no bribe me, Sutherland! I'll no do business with a man who harbors deserters, or who abuses king's officers in times as these!"

Sutherland motioned toward his boats. "There's not a deserter in sight, McAllister; see for yourself."

The miller grudgingly looked at the men with Sutherland. He did not recognize Corporal Duff sitting in a blanket near the boats, nor any others who had fled Stanwix, because they all wore boatmen's stocking caps, buckskins, and scarlet *voyageur* waist sashes. By now, Sutherland's men had skillfully turned the grassy ground between the river and the King's Road into an enticing exhibit of fine trade goods and expensive foods—bear meat, raisins, olives, and cakes—all surrounding the council fire and the tub of liquor. Combined with Mel's music, the sight of so much wealth and bounty was too much for the Senecas to resist. Even McAllister's wife had moved out of the cottage, awed, the little ones tugging her apron as she gave in to her curiosity. There had been no traders or tinkers this way since before winter, and she was drawn irresistibly toward the table where bolts of French cloth and kerchiefs from Quebec had been laid.

Sutherland saw the woman come, and he sniffed the air, saying, "Is that real Scots porridge? Aye! That's a dream to me, Mrs. McAllister! It's been more than a month since I've enjoyed a bowl of real porridge!" He removed his hat in her presence, and she blushed a bit, unsure whether to be kind or cold. Sutherland's good manners and compliments won her over, however, and when he offered to trade a pretty silk kerchief for a serving of her oats, she giggled.

"Those Injuns won't eat it, Mr. Sutherland, so you might as well have it all. But there's no need to trade—"

"I insist! My friend's wife, Hickory, will be happy to help you choose one for yourself, another for your wee daughter, and perhaps a pocket knife for the laddie."

Mrs. McAllister was excited and paid no attention to her husband's weak attempt at blustering. Indeed, the entire scene had changed from one of serious confrontation to a gathering of amicable trading and dancing. Bill Poole had shaken off his dread of attack and was jigging enthusiastically with a Seneca who had just received a pound of vermilion for ceremonial paint. The Indian held the jar above his head as he howled and hopped about. The only ones not in the party spirit were McAllister, puzzled and yet taken with Sutherland's charm, and big Manoth, who was silently contemplating how to reassemble his capering men into some semblance of fighting order without losing face.

As Hickory departed to help Mrs. McAllister choose her gift, Sutherland turned to using sign language with the Seneca. Though McAllister knew Seneca well enough, he had no understanding of signs and could not object when Sutherland suggested to Manoth that the whites and Indians toast in the name of the king. McAllister peered sulkily at Manoth, who was eyeing the liquor and wetting his lips. Then he saw Sutherland finish his hand signs, apparently reaching some agreement with the Indian.

McAllister protested, "Sutherland, I don't know what ye're after, but I warn ye this last time: Guy Johnson means business! He's coming upriver after ye, and if he catches ye serving that drink to these savages, he'll—"

Sutherland neatly slipped the whiskey back into the man's hands. McAllister sighed. He accepted the flask with a curt thanks, but insisted Sutherland would never persuade him to rent the carts that were kept in the shed near the mill.

"Ye'll no cross yon hill and pass the falls by my draft animals or cartage!"

Sutherland excused himself to have some porridge, which he ladled out generously. One by one, or in pairs, his men, who had not eaten that night, did the same. They might not have a chance to eat for many hours to come. Hickory, according to plan, went into the cottage with Mrs. McAllister and the children, carrying a few more items of trade to keep the woman busy. As soon as his wife closed the front door, McAllister took the opportunity to sample Sutherland's whiskey.

"Best I've ever tasted!" he said to himself, taking a breath. Then to make sure he was correct, he tried it again.

In the meantime, Indians were climbing down from trees, materializing from behind bushes, and coming up from where they had hidden down by the river's edge. The clearing was soon a swarming crowd of more than fifty men carrying muskets, hatchets, trade goods, or dancing to Mel's jig. Every Indian who came in eyed the liquor, then glanced questioningly at Manoth, who towered moodily above them all. But he said nothing, going on staring at the ground, perplexed.

The Oneida, Joe Onayote, was stirring the concoction in the tub, chuckling and humming to himself as other Indians drew near to watch. Whatever it was smelled powerfully good to him, though his tribe had sworn to their missionary they would not drink firewater. For several years he had been more or less faithful to this promise—at least on the Sabbath day—but his spirits were so high at this moment and everyone was becoming so jolly that he decided it was best to make certain these Senecas would think Donoway's potent brew tasty enough. After all, this risky plan would not work if the warriors refused to drink.

Joe looked up, seeing Sutherland again approach Manoth to converse in sign language. The Oneida made sure Hickory was in the cottage and could not scold him for imbibing against his people's rules. Anyway, he would not taste very much. He tried some, and his eyes closed and opened. Smacking his lips noisily, he grunted an approval that made Senecas nearby applaud and jostle closer to the tub.

By now, Angus McAllister was sitting in a shed on one of his wagons, sampling several times more the whiskey Sutherland had given him. He was feeling unusually sleepy, but otherwise was contented enough. After all, it was a bright, sunny morning, and it had been far too long since there had been so much company and such good music here. He drank once more, surprised that he was so vulnerable to the old local water. Too many years in America, he presumed. He almost lay back in the wagon but resisted the urge. Instead, he closed his eyes, just for a moment, and listened to the droning sound of men's voices, to the cheerful violin, and to the rushing, rushing of water thundering through the gorge, that constant, soothing sound of his home in the valley.

Somewhere in a foggy corner of his mind, he heard Sutherland shout a toast to King George. McAllister muttered to himself, "Hear, hear!"—a little later than the host of men who said it in unison. He should have taken a drop, as was fitting, but for some reason could not get the flask up. Then he realized he was lying back on the cart, more or less aware of the tranquil blue sky and white clouds drifting slowly, peacefully, by. Sutherland was offering another toast, this time to the memory of Sir William Johnson, and the Indians howled their approval. McAllister knew then that this whiskey was something far more than the old local water, knew, too late, that the Indians were also toasting with . . . with . . .

He tried to sit up. Even Manoth himself was grumbling a toast now—and to McAllister's dismay, it was to Owen Sutherland!

"Donoway! Bearer . . . of gifts! Friend of the Injun . . ." Manoth's voice was far, far away, but even the drowsy McAllister knew it was too thick, too slow, too . . . The miller passed out.

Moments later, Indian after Indian found a place to sit or lie, to contemplate happily his new gifts, to think of how pretty his wife or child would be in a shirt or ribbon he had been given by the famous Donoway. Off near the river's edge a yawning warrior was thumping languidly on a handsome brass kettle that would replace the tin one his wife now used. Nearby, his cousin plucked clumsily at a Jew's harp, rattling his teeth but not feeling it. Another Seneca was there, slumbering in the grass, a happy look on his face.

Soon only Manoth still stood, though his black eyes were glassy, fixed on the far side of the river, where the cliff rose gray and steep, sunk in the shadows of early morning. Sutherland was near him, tense and ready, for if Manoth noticed the condition of his men, he might have a few moments of violence left before the laudanum took effect. He was big, and it required more than the usual dose to drug him.

As Manoth stared across the river, his grimy hands sluggishly fondling a woman's silver hair comb Sutherland had bestowed on him, the whites quickly went into action. They caught four horses

in the corral next to the cart shed and set to work hauling the two
carts onto the road. There was no time to lose, for Guy Johnson's
force might top the ridge at any moment. Manoth swayed forward.
Sutherland readied to catch him, and Bill Poole stood waiting on
the other side.

Hefting an Iroquois war club he had taken for a souvenir, Poole
asked, "Can't I help things along a bit, Owen? One tap . . ."

Sutherland said, "No. Nobody gets hurt—"

The door of the cottage was suddenly flung open with a bang
and out rushed Mrs. McAllister, shrieking her husband's name,
hands clutching her face. She was wild with fear to see all the
Indians strewn about, and only the absence of blood kept her sane.
Hickory grabbed her by the shoulders, trying to calm her down
and saying it was only a sleeping potion; but the woman ranted,
tearing the new silk kerchief from her shoulders and dashing to
her husband, who was being carefully lifted from a cart.

Manoth half turned at that, regaining some of his senses. He,
too, realized what had happened. He growled like a mad dog and
began to shake violently, lifting his great arms with the comb still
in one hand. Poole and Sutherland were trying to hush Mrs.
McAllister, who was being held back from pummeling the men
carrying her husband, when suddenly Manoth threw himself across
the clearing. Three mighty strides, and the Seneca was upon Sutherland, but the Scotsman sidestepped, and the drugged Manoth
kept reeling forward, unable to stop until he slammed face first
against the edge of the turning water wheel. He received a wicked
blow on the chin that sent him stumbling backward until he fell,
unconscious but otherwise unhurt.

The screaming woman was borne back into her home. After
instructing his men to get the boats across the hill quickly, Sutherland went into the cottage, which was clean and prettily decorated, with new plaster walls, spring flowers, some framed
needlework, and a couple of pieces of Albany-made furniture. It
was a good house, and for an instant he thought of Valenya. The
two children were in terror as they clutched their mother's neck,
all of them huddled on the double bed against the southern window.
Hickory was there but was more upset than helpful, for the Scots-
woman's distress saddened her.

This was difficult for Sutherland, and it pained him. The children called up visions of Benjamin and Susannah. He approached
the trembling, weeping woman, and bent over, handing her a small
pouch of silver coins.

"For the rental of your wagons, ma'am," he said gently. "We've done no lasting hurt to anyone—"

But she slapped the pouch to the floor, then glared so hatefully at Sutherland that he straightened up, feeling profound sorrow. He should have expected this, but it was a bad moment for him.

Mrs. McAllister said with a hissing voice, "You and your kind *are* doing our country a lasting hurt! Loyal folk won't stand for your kind tearing our country apart! We'll fight you to the death! And we'll beat you!" Her face was streaked with tears, the sunshine glinting on them as she rubbed her forearm over one cheek.

"None of us wants war, Mrs. McAllister," Sutherland said slowly. "It needn't come upon us if we can compromise, if we can reason. It's time to bring in a new order in America, a new day."

She covered her ears, and closed her eyes, the children whimpering, both gaping at Sutherland. "No! I will not hear ungodly treason spoken in my own house! Begone, you devil! Take what you want from us! But begone from the sight of honest folk!"

Then her unconscious husband was carried in, and with a cry she rushed to his side as he was laid on the bed. The frantic children joined her in trying to awaken their father, and Sutherland motioned for his people to depart. Just before he closed the door, he took a long look at this sad sight. How easily bitter enemies were made. Why was it that good people such as the McAllisters and those on his own side could not come to terms without fighting?

He closed the door and paused to see his men lugging the unconscious Senecas into the barn, laying them in rows on the hay. His gifts were left at their sides, but these would do little to mollify their fury when they awoke. A cart drawn by two horses, carrying the first flatboat and a sleeping Joe Onayote, thundered past and on up the road. Sutherland watched, as in a dream, knowing full well that this was the prelude to war.

Working fast and with the knowledge that Guy Johnson's party might appear down the road at any time, Sutherland's men transported the boats and furs around the falls within two hours. In that time, the drugged Indians would remain unconscious, as would McAllister, but not much longer. Sutherland wanted to be well on his way before the Indians pursued.

The river widened into flat, wooded country opened up by fields and orchards. His weary men pressed on, keeping to the right side of the river whenever possible, and soon they came in sight of a large group of people coming up the King's Road on the opposite bank. There were four or five hundred, mostly whites, but Hickory recognized some Mohawks among them. Driving cattle and horses, pigs, goats, and sheep, these were Johnson's Tories. Because they feared growing Whig power in Albany, they were abandoning their homes, taking what they could in scores of wagons crowded with young children, furniture, household goods, and crates of clucking chickens.

At the sight of Sutherland's convoy, two men on horseback rode ahead of the train of people and came close to the water to stare. Sutherland immediately recognized Lieutenant Davies in his scarlet tunic, and the Indian Superintendent Guy Johnson in a rich frock coat that told of wealth and influence. To these men came another man on foot. This was a tall, regal Mohawk, who glared at the Scotsman's boats and spoke to Johnson as though making plans. Davies stood up in his stirrups, obviously anxious to do something to stop Sutherland from getting downriver. But Johnson seemed placid, ignoring both subordinates, for they had no boats, and they were pressed to keep moving before Albany rebels came to arrest Johnson. This was as Sutherland had hoped. He knew that if he got his men around the falls and back into the river, as they now were, Johnson would not be able to stop them. As Sutherland watched these three, he realized the Indian was none other than Joseph Brant, a noted leader of the Mohawk, and a close friend of Peter Defries's. But many friendships were dying these days, and the well-educated Brant was Johnson's private secretary, putting him on the wrong side for Defries. Sutherland heard Johnson shout, "I'd hoped to meet you again, Mr. Sutherland. Will you not come ashore and talk?"

Cupping his hands, Sutherland yelled, "Meet me in Albany, Mr. Johnson; I've an appointment there!"

Johnson paused a moment before replying, "I've an appointment there myself, Mr. Sutherland! Be sure I'll keep it before long, and if you're there as a rebel, I'll make certain to find you!"

Sutherland's men rowed hard, pulling away from Johnson, who, with his dismal fugitives, was soon left far behind. The bateau convoy was through the worst, because Johnson and Brant must hurry on upriver for the council with the Iroquois. No doubt the Indians would join him, and if Johnson had it in his power, he would come back to the valley of the Mohawk with an army of regulars and Indians to wipe out rebel Whigs, and his goal would be Albany itself. Sutherland hoped Congress had the strength

to stop him. If not, then the Hudson River and the waterway to
Canada would become a route of invasion. New England would
be sliced away from the rest of the colonies, and the uprising
doomed to failure.

It took a week for Sutherland to pass the rest of the Mohawk
Valley, but there was no more danger of loyalist attack. After
portaging his bateaux and canoes around the spectacular Great
Falls of the Mohawk at Cohoes, he put his convoy back in the
water, floating out of the Mohawk, past Van Schaik's Island, and
down the Hudson River.

North of Albany, the country was well wooded, with prosperous
farms on both sides of the river. The left bank became much higher
than the right, which was swampy and overgrown, and it was on
the road running along the left bank that considerable military
activity could be seen. Rebel militia companies were marching
northward, probably to garrison Ticonderoga, which Sutherland
had heard from passersby had been taken by New Englanders.
Beside the troops military transport wagons lumbered along, drawn
by oxen, making only a fraction of the time of the hurrying soldiers.

The river was also busy with traffic—canoes, barges, whaleboats, and small ships plied back and forth, some laden with troops.
Whenever Sutherland passed craft transporting men he called out
questions to sailors and soldiers, learning who they were. Though
few rebels had real uniforms, he soon came to recognize those
that did: Detachments of Yorkers were in buff coats faced with
green, Connecticut militia wore blue and red facings, and a company of smart New Haven troops appeared very much like British
regulars in scarlet coats, buff facings, and white smallclothes.

It was apparent that the majority of the rebels had agreed to
wear similar rough flax hunting shirts, dyed blue or brown to
match fellow troopers. In both the uniformed and less formal
regiments, officers were designated by cockades on their hats.
Field officers wore red or pink, captains yellow, and subalterns
green. At midday, while sharing the same resting place on shore
with some New Haven men, Sutherland learned that George Washington would soon be in command of the rebels besieging Boston.
The Virginian had immediately regulated the Army of the United
Colonies—or, as some called it, the Eight Months' Army, because
enlistments were generally for no longer than that. Sutherland
recalled meeting Washington at Fort Pitt a few years ago, and
though he knew that gentleman's military record was spotty, he

could well imagine him a forceful, dynamic leader of raw troops.

By contrast with the tense, hushed atmosphere of the Mohawk Valley, the country around Albany was aswarm with proud and cocky rebels. Well-fed and confident, they sang the war songs of their fathers, mostly British military airs with new words adapted to them. Sutherland heard the new rebel version of "Yankee Doodle," which formerly had been despised by American militia because Redcoats had sung it to deride them. Mel, in particular, took delight in this new version because he had always liked the melody but had felt it was wrong to play it on his tin whistle whenever an American was at hand.

The New Haven men sang the cheerful words about General Washington riding through the vast rebel camp outside Boston, and Mel picked it out on his whistle as he leaned back against a tree, Hickory sleeping on his shoulder. Watching soldiers pass by on the river road, Sutherland could well believe the song was accurate when it told of rebels in numbers "as thick as hasty pudding." It was a new day in America, the beginning of a movement of tremendous strength, one which even the might of the British Empire would be hard put to defeat.

Yet Sutherland felt a nagging worry for the cause, because these inexperienced soldiers were a long way from being a dependable fighting force. As he and his boatmen sat with the Connecticut troops, he watched a party of Yorkers come strutting along, looking like farm boys out for a Sunday jaunt or a turkey shoot. Sutherland had been a professional soldier, had fought the French on the Continent, had tasted blood and powder and fear, and had seen friends die at his shoulder. If not for fine junior officers and gritty noncoms, the British Army could not have built the Empire—but how few of these robust American fellows understood the meaning of discipline or respect for officers?

They came swinging past, laughing and chattering in the ranks, walking with muskets casually over their shoulders or carried in the crook of their arm. Militia officers in particular gave Sutherland little confidence, for they were elected by their troops, who were friends and neighbors. Striding alongside men in the ranks, these officers talked and joked with a familiarity that British regulars would have thought absurd.

Could they command under fire? That soon would be seen. Sutherland knew these men were brave and had the makings of good soldiers, but would Britain allow Washington the time needed to whip them into shape? And what would these rebels fight with?

Had Peter Defries succeeded in buying munitions and arms in
Europe? Feeling restless to push on, Sutherland hoped to find out
the answer to this last question when he went to the Defries residence in Albany. No matter how confident and brave these volunteers were, they would be useless without supplies and equipment,
which the British Army had in great quantity.

Even with such fears, Sutherland liked the looks of these men
as they marched past, singing, some shouting good-natured insults
at the Connecticut men, who gave as well as they took. They
would fight when it came to it, but fighting was only a small part
of making war. The rest was unpleasant drudgery, boring en-
campments, sentry duty, hunger, disease, cold, loneliness, worry
about family, and gnawing fear of a bullet from an unseen enemy.
To master these things required discipline, and discipline came
only from good officers.

Sutherland knocked the dottle from his pipe as more soldiers
tramped by, and he noticed the one thing they all had in common:
the three-cornered hat. Rather than allowing the brim to lie flat or
shaping it into only two cocks, they wore their hats this way to
achieve some semblance of uniformity. Other than this, however,
the rebels were little more than an organized mob, and not very
organized at that. Yet there was an easygoing kinship in the air,
shared by men from Massachusetts, New York, Rhode Island, and
Connecticut. This was unusual, because colonials were known for
bitter feuding and mutual distrust. These troops of many different
colonies seemed to have put aside their differences temporarily,
thanks to the triumph of taking Ticonderoga, known as the Gi-
braltar of America.

Sutherland learned more about the fort's capture from the resting New Haven troops, who were headed there. One cried out,
"Ti is commanded by our own Colonel Benedict Arnold!" Fort
Ticonderoga, up on Lake Champlain, had been taken by Massachusetts militia and rough backwoodsmen from the Green Mountains of the Hampshire Grants. Led by Arnold, a New Haven
druggist and merchant seaman, and by a Green Mountain Boy
named Ethan Allen, these country folk had captured the garrison's
few dozen regulars in their beds, without firing a shot. This was
amazing to Sutherland, because the name Ticonderoga meant death
and slaughter to Scottish Highlanders, who had been cut to pieces
nearly twenty years earlier while attacking the fort, which belonged
to the French. Sutherland's former regiment, the Black Watch,
had been decimated in reckless assaults upon the stout defenses,

and the British Army had withdrawn in defeat. He had been out of the army several years by the time his regiment was nearly wiped out at Ti, as the fort was called, and now he pondered whether he would have been imprudent enough to attempt such a brutally insane frontal attack.

Taking Ticonderoga was excellent strategy on the part of the rebels, because it blocked the main corridor of invasion between Canada and the colonies. Though the fort was in a state of disrepair, reconstruction would make it a key staging point for offensives and an essential rallying place for defense.

The Connecticut soldier telling about the rebels' remarkable success was a sturdy barrel-maker of about forty, clean-shaven and well dressed in a brown hunting shirt and soft breeches. He knew Bill Poole, also a New Haven man, and together they roared with laughter over the description of a British officer trying to shout down armed, unruly rebels as he stood at his door without breeches. These Britishers had been easy to capture, even though there had been considerable dissension in the rebel ranks.

The barrel-maker became serious. "Colonel Arnold had some real trouble with them ignorant Green Mountain Boys under that fella Allen. They wanted the fort for themselves and wouldn't listen to Arnold's order no way!"

He said Benedict Arnold had prevented pillaging of the belongings of the soldiers and their families, and as a result there had been dangerous altercations between him and the men from the mountains.

Chewing tobacco and spitting into the river, the Connecticut man said with some annoyance, "One drunk Bennington boy put a loaded musket against Arnold's chest and told him he had to give over the command and all honors to Allen."

Poole's face took on a look of anger, and he said, "If I know Arnold, he spat in the swine's eye!"

"Almost," another said, getting up as their officer asked the company if they were ready to embark in their whaleboats. "It were touchy, indeed, and that's why we're all itching to join up with the colonel to see such an insult don't happen again—not without a few Connecticut boys at Arnold's back."

Ethan Allen's Green Mountain Boys stood in sharp opposition to New York, which claimed their lands and considered them outlaws who had no right to settle in the Hampshire Grants. Allen's men had joined the Ticonderoga expedition mainly to consolidate their claims to the region east of Lake Champlain. Indeed, the reasons Americans were in arms differed greatly, and not everyone was crying for liberty and representation.

The Connecticut soldier's friends joined in boasting about rebel successes. First Lexington and Concord, now Ticonderoga, and the whole British Army save for two regiments in Canada was bottled up in Boston. Even Sutherland could not help but be impressed by the strokes against Parliament's soldiers.

Would the rebels try to take Detroit? The very thought of carrying the rebellion to Detroit and fighting men he knew well was totally strange and unreal to Sutherland. Yet it could happen. Before it did, however, he must get his loved ones to safety. Also, he must soon decide how he could best support the uprising—as soldier or merchant.

Parting with the New Haven soldiers, Sutherland's group prepared for entry into Albany. They washed and shaved, changed into clean clothes and their best city shoes, and were ready to be paid off. For a few carefree days most would celebrate their journey's end roistering and drinking, but not Bill Poole, who was joyful at the prospect of going home to his family. Then he would join Connecticut troops to fight the British Army.

Save for the somber Sutherland, the convoy was in high spirits as it went downriver to Albany. To his rebel boatmen the world had not seemed so fine a place in much too long a time. Perhaps it was because the British Army was being humbled by provincial militia, who had been unfairly reviled and scorned by Redcoats for more than a century.

The flush of victory was on every rebel face, and before long Parliament would learn that Americans who took up arms meant to fight, and fight until they won.

chapter 17

TURNCOAT

Bradford Cullen's company offices had a perfect view across the Charles River toward Breed's Hill, where hundreds of rebels had dug in during the night. The merchant turned his chair to the window, and comfortably prepared to watch the British Army attack the enemy, who had so insolently fortified the green hillside above Charlestown with trenches and a small earthworks.

Boats full of Redcoats were rowing across the Charles, landing men on the beach to assemble for the attack. In the harbor several warships were hammering the rebel positions, naval guns booming in steady, loud claps that shook Cullen's building, rattling the glass.

Cullen thought the rebel officers very stupid, because a few hundred soldiers landing behind them on the narrow neck of land connecting their hill to the mainland would cut them off. Several hundred yards across the shimmering water, the Charlestown peninsula belonged to the rebels, and that annoyed Cullen, for the army should have built its own defenses there after the retreat from Lexington. Yet the generals had been complacent, and now the enemy had moved in force onto Breed's and Bunker's hills. Those knolls above the pretty village of Charlestown, where Cullen had a magnificent residence, commanded the Mystic and Charles rivers as well as much of the harbor, so the rebels had to be dislodged.

Cullen and his family had moved from Charlestown into Boston soon after the April fighting began. Knowing that in Charlestown they might be vulnerable to rebel raids, and since the British and loyalists were crammed into Boston, the city was the safest place for him to live.

This room was large, with a high ceiling and several windows, but since it faced north, the light was weak, even on this sunny June day. Painted all white on ceiling and walls, Cullen's place

of business was a testimony to his Puritan taste for simplicity—
costly simplicity though it might be. The woodwork and moldings
were thin and plain, without the usual ornaments so popular with
other wealthy men of the day. The rug was expensive, but also
unadorned, colored in shades of brown and deep red. Even the
desk top was bare, except for a brandy decanter, a silver tray
holding crystal glasses, and quill, ink, and paper.

In contrast, Cullen's delight in fine furniture was apparent in
the exquisitely carved and velvet-upholstered Chippendale chairs
and matching settee placed around the carpet before the massive
mahogany desk, where he sat. It was said that wealthy Puritans
had a special vanity for excellent furniture, and in this otherwise
dreary room, the chairs were like brilliants in a dull setting.

The only real decoration was a large portrait of King George
III on the wall opposite Cullen's window. It was a copy of one
His Majesty had commissioned after the coronation in 1760, and
showed a youthful king in striking orange-gold garb and flowing
ermine robes. He seemed farseeing and impressively potent as a
young, benevolent ruler of the world's greatest empire. Now his
generals were bent on holding that empire together, and today's
attack across the river would begin that undertaking.

Beneath Cullen's private office was the family residence. Below this were offices for Cullen and Company's public business.
Staring attentively through a telescope, Cullen was at the top of
one of the tallest buildings in Boston, and nowhere in the city was
there a better view of the unfolding drama.

Down at the river wharves, more British troops were crowding
into boats to row across the river. Between thunderous cannon
salvos could be heard the steady tramp of marching feet on cobblestone, the brave whistle of fifes, the roll of drums, and shouts
of excited officers. The men were hungering to take revenge for
the slaughter of their friends during the shameful retreat from
Concord and Lexington two months earlier. It would be hot work
on such a sweltering, humid day, but the bayonet would swiftly
and decisively end matters.

Though Cullen was understandably concerned about his mansion over in Charlestown, he doubted the battle would last very
long. The British troops had those scoundrels by the throat now
that the amateurish rebel officers had picked the wrong place to
fortify. The Whigs were as good as dead or in prison now, and
Breed's Hill would be their last stand against Parliament's army.
Once the radical New Englanders were whipped, other rebels would

be cowed into surrendering or taking flight. A number of leading rebel prisoners would be strung up as fitting examples to anyone else who considered taking arms against the government.

Cullen laughed to himself and poured another glass of brandy. Among the loyal American merchants in Boston he was the most influential, and a rebel defeat today would put him in an enviable position. The British must choose faithful Americans to rule, and perhaps he would be offered the governorship of his native Massachusetts. But he would refuse that post, for what he craved was the northwest. How he longed to rule that vast and bountiful territory, from Canada to Ohio, from western New York to the Mississippi.

Brandy and visions of triumph lit Cullen's mind. He burned with a smoldering passion to dominate the endless land beyond the frontiers. And as governor reigning in Montreal, he would lord over Owen Sutherland in particular, counter his every effort in the rich fur trade, and ultimately destroy him. Then, remembering a letter he recently received from England, Cullen realized Sutherland might not be alive to oppose him. The evidence uncovered by Hugh Meeks accusing the Frontier Company of smuggling munitions condemned Sutherland as a traitor to the king. After a British victory today, with the army soon in firm control of the colonies, Sutherland would be arrested for high treason. The Scotsman would kick away his life from a noose, and no one would prevent Bradford Cullen from grasping complete control of the entire northwest.

Then he winced as a British cannon was fired nearby. Already the rebels had suffered a tremendous pounding from the warships in Boston harbor and from a battery of heavy guns that stood on Copp's Hill, just a hundred yards to the right of Cullen's quarters on Lynn Street, near Hudson's Point. The merchant was surprised the Americans had kept on digging in, despite the bombardment, but their boldness would mean nothing when they saw two thousand regulars come at them.

As he watched the soldiers below cheered on by thousands of loyalists lining the wharves and streets and packed onto roofs of buildings, Cullen was sure the rebellion's end was at hand. He had chosen the correct side after all, though there had been moments when he had not been so sure. The months of Whig swaggering and Tory cringing were at an end, for no half-armed rabble could withstand trained Redcoats whose blood was up.

Soldiers in barges wore flowers on their heavy packs, tokens from families and sweethearts who made up a considerable part of Boston's besieged population, for most men had been stationed here for seven years. A large number were Irishmen who had joined regiments to escape poverty, and many were native Americans recruited to fill out companies to full strength. All were eager to engage and punish the rebels. Cullen's spies out in the countryside had told him the rebels were poorly supplied with powder and ball, and their gunners manning the couple of cannon near Charlestown had little or no experience. It would be a walkover.

There came a knock at the door, which was immediately thrown open by a skinny old woman, bustling and severe, who hastened into the room. Helen Cullen wore her hair tied in a bun, without a wig, and had on a dark gown that touched the floor. Shunning jewelry and makeup, she held firmly to her own Puritan heritage of strict, harsh modesty. Though she was the wife of a corrupt and ruthless man—one who mouthed regular platitudes to his Puritan heritage, however—she maintained the family's public image of piety and propriety. Well over sixty, Mrs. Cullen was a force among Tory women of Boston and stood firmly behind her husband's professed loyalty to the crown.

As she came in, Helen Cullen was excited to see the soldiers preparing and, though she did not like to see her husband drink, ignored it this time and took a chair nearby.

"Now we'll see those rascals get what they deserve," she croaked, taking the spyglass from her husband and looking out the window, where the heavy velvet curtains were tied back out of the way.

A tremendous blast from the cannon battery on Copp's Hill rattled their room, cracking a window pane. "We'll report this to General Howe, or Clinton, or that Burgoyne! They'll pay us for whatever they damage!" Mrs. Cullen squawked in anger, referring to the three generals who had arrived that spring to assist Gage.

"It can't be helped, Mrs. Cullen," her husband said languidly, smacking his lips as he sipped the drink.

They heard someone else at the door and turned to greet their middle-aged daughter, Linda, who came staggering into the room, hands on her ears as the cannon blasted away once again.

"Papa, Papa! Can't you please tell them to move those guns away?" She was a melancholy woman, with thick features, dark eyes and hair. A baleful expression of self-pity and a stocky body made her all the more unattractive. Even her voice was unpleasantly pitched. "Oh, it's dreadful, this din! I feel positively ill!"

Linda began fanning herself furiously as she collapsed into a chair beside her father, who ignored her and squinted out at the masses of scarlet rowing across to the beaches of the Charlestown peninsula.

"Don't fret, girl," Mrs. Cullen said gently, using her own fan. "It'll be over soon. I just hope none of your officer friends will be injured today."

In the year they had been back from Montreal, the Cullens had done their best to marry Linda to a British officer or a leading Tory, but without success. Cullen's immense wealth and power had persuaded several to examine the wares, but Linda's eternal complaining, frequent sickness, and desperate reliance on her mother kept even the most ambitious suitors at a distance. Unlike the aged Helen, who was proud, vengeful, and stoic, Linda was helpless, and more than one male acquaintance thought her simpleminded—though none dared hint such a thing publicly for fear of Cullen's retribution.

"What on earth's taking them so long?" Cullen muttered, his face red from heat and brandy. He mopped his brow, saying, "These dratted guns are jangling my own nerves in this cauldron! Go on, Lord Howe, surround those blasted rebels and be done with it!"

A grating, deep voice at the open door said, "I've been thinkin' just that very thing, Mr. Cullen."

They were startled to see big Hugh Meeks, brazen and grinning, standing in the doorway. He had his hat in hand and wore fine new clothes of gray broadcloth, with a lace ruffle at his massive chin. Linda gasped. She had never met Meeks before and thought him an incredibly lusty figure of a man. She began fanning herself almost frantically, and Meeks noticed her bewilderment.

Bradford Cullen raised a hand to invite his man inside, chortling that he was glad to have the sailor back again. Meeks bowed to the women, the cutlass swaying beneath his coat. He, too, was hot, beads of sweat dotting his face and staining the fine white blouse he wore. Linda watched his every move as a yarded doe might watch a wolf.

Meeks cackled, "At yer service, ladies, Mr. Cullen, sir. It's good to be back. And as I were remarkin', Lord Howe be over there hisself, bound for glory, ye might say!"

Cullen declared, "Ladies, this is the famous Captain Meeks I've spoken so much about. He's done us great service overseas!"

Linda fluttered her eyes, and Meeks bowed again, his strong white teeth flashing as he smiled at her. Helen Cullen took note of this exchange, and her thin mouth turned downward. She gave a haughty but correct greeting to the pirate. Helen knew her impressionable daughter well enough to recognize the familiar signs of infatuation she felt for practically any man who looked at her—and this gross character was looking at Linda as though he would ravish her at the first opportunity.

Linda listened intently as her father introduced Meeks as a man of the seven seas, a brave adventurer who had done the company proud. Though Meeks did not return Linda's wide-eyed gaze, he was clearly aware of it and of Helen Cullen's disapproval. To Meeks, Linda was a direct route to fortune and power through the Cullen family, and his agile mind quickly assessed the woman, who was like a vulnerable galleon becalmed in the Atlantic doldrums.

"Ye do me too much honor, Mr. Cullen, sir," Meeks grinned, bowing again and thinking how to take this prize. Helen Cullen, however, made a formidable guard. Meeks glanced at Linda and knew she was the kind who'd favor anyone bold enough and with stomach enough to take her. Turning, cocking his head, he squinted at Helen Cullen, who was looking uneasily from him to her daughter and back again.

"Dash my buttons, Mrs. Cullen, ma'am, if I ain't blessed to be back in Boston in company with our own dear gracious ladies! At yer service, ma'am!"

It would have been proper for Mrs. Cullen to offer her hand for Meeks to kiss, but she made her opinion of the seaman clear by nodding curtly and looking away. Cullen hardly noticed, for he had taken another glance out the window at the military developments. Nor did he see Linda float her stubby hand toward Meeks, who gallantly took it, held it just a moment longer than was appropriate, and kissed the knuckles. Neither he nor Linda acknowledged Mrs. Cullen's hiss of dismay. Meeks gazed at Linda, who was lost in a kind of rapture that spoke eloquently of her desire for a man, any man.

Turning from the window, Bradford Cullen went on. "At last, Mrs. Cullen, I've found an assistant I can rely on!" He beamed at Meeks, motioning for the man to take a chair, have some brandy, and stay to watch the imminent battle. "Yes, Captain, you've served me well indeed! I've just received word of your clever discovery of Frontier Company smugglers. Our agents in England said no effort will be spared to prevent Sutherland's ship from escaping to America! You've done well, indeed!"

"Aye . . ." Meeks cleared his throat and sat down between Cullen and Linda. "Aye, that's one reason I come to see ye soon's my ship was tied up, Mr. Cullen—"

Another terrific boom of cannon shook the building, and the shock threw poor Linda from her seat. She shrieked and fell clumsily against Meeks, who caught her. Eyes rolling, Linda fanned herself as she pressed against the seaman, who swallowed hard, not sure what to do. His big, gnarled hands pushed Linda awkwardly back to her chair, and Helen Cullen hovered about, keeping her daughter away from him.

Cullen seemed unaware of this little scene, for suddenly he smashed the arm of his chair with a fist and cried, "In the name of Jehovah, what *are* they doing?"

To Cullen's surprise, the soldiers had landed on beaches at the right of Charlestown. Instead of rowing completely around the peninsula on both sides and simply cutting off the rebel troops, who could be starved out in a few days, the regulars seemed strangely to be preparing a frontal attack up the steep slope of Breed's Hill. That was not possible! That was madness!

Out the window they saw British soldiers formed up in long, scarlet ranks, about to assault the rebel earthworks from the beach. This maneuver went against all good military sense, for these three long ranks would be vulnerable to volleys that would cut men down in swaths. Thin British lines stretching bright red upon the green slopes were a brazen, ignorant, and foolish order of battle.

Meeks shook his head and said, "Howe underestimates 'em rebels, I'm thinkin'. It ain't gonna be nice."

Cullen was quivering. "They can't do this. They're fools! They must go around! Around the peninsula! Cut them off from behind, not charge—"

But General William Howe did charge. He led his men up the windblown, grassy slope, bathed in torrid sunshine that glinted off bayonets and brass. His troops wore their full packs and full-dress uniforms as they broke ranks, struggled over fences, and formed up again. Partway up the steep hill they stopped, forming one long stream of scarlet, and fired a volley that rose in fragile white puffs to drift out over the harbor. The guns of the ships and Copp's Hill fell silent to allow the Redcoat infantry to attack.

Up the hill they surged, disciplined and courageous. The breast-works filled with rebels lay still. The Cullens and Hugh Meeks gazed in astonishment at British confidence, but as the soldiers advanced unopposed, it appeared that the rash strategy of the king's generals was actually a clever decision. Cullen began to think the rebels would be so terrified by a tide of massed Redcoats coming at them that they would despair, lose heart, and flee for their lives. The merchant's fear that the generals had blundered melted away with every step the soldiers took, with every heartbeat.

"Yes," he whispered. "Yes, that's it. You'll soon have them! Yes!" The soldiers were moments from the earthworks, and not a shot had been fired at them. Cullen would toast Gage, Howe, Burgoyne, Clinton! They had been right all along! He released his breath in a long, satisfied sigh of relief.

Closer marched the scarlet ranks toward the brown trenches. Linda chattered, "The rebels are afraid to fire because they dread the anger of the troops!"

Helen said, "The rascals must flee now if they expect to get away!"

But Hugh Meeks had another opinion. Downing a stiff drink of brandy, pain on his face, he rasped, "No, b'gad! Them rebels knows what they be doin'." Cullen looked sharply at him as he said again, "They knows, b'gad!"

The merchant spun away to watch, one hand clutching the chair, the other holding the spyglass to his eye. Still nothing. The rebels surely were overawed, as the Redcoats had intended them to be. *They must be!* Again he whispered the soldiers would make it. Only a few more steps. If the rebels had meant to wait with their volley, they had waited too long— Then there came a silent ripple of flame and blue smoke from the rebel works. Cullen caught his breath as he heard the faint crackle of distant musketry. The long scarlet line shivered like a ribbon in the breeze; it wavered, recoiled, and tore to shreds, blowing back down the slope. Scarlet bodies lay all along the hillside.

Cullen howled, smashing his fists against the chair, banging the desk, then hurling a glass against the wall, just missing the portrait of the king. His wife calmed him, speaking carefully. She was the only person on earth who could influence Cullen. If it came to it, she could even govern him, but he did not know it.

Breathless, Helen said, "They'll go up again, you'll see. They'll go! That was just a test of enemy strength."

"Ah, some test," Meeks muttered. "There be hundreds of done-for Redcoats lost in that there test."

Through the spyglass Cullen observed the green swath of meadow cluttered with dead and dying men. The rest were fleeing down to the beach, re-forming in clusters of scarlet and white.

The battle was too far off to hear the cries of wounded or the commands of officers, but the wailing howls from the people on the street below drifted up to the Cullen chamber. The slaughter had been terrible, and friends and relations of soldiers were becoming hysterical, especially because everyone knew the troops surely would go up again.

Cullen shouted, "Go around them, Howe, you blasted martinet! Go around them and take them from behind! In the name of —"

"Husband!" Helen touched his arm. "Take not the name of thy Lord in vain!" Then she saw fire erupt in Charlestown, throwing black, oily smoke into the sky, and she moaned, "Oh, my God! Not my lovely house. . . ." Grabbing the spyglass, Helen gave a low whine as she saw smoke and flames spurt from the windows of their very own residence. She fell back into her chair, whimpering.

Snatching the spyglass from his wife's limp hand, Cullen leaned forward, his belly hanging in folds before him. He cursed and shook the glass, his hand clawing the air. Even he, no military man, saw how the British were indeed preparing another frontal attack, rank on rank as before. He howled that the soldiers were still compelled to wear their enormous packs.

"Fools! How can we put ourselves in the hands of such fools as these generals?"

"How can those men do it?" Linda gasped. "How can they go up again?"

"They're made to follow," Cullen said, and Linda understood that. Neither Cullen nor his dazed wife had noticed the looks passing between Linda and Meeks. As hot as the day was, the fire smoldering between these two was more intense.

The savage repulse of a second disastrous assault distracted Linda's parents, who howled to see a murderous wall of flame and gunsmoke sweep the soldiers away. Swearing and spluttering, Bradford Cullen accused the British commanders of every ignorance and stupidity his tormented brain could rake up. Helen was wailing. She cared little for the men dying and suffering out there, but she knew well the meaning to the loyalist cause of this impending disaster: Rebels would rise in even greater numbers; a civil war would begin in earnest, which the government would eventually lose. That catastrophe would put loyalists like Cullen to flight, and all he possessed in America, including his hopes for governing the northwest, would be lost to him forever. Even the slaughter of the troops would give heart to the rebels, who had already done much to enhance their prestige.

Her thin hands in fists, Helen urged the army on to the attack. Now neither she nor her husband cared how it was done, with skill or blundering courage, but she wanted those rebels driven out, pushed back across the neck onto the mainland, pursued, and ultimately destroyed to the last man.

Hands trembling, Cullen peered through the glass. "The soldiers are throwing their packs aside," he said. "Some of them had been getting in the boats, but they've come back on land. There's hardly any officers left, but my God, they're forming up again! Look, they're not marching in rank this time! They're charging the hill in groups, firing as they go! Look! They're getting up there! See! They're getting up there!"

The first mass of soldiers surged up the slope, staggered under one final rebel volley, and kept on going. The rebel fire was scattered and weak, then nothing at all. Over the brown earthworks the Redcoats went, attacking with the bayonets, determined to kill.

Still the attackers advanced only frontally, however, doing nothing to stop the main rebel force withdrawing rapidly through the back of the earthworks. Cullen saw with disbelief that the British had not sent flanking companies behind the defenses to cut off escape.

"In the name of the Almighty, they're all getting away! They're getting away!" The mass of rebels scattered like ants out of the Breed's Hill redoubt, though maintaining reasonably good order. Joining retreating rebels on Bunker's Hill, which stood behind Breed's, the defenders streamed across the thin neck of land joining the peninsula to the mainland. Cullen threw the spyglass crashing to the floor.

That brave frontal assault had cost a thousand dead and wounded, but the rebel army was escaping unharassed. Although the British had won the battle, it was really a victory for the audacious rebel forces, who had stood up to the finest troops in the world and repelled them twice. Cullen could see the rebels were slowly becoming an army—a strong and brave army willing to stand toe to toe with regulars.

The debacle dismayed and frightened the Cullens. They well knew that the side they supported would never win if it conducted war like this. Meeks, however, was calm, for he had witnessed considerable death and disaster before. Also, he had more bad news that made him chafe to keep it in. He cleared his throat, about to speak, when Cullen interrupted.

"Captain . . ." The merchant's voice was hoarse, unsteady. "Captain Meeks, I want you to find our man Jones in Albany. I'm afraid we'll have to reconsider matters now."

He looked unhappily at Helen Cullen, who got up, hiding her face with the fan as she wept. Helen guessed what her husband intended to do, for Albany was a rebel city. She tugged at Linda, who got up and followed. The woman gave Meeks a lingering glance before she and her mother departed and closed the door.

Lost in thought, Cullen asked absently, "What do you think, Captain? What are our chances for victory over these rebels now?"

"Well, sir," Meeks shifted one foot beside the other. Scratching his cropped gray head and chewing his lower lip, he considered how best to reply. "I reckon our chances'd be a damned sight better if the damned poxy Royal Navy'd cut off Sutherland's damned sloop, sir!"

Cullen's eyes widened and his mouth dropped open, but he did not speak. Uneasily, Meeks maintained composure and went on.

"Ye see, Mr. Cullen, that there Sutherland sloop got through an' brung enough powder and arms to equip an army!" Cullen made no response, but there was anger in his eyes. Meeks struggled on. "An' as ye can tell, 'em British're willin' to make every Yankee shot count, so as ye can see, sir . . ."

Meeks waited for Cullen to reply. He stared out the window, speculating on how best he could save his own skin if things went badly for the loyalists—as surely they would now that the British had proved to be ignorant, overconfident fools when it came to putting down this revolt. In his view was the glassy water, a blue sky stained by smoke rising from Charlestown, and the distant green hillside with its crowds of scarlet blossoms. Meeks, however, saw none of these things. Instead, he envisioned Linda Cullen beckoning him—an image that was not pretty, not even desirable, but without doubt very, very appealing.

Suddenly, Cullen grabbed the shipmaster's sleeve and pulled him forward. With great effort, Cullen said in a fierce though aged voice, "I depend upon you, Captain! Get to Jones in Albany! I'll give you a confidential message for the Whigs there! Jones will know who must receive it, but do not let him fail me—or fail us!"

Cullen was pale, dazed, as he leaned back in the chair. He seemed terribly old, but Meeks knew well the man's force of will and mind were as keen as ever, perhaps more keen than ever before, because he was at bay and dangerous. Meeks deftly poured a brandy and gave it to Cullen, who nervously slurped, sweat pouring from his face. Outside, the streets rang with people lamenting. Women screamed, men shouted oaths against the lunatics who ran the army.

Cullen closed his eyes and began to regain mastery of himself. Meeks fixed that brazen squint on his face, threw out his chest, and exclaimed, "Don't make no nevermind to me, Mr. Cullen! Ye can count on me, sir! Rebel or loyal, I'm with ye!"

The town of Albany, which spread up from the river to the top of a knoll, was far different from what it had been when Sutherland was here last year. Though there were still only three hundred stone houses in the old Dutch style, with steep red roofs and gables facing the street, there were many more people here than before.

In Albany sat the colony's revolutionary Committee of Safety, deciding matters of defiance against Britain and making preparations for war. The Committee of Safety of New York had become the real government of the province—as had most committees like it in other colonies. To this committee's meetings came those who wanted to lead regiments or replace Tory officeholders who had fled. Applicants for political favors, for financial support, for arms, supplies, and guidance came to Albany by the hundreds. They crammed into houses, inns, farms, barns, sheds, and warehouses while they awaited the decision of the committee. There was no room for them all, and some even slept in tents with soldiers they knew.

The most important rebels from hundreds of miles around converged here, along with growing numbers of militiamen from the New England colonies, Pennsylvania, New Jersey, and even faroff Virginia and Maryland. There was rumor of fortifying the Champlain and Mohawk valleys, thus preventing British counterattacks from neutral Canada, which gave no support to the uprising and might serve as an enemy base.

From the moment his convoy drew alongside the docks, Sutherland felt a heady exuberance in the air. The Mohawk Valley had been a place of doubt and fear, conspiracy and suspicion, but the Hudson Valley and Albany were thronged with Congress party supporters expecting victory.

Albany was a gateway to the northwest and in a key position to command the Hudson and Mohawk valleys. American and British forces of the French and Indian wars had massed at Albany, bought goods and equipment here, and thereby enriched the res-

idents, who had often profited from war, and now would again.
Its three thousand residents were generally in favor of Congress,
and the few local Tories, including the city's lord mayor, had
either been arrested or warned to keep quiet.

After paying off his men and seeing Gavin Duff taken to the
large hospital on the hill, Sutherland had the pelts safely stored
in a secure brick building belonging to the Frontier Company. He
went to the empty Defries home, just off the broad cobblestone
central square in the heart of Albany. Using his own key to the
neat, clean brick house, which had a colorful garden, he found it
a welcome haven. With Mel and Hickory, Sutherland would reside
here while trying to find a buyer to take the enormous shipment
of pelts.

Soon after moving in, a letter came from the Defrieses in
Philadelphia, saying they had arrived safely, with "flammable
goods," and Sutherland exulted to know they had succeeded in
their mission. There were oblique references to Jeremy Bently,
but Defries did not say Sutherland's stepson had chosen to stay
behind because of an English love.

Sutherland was more anxious than ever to get down to Philadelphia and see Peter and Mary once more. The nagging, frustrating task of finding someone wealthy enough to take his pelts
immediately became a burden, for none of the merchants he met
were able to offer the thirty thousand pounds sterling. Further,
few were even sure they could find a market overseas, because
British warships might intercept American ships trading illegally,
resulting in confiscation.

During the many trips to merchants in those days in Albany,
Sutherland often observed ambitious young rebel militiamen drilling clumsily, but gamely, wherever there was open ground—
preferably in sight of local girls. That the women in Albany were
mainly Dutch-speaking and knew very little English mattered not
to hearty volunteers, in the full bloom of health. Preening and
sporting military bravado like so many peacocks—uncolorful
though most were—each colony's militia tried to outdo the other,
and there were frequent brawls among them, some serious, some
routine.

On one sultry July afternoon, as Sutherland tramped through
the crowded waterfront on his return from an unsuccessful attempt
to sell his pelts to a merchant from the West Indies, he saw a few
New England militiamen being chased along the narrow street. At
least twenty half-drunk York militia were in hot pursuit, clubs and

fists threatening to pulverize the Yankees for some reason. To Sutherland, the nature of this conflict did not matter. He was furious, upset that there was not better control of the rebel forces. Until its commander, General Philip Schuyler, reached the city from Philadelphia, there was no overall leader in Albany.

Sutherland whipped out his claymore and sprang in front of the mob, whose ringleaders pulled up short at the sight of cold steel. But the numbers were too many, and when Sutherland told them to back off and behave like soldiers, they laughed roughly and began to threaten him, also. The timely arrival of some York and Connecticut officers cooled matters somewhat, but the rowdy militiamen wanted their sport and seemed about to defy their superiors and push on after the New Englanders.

The officers were nervous and inexperienced, but Sutherland stood fast, shouting at the troops, "If you call yourselves supporters of the cause, then obey these officers Congress has put above you! If you won't, we're lost!" He glared at them, these farm boys and carters, workmen and artisans, many of them lads away from home and family for the first time. He knew they would be brave enough when the time came, but as undisciplined as they were, they could not serve the cause, and he told them so.

"If you won't unite and obey officers, you'll be swept aside by a better fighting force than you'll ever hope to be!" They grumbled and complained at that, but his sword kept any from moving against him. "The result will be a bayonet in your gut— those of you who don't take it in the arse as you run! And those who live will be remembered with shame by their children, remembered as traitors to the king, who were strung up on gallows trees! Fighting each other, you're worse than useless as soldiers! United, you can triumph over the mightiest empire the world has known—triumph as Americans!"

A great, deep voice shouted, "Well said, Mr. Sutherland! Well said, indeed!"

Standing on a pile of baled goods nearby was a tall officer in dark blue, wearing white breeches and soft, shining boots. Sutherland recognized General Philip Schuyler from past business they had transacted here in Albany, where the general reigned as one of the leading Dutch noblemen, called patróons. One of the wealthiest men in America, Schuyler was a delegate to Congress, and had been named commander of the rebel northern army because he was admired and respected by York troops, who would make up the bulk of the force.

Fury showed in the general's angular face, which had the likeness of a hawk, with eyes set far apart and a long Roman nose. Schuyler shouted for off-duty soldiers to clear the area immediately. Seeing him and hearing his threats to jail them and drum them out at once, the Yorkers rapidly dispersed. Schuyler stepped down from where he had been standing and came to Sutherland. The general had a regal bearing, well suited to such a critical command. At hand was a staff of three splendidly dressed and mounted officers, who waited while the general shook Sutherland's hand, apologizing for the behavior of York colony's forces.

Schuyler added, "I just reached the city from New York Town, and before that I was in Philadelphia, where I met a mutual friend of ours—Peter Defries."

Sutherland was excited when Schuyler said the fellow would be back in Albany before long. "Peter said you'd be in the city with your pelt harvest, and I meant to seek you out immediately; it's good fortune to have found you, Mr. Sutherland, because I've a rather delicate subject to discuss with you. . . ."

Sutherland waited for Schuyler to choose his words as all around them the raw troops of many colonies gawked and stared.

After a moment, the general sighed, as though at a loss for appropriate words, and said, "I'll get right to the point." His voice was soft, so no one else could hear. "Would you honor me as my dinner guest tomorrow evening? I wish to discuss military affairs with you and ask about an acquaintance of yours." Schuyler looked pained and pursed his lips, saying, "The Boston merchant, Bradford Cullen, has an interesting proposal for the cause—"

Sutherland's eyes hardened, and Schuyler could tell the Scotsman was upset.

"Mr. Sutherland, this is not a subject to discuss in public, but I value your judgment, and it's critical to the cause that we make no mistake in what we do."

Sutherland already guessed what might be happening: Cullen was turning his coat. Governing his mounting anger, he said, "At your service, General Schuyler; but if you're looking for some recommendation of the man, it'll not come from me."

Schuyler nodded and swung up on his huge horse. "That's what I expected, Mr. Sutherland." He saluted by removing his hat and holding it out to the side, military fashion. Sutherland did the same. "Until tomorrow, sir. Then I'll also inform you of how Dr. Franklin looks out every day for your arrival in Philadelphia. Our conversation, Mr. Sutherland, will not be wholly unpleasant!"

The general rode off, his party thundering along the cobblestone street, and Sutherland felt relief that such a reliable, honest man was commander of the northern theater. But much responsibility would rest on Schuyler's shoulders. Sutherland hoped Bradford Cullen's intrigues would not make the patroon's awesome task even more difficult.

A little later, as Sutherland walked back to the Defries house, his mind turned over the many considerations that plagued him. How he wanted to get to Philadelphia and then back to Detroit! But he must sell those furs before he could go. Hardly conscious of where he was, he strode through the crowds with head down, thinking hard. Then, as he opened the white picket garden gate to the house, he had the sensation of being watched. Acting casually, he straightened his wide-brimmed hat and took in the neighborhood, which was full of carts, soldiers, children playing and chasing hoops, and respectable Albany families on daily errands.

It was not the casual glances of these people that had stimulated Sutherland's woodsman senses. He was sure someone had an eye on him—someone who did not want to be seen.

Then he spotted a figure lurking in an alley across the street. It was smallish, furtive, and nervous, somehow familiar to Sutherland. Pausing just a moment to make sure this fellow was indeed spying on him, Sutherland closed the garden gate, then turned and walked briskly for the alley. The figure vanished back between the buildings. Sutherland shouldered through a crowd of startled soldiers and dashed into the alleyway in pursuit. The man went around a corner thirty yards down the narrow alley, and Sutherland flew behind him, whirling along among back sheds, trash bins, and a row of fenced kitchen gardens where tied dogs barked frantically at his appearance.

He stopped, looking around for some sign of his quarry. But there were only blank walls, doors, windows, and noisy dogs. No one suspicious was in sight. Whoever it had been must have taken one of a dozen rear doors visible from where Sutherland stood. This alleyway ran behind houses and shops, and by now the spy could have slipped back onto the main thoroughfare.

Returning to the busy street, Sutherland realized the smuggling that Defries had carried out had marked them all for watching. He wondered uneasily whether Ella and the others at Detroit would be spied upon. And who was it on his trail?

chapter 18

THE ORCHARD

The Sutherland homestead at Valenya was thriving. An apple orchard had been planted that spring a hundred yards behind the big house, and Ella took as much pride and joy in it as in her colorful flower garden surrounding the house. Nowadays there were hired hands to tend the vegetable gardens and the fields of grain, wheat, and oats, but the care of the two hundred young apple trees was a responsibility Ella took as her own.

Ella, Sally, and the children were kept busy watering and mulching the newly planted trees. Set in good, well-drained soil on a west-facing slope, the orchard flourished from the very start. Ella had purchased the saplings from a Frenchman downriver, acquiring several varieties, some good for eating, others for baking and winter storage. It was easy enough to buy cider, vinegar, or apple butter made by French or Indians, so Ella wanted her orchard to be the kind that produced only sweet fruit.

Throughout the summer, she and her family gave themselves over to the care of the orchard, and it was a welcome distraction from missing Owen. Near the orchard Sally had started two colonies of honeybees—white man's flies, as Mawak called them. The hives were set between the orchard and the two-acre garden laid out alongside the apple trees. Sally was so naturally adept at beekeeping that she seldom wore protective netting or gloves when she tended the hives. A new veranda overlooking the straits had been added onto the house. It was not yet painted, but already Ella enjoyed sitting out there in the evening, viewing the broad, beautiful river to her heart's content. Benjamin had learned much while assisting the carpenters who had built it, and for her part Susannah was almost as good with bees as Sally. How the children were growing! When their father returned he would be delighted and amazed at their change.

This afternoon, as Ella toiled in the orchard, the late July heat was oppressive; but a fresh breeze wafted in from the river, and it was easy enough to make some worthwhile progress. She wore a broad straw hat and light linen work dress and apron, with soft flannel gloves and wooden shoes—sabots, the French called them. It felt good to be out here among the trees, for every small thing Ella did to give life and nourishment to Valenya meant she and Owen put roots a little deeper into the land they loved. All around her were green and healthy saplings as tall as she. After all she had done, they were dear to her, and by now she might have known every leaf, every twig. Susannah and Benjamin were on their knees a little way off, packing earth around a sapling that had been transplanted to better soil. Near the vegetable garden, where an aged French hired man hoed between squash plants, Sally and Tom were busy with the beehives. Actually Sally was the one busy with the hives, while Tom stood back a safe distance, careful not to talk too loud or make any sudden movements. As she replaced an empty jug of sugar water given as food, Sally said the bees would have plenty of nectar this year from the clover meadow beyond the orchard, where a herd of cows grazed peacefully.

Ella paused to look around, pleased at all she saw. She felt like singing and was especially glad the absence of her husband had not left her so gloomy. Because of the family and Valenya, she could still be happy, even without Owen. As she let her eyes rove over the house and the river, Ella noticed Heera lying in the shade of an old maple, undisturbed by chickens that clucked around the woodshed and about a small barn built to the left of the house. Though the colonies might be at war, fortunately Valenya was still peaceful.

The peacefulness was tinged with loneliness, however. Many folk at the fort refused to converse with Ella because Owen was a known Whig, even though no one as yet could accuse him of being a rebel in arms. If they could, Valenya would surely be seized in punishment. Ella herself was not sure where Owen was or what he was doing about the widening war. She kept informed of the eastern uprising by reading newspapers and talking with trusted friends who traveled back and forth to the colonies. Though she had not heard from her husband since he sent a note from Oswego, she knew he fully supported the siege of Boston and wondered how he would act if the warfare came close to him. Ella spoke of it to no one, but she was deathly afraid for Owen.

Few letters had come through to Detroit from the colonies since the loyalists and their Indians had fled the Mohawk Valley and set up bases at Niagara and Montreal. Now the frontier between Whig-held Fort Pitt and Detroit was a very dangerous place, for when groups from one side encountered individuals from the other, there were arrests and often bloodshed. Couriers bearing the colonial post did not pass through that lawless region or through the Mohawk Valley, and thus the only communication with Detroit was across the lakes from loyalist-held Montreal.

At Valenya Ella was cut off from the rest of the world, yet she knew Owen would somehow find a way to write her or to tell her what she must do. Several Whig families had already sold all they possessed—always at a loss—abandoning the straits for a more sympathetic settlement. Most had left quietly, but others had been harassed by ruffians or the lower sort of loyalist as they attempted to leave for the colonies or eastern Canada.

As long as she did not think about these unsettling things, Ella was content enough. The homestead took considerable attention and energy, and it was time well spent. After the turmoil died down, she would have weathered it fruitfully and well. Now and again she wondered what would happen to Valenya if she was forced to flee in a hurry. Who would care for it? Their French and Indian friends had promised to watch Valenya as best they could, but there was always the danger that some vengeful loyalist or soldier might amuse himself by slipping across the river and committing some mischief.

Leaving off pruning a sapling, Ella stood up and wiped her brow. Unbidden, a vision of Valenya in flames came to her, and she closed her eyes to shake free such painful thoughts.

She moved on, carrying a small pruning saw and a bucket of pitch used to smear cuts and to protect trees from disease. Then Ella noticed a canoe approaching from across the river. In it were several Indians and a soldier, whose red coat blazed against the shining water. In the distance was another boat. This one was a whaleboat under sail, and it also seemed to be making for Valenya. Ella cleaned her hands on the apron, called to the others, and went down the slope leading past the house to the landing. Sally and Tom finished with the bees, and the two younger children ran excitedly after their mother to see who was coming to visit.

Tom was in no hurry to accompany Ella, and he lingered with Sally, glad to be alone with her for a while. Sally was cheerful as usual, but Tom sensed a certain distance about her, as though she was thinking of things other than bees or him. Tom was restless these days, anxious to contribute to the rebellion in any way possible. He had been involved in several clandestine shipments of company goods to rebel settlements that were fortifying themselves along the Pennsylvania frontier. Though he wanted to go, he never traveled with those goods, because he was needed here, to keep watch on company matters and Valenya.

Feeling wasted while others back east were joining militia regiments to prepare for an expected British counterstroke, Tom was frustrated and ever ready for an argument. He, too, knew well they all might have to abandon Detroit, and that gnawed at him, day in, day out. Until something decisive happened one way or the other, he was at peace only in Sally's company, even if it meant no more than watching her work with the bees. He could not bear it whenever she appeared as distracted as she was this afternoon, and he felt he had to say something. As Sally finished replacing a jug of sugar water, Tom asked whether she had heard from Jeremy yet.

She shook her head, not looking at him. "These are uncertain times, Tom," she said with a shrug. "No one knows whether the post gets through at all anymore. He surely has written, but since he's American the British could be intercepting his letters, to see if he writes about war things, such as troop embarkments or—"

She stopped. Tom knew she hardly believed what she was saying, for others recently had received letters from Britain through Montreal.

He said, "Jeremy must've wrote you this winter, to be sure, Sal. Don't fret, you'll hear soon enough." Without thinking, he took her hand, and they walked down toward the beach. Ella stood there with the children, watching the canoe come alongside the landing. Tom added, "Not even Ella and Owen've heard yet, so my guess is something went wrong with the post; or then, maybe he's so danged busy with all that anatomy and such that he ain't got time to write us."

Sally said, "I've sent a letter to him. I was waiting to send two more I've written until I heard from him, but I think I'll send them anyway, with the next post Ella sends out. I'd have thought Jeremy would've sent us word as soon as he arrived there last year."

"Don't think about what might be, girl! Come on, let's see what this lobster wants—"

Sally yanked him back, fear in her voice as she said, "You stay here, Tom! You're always baiting these soldiers, and I don't want you in trouble, hear?"

"Aw, Sal, I ain't gonna bait nobody, not even that lobster— Hey, look! It's the very one Owen roughed up! That Lieutenant Davies—and he's lookin' mean! I heard he'd been brought back to Detroit because the army wants him to do a war dance with them redskins and rally 'em round the king."

Sally gripped Tom's arm, insisting he stay away, but he would not allow Ella to confront this soldier alone, especially since there were several Indians with Davies.

On the landing, Ella was as angry as she was afraid, but she stood her ground. Lieutenant Mark Davies, tall and severe in his immaculate uniform, was waving a document at her, saying he had come to search Valenya.

"Your husband is known to be a rebel sympathizer!" Davies's voice was high-pitched, his eyes shining unnaturally. Behind him stood the horribly tattooed Manoth, painted hideously and armed with scalping knife and tomahawk. "I've come with my scouts here"—Davies indicated two other grinning, ugly Senecas, who were climbing from the canoe—"with direct authorization from Governor Carleton at Montreal to search your residence thoroughly. And if we find any indication of treason, collaboration with rebels, or traffic in arms, your house will be confiscated, and you and your family will be obliged to find other quarters."

Ella fought back the dread that wrenched her inwardly. Surely Davies did not know that she and the other radical members of the Frontier Company had secretly sent goods and foodstuffs through the wilderness to Fort Pitt for the use of Congress supporters there. With the aid of Jeb Grey, secret shipments of gunpowder, provisions, and medicine had gone by canoe and packtrain to the nearly destitute rebels who populated backcountry forts and were so very much in need of supplies. If Davies knew of this, he would not be putting on this show of legal authority, but would have simply ordered the house locked up and Ella thrown out.

There were careful records of these transactions, so that when the war was over Frontier Company partners might be remunerated for their costly contribution to the cause. One copy of those records was with the militia commander in Fort Pitt, and the names of the donors were kept completely secret. These same records were also entered in code in Frontier Company books, so if they were examined by Davies, he would suspect nothing.

But it was not the chance uncovering of the real conspiracy that troubled Ella. It was the officer's rudeness and the dangerous looks of these Senecas that made her stomach tense and ache. Though she had not learned of Owen's drugging of Manoth in the Mohawk Valley, she could tell these Indians and Davies had come to Valenya with the aim of starting serious trouble. She wanted to avoid anything that would mark her for punishment by the army, but it would be difficult to see this through calmly if Davies or the Indians dared insult her.

Keeping her hands from shaking, Ella took the search warrant, saw it was in order, and handed it back, saying sharply, "Have your inspection, Lieutenant, for you'll find nothing amiss; but if you enter my house, you'll wipe your feet! And keep those Indians out!" The Senecas understood enough English to look at one another and jeer in their own tongue. Ella did not waver. To Davies she said, "You'll observe the law and remain in their presence wherever they go on my property; otherwise I'll report you to Commandant Lernoult!"

Davies scoffed. "You'll not be so haughty, wench, when I'm finished here." Pushing past Ella, Davies found Benjamin blocking his way. The lad stood with feet apart, hands on hips, glaring at the soldier's chest. Davies thrust him aside, and Ella just barely grabbed Benjamin before he sprang onto the soldier's back. But she was too late to stop Susannah.

Petticoats flapping, pigtails flying, Susannah shrieked like an Ottawa and leaped at Davies, who turned just in time to catch her in midair. Kicking and scratching, the girl knocked off Davies's hat and wig before he dropped her to the ground. Manoth stood back with his friends to chuckle at such humiliation. Davies blazed with fury, and he cursed loudly as he recovered his hat and wig.

Then matters became more serious. Heera was bounding across the lawn, snarling. Ella had just retrieved Susannah and did not see the attacking dog until Manoth shouted a warning to Davies, who had an instant to draw his sword as he spun at the animal.

"Heera!" Sally screamed, and commanded the husky in Ottawa to stop. Perfectly trained, Heera skidded to a halt, just yards away from Davies. Nonetheless, the officer moved at the confused animal, sword raised. At that moment Tom Morely ran down the slope, shouting for Davies to hold. The lieutenant hesitated as Tom grabbed the growling dog by the collar. Tom was hot, and stared down the officer. Manoth came to the soldier's back, eager for a fight.

Davies said through clenched teeth, "I'll arrest anyone who resists me, Morely. Would you like to be first?"

Davies was smiling coldly. Sally took Heera, and Ella stepped between the officer and Tom as did the two children; but Tom moved them away and faced Davies, who brought his sword up to waist level.

"So," said the lieutenant with a snicker and a glance at his men. "I knew you were a rebel like the rest!"

The Indians ranged themselves in a semicircle. Tom prepared to take them, though he was unarmed.

Ella suddenly cried, "You'll have to fight us all!" Heera struggled to attack, as though understanding her words, but Sally held him.

Davies hissed, "That'll do me fine—"

"Hold! Hold there, all of you!"

From a little way offshore Dawson Merriwether stood up in his whaleboat and yelled for Davies to back off. As the boat's hired tillerman maneuvered into shore, Merriwether shouted angrily, "Control yourself, Lieutenant Davies, or I'll report you to Lernoult myself!" He climbed from the boat onto the landing with surprising agility.

Davies raged. He knew well that Merriwether was the leading loyalist in the entire northwest and was a witness who would speak the truth.

He shouted, "This affair is under my control, sir! This rebel has defied my search party, and I intend to arrest him on the spot. Do not interfere, Mr. Merriwether!"

Merriwether limped rapidly toward them, placing himself between the soldier and Tom, who was just as willing to fight as Davies.

"Keep your head, man!" Merriwether roared at Davies. "Do your duty, but cause no unnecessary bloodshed!" The Virginian glanced over his shoulder at Tom, saying, "And you, son, be still! The army will conduct this search. I can do nothing for you if you stand in the lieutenant's way."

Tom said slowly, "If he tries to arrest me, I'll kill him first."

"Tom!" Sally cried, and grasped his arm. "Let it be, please!"

"There, Mr. Merriwether," Davies said with a sneer. "He's asking for trouble."

Ella broke in. "Not if you don't try to arrest him! He'll not fight you if you behave like an officer instead of a bully!"

The lieutenant said in a slow voice calculated to intimidate,

"Before winter, I'll find a way to arrest everyone who ever had anything to do with your husband, and I'll see to it this place is confiscated for crimes against the king!" He glanced triumphantly at Merriwether, who was astonished to hear an officer so governed by hatred that he had lost sight of justice. "Suffice it to say," Davies went on to Ella, "that this pretty residence will not be yours much longer!"

Tom moved abruptly at that, but Ella blocked him as she replied, "Whatever your intentions, Lieutenant, you'll not find easy prey here."

"Enough!" Merriwether burst out. "Davies, be about your duty, or I'll personally press charges against you for insulting these people! If you try to arrest this young man, I'll stand in your way myself!" He brandished the cane. "This is no blade, my man, but do not underestimate its potency."

Merriwether gave another flourish of the cane, showing that he could use it with effect. Davies restrained himself. Ramming his sword in its scabbard, he spoke curtly to Manoth and the rest, telling them to search the grounds for anything suspicious. The Indians sauntered off to look among the sheds and fields. Tom followed, picking up a nearby ax so they knew he meant to keep an eye on them. Sally went with Davies up to the house, the dog at her heel.

Before Ella went to her house, she thanked the kindly Virginian, who seemed to have aged so in the past half year. His hair was pure gray, and he seldom wore one of his many elegant wigs these days. As the children looked on, Merriwether nodded and kissed Ella's hand.

"Whatever we are to become," he said, "I shall do my utmost to see that our honor is not destroyed."

"Bless you, sir." Ella firmly held his wrinkled hand. A profound melancholy came over her just then, for she knew now their time in Valenya could not last. Dawson Merriwether could not hold back the likes of Mark Davies for long, and it was only by good fortune that he had learned of this search in time to oversee it. Caring about the Sutherlands and knowing what Davies was made of, Merriwether had hurried to Valenya in order to prevent persecution.

Whatever Owen was doing in support of the rebellion would surely become known to the British and to Merriwether, Ella thought. When that happened, they would lose Valenya. That could well happen before very long.

"Mr. Merriwether," she said, both of them watching Sally and Davies enter the house. "Sir, I fear that what we have made here is in jeopardy of being destroyed. If matters worsen and I have to go, I pray that Valenya will continue to be—even though it's no longer mine." It hurt so deeply to say that, and Ella almost began to cry. She looked away to conceal the tears, but was upset to see the Indians roughly pushing their way through the orchard, looking for nothing in particular, laughing and joking. Tom watched them, however, and saw they did no damage to the trees.

Merriwether said sincerely, "Whatever I can do, Mistress Sutherland, I'll do for you." Then he gave a searching look that told Ella he suspected she and the others were doing something for the rebellion. That look passed, and, sighing, he said, "Even if we become true enemies one day, I'll try to protect this place, for I'm a man who cannot bear to see honest work wasted or ruined."

Merriwether and Ella walked with the children up to the house. In a sad, helpless way, Ella sensed her fate was already sealed. After all the sacrifice, labor, and joy of building Valenya, it was no longer theirs.

Jeremy Bently and Penelope Graves were engaged to be married when Jeremy's studies were completed next year in the spring of 1776. The Graves family and the Gladwins could not have been happier, and a wonderful party was held at the estate in Derbyshire. Though there had been a few questions about the journey to Birmingham, the matter was not pressed by Penelope's parents, who admired and liked Jeremy very much. They knew nothing of his or Penelope's involvement in the narrow escape of Peter Defries from the Severn estuary.

For weeks the conversation at Derbyshire concerned the apparent cooperation of the Frontier Company with American rebels, and everyone was in deep gloom over it. Richard Graves, Penelope's father, was sorry his friends and former partners in the company had broken with him—a break that now seemed impossible to repair. If Sutherland and Defries were arrested after the rebellion was put down—as most people in Britain were convinced it soon would be—they faced a long prison term or even execution.

The Gladwins and Penelope's family feared for their relations in the colonies, so there was profound relief among them that Jeremy repudiated the violent acts of the rebels. They thought him a shining example of a loyal American, and even conceded that he was right when he said Parliament's bumbling rule had brought on the rebellion. They admired and applauded him for opposing outright rebellion as a way to correct the government's mistakes.

During that bittersweet spring and early summer of 1775, Jeremy was buffeted between the joy of Penelope's love and the fierce urge to go home immediately. He longed to learn precisely where his family stood and what they were doing. They had sent letters with the first ship out that spring, but these letters had been written before the critical April fighting in Massachusetts. Where did they stand now? His family had spoken of factional hostility at Detroit and of the tragic murder of Mrs. Merriwether, but otherwise they had sent optimistic, newsy letters that normally would have been uplifting had it not been for the dark and dangerous side of life not mentioned.

Sally had written a letter that was somewhat of a relief for Jeremy, because its tone was not that of an anguished young thing waiting breathlessly for her sweetheart to return. Her letter was breezy and entertaining, and by the time Jeremy had finished it, he was sure Sally was not as vulnerable as she had seemed when they parted in Philadelphia. He did not allow himself to admit that Sally Cooper was always unselfishly cheerful and would never let him know she was pining for him.

After learning of the loss at sea of the earlier letters home, Jeremy had written again. This new letter to Sally was lighthearted and impersonal and carefully avoided any sentiment that might give her the wrong idea about his feelings for her.

But now that marriage with Penelope was impending, he had to write still again. He tried so hard to be tactful about the engagement that he had to write and rewrite the page:

You would love Penelope, too. She is like you in many ways, but thoroughly English—only the best qualities of this island race, however! When you meet her, dear Sally, you'll both become fast friends, I'm sure, and you'll take great pleasure in teaching her our ways. Perhaps you'll come here to Penelope's ground one day, and she'll do the same for you. Am I suggesting I'll stay in England? Doubtful. I hope the trouble in America has passed before the next spring, for we wish to come over to see you all. If Penelope can make a go of it, we'll live at Detroit, and you'll have a friend who'll make the best companion in the world.

Jeremy had inserted this news among other items of interest—
such as the many remarkable artifacts in the university museum
above the library. He told of a crooked horn cut out of the head
of an old woman who lived twelve years afterward. He wrote of
how he had interested the soldiers at Castle Rock in taking Indian-
style sweat baths with him in an unused dungeon. There they built
a fire, heated up a pile of rocks, and poured water over them,
causing steam that cleansed the body and soothed the mind. Also,
he said he ran for distance around the city at least once a day to
maintain his conditioning. Often he practiced with officers to keep
his swordplay keen, and somehow even made the time to enter
the occasional athletic contests beloved by the Highlanders. Having
been brought up with Scottish soldiers at a military post, he knew
how to toss the caber and throw the hammer, and he always did
well.

He told Sally of his desire to come home soon, but added that
he would be of most value to their country after he finished his
studies next spring and was better qualified as a medical doctor
and surgeon. By now he was quite accomplished at both. Before
the term at Edinburgh resumed, he had apprenticed himself to a
surgeon in Derbyshire. Though he spent what time he could with
Penelope, he threw himself with a fury into his work with the
surgeon at a nearby hospital. In a month he learned what most
aspiring surgeons required years to learn, and he became a favorite
with the soldiers and sailors who were the majority of the patients
in need of surgery.

While studying at Edinburgh, Jeremy had often assisted one
of the city's finest medical doctors and had labored long hours
among the poor folk there. Furthermore, his scholarship was good,
for he had achieved much during those years studying in Philadelphia, and few young men working toward a degree as doctor
of medicine could compare with Jeremy Bently for either book
learning or practical experience.

It was apparent to everyone who knew him that he worked this
hard because he wanted to get back to America as soon as he
could. Penelope understood and had already told him she would
be delighted to marry and go to Detroit whenever he was ready.

Much of that spring and early summer was spent in her company, with the distant American war only a shadow, a cloud
passing over the sun. Though there was always the anxiety about
his family, Jeremy had never been happier. Penelope gave his life
meaning, and when he wrote his parents, he poured out expressions

of love and respect for her. Right after the Defries adventure, Richard Weston had left England carrying the letters announcing Jeremy's engagement. Weston would be stationed at Detroit and would bring the letters telling about Jeremy as well as Ella's brother, Henry Gladwin. Jeremy was relieved to know that Gladwin had refused a promising offer of advancement and profit through taking a field command with the army being assembled to embark for America.

In Jeremy's letters to his parents, he explained that Henry Gladwin could not bring himself to make war against a people he had served and protected throughout the cruel wars against French Canada and the Indians. Jeremy also explained his own reasons for standing against the methods of the Whig rebels. He made it clear that most leading Americans living in Britain agreed with him—including notable ones such as the famous painter Benjamin West, who lived in London and was considered the greatest living artist of his day.

I met West and John Singleton Copely on a recent visit to London, and they believe that many leaders of the rebellion are no better than those they mean to overthrow. Like myself, these two men are loyal to America, their home. Surely any rational, calm thinker would feel the same as they. It may be that the rebels have strong influence over the colonies today, but that will soon change. After all, it's well known that rebels represent no more than one-third of the three millions in British America. One million are loyal and opposed to the rebels, and the third million are trying to keep out of the road of the warring parties.

In his letter, Jeremy said he hoped the Sutherlands would remain neutral. Though he knew well they were active rebels, he dared not write such a thing in a letter that might be intercepted and read by government agents. Just then nearly every American in Britain was under suspicion as a rebel spy, so if he let slip any hint that his family's company was supporting rebels, there would be serious repercussions at home.

Mother and Father, it breaks my heart to hear about my beloved America. I tremble for you all and am sick whenever I think of the consequences of such misguided idealism. Forgive me for addressing you, whom I respect, in this way, but in these harsh and brutal times I must voice my innermost distress.

I stand for the king and for the restoration of harmony at home, but I fully support the movement to establish an American Congress that will govern our country as a body equal to Parliament, both under one British king. Surely you see that taking up arms must destroy that movement, and if there is no way to avoid further bloodshed, then America will be even more sorely enslaved by a vengeful Parliament!

His hand shook with emotion as he wrote this. Then he assured his family that as a physician he was sworn to save lives and therefore would never take up arms against the rebels, even though he vehemently opposed them.

When Jeremy wrote these letters home, he had heard nothing of the slaughter at Breed's Hill. The full truth of that butchery—a thousand British soldiers and four hundred colonials dead or wounded—was reluctantly revealed by the military to the people of Britain. It was not until July, when Jeremy was back in Edinburgh, that he learned how his letters had been dreamy and unrealistic in their hope for reconciliation.

He was reading in the university library, sitting at an oaken table in the hushed atmosphere of scholars and books, stared down upon by the portraits of well-known princes and religious and scientific reformers of the world. Before him was the thick *Edinburgh Pharmacopoeia*, considered the standard authority on herbs and medical concoctions that must be memorized by any hopeful doctor worth his salt. Jeremy's tired mind wandered, and he noticed that a fellow student's books and papers included a recent copy of the London *Morning Chronicle*. Idly reading the headlines from a distance, he gave a start to see the paper had a report on the battle, of which he as yet knew nothing.

Fascinated, he borrowed the paper and, with heart pounding, read of the tremendous loss of life on both sides. Harshly attacking the government, the paper contained letters about the battle from both Whigs and Tories in America. It denounced the generals, saying, "A few such victories must nearly ruin the victors." One despondent Boston Tory wrote, "Poor Old England," and a dying British officer was quoted as having said, "My friends, we have fought in a bad cause, and therefore, I have my reward."

Jeremy was dismayed, completely shocked to learn of full-scale war breaking out. He could no longer go on as though matters at home soon would run their course. He pushed his chair away from the table and, breathing hard, stood without leaving. The scholars and professors sitting about glanced up to see his extreme agitation, and someone asked if he were ill. Barely composing himself, newspaper in hand, Jeremy strode from the library hall, impatiently hovering about until the old doorkeeper unlocked the wire gate that prevented theft of books or the entry of anyone who had not paid his dues that semester.

Swiftly he paced outside into the raucous din of the city at midday. Shouldering past workmen and shoppers, he hurried away, mind spinning. He was not making for anywhere in particular, but just wanted to move. The winding streets were more confining than ever before, and he was frustrated by the crowds, filth, and noise. He thought over and over about the terrible Battle of Charles-town, or Bunker Hill, as some called it. Now the war would go on for a long time. It meant he could not dally here in Britain. The land he loved was undergoing far more than minor growing pains. He must go back! He had to go right away. He had no clear idea what he would do when he got home, but he must do something—anything. He would see Penelope, take the next ship from Bristol to Montreal, then on to Detroit. If Penelope refused to join him, he would postpone their marriage until he returned to England.

Soon he found himself striding rapidly up Arthur's Seat. He was sweating, though it was a misty afternoon and fairly cool. He paused where he and Penelope had stood. Somewhere a piper was playing a cheerful melody, but Jeremy hardly heard the tune. Nor did he see the city far below, engulfed in fog and smoke, its red-tile rooftops like smoldering embers of a great fire. In his hands was the wrinkled newspaper he had just read, describing the Breed's Hill slaughter. The piper played on, and Jeremy noticed a military parade passing through the city far below. Drums rattled and beat in cadence, and he could hear the soldiers' proud song rising above the city. Crowds were clapping and cheering as their young men went off to America, off to war against Jeremy's own kind. The gray street was like a gutter, and along it flowed a stream of soldiery in scarlet and tartan. Like a gutter. And the scarlet was blood, flowing toward the sea, leaving Edinburgh cold and ashen, and older.

* * *

Farley Jones was terrified. He had dared to follow Sutherland through Albany, as Bradford Cullen ordered, but when the Scotsman had nearly caught him in the alley the other day, Jones swore to get out of the city while he could.

It was evening, and Jones sat in the cabin of a Cullen and Company sloop anchored in the Hudson River, near the city. Hugh Meeks, huge and fierce, stood over the trembling clerk. Meeks had been here several days, having brought Cullen's offer of alliance to the rebels; now he awaited an answer. Jones had been the one to deliver the formal letter from Cullen, but tonight he refused to go back into the city because Sutherland was there. Meeks was disgusted and angry at the clerk for his cowardice. Swearing, he raised his hand to slap Jones, who cringed in the chair, begging to be left alone.

"I can't go back there!" Jones wailed. "Sutherland'll have me jailed for what happened at Detroit! Please, Hugh, have mercy!"

With a snarl, Meeks booted Jones in the shins, and the clerk howled, falling to the floor and scrambling away as the seaman took another wicked kick at him.

"I should fling ye to the fishes, blast ye! What good be ye to us? Mr. Cullen wants spies, not slinkin' yellow dogs! Ye'll not let us down again, hear?"

"Wait! Wait!" Jones wailed as Meeks made to boot him once more. "I know how I can serve! Listen! No, please don't hurt me again!"

Meeks held off, though he longed to smash Jones in the face. "It better be good, or Cullen'll be praisin' me for slittin' yer throat! Pipe up, dog!"

"Montreal!" Jones croaked, shielding himself with his bony hands. "I'll get to Montreal! I know people there, lots of people!"

"Stupid swine!" Meeks roared. "Cullen's turnin' rebel, don't ye know? Montreal's full of loyalists and king's troops! What good'll ye do there?"

Quaking, rushing to speak, Jones blurted out that he would be a worthy spy in Lower Canada. "I could do in secret whatever our master asks! He'll have someone to trust up there! Think! Think! Tell Cullen it was your own idea! I'll say it was! He'll call you a genius!"

"Pah!" Meeks turned away and paced the floor. Jones had a good point, but Meeks did not like to admit that the clerk was as crafty as he.

Both knew Cullen meant to rule Montreal eventually, after the rebels accepted his offer to join them. Jones could lay the groundwork for Cullen, spying out the latest political and military situation—particularly the new trading partnership known as the Northwesters. By the time Cullen arrived in that city, Jones would know whom to overpower, whom to hire, and whom to accept as a supporter. Much had changed in Montreal since the outbreak of hostilities. The small rebel faction there was hoping for an invasion from the Whigs in the south, and the loyalists were Anglo businessmen who wanted to be left alone—yet most loyalists were determined to fight any rebel invasion. The nervous French were anxious to choose the right side—the stronger side—and whoever won them over first would triumph.

Meeks rubbed his jaw, which needed a shave. He eyed Jones, then snorted and yanked the little man to his feet.

"Ye're on!" he declared. "Hang me if ye ain't been no account to us here in Albany! Ye can't be no worser in Montreal! But don't fail me, for Mr. Cullen'll hold me liable for not doin' for ye here and now!"

"You won't regret it, Hugh!" Jones was ecstatic, shaking all over.

"By thunder, Jones, ye've given Cap'n Meeks a chance to show Cullen there's other cunnin' lads besides him in the colonies!" He clapped Jones on the back, and the clerk staggered, nearly losing his teeth. "Aye! That there Cullen'll look with favor on Hugh Meeks! Might even forgive me for a small indiscretion with his daughter! Hah!"

Jones ducked the next clap and scurried away to fetch rum from the bottle that hung by the shipmaster's rumpled bunk.

Meeks rocked on his feet, cackling to think of how Helen Cullen had found him and Linda alone in a room of the Boston office building. Fortunately for the seaman there had been no more than holding hands and heavy breathing, but Helen had flared up and yanked her daughter away, with a sharp warning to Meeks that Linda was never to be touched again. Later, Cullen himself had given Meeks a tongue-lashing over the affair, and now the pirate was anxious to get back into favor with the merchant. He knew only too well that if he did anything to hurt or compromise Linda, he would be doomed; but if she was determined enough to take him for a husband, her doting parents eventually would relent. Before departing Boston, Meeks had briefly met with her in secret, and Linda had spoken of her desire for him. Now it was up to Meeks to convince Cullen that he would make an excellent son-in-law.

Though Jones did not know the entire story, he could tell Meeks was on dangerous ground. After slurping rum, the clerk asked, "Do you think Cullen'll forgive anybody making bold with that wench? You're playing with fire there, I'd say."

Meeks guffawed and stood with hands on hips, brazen and confident. "They ain't gonna find another man as is willin' to take Linda to wife! Let old Helen stew all she wants! Linda favors me, to be sure, and she ain't ever clapped her black eyes on the likes of Hugh Meeks afore!"

He leered at Jones and motioned with his hand for a swig of rum, saying, "Leave off suckin' that bilge and give me a slug! We'll toast to Linda, the apple of me eye! The way to Cullen's heart—"

"He hasn't got a heart!" Jones hissed, then glanced sulkily at Meeks.

Meeks laughed. "Don't be sayin' such hard things in the presence of the good gentleman's future son-in-law, even if they be true! Ye'll be crossin' me, and I'll be forced to keelhaul ye to teach ye manners! Now, here's to Linda!" He leaned back and guzzled from the bottle, swaying as he drank.

Jones thought Meeks was the one who should take care of what he said. The clerk was glad to know Meeks was after Linda, for the man had revealed a weakness by such boasting. If and when it served Jones's purpose, he would use this knowledge against Meeks any way he could. He would bide his time, and from Montreal he could do much to win Cullen's gratitude. Perhaps it would not be long before he took revenge against Hugh Meeks, whom he despised as much as he feared. Bradford Cullen's son-in-law! That was laughable!

That night, lying in her bed, Ella thought the wind had changed and that it blew hard from the east by the sound of it. Sleepily she turned over in the darkness to face the shuttered window, which looked out on the yard, garden, and orchard. Her eyes were closed, and she was not sure if she was dreaming or not, but it was strange that the wind could be so loud, hissing through the trees, when it did not trouble the house or the closed shutters.

The house was tightly sealed, with every shutter barred, the doors locked and also barred. Since the threats of Lieutenant Davies and the appearance of Manoth, Ella would take no chances by leaving the house vulnerable at night. Even during the day she was inclined to keep a loaded rifle near at hand. There was not a moment when either she or Sally did not know where the younger children were, and everyone stayed close to the house just in case Davies or the Senecas or any loyalist tried to harass them.

Davies had found nothing in his search, which was a week past. It was fortunate for Ella that Dawson Merriwether had been there, for the officer would have conjured up false evidence to accuse her of cooperating with rebels.

Real evidence was there in the books, but so disguised as to be indecipherable. Ella hoped the goods the company had sent secretly to the backcountry rebel settlements had gone through safely, and that Jeb Grey, who had taken them, would return before long. She was glad Tom Morely came by Valenya several times a day to look in on them. He and Sally were really close lately, and it seemed the young woman had overcome missing Jeremy. That, too, was good, thought Ella. Tom did not stay with them at night, however, for he had his own family's homestead to oversee now that Jeb was away and James lived in the fort. Tamano's lodge was fairly close by, but Ella was uneasy in the evenings, for she was certain someone was trying to frighten them.

More than once in the mornings there had been strange moccasin prints around the house, where prowlers had tried to find an open window. Twice Heera had barked at night, and when Ella let him out, whoever was there had fled, likely down to a canoe at the riverbank.

Ella was dropping off to sleep, but awoke with a start. Heera was barking, yowling and yipping to get outside. Ella sat up in bed, heart pounding. The east wind was rushing so fiercely, hissing in the trees. It was a strange wind and still did not buffet the house as it ought to. Something was wrong.

Springing out of bed, Ella drew on a nightgown and hurried to the window. Throwing up the bottom half, she then opened the shutters, letting in a terrible blast of heat and light that staggered her. At that same moment she heard Sally scream from upstairs, and Heera was going wild at the back door. Reeling from the shock, Ella regained her senses, and Sally shrieked, "The orchard! Ella, they're burning the orchard!"

"No!" Ella cried, staring in horror at the fire and smoke beyond the barnyard. The sky was alight, the entire hillside ablaze. "No, they can't! They can't!"

Bewildered at first, she gaped at the silhouettes of Indians, who had poured pitch on the trees to create this surging blaze. There were three or four savages, and over the roar of the fire Ella heard them shouting and screeching with delight. Her terror and despair suddenly drove her to fury, and she whirled to grab the rifle that stood near the bed. Just then the door opened and Sally burst in, the two wailing children beside her. Sally was in tears, but Ella was resolute, breathing hard as she checked the rifle's priming. Seeing Ella so tenacious, Sally immediately took heart and hushed Benjamin and Susannah. Into the room came Heera, who stood yapping and whining with his feet on the windowsill. He wanted to leap out and attack, but Sally commanded him to stay with them.

The crackling glow of the fire filled the window and heated the bedroom. Ella went to the window, rifle in hand, and Sally fetched two pistols, loading them from a shot pouch and powder horn that hung behind the door. Trembling with anxiety, Benjamin and Susannah stood beside Heera, illuminated by the flame as they stared outside.

"They're coming," the boy cried out, and picked up a poker from the iron stove; Susannah drew a shuddering breath, but refused to show fear. Sally and Ella moved the children aside and looked out. Three men with flaming torches were advancing down from the ravaged orchard. Like black ghosts against the flames they came on, unhurried, as though enjoying themselves and confident that there was no one to stop what they intended to do.

They walked like Indians, flat-footed and leaning forward. They came closer, and from thirty yards off one yelled, "Rebel dogs!"

Another cried, "You roast! Come out, or we burn you out!"

Ella recognized Manoth's husky voice and could tell which was he by his immense size compared to the other two figures. She brought Manoth into her rifle sights, quite prepared to kill him. Another few steps and they would be near enough to hurl the torches at the roof of the house. But first Manoth would fall. Ella had no doubt about that and aimed at his chest. The bright fire behind him made it hard to concentrate, but she held her aim. Another moment—

Sally cried out. Ella saw one of the other attackers run forward, whipping the torch in a circle over his head, about to hurl it onto the roof. Ella fired, the recoil and smoky blast throwing her back a few feet from the window.

"He's down!" Benjamin screamed. "You got one, Ma!"

Sure enough, the man was writhing on the ground, holding his leg, shot in the thigh. The other two fell back in surprise, uncertain what to do next. Ella reloaded as swiftly as possible. She rammed the cartridge down the muzzle and poured powder into the priming pan, but the one she thought was Manoth gave a horrible shriek and began to come forward with his torch. Sally had her pistols leveled. The first one banged, and Manoth ducked. She fired the second, and he scrambled back. He had not expected this, and with his companion quickly carried the third man out of the yard. They were still silhouetted by fire, and Ella drew a bead on them. A Pennsylvania rifle was deadly even at three hundred yards, and these targets were less than one hundred away.

Suddenly there was a burst of gunfire from somewhere. Ella looked out the window to her right and saw two men across the barnyard, rushing through the fiery light. It was Tom and Tamano, charging the Senecas. Ella brought the rifle around again, but the Indians had fled, taking the wounded man with them.

The children and Sally rushed to Ella and embraced her, sweat and tears running down her face. She felt weak in the knees and shivered. They looked out at the burning orchard, the red glow playing over their sorrowful faces.

Susannah spoke first. "Why, Ma? Why do such a thing? Why waste such a beautiful, beautiful orchard?"

Ella held the two children against her side, and a sob rose, making her shudder. She sighed and shook her head, saying, "This won't stop us. We'll plant another. We'll start again . . . we'll plant again!"

Heera looked up, eyes baleful, as though he understood. Sally leaned against the window sash and stared for a long time at the destruction. Tom and Tamano had vanished in pursuit of the Indians, and there was no sign of life outside at all, only the roaring fire.

A little while later, as Ella, Sally, and the children walked in a daze toward the inferno, Tom Morely came trotting back.

Sweating and panting, he took Sally in his arms, relieved she was safe. He had been walking a nightly patrol downriver and on seeing the blaze had awakened Tamano. To Ella he said hoarsely, "They got away, and we can't prove who it was. Do you know?"

"I'm sure it was Manoth," Ella said.

Tom spoke with a snarl that chilled Sally: "I'll kill him!"

Then Tamano was there, also sweating from a hard chase. "No

kill Seneca," he said. "If you kill favorite of British Army, Donoway lose all, lose it quick, and they hang you quick, friend."

The Chippewa's grim face was lined with shadows in the firelight. They all knew he was right. It was not yet the moment to punish Manoth for this.

Ella said wearily, "We can't do anything except defend ourselves until we hear from Owen; we must know where he wants us to go and must not be forced out before we're ready."

Sally gasped, "Then you're sure we'll have to flee? Oh, Ella!" She threw herself into Tom's arms again, and he held her close.

Tamano said to Ella, "It must be soon; Donoway must send word soon. You cannot wait much longer."

Gazing at the fiery orchard, Ella said, "They can't scare us away, Tamano! We'll beat them—"

"No," Tamano said with much anger in his voice. "You cannot beat them! They rule here, not your rebels! One day they come for you, and Valenya will be theirs. You cannot beat them, Ella. If you fight, then choose a good day for dying!"

He looked at all of them: the children holding on to Ella's nightgown, Tom and Sally staring blankly at the fire. Ella looked proud and fearless, but she could not deny the truth.

Tamano said, "You can only wait until Donoway calls. Meantime, I will build a lodge beside your house, and with my family guard you from Senecas. But I cannot guard you from Davies. He is a soldier-devil and thirsts for the blood of my brother, Donoway. Until he has drunk it, he will take revenge where he can." He spoke slowly, repeating, "Where he can."

PART THREE

Blood Enemies

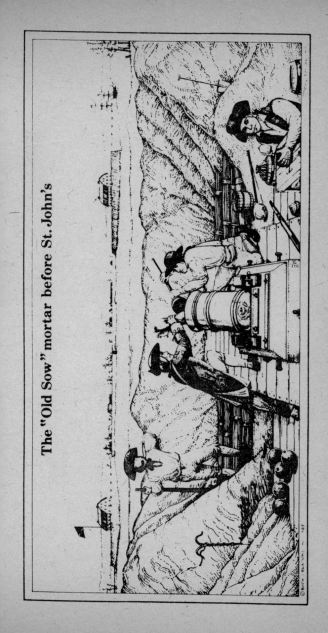

The "Old Sow" mortar before St. John's

chapter 19

PHILADELPHIA

Sutherland was on the wharf at Albany, about to board a sloop and head downriver to rebel-held New York Town. From there he would cross overland to Philadelphia, because the sea was controlled by the British, and ships often were stopped, boarded, and searched. If the Royal Navy suspected that a ship belonged to rebels, it would be impounded, with passengers imprisoned under the charge of treason. Mel and Hickory were to make this trip along with Sutherland, excited to be going to the greatest city in America.

For Sutherland, the days in Albany had been busy and productive. As General Schuyler had said, Bradford Cullen was turning coat and offering military supplies to the rebels in order to take his place among leading Whigs. But of more immediate importance than this news about Cullen was Sutherland's success in finding a wealthy New York financier to act as his agent for the sale of the pelts. Haym Salomon, a Jewish merchant with Spanish and French clients, agreed to take the pelts, and gave Sutherland a bill of exchange for the full thirty thousand pounds Sutherland had hoped to earn. This note was virtually as good as money; Sutherland could draw credit on it from Salomon's merchant house, and would be able to pay the partners of his own company.

Before the Scotsman left for Philadelphia, General Schuyler had offered him a captaincy in the New York Batallion of Rangers for the coming critical campaign against Lower Canada. Sutherland declined the commission, however, for it was urgent that he attend the meeting of Congress, then return to Detroit to fetch his wife and family.

As their ship made ready to get under way, Sutherland and his company bade farewell to General Schuyler, who stood on the crowded wharf, his staff waiting nearby. Mel and Hickory went on board, where seamen were busy securing hatches and hauling away at cables, and Sutherland and the general were left alone.

Then there came a loud hurrah from down the street, and everyone looked around to see a regiment of Pennsylvania troops come swinging along, resplendent in blue tunics, white small-clothes, and sparkling brass. These were the men of city and farm—German, Irish, Scottish, English, and Swedish descendants from the most prosperous colony in America. They strode in perfect order to the sharp rattle of snare drums, and their fifers played "Yankee Doodle."

People all around hurried to line the streets, applauding and cheering the marching troops. Room was made for General Schuyler to stand on the ship's gangway and overlook the parade, and he asked Sutherland to join him. The rebel regiment, six hundred strong, was a thrilling sight. They looked smart and brave, white belts crossed over the chest, red facings bright against new blue coats. Muskets with glittering bayonets leaned at the correct angle over their shoulders, and each man carried a backpack holding food and gear.

The street, the wharf, the entire city reverberated with the tramp of the Pennsylvanians, who had reached Albany two days earlier. At their head marched an elderly, robust colonel, beaming and proud, leading them toward bateaux that would transport them north to Fort Ti, the staging area for the Canadian invasion. Their regimental colors of dark and light green with the symbol of a tiger in the center snapped in a gusting breeze off the river, and Schuyler leaned toward Sutherland, saying it was a pity that no flag of the Continental Army had yet been designed or authorized for every regiment. In the interim a scarlet flag was carried as the color of the army, the color of rebellion.

Schuyler himself was an imposing figure as he stood with hat held out from his side in salute. As the regiment's colonel passed, he saluted in this same way, and his men obeyed the sharp command to turn eyes left toward their general officer.

"Now, these are soldiers!" Sutherland said to the general, a rush of patriotism and admiration filling him. "We'll show Parliament we mean business! You'll easily take Saint John's, and then down the Richelieu River toward Montreal! The British'll be unable to collect the force to stop you!"

Schuyler said he was also confident, and grinned broadly as the troops marched past. Up on deck, Hickory ululated in a squaw's cry of joy, and one or two backwoods Pennsylvanians whooped back, only to be silenced by their officers. Sutherland liked to see that kind of discipline, and the Pennsylvania rank and file took pride in it. He thought it amazing that such a stout body of well-trained troops could be raised so rapidly from militia companies. It was testimony to Pennsylvania's commitment to the rebellion, and Sutherland was excited to see the heart of a regular army taking shape. Without units such as this, there was no hope of victory.

"On to Canada!" Mel shouted from up on deck, and some York troops standing nearby removed their tricornes and took up the cry. The entire crowd began to shout the same way, and then there arose a deeper, thunderous chant that hushed them, awed by the rhythmic shouts of the marching Pennsylvanians:

"Que-BEC, Que-BEC, Que-BEC, BEC, BEC! Que-BEC, Que-BEC, Que-BEC, BEC, BEC!"

Soon the entire mass on the wharf and in the street joined in; all Albany was buoyed by the tumult, as more and more people threw open windows and crowded rooftops to wave and cheer. Sutherland was sure the rebels would make a name for their regiments if well led. Congress's choice of Schuyler as commander and a former British Army captain named Richard Montgomery as second-in-command convinced him they would be led to Montreal with courage and wisdom.

Sutherland had not met Montgomery but had heard praise of him. Brigadier General Richard Montgomery was an Irishman, son of a British peer, who had moved to an estate in New York Colony only three years ago. As a respected Whig and staunch supporter of the rebel cause, Montgomery had been elected as a delegate to Congress. He would be the field commander of the invading army while Schuyler was in charge over the entire northern theater of war.

At that very moment Sutherland saw up the street to the left a dashing man astride a charger, intently watching the regiment's procession. The gentleman wore a cape over what was obviously a blue uniform, but from this distance there was no telling his rank because the crowd was too dense and the cape concealed any symbol he might have. The Scotsman could see that this was no common man.

To Schuyler, Sutherland said, "If that's Montgomery, I'll wager he'll live up to his reputation as a leader!"

"Yes! He's arrived at last!" Schuyler grinned and looked at his subordinate with esteem. Montgomery noticed the general and, removing his hat in salute, smiled confidently, approving what he saw in these troops.

Montgomery was thirty-seven years old, tall and dark, with refined features that were reassuringly tranquil. He looked like a true soldier as he watched the men who would fight and die for him. The troops marching past did not notice their leader in the crowd and did not accord him the respect given Schuyler. As the Pennsylvanians began to sing "Yankee Doodle," Sutherland saw the brigadier smile wistfully.

Montgomery would have to deal with more than well-trained Pennsylvanians, however, before this coming campaign was won. In the northern army were hundreds of raw militiamen, just as cocky but not as steady as these soldiers. Many militia enlistments would be up in December. Would those men stay on if the weather was bad, the fighting hard, victory not certain?

How Sutherland wished the rebels could have the time to train and equip a fighting force ten times the size of this Pennsylvania regiment! But it would take two, perhaps three years of dedication and patience to create such an army. Could the rebels hold on for so long? The answer depended on these bold Pennsylvanians and on the uncertain, though courageous, militia of every colony.

Sutherland heard someone call his name and saw Corporal Gavin Duff come through the crowd. They shook hands and Duff saluted Schuyler. The corporal was pale, but clearly on his way to recovery. He wore his buff and green York uniform, which was clean and mended. Sutherland introduced him to Schuyler as a veteran member of the colony's own professional companies.

Sutherland said, "When will New York supply a regiment like this one, Corporal?"

Watching the Pennsylvanians with obvious admiration, Duff replied, "Give me good Yorkers, and I'll whip 'em into shape, Mr. Sutherland, sir! The militia lads you chided the other day already've quieted down, and most're willin' to learn how to soldier."

General Schuyler leaned over to Duff and Sutherland, asking whether Duff was an experienced drillmaster. Self-conscious, but very correct, Duff said some thought him capable and ended his reply with, "At yer service, General, sir!"

"Are you enlisted in one of our new line regiments, Corporal?" Schuyler was told Duff intended to enlist within the hour. The general asked Sutherland whether he would personally recommend Duff to him.

"With honor, General," Sutherland replied. "Corporal Duff would do any company credit as its commanding officer, if I'm a judge of men."

Duff stiffened and flushed in embarrassment. Schuyler nodded, looked him over, and then told him to come to headquarters that afternoon.

"We need lieutenants, Corporal," Schuyler said. "After our interview today, I'll appoint you either lieutenant or else as an ensign with a quick chance at advancement to lieutenant."

Duff was aglow with happiness. He saluted again, clicked his heels as Schuyler dismissed him, then shook hands warmly with Sutherland.

"When next ye meet my York troops, Mr. Sutherland, ye'll think these Pennsylvanians only schoolboys at play!"

Sutherland laughed and said he hoped so. Duff departed, and Sutherland bade farewell to General Schuyler. The regiment was past now, the milling crowd dispersing from the wharf and street.

Schuyler wished Sutherland a safe journey to Philadelphia. "And do not take it amiss if our Congress decides to enlist Mr. Cullen," the general added.

Sutherland nodded once, and they shook hands. "I have my own task, General. I'm not marching against Canada, and I'm not about to occupy Montreal with you, so Cullen won't be my affair until times change and we return to peace. Then I'll see Cullen in court for what he's done in the northwest. General, I wish you good fortune, and may Montreal be yours by September. I pray it will fall without serious fighting, for everyone's sake."

Schuyler watched Sutherland go up the gangplank, which then was raised, and seamen cast off lines as a whaleboat hauled the ship's prow into the river. Sails were unfurled, and the vessel drew away from Albany. Sutherland watched from the ship's side as on the wharf Schuyler met Montgomery. They were the sort of leaders the rebellion required. The rebellion would succeed as long as men such as these fought for it.

In another week, Sutherland, Mel, and Hickory reached Philadelphia. If Albany had seemed bustling and excited, Philadelphia was tumultuous. Its harbor was thick with shipping of many nations that formerly had been forbidden to trade directly with America. The demands of waging war and the fear of famine or shortages had caused American merchants to increase their orders from abroad and stockpile goods for the future.

Spread along the western shore of the broad Delaware River, Philadelphia contained nearly thirty thousand people and was the second greatest city in the British Empire. Only London surpassed it in size and wealth, though Philadelphia's future was considered so glorious that many believed she would one day outstrip even the British capital. Sutherland had been here several times in the past and knew the city well, but though he searched hard, he, Mel, and Hickory were obliged to settle for lodgings in the northern quarter, near the shipyards. This was not a desirable location, for the stench of paint and tar and the steady rattle and drum of hammers made the neighborhood less appealing than were the western outskirts, where the wealthy lived on great estates.

Sutherland could find no better dwellings, however, for Philadelphia was mobbed with delegates to Congress, their entourages and assistants, merchants vying for government contracts, soldiers seeking appointment, politicos after congressional favor, and adventurers determined to make their mark on the momentous events of the day.

That first hour in those shabby lodgings was spent arranging for clothes to be cleaned, essentials to be purchased, and in hiring boys to run errands and carry messages. Sutherland paid his respects by letter to Benjamin Franklin, sending it with a son of his landlord.

Franklin had recently come back from London, where he had been the representative of several colonies, including Pennsylvania. From reading periodicals, Sutherland knew Franklin had labored hard to convince British Tories as well as many British Whigs that America would not sit still while Boston and New England were punished. Franklin had been rebuffed by Parliament, however, and now that he was back in Philadelphia for the Congress, the old philosopher and statesman would be a guiding light in any decisions taken by the rebellious colonies.

Hickory was absolutely awestruck to be in such a vast metropolis; from the moment their ship came in sight of Philadelphia to the time Mel took her to their room in the three-story boarding house, she said nothing at all. While riding there in their carriage, she had huddled against Mel, intimidated by the noise, the sights, the strange sounds and smells. To Hickory it was as though she had descended into some strange netherworld, where demons were all white and not an Indian was to be seen.

Once she reached the safety of their small room, Hickory ranted on in astonishment about all the things she had witnessed. Mel was at home in the city, having taught here at the Academy on and off for several years. Excited to be back, he explained things to Hickory and promised to show her estates greater than that of Sir William Johnson. He would walk with her along the waterfront, where masts were gathered thicker than an Iroquois forest, and he said she should not be afraid of the strange men in black with the big flat hats, for they were Quakers, who were kind to Indians.

As Sutherland soaked in a copper tub of hot water and soap, hearing Mel and Hickory through the wall, he recalled how twelve years ago he had come to Philadelphia with Ella, then his new bride, and they had honeymooned in a fine, elegant house. Those days were long past, but Sutherland wished he had his beloved wife and family with him now. Had he known fighting would break out in New England, he would have taken them all with him. He was impatient to get back, no matter what the risk to himself, and bring them out, even though it meant abandoning Valenya and breaking up the company temporarily. Once his position as an active rebel was revealed at Detroit, all he owned would be confiscated anyway, and he would be marked for arrest.

There was a knock at the door, and Sutherland called for the visitor to enter. He was shielded from the door by a folding screen but recognized the voice of the boy he had sent with the message to Dr. Franklin. The statesman had been at home and had immediately penned a reply, saying he hoped Sutherland would come directly.

Sutherland told the lad to fetch their carriage, then quickly dressed and went to Mel, who was sitting with Hickory at a window looking over the gray Delaware. The sultry heat of early August laid a haze over everything. Ships and barges plying the water seemed to shimmer, and the cobbled pavement of the street was hot. Red brick and tile roofs were hot; draft animals, laborers, and passersby were hot. But Owen felt refreshed and excited to be near the end of his mission. In a few days he would have addressed Congress and at last be on his way home. Sutherland's bath had purged him, cleared his head, and cleansed him of all the murky thoughts.

"Why don't you both take a bath, too?" Sutherland asked as Hickory helped adjust the white linen cravat at his neck. But both she and Mel had other ideas than bathing.

"Will you take us along?" Mel asked. "You promised to introduce me to Dr. Franklin, Owen. I know you'll both be busy with Congress affairs, and he might not have time to discuss levitation devices, but at least introduce me, and we'll leave right after I've asked him to correspond with me."

Sutherland said he would take them, and together they went downstairs to the street, which was a hubbub of carriages, carts, and pedestrians coming and going. The dust in the muggy air was choking, but fortunately a watering cart came by. An old man with a hose laid a fine mist over the street while two boys on the back of his wagon flailed away at a two-handled pump, like a seesaw. Hickory took delight in this and sprang out under the spray, closing her eyes and savoring the cool water. The Phila-delphians nearby laughed and applauded at the Indian woman's exuberant innocence, but Mel was a bit embarrassed.

In a moment their hired carriage came around the corner from the stable. Just as they were boarding, with Hickory happily soaked and feeling much cooler, a loud cry rang out, "Stand back! Stand back! Here comes the Flying Machine!"

At that, Mel gave an exclamation and leaped from the carriage, looking straight up at the clouds and seeing only blue and white. There were screams and shouts of warning, but Mel could see nothing as he staggered about the street, eyes gazing upward. Then Sutherland jumped out and dragged him aside just as a thundering stagecoach with a team of six fast horses pounded past.

He and Mel crashed against a brick wall, narrowly escaping the iron-rimmed wheels. At the last moment they got a glimpse of ornate lettering on the side of the high coach: "The Flying Machine, Mailcoach, New York Town–Philadelphia." Chuckling, they dusted themselves off and went back to their carriage, where the prune-faced old driver eyed Mel as though he were a lunatic. Sutherland asked the craggy fellow how long the Flying Machine took between cities. "Two days."

"Indeed!" the Scotsman declared. "Mel, you'll have to go some with your levitation inventions to beat that."

Mel, shaken but unhurt, said, "Someday an air balloon might sail from London to France in less time! And it could carry the mails, too." He became lost in thought and excitement. "Carry the mails by airship . . . what a fantastic idea! Why, a fellow could make a fortune that way! He could decide the fate of parliaments and kings!"

Mel chattered dreamily as they set off for Franklin's house on Market Street. On the way, bells in all the churches and at the statehouse struck noon, and the deafening clamor confirmed to

Hickory that this was indeed a white man's underworld. She held her ears at the raucous din, though Philadelphians seemed not to mind. From the Christ Church belfry and St. Peter's, from the top of the Presbyterian church, the steeple of the Roman Catholic church, and the Lutheran house of worship, bells tolled and tolled. But none was louder than the monster in the bell tower of the Pennsylvania statehouse. High above the great red-brick building, in a white cupola with a weathervane on top, the mighty bell pealed like thunder as Sutherland's carriage passed by a few streets to the east. Even the tremendous rumbling of wheels and the noise of hawkers, workmen, and drilling soldiers were drowned out by the bells.

Sutherland asked the driver to slow the carriage as it passed the enormous statehouse, and they looked out at the lovely grounds to see a militia company known as the Philadelphia Associators marching among the shade trees. They were all sincere and ambitious, even though they had no other uniform than a tricorn. Previously, he had seen other marching militiamen, including the Quaker Blues, a smart, well-dressed company that had been cast out of their pacifist religion because of their warlike stand. Only Philadelphia could provide such a variety of supporters of the cause.

Before the carriage went on, a wealthy group of young men known as the Silk Stocking Company came marching by, very conscious of the envious eyes of the Associators. The Silk Stocking Company wore handsome light-green uniforms, crossed with white leather belts. They had green leather jockey caps, with ear-flaps folded up, and their cartridge boxes bore the word "Liberty."

Sutherland had noticed this same martial spirit in Kingston, New York Town, New Jersey, and all along the Delaware River. The country was in arms for the rebellion, and those who opposed it were either departing for loyalist regions or keeping quiet to avoid arrest. Philadelphia was the focus of that rebellion, the nerve-center that gave direction to those limbs and members that could be governed. For anyone to influence the rebellion, this was the place to be.

Turning down wide Market Street, Sutherland's coach stopped at a fairly new, modest house of brick, where there was little to indicate this was the residence of one of the most famous and influential men in all the world. Sutherland was greeted by Franklin himself, who embraced him as though he were a prodigal son.

The aged man, who was a spry seventy, with long, gray hair, seemed more weary than Sutherland remembered, though as alert and vigorous as ever.

"I knew you'd join us, Owen!" he declared and clapped Sutherland warmly on the back. "The men of vision of your generation are flocking to our side, but too many old fogies like myself are quivering under their beds at the thought of—"

He noticed Mel and Hickory, gazing with reverence from their places in the carriage. Learning from Sutherland that they were friends, Franklin immediately invited them in but warned that they could not stay, for he and Sutherland had confidential affairs to discuss, "Matters which must not be heard by Indian princesses or missionaries."

"We're neither of the sort, sir," Mel asserted. "My wife here's the daughter of an Oneida medicine man, and I'm an inventor, like you!"

Still standing in the doorway of his house, Franklin eyed Mel closely. "What've you invented?"

Mel was somewhat reluctant, but said, "I'm in the process of inventing a, ah . . . a levitation machine!"

"Levitation machine! Yes . . ." Old Franklin's face lit up, his wide eyes behind the octagonal spectacles sparkling with excitement. "Well, well, here I've been these past six weeks in Philadelphia, trying to keep indoors to give myself time to think—" To Sutherland he said, "—and to let the conservatives see I didn't come back just to heat up this revolution as soon as I stepped upon my native soil—" To Mel: "—but I hadn't imagined one of my own countrymen was discovering the lure of flight! Come in, come in, young man! We'll partake, and you'll tell me more!"

With an arm over Mel's shoulder, Franklin guided Sutherland's party into the cool house. It was comfortably furnished, light and airy. The rugs were from Persia, the tables and chairs came from England and Philadelphia, and the clocks were French and German. Shelves full of books lined the walls of a neat, sparsely furnished sitting room where Franklin brought his guests. For a moment, Sutherland was almost forgotten as Mel and the doctor fell into a deep and convoluted discussion of flying machines.

Sutherland and Hickory took chairs to let this talk run its course, and a butler brought a tray of refreshments, including brandies, Madeira, cider, and some sweet cakes. Franklin and Mel hotly debated a detail on a Leonardo da Vinci sketch. Mel said it could not work; Franklin said it had to work according to theory and mathematical calculations completed by a noted Frenchman experimenting with those very same designs.

Mel declared loudly, "I say it can't work, and won't work, because it didn't work for me!" He might have been a boyhood chum of this distinguished gentleman.

Franklin did not recoil at such impertinence, but asked, "You proved it can't?"

With that, Mel held up his left hand. The little finger was out of joint slightly and did not bend all the way closed.

"I fell twenty feet, almost straight down, using that very same contraption—in every detail! This finger was broken, although it was not all so bad, for I met Hickory, my wife."

Franklin looked from Hickory to the finger and then to Sutherland. He peered closely over his bifocals, seemed to clear his head, and then harrumphed loudly.

"Quite, quite, Mr. Webster." He poured himself and Mel glasses of Madeira. "No proof quite like failure—none better!"

Then to Sutherland, he said, "You'll agree, my dear friend, that Congress and our radical Whigs are about to put their own inventions to a test. But I daresay the drop is somewhat greater than twenty feet!"

It was Hickory who spoke, as though without thinking, "Drop greater than Date-car-sko-sase, in the land of the Senecas."

About to drink, Franklin hesitated. Squinting, he asked what she meant.

Mel said, "Niagara waterfalls; that's how far Congress'll drop if it fails."

Later, Sutherland asked Franklin whether he knew about Peter Defries's arrival in Philadelphia, and the secret shipment of munitions. Franklin said he did, for little escaped him if it was so important to the rebellion.

"A good man you have there in Defries," Franklin said over his Madeira. "Pretty woman, too. I had them for tea one afternoon, even the little daughter." He chuckled and said Jeanette would make an excellent delegate to Congress, she was that smart. Then he became serious as he said, "Defries has gone back north again. I recommended him to Schuyler, who knows him well, of course. Peter'll make a good commissary for the army going against Canada." Franklin eyed Sutherland closely, as though thinking how to phrase something troublesome. After a moment of silence, he asked, "Are you in battle trim these days, Owen?"

Sutherland sat back in his chair and shook his head. "There's more need of me in the supply and financial end of this rising, Dr. Franklin. I'd be just another soul to feed and clothe if I took the field."

"So you didn't accept Schuyler's commission?"

Sutherland was surprised that Franklin knew about the offer of a captaincy in the York battalion of rangers, and he said, "He won't need me as a scout, and from what I've heard, the British haven't raised many Indian levies yet—at least not enough to harry the two thousand men under Schuyler and Montgomery."

Franklin thought about that, harrumphing again. "Yes, well, perhaps you're right, Owen. Perhaps. Anyway, at the moment we have other affairs to chew on. No use you hurrying away north just to keep those troops from getting lost in the woods and capturing Boston instead of Montreal, eh?"

Sutherland suspected he had not heard the last of this, but as Franklin had just pointed out, they must discuss how Congress would be told about the political and commercial situation in the northwest. Franklin asked that Mel and Hickory excuse them, because matters of state and war required that the discussion be private.

"I gather from what you've said, Mr. Webster, you're neutral in this rebellion, and I have no quarrel with that." Franklin saw Mel and Hickory to the door. "I admire a man who's determined to create new machines as much as I admire one who'll create new nations. We need the one to have the other, and I'd be honored if you'll come back tomorrow to tell me more about your work."

Enthusiastic, Mel shook hands in farewell, saying, "I have no passion for civil rebellion, Dr. Franklin; I simply want to do the right thing, peacefully, as I see it."

Franklin nodded, obviously taken by Mel and Hickory. "Then you'll be better not to know what Owen and I say today—innocence is its own defense."

Mel smiled and replied, *"Poor Richard's Almanack,* back in '35, I believe. I've read them all."

Franklin laughed. "Well said, but it was '34, and since it's the only 'Poor Richard' I can remember these days, I use it whenever I can—especially when Parliament asks me about American political ambitions. You see, they think we mean to have independence."

Late that afternoon, after considerable discussion of the northwest and of military affairs, Franklin suggested he and Sutherland take

a carriage into the country for "an airing." Before long, they were
seated in a one-horse, hooded shay, Sutherland driving westward
through the city out High Street, toward the ferry that crossed the
placid Schuylkill River.

By now Franklin knew Sutherland had bitter relations with the
newly rebellious Bradford Cullen, and that Sutherland would oppose any plans of Congress that would ruin the fur trade or Indian
country. Franklin made no objection to either stand, but said the
rebellion needed wealthy supporters, whoever they were. And if
Sutherland suggested plans for the rebel capture of the northwest,
Franklin would support it wholeheartedly before Congress.

Both spent considerable time commenting on the amazing growth
of the city in this westerly direction. Sutherland had been here last
autumn, but this was the first time Franklin had been back in
Philadelphia in more than ten years. His wife had died less than
a year earlier, and now he seemed somewhat lonely. No doubt,
thought Sutherland, the weight of the world—the new and the
old—lay heavy on his shoulders.

Speaking softy, Franklin said, without having led up to it, "You
know, Owen, I tried to talk my son William into joining us, but
he refused; as royal governor of the Jerseys he believes he has an
obligation of honor to carry out his duty and oppose Congress.
Ah, it pains me deeply, Owen, but he will not resign his post."

Sutherland was aware of the sorrow in the old man's heart.
They had done now with abstract talk of war, campaigns, and
politics. The struggle touched on reality, including Franklin's family. As the statesman had said, his son was a stolid Tory who
might take up arms if need be to quell the insurrection in the
Jerseys. Franklin sighed shakily. Better than anyone else in America, he knew the power of the British, knew that America was on
an unwavering course to total, bloody civil war.

Sutherland thought of his own stepson, Jeremy, far across the
sea. He had not received a letter from his stepson in all the time
Jeremy had been away but was certain the young man would
support resistance to British tyranny. Sutherland had recently written a letter to Jeremy and had sent it to England from New York
Town. The letter explained his hopes for a better world and had
asked Jeremy for a direct answer as to his opinion in all this.

After a while, Sutherland turned the horse around, and the
reddening sunset swung behind them. He sent the shay back on
the road to Philadelphia, toward gathering darkness in the east.

Unexpectedly, Franklin said, "The world will never again see the likes of our cause, Owen! Though it costs us loved ones and even our lives, we will herald a new age, a new republic that the greatest powers of Europe one day will honor!"

Sutherland needed to make no reply. Franklin was looking out at the neat fields and well-tended orchards west of Philadelphia. Ahead were the spires and steeples of the city, rising over a line of trees, gleaming in the lowering sun.

In a shaking voice, Franklin said, "I only wish that my dear boy Willie were with me in this experiment! Ah, but he's a bold lad, Owen! He was there that night in the lightning storm . . . helped raise the kite with me!" Franklin recalled the experiment that proved lightning to be the same as electricity—the experiment that won him international fame as a scientist and made him the darling of European philosophers, writers, and royalty.

Franklin sighed. "Ah, my Willie . . . what is to come of us?"

Sutherland looked over and saw, in the shimmer of sunset, light glinting off a solitary tear on Franklin's cheek.

Never in his life had Jeremy Bently been so overwhelmed by the conflicting emotions of happiness and sorrow. Penelope and he had been married a week earlier, and that was a soaring joy above everything else. Her cheerful willingness to sail with him to Montreal and then on to Detroit had made Jeremy a happy man. Fortunately, Penelope and her family understood his tremendous impatience to return to America and sort out those fragments of his life that remained there.

The wedding had been small but beautiful, in a quaint village church near Stubbing. For three enchanting days the lovers had cast aside every woe, and their brief honeymoon in a hidden cottage in the Midland hills had been a time of magic and delight. Sniffer had been with them, and their faithful friend, although weakening and aging, had been contented despite the abrupt change of scene from the palatial Gladwin mansion to the rustic cottage.

The newlyweds had come back to Stubbing and swiftly prepared for a trip to Bristol, where a ship was due to depart for Montreal late in August. Jeremy's affairs as a student were placed in a temporary state of limbo until his anticipated return in a year or so, when he would resume his study to become a physician. Though he was not yet certified, he was very skilled, and all that was needed was another term at the university to make him officially a doctor of medicine and an apprentice surgeon.

The happiness of marriage and of preparing to settle matters at home in America had been shattered, however, when Sniffer fell ill a week before their departure. Penelope and Jeremy labored without letup over the otter; friends and relations took charge of the many preparations for travel, while the newlyweds did all they could to help Sniffer recover. Old Sniffer might not survive the taxing six-week crossing if he was not in good health at the outset.

In their chamber at the Gladwin mansion, they concocted potions and teas, applying poultices and rubs, while Sniffer lay in his cushioned basket near a bright window. His eyes glazed, he would eat or drink nothing and made hardly a sound except for an occasional friendly sniff, though always a weak one. Jeremy was determined to take him back to America and desperately tried to cure whatever it was that had caused Sniffer to fall ill.

Just before dawn, nearly fifty hours after Sniffer had first taken sick, Jeremy sat, half slumbering in an armchair, while Penelope took her turn rubbing a mint ointment into the feeble otter's chest. She sang an old English song, and the animal gazed up at her, his eyes big and round. Sniffer seemed inspired by Penelope's song, for she felt his heart beat faster, and hers did the same.

"Sniffer! Ah, old friend!" A mingling of relief and happiness came over her as the otter blew through his nose in that soft way he had of acknowledging pleasure. "It'll be a long way home, Sniffer, but you'll be happy to be back."

Penelope called to Jeremy, who stirred, rubbed his eyes, and saw the otter looking at him. Jeremy hurried to the otter's side. Sniffer gave a little snort and licked Jeremy's hand as his master touched his dry nose. The couple thought he would be fine.

But it was really the end for Sniffer. He died that night, far from his northwest home, but in a house where he was well loved.

Days later, Jeremy stood on the deck of a schooner sailing down the Severn estuary toward the sea and thought fondly of his otter. Staring at the land passing by, Jeremy stood in a warm summer wind, thinking how Sniffer had for years given delight to so many, including Penelope and their friend Richard Weston, who was already in America. Jeremy's life had altered greatly in that time.

As England drifted by, rising and falling with the pitch of the ship, Jeremy knew his time here had been an amazing episode of transformation. He had strong new ties, new links to Britain that he wished to nurture and develop. One day he would return to resume his studies and learn all he could to take back to the northwest, which would always be his first home.

Just then Penelope came to his side and held his arm. They were dressed lightly, in beige linens and taffeta, and the balmy sea breeze was soothing and renewing. Penelope noticed the thoughtfulness about her husband.

"Thinking about Sniffer?"

He nodded. "Perhaps he never could have returned to the primitive life he knew before Uncle Henry spoiled him and made him an otter of leisure."

They both smiled ruefully at that, guessing Jeremy was probably right. They missed the otter, but already Penelope was thinking about children who would require so much attention and love. That thought made her a little sentimental, and she leaned close to her husband's shoulder.

Kissing her forehead, Jeremy asked, "You crying for Sniffer?"

She shrugged. "For him, and lots of things . . . not all sad."

He put an arm about her, and they watched as England passed away and dwindled to the horizon. They had much to remember, much to hope for.

What the situation would be when they reached America, no one could guess, but Jeremy had heard the rebels might attack Montreal or Quebec. He intended to head westward from Montreal, taking a boat to Niagara, and from there go by ship to Detroit.

He would not join the rebellion, but did not intend to fight actively against it. He would do his utmost to protect his family and Valenya against outrage or brutality from either side. As far as he was concerned, there were good points in both rebel and loyalist arguments, but if either side endangered his own family, he would become its enemy.

Penelope broke into his thoughts. "Perhaps your family will think you've been spoiled, too—I mean the way Sniffer took to England is the way you've taken to it, as well. They might find you different now—or am I being too anxious about that?"

Jeremy pondered a moment, then said, "We've all changed—they and I. Let's hope we haven't changed too much."

chapter **20**

CONTINENTAL CONGRESS

Early in August, Franklin and Sutherland strolled beneath shady sycamores on the way to the Philadelphia statehouse. They were coming from City Tavern, where they had breakfasted and discussed the testimony Sutherland would present to the forty assembled delegates of Congress that morning. Dressed in the finest gray broadcloth, Sutherland looked nothing like a frontiersman. He wore a cocked hat and a new-style collarless coat with a short skirt and high waist. His soft velvet breeches were a lighter gray, and his stockings matched the coat. He wore no waistcoat, as many younger men now chose to do, and his ruffled white blouse hung down over his waistband.

Walking beside him, in remarkable contrast, the rotund Benjamin Franklin wore a traditional brown Quaker frock coat that was a bit longer than his ample waistcoat of the same material. On Franklin's head was a wide-brimmed Quaker hat, uncocked, heedless of the rebel preference, and his gray hair straggled to his shoulders.

Sutherland and Franklin passed the people of Philadelphia, who paused to stare at them or greeted Franklin with either great reverence or familiar neighborliness. Both greetings Franklin returned in kind, saying to Sutherland it was good to be back home again.

Sutherland was tall, handsome, and physically strong; Franklin was of medium height and unassuming. They were a strange combination as they went along the gravel path leading to the magnificent statehouse, an edifice that was unmatched anywhere in the colonies. In the clear, warm sunlight of a perfect summer's morning, the white cupola high above Chestnut Street shone as though it had a light of its own. From the moment Sutherland came in sight of the statehouse, he wondered whether the sophisticated, cultured men who sat in such a grand place could understand the true worth of the virgin northwest wilderness.

For the past three months leading Whigs had wrestled and debated hundreds of great and small questions, the answers to which could determine the life or death of the rebellion. They had raised an army, adopted a united front against Parliament, chosen political leaders and military commanders, and fruitlessly appealed to Britain for peace. The delegates had struggled to forge some temporary understanding among squabbling colonies who never before had imagined themselves in any alliance with the others. How could these men, the wealthy gentry of the East, fathom the need for holding the northwest to the new nation that would grow out of the ashes of war?

Fifteen years earlier misguided French ministers had surrendered to England all claim to Canada and the northwest—which France now deeply regretted—considering it nothing but a trackless, frozen desert. These American statesmen might hold the very same notion about Sutherland's homeland. They might not fight for it in the future peace negotiations, might not try to persuade Britain to give it up. Sutherland would explain that the future of America lay to the boundless west—as did her ultimate strength, destiny, and greatest wealth.

While the delegates Sutherland would meet today risked their lives to represent their colonies in a united assembly, they were mainly cautious men who might not care if Detroit, Pitt, Niagara, or the endless wilderness beyond the mountains were ever part of their own colony. Other delegates, not so conservative, would claim great stretches of the northwest, which their colonies would fight to take—fight Britain, other colonies, or even France or Spain, who also had ambitions there. Such future warfare must be prevented.

First, however, Congress would have to struggle fiercely to win liberty for the thirteen colonies, whatever the fate of the northwest territory. Yet Sutherland was determined to persuade them to try to take this vast land, which one day could be greater than even the most prosperous of the colonies. He was thinking hard when Franklin touched his arm, and looking up, realized he was already in the large hall outside the Pennsylvania Assembly's chamber. There was no one else there but a wizened footman, who bowed and opened the great doors. Sutherland went in first, Franklin following, and they entered an enormous, beautiful room, lined by windows on two sides.

The chamber, paneled and painted white, was filled with men

of nearly every age, size, and description, all buzzing in conversation as they waited for the president to bang the gavel on his desk at the right and begin the meeting. Upon the arrival of Franklin and Sutherland, all heads turned their way, and the Scotsman felt his heart leap to be the center of attention in such a distinguished gathering. Smiling, Franklin acknowledged greetings on every side, and Sutherland heard a few murmurs mentioning the name "Quill," the famous pseudonym he used as a political essayist.

Apparently he was well known here because of those writings, and because he was a member of the Frontier Company, which had already done so much for the rebellion. To his surprise, hand after hand was offered in congratulations for his support of the fight for liberty. Men rose singly, and in twos and threes. Franklin introduced them, and shortly Sutherland was nearly overwhelmed as it seemed everyone came to him. He knew little more about most of the delegates than fat hands or thin, strong hands or soft, firm, gentle, or overbearing. In that sudden swarm of dignified humanity, he heard Franklin say the names Jefferson, Hancock, Mifflin, Adams, Adams—he made note of Sam, the dark, bulky one, who seemed less an ogre than he had expected—Duane, Livingston, Morris, Lee, Jay.... These were the names of the finest minds in America, men who were changing the world, and Sutherland was caught up in a heady whirl of kind words, compliments, and generous welcome.

In that moment, Owen Sutherland knew what it was to be an American. Philadelphia was as much his home as Detroit, as much as Boston, Albany, New York, Savannah, Charles Town. The men of the Continental Congress welcomed him as they might a companion-in-arms. They would listen, would hear him, and would recognize the importance of the northwest territory to the colonies that Sutherland believed must someday unite and form one nation.

The delegates comprehended Owen Sutherland perfectly. They agreed that the great northwest would make America a mighty world power. No one expected Britain to readily surrender that territory. Only after the invasion of Canada succeeded would there be any hope of a military conquest of the northwest, for once Montreal was taken, supplies to the British forts would be cut off, and garrisons there would have to surrender or starve. If that happened, Sutherland believed an attack on Detroit from Pitt next year would meet little resistance.

During his testimony he was told a grave secret: A second

invasion of Canada soon would be launched by Colonel Benedict Arnold, this one through the uncharted wilderness of northern Maine. Arnold would daringly strike with twelve hundred well-equipped men--—including some of the finest Pennsylvanians—against the city of Quebec, at the same time that Schuyler and Montgomery attacked Montreal. These campaigns, however, combined with the heavy cost of supplying forces to besiege Boston, would leave neither the manpower nor the funds to support a third invasion force advancing from Fort Pitt toward Detroit.

The Indians in the Ohio country were being won over to the loyalists and the British Army, and those around Detroit were gathering for councils with officers there. They could ambush and wipe out a small invasion army, but any larger force would be too expensive to equip and supply over such great distances. Besides, Sutherland was told, every effort was being thrown into invading Lower Canada. Other than those troops and the army besieging Boston, every regiment that could be raised was opposing loyalist strongholds, such as that in the Mohawk Valley.

After three hours, Sutherland had answered a hundred questions about the northwest, asked many of his own, and accurately informed the Congress of Indian relations and loyalist sympathies in his home country around Detroit. The delegates came to realize how essential it was to establish a consistent Indian policy to speak with one voice for all the colonies and persuade the warriors to keep out of the war completely. Sutherland was requested to meet in committee with Franklin and others working on Indian affairs, but for the time being this was all that could be done with regard to the northwest.

He understood. It was clear that the fate of the northwest hinged on Montgomery and Schuyler capturing Montreal, even taking Quebec. There would be no immediate assault on British posts in the northwest, and that meant Ella would not be trapped between armies—a great relief to Sutherland.

Sutherland had done all he could in Philadelphia. His visit had been timely and necessary, for a seed had been planted in the mind of every man who had heard him speak. By the time he left the assembly hall, Sutherland had received promise after promise that his hopes for the northwest were in complete accord with those of nearly every delegate.

He and Franklin departed to lunch at the India Queen Tavern, where years ago they had often conversed over good food. As they came to their carriage, Franklin touched Sutherland's shoulder and said with a grin, "You've made many friends for your northwest territory this day, Owen! They've always liked to read Quill, but now that they know he's flesh and blood and comes from such a splendid land, they'll pay even more attention when he addresses them—in writing or in person!"

Sutherland was glad to hear that. He settled into the carriage, and Franklin joined him, humming to himself as they swayed off. Franklin's contentment at making an impression on Congress was not fully shared by Sutherland, who was distantly thoughtful, staring hard out the window at Philadelphia. After a while, the statesman looked closely at Sutherland, who sensed it and turned.

"Forgive me, Dr. Franklin. My thoughts are elsewhere."

"In Detroit?"

Sutherland nodded.

"You mean to return now?"

"To fetch Ella and the children before winter sets in."

Franklin said nothing, but thought a little longer before asking whether Sutherland would take them eventually to Montreal. He was told that would be done after the city was won by the rebels. In Montreal Sutherland would reorganize the Frontier Company and prepare for the fall of Detroit.

Franklin then said, "Why don't you help Schuyler capture Montreal? Then your family can come to you there sooner."

Sutherland glanced out the window. He knew Franklin wanted him to accept Schuyler's offer of a captaincy. It was true the rebel army needed seasoned officers, but Sutherland could not imagine the undermanned British forts successfully repelling as strong a force as Schuyler's.

He turned and said, "By the time I get to Detroit, Schuyler will be in Montreal, and I'll come down to join him there; there'll be plenty of fighting to be done once the British launch a counterattack in the spring. I'll accept the commission then—once my family's safe—not before."

Franklin spoke softly, "I'd do the same. Perhaps. But you'll be in danger if you go directly northwest from Philadelphia, because British agents are stirring up the Shawnees and Delawares. You're known to them, Owen, and they'll take you prisoner if they can."

Sutherland made no reply.

Franklin went on. "You know the chances are poor that you'll even get through at all. What good will your death be to your wife and children?"

"Then I'll take the northern route," Sutherland said. "I'll follow the Mohawk Valley—"

"Owen . . ." Franklin removed his bifocals and rubbed them with a handkerchief while Sutherland waited to hear what he had to say. He replaced the spectacles and looked squarely at Sutherland. "I ask you to give of yourself for our country's sake, Owen. Join Schuyler, immediately."

Sutherland showed no emotion, but his heart was wrenched at this.

Too many of Schuyler's troops were woefully green, Franklin said, and his officers did not have the battle experience needed to manage the men in critical situations.

Sutherland replied, "They'll only follow their own colony's officers, Doctor; why would they follow me?"

"Not the troops, necessarily, Owen, but the officers will heed you if you show them the way. In the field, Montgomery's the best we have—he and Arnold—but they need the support of subordinates who'll set an example, and by doing so allow the generals to command instead of trying to persuade privates to obey.

"Owen, I fear for the frail health of General Schuyler, and I doubt the militia troops will like Montgomery's strictness. If we fail to take Montreal before winter, we cannot take it next spring; the British will arrive in force, to ascend the Saint Lawrence with an army, and will drive us like sheep. You know what will happen after that."

Franklin was right, but to join Schuyler meant Sutherland would not be able to go for Ella until very late in the year.

Franklin interrupted his thoughts, saying, "Once Canada is ours, I intend to journey overland to Montreal myself and urge the Canadians to join us as the fourteenth colony against Parliament."

Sutherland was shocked. "Sir, at your age, that journey could be your death! It's a grueling one for any man."

Franklin wore an expression of amusement. "It very well might be so, Owen; but if I succeed in bringing the French of Lower Canada to our side, I'll have died in triumph. The rebellion will be won by next summer."

He looked at Sutherland with those keen, all-knowing eyes, and the Scotsman was moved to have such a great man as a friend and as the leader of their cause.

"Sir," Sutherland said quietly, "with or without Canada beside us, you cannot leave the world until you've seen through what you've helped begin." They both grinned at that. "There'll be more to do in America after the fighting's done."

Franklin chuckled. "By this time next year, my friend, Canada as our ally or no, I do indeed intend to see something through: a declaration of independence from Great Britain!"

Thrilled, knowing Franklin meant every word, Sutherland sat back in his seat as the carriage swung around a corner and drew up beside the busy India Queen Tavern. Franklin was watching him, waiting.

There was only one possible answer. Sutherland knew he must immediately send Mel and Hickory to Ella. These two were neutral and could travel safely through Indian villages. They would tell Ella of a plan he had devised for his family's safety in his absence, informing her that he had made up his mind to go northward again, to Schuyler, and do whatever he could to help capture Montreal.

He looked at Franklin and said, "I'll serve with the invasion force until November—no later, for then I must go for Ella and the children."

Franklin held out his strong, slender hand and took Sutherland's. Neither said a word. There was much to say, but at that moment, their silence was eloquent enough.

Tom and Sally were finished planting for the day and had done well. One hundred new apple trees stood out on the slope, green and promising against the charred earth. Both of them were black and sweaty, happy that at last they had finished replanting the orchard. It was a cloudy, mild day in early September, about three weeks after Sutherland had met with delegates of Congress. Ella was down in the house, preparing dinner, and Susannah and Benjamin were fast asleep with Heera under the yard's big maple. The children, too, had labored hard for the past weeks to restore what had been destroyed.

Sally stood up straight and worked her sore back, a contented look on her face, which was smeared with soot. Tom put hands on hips, saying, "You look like a spaniel hound I had once, or maybe a raccoon!"

Sally saw that her filthy hands were covered with the soot and muck of wet soil and ashes. Her legs, arms, apron, and face were indeed black, and she could not help giggling. Suddenly, Tom drew her against him, not caring that they were in full view of the house and the river. Sally suddenly stopped giggling, her large eyes meeting his, her heart beating with unexpected speed.

"A real pretty raccoon."

"Tom . . ."

He kissed her roughly. Her hands went out at her sides, fingers spread, but she did not resist.

"Oh, Tom Morely!" she whispered, and threw her arms around him, kissing him, then drawing back to look at him. Then she said, "I think I love you."

She had never seen Tom speechless before. Tom, who always had a quick reply, ever the one to make light of things, was at a loss for words. He did not even smile, or tell her he loved her, too, though she knew he did. He simply stared, eyes wide and white in the soot that streaked his own face. His strong arms enclosing her seemed to tremble as Sally put her fingers to his lips. Her hand was trembling so.

He said, "You're cryin'."

"I am?" She bit her lip, tasted tears, and with a breathless voice replied, "No, I'm not!" She laughed through her tears, a burst of joy released, and then was lost in his tender kiss. Closing her eyes, Sally pulled Tom's head to her shoulder and kissed his cheek. Shivering, laughing, Sally understood how much in love with Tom she had been for such a long time. It was not that her love for Jeremy had disappeared, but rather that it was understandable now, and completely different from what she felt for Tom. Her love for Jeremy had been a young girl's dream, childish compulsion. Loving Tom was real, easy, and right—a woman's love.

He looked at her, saying, "There'll be a letter from Jeremy one day. You know there will."

She smiled, gazing at his beautiful eyes. "I know, but that won't change anything. Not if—not if you love—"

He kissed her passionately and whispered that he loved her more than anything in the world. Sally's joy opened from within like a blossom. He was fine and good, and she needed no more than that, wanted no more. She was content. She did not notice the children watching, smiling, wondering what it was that made grown-ups so emotional.

Looking through the kitchen window, Ella let the cabbage she was cleaning drop into the sink. She leaned on the windowsill and saw the young couple embracing in the middle of the charred orchard, the new orchard. It was a wonderful sight, and her heart was glad. This was how it had to be. She sniffed, taking a long breath, thinking how life goes on, must go on! There must always be young ones to carry life forward, to plant new orchards, and give hope and inspiration to their elders.

The soup pot on the fire hissed, and its lid clattered as the water came to a boil. Ella sighed wistfully and returned to her cabbage, chopping it, then putting it in the hot water. She was dreamy, like a girl who had just seen an elder sister fall in love. Ella smiled to think that. She felt indeed like the sister who wondered when her own Prince Charming might find her. She hoped it would be soon.

Heera began to bark furiously, and the children were shouting. Terror gripped Ella, thinking Manoth and Davies were returning. She dropped everything and snatched the loaded rifle from where it hung above the mantelpiece. Fear surging through her, she dashed out the front door and looked at the landing.

"Mel! Hickory!"

Ella was overjoyed to see the couple disembark from a canoe. Owen was not with them, but they must have word from him. Finally! She carefully laid the rifle on a bench and raced down to greet them. Now she would know how to find her husband once again.

They stayed up late that evening, listening to Mel and Hickory relate news of their adventures. Ella heard that Owen was with the rebel army moving against Montreal, and although that frightened her, at least she knew what his plan was. He had written a letter that said she and the family must set out for Montreal as soon as they learned it had fallen. They should travel in the ship *Trader* as far as Fort Erie, which formerly had been called Fort Little Niagara. They would cross this portage to Fort Niagara, then hire whaleboats to take them down to Montreal. He told her:

Travel with as many folk as possible, with the usual traffic coming out of the northwest. The British have enlisted some Indians, but the lakes and waterways between Detroit and Montreal are patrolled by British Army whaleboats, and no pillaging of our people is permitted (as yet). The few Indians who have joined the loyalists are mainly in the Lake Champlain region, so they surely will not trouble you. I am concerned, however, about threats from Indians at Detroit.

My darling, use the greatest caution! Take no risks! If for some reason you cannot get to Montreal, then go to the Apostle Islands on Lake Erie, to the one where we sojourned with the Huron Ido-lana some winters past. I'll come for you there if you send a message to me. Have Mel and

Hickory stay at Valenya until you are ready to get word to me through them. Tamano and Mel will see to it you are well protected until I arrive. If necessary, the Morelys and Greys will also be safe on that island.

Ella, I know you will understand why I am delayed in coming for you. It is in the best interest of us all that I undertake this duty, and it is my fervent hope that it ends the fighting that much sooner.

The letter went on to explain that Ella should speak of their plans to no one, and it carefully avoided saying that Sutherland was a captain in the New York Battalion of Rangers. If the letter were to fall into the wrong hands and he were exposed as a rebel in arms, the consequences for Ella would be severe. Therefore, it was best that Sutherland's participation in the Canadian campaign be kept secret as long as Ella was at Detroit.

She realized clearly that her days at Valenya had passed. There was no doubt now that loyalists eventually would confiscate the homestead. Even a rebel victory could not guarantee a safe return to the northwest, which might remain British. Ella prayed for peace and that one day they would come back. She suspected, however, that this hope was a candle in a windstorm. Every shot fired between loyalist and rebel would cause the small flame to diminish, one day to die.

In late September, Sutherland arrived by whaleboat at the American camp besieging the British fort at Saint John's, about twenty miles north of the border between New York and Quebec provinces. He was cold, tired, and hungry from his long journey northward, but more than that, he was deeply worried.

Ever since leaving Philadelphia he had seen how poorly prepared for war the rebels were. The single fine Pennsylvania regiment that had marched out of Albany weeks ago had gone eastward to Boston or to join Arnold, and there was no unit like it in the army attempting to take Lower Canada. Instead of well-equipped, well-fed, confident troops, Sutherland had met mostly angry men, badly fed, poorly supplied and equipped, unpaid, undisciplined. They were disheartened by the inadequate support they had received so far. Sullenly suspicious, they trusted no one who was not from their own colony, their own county, and, when it came down to it, from their own village or farmyard.

Traveling swiftly, he had stopped at Fort Ticonderoga, between

Lake George and Lake Champlain, and there found General Schuyler suffering from fever and gout. The sick general was bearing up courageously, doing his best to persuade touchy, bickering subordinates to send any available food, ammunition, and money up to Brigadier General Montgomery's seventeen hundred soldiers from New York, Connecticut, Massachusetts, and New Hampshire. Schuyler's terrible physical condition paralleled the awful, desperate state of the rebel army at Saint John's.

There was not a day to be lost in this hasty gamble to capture Lower Canada, but Sutherland could see that weeks had already slipped away because of incompetence, well-meaning mistakes, and a pronounced lack of military organization to make war. The first flush of rebellious enthusiasm had passed, and the achievements at Lexington and Bunker Hill could not feed or clothe hungry, cold, and sickly men, who blamed Congress for their despair, believing the delegates did not really care about them. It had become a war of commissaries and of supply, and a battle to win over the thousands of French and Indians who populated the north country. As yet wavering in allegiance, these inhabitants held the balance of power. Whoever they chose would be the victor, and with every day that the besieged British held on to the fort at Saint John's, confidence in rebel power waned among these volatile, hardy folk.

From the moment Sutherland's whaleboat drew into the low-lying, swampy shore on the west side of the Richelieu River, he noticed the lackadaisical attitude of sentries, the discouraged looks of troops manning muddy entrenchments, and the bad condition of weapons and clothing. Sick men were everywhere, lying in lean-tos, ragged tents, and shacks. The wooded shoreline was thick with rebel soldiers, sallow-faced and morbid, wrapped in blankets against the damp chill, trying to keep warm at smoky campfires. Everyone seemed to be wondering if he would be next to fall ill with dysentery or worse. Few had died in battle, for the enemy was keeping well inside the fort—but hunger, disease, and cold were deadly foes.

Sutherland ordered his three hired crewmen to begin unloading the whaleboat and said he would be back to have his tent set up somewhere in the encampment. He had brought a large amount of food, several blankets, shoes, and clothing for himself and for Peter Defries, who was somewhere with the army. Also, he had a chest of medicines that would be useful in tending to the needs of this sickly, doleful collection of rebels. He would report to

Montgomery first, because he was also carrying dispatches from General Schuyler, and later he would find Peter and have the three boatmen join them.

The ground Sutherland crossed on foot was deep with slush and sucking mud. It was a desolate scene. Trees were slashed and hacked for firewood or shelter, shallow latrines stank without enough quicklime to treat them, and everything was a murky shade of gray. The groans of ill and wounded mingled with occasional bits of homesick song or bursts of ill-tempered argument, creating a melancholy atmosphere that smelled too much of defeat. Sutherland's dispatches from Schuyler would not cheer up Montgomery, for they explained that reinforcements being assembled at Ticonderoga had refused to sail north until their own commanding officers caught up with them. Schuyler urged Montgomery to attempt the capture of Saint John's and its five hundred defenders—most of them regulars—without additional troops. So far, the rebels had been before the fort for three weeks without the least success.

An occasional thud of artillery and the pop of random musketry told Sutherland the foremost rebel trenches facing the fort must be near, and he hurried to take a look. He was trim and clean in buckskins and leggins, the claymore at his side. The Pennsylvania rifle was slung over his shoulder, and he had a warm fur cap against the unseasonably cold, blustery weather. The troops contemplated him idly as he passed, some remarking that he soon would be filthy and tattered like them. Others called out, telling him to be gentlemanly and keep his nice sword out of the mud.

Following directions to the tent where Montgomery had his headquarters, Sutherland passed six-foot-high earthworks, thrown up a few hundred yards from the fort. He stopped to climb a mound and gaze downriver, through thin birch and maple saplings. There stood the British stronghold. It consisted of two square enclosures of sod and earth, each one a hundred feet on a side and twelve feet high. These two compounds were linked by a stockaded corridor three hundred feet long, and in each was a large brick building—one a house, the other a barn—where British regulars, loyalists, Canadian supporters, and their wives and families were huddled under the sluggish, ineffective fire of the few rebel cannon.

Sutherland saw the Union Jack snapping on a mast in the left-hand compound, and it painfully occurred to him that the people besieged were his own countrymen. For a fleeting moment, his heart sank, and he was struck by the tragedy of it all. But those besieged people were his enemy, and if they held this fort much longer there might be no further march northward. Winter would close about the American rebels, and few ever would get home again.

Sutherland studied the fort and saw a newly built sloop of war anchored in the river beyond the works. A surrounding ditch full of water protected the compounds, and with a broad open marsh-land of brown grass on three sides, a direct attack would be costly if the British fought hard. There was a loud boom, as rebels close at hand fired a fat, aged mortar, its massive shell visible as it arched over the fort to burst harmlessly in the river.

"Old Sow!" a gunner yelled in anger. "No wonder ye're called Old Sow! Ye're blind as an old sow, and twice as stubborn!"

This burly fellow with a black beard gave the mortar a savage kick, and his fellows grumbled in agreement that the squat mortar was unbelievably poor at hitting its target.

Sutherland recognized the gunner with the beard, and shouted, "Since when does a blacksmith know anything about sows, let alone mortars?"

Bill Poole spun at this mocking remark, but when he saw who had said it, he howled with delight and ran to greet Sutherland. The Scotsman laughed happily to be in the company of this man, whom he regarded highly. He was startled, however, that the best the rebels could do for an artilleryman was the inexperienced Poole.

"Owen!" the blacksmith declared, "it does my heart good to see ye, lad! I'd heard tell ye'd joined up with 'em mangy Yorkers!" He introduced Sutherland to his Connecticut friends, one a brother who was as thin and sallow as Poole was robust. The gunners gave a silent nod of greeting. "Yorkers loaned us this useless hunk of scrap iron! Yorkers who didn't have no other use for it but to stash potatoes in!" He gave the mortar another kick and declared that as hard as they tried to aim it, they could not hit the fort.

Sutherland looked closely at the gun. He was familiar with cannon from his days as a merchant seaman and knew it could do tremendous damage if used properly. He inspected the elevation of the gun, which was controlled by jamming wedges of wood under the breech. It was badly aimed. With the Connecticut men voicing some suspicion, he maneuvered a wedge around and said, "This gun must always be aimed at forty-five degrees, and you'll get the right range by experimenting with the proper amount of powder in the charge. Once you sight her properly, paint a white line down the top surface of the barrel, make it align with a plumb line somebody holds between the gun and the target in the fort . . ."

As he spoke, he deftly loaded a cartridge cloth with powder, carefully measuring how much he used. Then he walked to the front of the mortar and hung a bullet on a piece of string as a plumb line to determine his aim. In this way, the gun could be checked after every shot and would be kept on target.

At Sutherland's request, Poole had the gun loaded with the charge just made; a hollow shell filled with gunpowder was dropped down the muzzle and rammed firmly home. Taking the slow-match linstock from an openmouthed amateur gunner, Sutherland lit the touchhole. There was a hiss and a deafening boom as the mortar shook the ground and caused ears to ring. The whistling shell arched languidly through the sky. Again Sutherland had that gnawing feeling that he was attacking his own people.

The shell crashed through the roof of the house in the lefthand compound, and the following explosion blew the inside of the building apart. Windows belched smoke and debris, the roof was lifted almost completely off, and doors were blown out. Only the brick walls were undamaged.

Sutherland gaped. How nonchalant and professional he had been! All around, men were yowling in delight, crawling out of tents to view the success. Ill soldiers were dragging themselves to the top of entrenchments to watch smoke and dust rise from the house they had failed to hit after weeks of futile trying.

Poole was the most excited of all. He slapped Sutherland on the back, saying, "Resign that damned York commission, Owen, and join us! I wish to hell we had enough ammunition to take pot shots all day until there ain't no fort left at all! If we could get the black powder and shells, you could aim, and it won't be no effort to smash them Britishers to smithereens!"

As would-be gunners swabbed out the barrel of the Old Sow and prepared another cartridge, Sutherland told Poole he had to confer with Montgomery, adding, "If you build yourself a strong platform for a flat firing surface, and you line up the barrel with a plumb, you won't need my help. Remember, the amount of powder in the charge determines distance."

Poole waved as Sutherland left, saying he should share mess with them tonight, for Montgomery ate no better than the troops, and one of his New Haven men had liberated a few chickens from a loyal French nobleman's house. Sutherland thanked Poole and hurried away through the streams of curious men coming forward to watch the exultant gunners try again.

Sutherland found Montgomery's tent and was told the general was away, reconnoitering downriver. He left word with the general's secretary that he would return with dispatches as soon as the commander came back. Then he asked for the whereabouts of Peter Defries, who was acting as commissary for one of the York regiments.

Hearing Defries was sick, Sutherland hastened through the camp and found him in a small lean-to near the river's edge. Defries was astonished and delighted to see his old friend, but Sutherland could not believe how awful the man looked. Defries was not the hearty, hale fellow he always had been. Instead, he was feverish and coughing, lying on a torn blanket over dirty straw. Sutherland saw by the bedrolls that at least eight other men were sheltered here at night, though there was room for only three.

"Owen!" Defries gasped, trying to sit up. Sutherland pushed him down again. "I thought you was dinin' with Congress folk!" The Dutchman's voice was weak and hoarse.

"Peter, laddie! What's the matter? How did you let this happen to yourself?" Sutherland laid the dispatches aside and began to rummage through his heavy knapsack. He had plenty of food and equipment back in the whaleboat, but in the knapsack was a bottle of Scotch, and Peter's eyes lit up to see it.

Defries drank a solid shot, lay back, and smiled with a sigh. Sutherland feared he had dysentery and said so, but Defries strained to sit up and shook his head.

"More like feverish pneumonia," he rasped. "Ain't got no bloody discharge, but I'm weak as a mouse, and I can't eat! Good thing I can drink!" He had another swig and closed his eyes.

This feeble, pale, and haggard Peter Defries was something Sutherland had never imagined possible. If even Defries was like this, it was no wonder Montgomery's army was so bedraggled and full of disease. The Old Sow blasted away, followed by the scream of the shell and a distant explosion. It must have been another hit, for the entire rebel encampment howled and roared in joy. Sutherland cared nothing for that just now. He had to help Defries.

"I've got medicines aplenty in my boat," he said. "We'll have you up and around in no time. We'll make our own camp away from all these sick lads, and I'll nurse you like your dear Dutch mother would! Aye, and be just as hard on you, too!"

Defries grinned weakly, his spirits already lifted. Sutherland went off to fetch his men and gear, and soon Defries was comfortably settled into a clean, dry tent on higher ground, exposed to the southern sun, or what little there was of it in this dreary, cloudy weather. Defries lay in the tent, covered with blankets, sleeping soundly, while Sutherland prepared a hearty meal of boiled beef and cabbage, with lemons bought in Albany. He suspected Defries might be suffering from scurvy as well, as so many others at the miserable encampment seemed to be. He resolved to do what he could to have his boatmen go down to Albany and buy up citrus fruits and juices at the busy market there. He would dole out this scurvy remedy to as many as he could.

Late in the afternoon, when a British mortar shell burst with a resounding boom nearby, Defries awoke and sat up in his blankets.

"You look better already," Sutherland said, and brought over a spoonful of Stoughton's Bitters to induce purging; Defries recoiled at this disgusting medicine, but Sutherland insisted. "Come on! Get it down! Just like your Dutch mother I'll be, till you're on your feet again! I need men I can count on!"

Defries gagged, but took the foul stuff, following it with fresh water Sutherland forced on him. A little while later, they sat before a roaring fire, desultory cannonading going on not far away. Defries revealed the sorry campaign in full.

"Damned New Englanders!" Defries hissed, and sneezed with the effort to talk. "These damned Yankees think they're at a town meetin', not a war! Officers got to get together with privates to ask politely whether they would mind marchin' around Saint John's! Or would it suit 'em to muster this mornin'? Or perhaps they'd be so good as to take a shot or two at 'em British over in the fort!"

Sutherland heard that the troops had twice loaded into boats in a panic during the early investment of Saint John's, refusing to go on with the fight because they heard rumors that the enemy had an overwhelming force on the way. Only the pleading of General Montgomery and a few other responsible officers had persuaded them to come back and eventually surround Saint John's.

"I ain't foolin', Owen, Yankees won't do nothin' without everybody at a council of war first!" Defries spat and stretched his aching muscles. "And when they say council, they mean every last man jack down to the young lads rappin' on drums! An' if drummers don't agree with officers, they all just get up, pick up, and pack up to leave till the officers give in! I swear, the only reason half of 'em still hang about is that they're too sick to go!"

Defries had plenty to complain about, but by the time he had told of the army's refusal to assault the fort when Montgomery called for it, or even to sign the articles of war enlisting them formally into the new Continental Army, Sutherland well understood their bad frame of mind.

For one thing, they had not been paid and were suffering from a lack of everything necessary to fight. For another, winter was fast closing in, and they rightly feared they might be left up here to freeze and starve, without hope of escaping if they failed to take Saint John's. Also, there was no certainty that the French peasants would rise and join them as had been hoped, and there were rumors that Indians were preparing to attack their flanks and force them to break camp and flee. If the army was routed, there were not enough bateaux to get them all away, and Yorkers suspected Yankees of wanting to run first, while Yankees were sure the Yorkers would leave them behind as a sacrifice if they could. No one had confidence in his comrades, or in Congress, because of the shortage of supplies. Congress had promised, but because of inadequate war readiness, had been unable to deliver essential food and equipment.

Defries had no sympathy for the suffering troops, however. "They don't trust their officers, not even Montgomery, and he's a hell of a man! Why, if we get shot at when we send troops on the move, somebody sure enough declares Montgomery's a Tory in disguise who means to lead us to defeat! If guns don't work, they blame Montgomery! If it rains, they blame Montgomery! And if they ain't got food, they blame Congress. There, though, I can't say I blame 'em."

At that he sneezed, and it sounded like "Shitoncongress!"

Sutherland said, "There's some food and clothing on the way, but little black powder to be had until our own mills are set up to make it—and none to replenish what you've used so far."

Defries lamented that. "It's one thing that we've been on half rations of pork fat and peas ever since we got here, but we can't fight without powder!"

In the course of the conversation, Sutherland learned that rebel scouts and recruiting agents were passing through the country between Saint John and the Saint Lawrence, trying to persuade the hundreds of Canadian and Indian fighting men in the region to support them. There was a deep fear in the camp—justified by reality—that if those people saw things going badly for the rebels, they would join the British and it would be over for Montgomery's little army.

"It's a razor's edge right now, Owen," Defries said. "Go out to the villages and farms and say you're a Whig, and they won't give you the time of day. That's why so many of our hungry boys got to *take* the necessaries, 'cause there ain't no cash to pay for what we need."

Sutherland could see the chances of his getting to Detroit before winter were remote, unless this fort fell soon. The British and loyalists inside were said to be starving, also, and were crowded, cramped, and in danger from the few shells the rebels could afford to spend. But they would not surrender unless they had to, for they had confidence that the inexperienced rebels could not hold on once the anticipated relief force came upstream from Montreal.

Leaving Defries to recover and to digest more Stoughton's Bitters, Sutherland went to General Montgomery's tent and found the officer back from his trip. After turning over the dispatches to the tired and haggard commander, he explained an idea he had, which, if successful, might convince the defenders of Saint John's that the end was near.

chapter 21

A BRITISH STANDARD

Ten miles north of Saint John's was a second British fort, called Chambly. It was manned by nearly one hundred regulars of the Seventh Welsh Fusiliers, who were amply supplied with food, munitions, and warm clothing. After Sutherland carefully scouted this post, he saw that even though it was built of masonry, its walls were not thick enough to withstand accurate cannon fire. Conferring with Montgomery and the captain commanding York artillery, he won approval of a plan to slip bateaux loaded with cannon downriver, past Saint John's, at nightfall.

It was a dangerous task, through foaming rapids that ran most of the ten miles between the forts. The cold river was swift and deep, noisy, and clouded with icy mist. It required great skill and courage to get the bateaux downstream that night. Sutherland chose men he knew, including Poole's gunners and some men from the northwest who had served with him through the Mohawk Valley episode. Also along were some of the York troops he had run up against during the near-riot in Albany. These Yorkers were led by Lieutenant Gavin Duff, the former corporal who had deserted Fort Stanwix to join the rebel army.

That long, black night they labored, poling, rowing, sometimes putting in to shore to edge along the bank with ropes lashed to trees. It was grueling, wet work, and hazardous. When the fall of the river became too steep and water raged savagely, the bateaux were landed and cannon placed on farmer's carts for the rest of the journey. At dawn Sutherland was joined by a mixed force of New Hampshiremen and three hundred French Canadian volunteers, who had been prevailed on to join the rebels, and the astonished British garrison was awakened by the frightening crash of cannonballs punching holes in their stone walls.

For three brutal days rebel guns battered Chambly, spending

precious powder but winning the admiration of Frenchman and
Indian onlookers alike. In the end, the fort surrendered and with
it an enormous store of precious powder, ball, and even warm
Redcoat uniforms and coats, which were quickly distributed from
the supply rooms. The ragged Americans looked comical in fine
scarlet coats and patchwork civilian breeches, but they were proud
of their triumph. Almost as thrilling as the capturing of powder
and supplies was the taking of the regimental colors of the Seventh
Welsh Fusiliers. This was the first battle trophy ever won by rebel
arms, and the troops were overwhelmed with joy that the fortunes
of the campaign had changed so much for the better.

When Sutherland's troops came marching back along the river
road through dense woods, they were met by Montgomery, with
a few officers riding beside him. The general had heard the exciting
news, and Sutherland saw how moved he was to be presented the
standard of the Seventh Fusiliers. Montgomery's horse was frac-
tious, and he had to struggle with it and with his own emotions
in order to display a proper military bearing as he accepted the
standard and unfurled it. It was a Union Jack, and in its center
was a rose surrounded by a garter, a crown above. The motto was
that of the legendary English Knights of the Garter, *Honi soit qui
mal y pense*, which might be translated as, "Shame on him who
thinks evil of what we do."

Sutherland saw irony in this, for there was no doubt that the
American rebels thought evil of the Redcoats barring their way to
victory over Lower Canada. In turn, these British soldiers and
their loyal adherents believed fully in their own cause, and were
wholeheartedly opposed to what Sutherland and his rebels were
attempting to achieve.

Montgomery held up the captured colors for all to see. The
narrow road was thronged with proud rebels and French *habitants*,
as well as with the many Frenchmen who had helped take Chambly.
These Canadians were beginning to believe the British Army was
not so invincible, and that this boisterous, audacious rebel army
might win the campaign after all.

"*Honi soit qui mal y pense!*" Montgomery cried, standing up
in his stirrups, raising the British regimental standard high. The
French cheered him, along with the victorious rebel troops, and
then Montgomery cried out an even more powerful motto—this
one also on the British royal arms: "*Dieu et mon droit!*"

Again the onlookers howled in excitement, and even Sutherland
was stirred to hear such venerable words applied to the rebel

cause—the American cause. "God and my right!" the motto declared plainly in the language of the *habitants*, who would consider it very soberly.

Montgomery passed the colors on to a subordinate, then removed his tricorne in salute as the victors marched off, having left a small garrison to hold Chambly and guard the prisoners still there. As Sutherland walked by Montgomery, these two former professional soldiers acknowledged each other. Both knew it was profoundly strange to have captured a British regimental standard. Every other former British soldier in the rebel force felt that way, for they had been devoted all their lives to the army and the king. The world would never be the same again.

A fifer played brightly, striking up "Yankee Doodle," and then Montgomery called out, asking Sutherland to come to his headquarters that evening for a private discussion. Sutherland touched his hat and strode on in time with the music. It was a good song, good enough to carry this tough little army all the way to Montreal and even Quebec.

Near nightfall, Sutherland was in Montgomery's large tent, in the flickering light of oil lamps and candles. He sat on a stool, the only chair, and Montgomery used a barrel, which was next to a makeshift plank table. There were maps and charts, records of daily regimental strength, a sword hanging by its scabbard over a neat cot, and some good French brandy was on the table. Other than writing implements and some books, there was little else in these spartan surroundings.

Montgomery was gaunt and pale, but though he was obviously weary, an inner strength seemed to radiate from him as he spoke. His voice was high-pitched and cultured, but also clipped and no-nonsense, in the manner of a veteran regular officer.

"I've fought alongside your former regiment, the Forty-second Highlanders," Montgomery told Sutherland, whose thoughts immediately wandered over the past. "They've been stationed in Ireland these past years, but since most of the regiments over there are being sent to America, I imagine they'll come here as well. Perhaps as soon as next year."

Sutherland said, "The coming of Highlanders would be a sorrow to me. It was strange enough to fight Welsh Fusiliers, but the Black Watch . . ."

He did not need to say he would fight them, too, if he had to. Montgomery understood, for there were plenty of native-born

Irishmen like himself in the British ranks.

After a brief discussion concerning Philadelphia, Sutherland was offered the rank of major in the First New York Regiment. He was surprised and was allowed a moment of thought by Montgomery. But he easily made up his mind.

"Some weeks ago," Sutherland said, "I agreed to come here at Dr. Franklin's request, but I agreed to serve no later than November, or before if Montreal falls sooner. My wife and family are at Detroit, and I mean to go for them before winter. General Schuyler accepted me on those terms, and that's how I prefer to remain, sir.

"It's a great honor, General, to be offered this rank, because I respect all that you and General Schuyler have done to get this far. I only wish we could take this fort and get on to Montreal. You see, I know of Arnold's secret march, and if you're to join him at Quebec before bad weather blocks the road, you'll have to break through soon."

Montgomery was startled that Sutherland knew of the army moving through northern Maine toward Quebec City. It was obvious Sutherland had powerful friends in Congress.

Montgomery replied, "Perhaps the fall of Chambly will clear the mind of the stubborn commander in Saint John's." He stood up. "Let's send him proof of his sorry plight, and pray he'll be accommodating enough to surrender forthwith."

The following morning, a captured Redcoat sergeant major was sent to Saint John's under a flag of truce. Making the most of the victory, Montgomery asked permission from the fort's commander to send the prisoners taken at Fort Chambly upriver in bateaux to remove them from the fighting. The general knew it would be a dismaying sight for the beleaguered defenders of Saint John's to see their comrades herded off, leaving them alone to defend Canada against overwhelming odds.

Yet Saint John's held on. Montgomery was sorely disappointed when he heard the commander's refusal to give in. Later, he stood with Sutherland near the Old Sow as Poole sent round after round screeching into the defenses. Well-supplied with captured ammunition, the rebel guns had been firing all day long.

"They're brave in there," Montgomery remarked. "I wish I had such disciplined men instead of a quarreling gaggle of civilians!"

Sutherland understood the officer's distress but said quietly, "They're still with you, General."

Montgomery listened closely as Sutherland went on. "They're not regulars, sir, and most never will be, but after what they've suffered here, the fact they're staying on with winter coming means they're the right sort. Think, sir, about the ones who don't complain, and consider what they're made of before you're too hard on them."

Montgomery relaxed, then jumped a bit as the mortar went off. "Yes, I've expected too much from them. I often forget they're different men from the professional troops I'm used to." He gave a little laugh and shook his head. "I'm learning about these Americans the hard way, but perhaps one day I'll be considered one of them."

"I think you've already earned the name American, General Montgomery." Sutherland smiled. "Parliament would surely call you one, though not meaning it as a compliment."

Just then Bill Poole strode over to them, touching his forehead to Montgomery. "Beggin' yer pardon, General, sir, but my boys'd like a word with Mr. Sutherland here, about the proper charge in the Old Sow—"

A tremendous explosion blew them all off their feet, and Sutherland reeled hard against a tree, staggering as the wind was knocked out of him. He regained his feet, and when the acrid smoke cleared, he knew the mortar had burst. Men were running everywhere and horrible screams of agony came from the wounded. Sutherland shook away the dizziness in his ringing skull and sought anxiously for Montgomery, fearing he had been killed.

The officer was all right, with only a few bruises and a torn uniform. He was with the injured near the remnants of the destroyed mortar, which had blown apart like a steel flower. Bill Poole, blood on his face and arms, came to the general, who was cradling a dying Connecticut man in his arms. It was Poole's brother. The blacksmith groaned and fell to his knees, taking his brother from Montgomery. Sutherland and the others regained their senses and did what they could to help the injured and carry away the dead. A man had an arm blown off, another was gutted. Four were dead on the spot, and others would die. In an almost bloodless, dreary war, as many rebel lives had been lost in this mishap as in an entire month's siege—without counting those who had succumbed to illness.

A somber mood settled over the men as they cleaned up debris and prepared to bury the dead. Most of Poole's gun crew had been wiped out, and he was the only man left who could stand. After

Poole's brother had been laid to rest, Sutherland took the weeping New Haven blacksmith to his tent and tended his wounds.

It was a small incident in a small battle of a nameless war that had hardly begun, but to Sutherland, this was the story of all war: inglorious, painful, and cursed with ugly sadness for those who did the fighting. The light hearts that had set out to conquer Canada had become dark and moody. The British and loyalists they had meant to chastise and humiliate were now hated blood enemies. He knew those suffering within the walls of Saint John's felt just the same about the rebels.

Dawson Merriwether came across the river on a sunny October day with a package from England for the Sutherlands. Merriwether was in good cheer, for he knew they all were desperate for these first letters from Jeremy, which had taken all this time to get here. He had decided to take the package personally to them when he learned from the postmaster it had arrived.

Ella invited Merriwether in, as though he were one of the family. He admired the new orchard, where Mel was busy trying out a new grafting technique. Then he commented on Sally and Tom walking hand in hand along the beach.

"I knew those two'd find some way to fall in love!" He laughed and followed Ella and the chattering children into the house. Ella fussed around the kitchen, attempting clumsily to put on water for tea, but she was so excited about the letters that Merriwether insisted she read them first.

Ella looked at him, thinking how decent he was and what bizarre times these were to put them on opposite sides in this conflict. As the children urged her on, she cut the string from the bundle of letters and unwrapped several layers of waxed paper.

Tom and Sally came in then, and Benjamin yelled in a voice that rang through the house, "Sally! Letters from Jer! Letter for you! Come quick!"

Sally gasped and ran forward, then felt Tom hesitate, and she turned to him. He smiled, saying he would wait outside until she read it.

Sally grasped his hand. "Stay with me, and we'll read together. There's one for you, too, see?"

Susannah gave each of them letters, which were the ones posted in early spring, before Jeremy knew he would marry Penelope Graves.

Sally and Tom sat side by side, each silently reading their own

letter from Jeremy. As she read, Sally felt a sense of relief at
Jeremy's nonchalance. Clearly, Jeremy was not expecting her to
wait for him.

Ella felt weak and happy all at once. Forgetful of the others,
she sat down at the trestle table and began to devour her letter.
How mature Jeremy sounded! How he had changed, though it had
been only a short time! She learned about Derbyshire, Henry
Gladwin, Edinburgh, and about Richard Weston, Sniffer's great
friend. Also, it was easy to read between the lines and tell that
the girl called Penelope meant something special to Jeremy.

"It's a wonderful letter!" she declared, and looked up to see
only her two children there. Merriwether was out on the veranda
petting Heera, and Tom and Sally were in the backyard, sitting
under the maple tree.

"Read it aloud, Ma!" Benjamin cried, and Ella sat them down
beside her. Jeremy spoke little of politics, but when he did, she
realized his opinion was sharply different from hers and Owen's.
No doubt that was because he had met so many British and saw
mainly their side of things.

Benjamin voiced his own concern, saying, "He sounds like a
loyalist, Ma!"

Hearing this, Merriwether turned to look closely at them, and
Ella felt self-conscious. The Virginian seemed to be thinking about
what Benjamin had said as he strolled away in company with the
dog.

"He's no loyalist, darling," Ella said. "He's just seeing things
from another perspective, that's all."

Susannah chimed in, "Does that mean he's not on our side?"

Ella felt a twinge in her heart. She did not want to hear this.
She would not hear it.

"Don't say such things! Neither of you! Now listen while I
read it all. Be still, and just realize your brother's in a different
country, with different people. He won't forget us, you know!"

"Just the same," Benjamin said plainly, "it doesn't sound like
Jeremy's on our side, Ma."

Ella looked at the lad imploringly, but he knew what he was
saying. Benjamin was growing up, too, and did not try to gloss
over things, not even when it came to so tender a subject. Ella
tried to shake off what the boy had said, but she read Jeremy's
letter with mounting anxiety. She could not deny that, indeed,
Jeremy did sound like a loyalist.

* * *

Ella and the children were accompanying Tom and Sally to Fort
Detroit one Saturday afternoon in October when a flotilla of Indian
canoes came downriver. Disembarking from their own craft, they
stopped to watch the arrival of at least a hundred birch boats full
of painted Indians and their families.

"Ottawas from up at Michilimackinac," Tom said. "Looks like
they've come for a parley with the British. Come on, let's stay
out of their way!"

They moved away from the landing and walked up the slope
to the fort's water gate, Heera bounding along with them. There,
another thirty or forty noisy, decorated warriors of many nations
whooped and applauded to see the arrival of the Ottawas. The
British soon would hold a major Indian council, and Ella feared
they would call upon the Indians to go to war against the rebels.
After the destruction of her orchard a few weeks ago, there had
been no other incident at Valenya, but since then she had avoided
coming to Detroit, so she did not know the exact mood of Indians
and loyalists near the fort. As she and the rest went through the
gate, however, she sensed hostility from those who recognized her
as a Whig.

Tom and Sally hurried off with Heera to visit the Lees, whose
new residence was a small cabin near the stables. The minister
had been put out of the unused barrack that had been his chapel
and apartment, because the army objected to his Whig leanings.
It was expected that before long no one left at Detroit would listen
to his sermons, not even Dawson Merriwether, his father-in-law.

As Ella walked through the fort with the two children, she gave
a start to see the hideous Manoth glaring at her. He was in a
cabin's shadow, with two of his Seneca companions. One had a
bandage around his upper thigh—surely the man she had shot!
Manoth wore a long scarlet plume attached to a round silk cap,
making him appear even more warlike. He made as if to step
toward Ella, to scare her, but she refused to flinch and glared back
at him. A few soldiers and traders were around, but that might
not stop Manoth from trying some harassment.

Ella pushed Benjamin and Susannah ahead of her, along the
busy, dirty street. She wished Heera had stayed at her side and
not gone with Sally and Tom. Then, as though she had been
touched, she felt a cold, threatening sensation behind. She whirled
in alarm to see Manoth very close. As she sprang back, Benjamin
bravely put himself in front of her.

With an ugly leer on his face, Manoth rumbled, "You be plenty fine white bitch. Make fine squaw for Manoth." He snickered as Ella readied to swing her carrying bag at him.

"Go!" she demanded, holding Benjamin, who would have charged, kicking and punching. In halting Oneida, learned from Hickory, she cried, "Go, before I get a gun and shoot you for the bad dog you are!"

Manoth's mockery immediately turned to rage, for Ella had insulted him with the worst of Indian epithets and had done it in an Iroquois tongue that his friends loitering nearby had heard.

The Seneca hissed, "Me dog? You bitch! I come get you some night! You be ready—"

Ella's heavy canvas bag flew in a sweeping arc and grazed his nose. Staggering a pace backward, cursing in English, Manoth would have struck her if a slim Redcoat officer had not pushed between them, shaking his fist at Manoth's tattooed face. This young ensign was half the size of the Indian.

"Leave off, Manoth!" the officer commanded fearlessly.

Manoth looked ready to break the fellow in two but restrained himself, knowing he would be punished if he hurt a soldier in the fort.

"If I ever see you insult a white woman again, I'll throw you in irons, and to hell with your friend, Lieutenant Davies! Leave off, I say, or even he won't be able to help you!"

Manoth hardly looked at the furious officer. Showing no emotion, the Seneca turned to swagger contemptuously away.

Bowing to Ella, Richard Weston introduced himself and said he was very sorry this unpleasantness had gone so far before he had arrived to halt it. At first Ella did not recognize his name from Jeremy's letter, but when she told him who she was, Weston staggered with surprise.

"Jeremy's mother! Why, Mrs. Sutherland, I've hoped to come across the river to pay my respects ever since I reached Detroit three days ago, but I've been kept too busy with a thousand tedious details!"

Weston's unexpected warmth was a relief to Ella. While other folk gave her sidelong looks and whispered behind their hands that this young officer soon would learn who was to be befriended and who not, they broke into a lively discussion about Jeremy and England. Ella now remembered Weston from her son's letter but had not expected him to be posted out here. Nor had he.

"Dreadful!" he declared. "I mean this is a beautiful place, to be sure, but I'd best not have much ambition as far as soldiering goes! I had hoped for Boston or Saint John's, where my regiment's main body is stationed, but it seems my fate was to meet you, and I daresay it's good fortune that it happened to be just now! By the way, I carry letters from Jeremy, and he's about to be—" Weston abruptly refrained from telling of Jeremy's coming marriage, deciding to let the letters speak for themselves. He did not know Jeremy was already married and on his way with Penelope to America. He said he would fetch the letters for Ella as soon as he was finished with the "greasy duty of welcoming Indian nabobs and bashaws and their retinue." About to excuse himself, Weston was interrupted by someone angrily shouting his name.

Lieutenant Mark Davies was storming toward them, and Weston showed puzzlement, wondering why the man was so red in the face. Weston had no knowledge of the hatred Davies bore Ella and was astonished when his superior officer demanded to know why he was talking to her.

"Personal matters, Lieutenant." Weston was far more the gentleman than Davies ever would be, and he curbed his rising anger. The lieutenant, however, lost his head and fumed sourly about niggling military matters that seemed of no great importance to the ensign.

"Those redskins will be here soon, and you're supposed to greet them!" Davies exclaimed. "Are you prepared? Have you learned protocol? Well, then, get down to the landing this very minute, you sluggard! Don't dally here with such despicable riffraff!"

Weston was cool, but touched his sword hilt. "Apologize to Mistress Sutherland, Lieutenant, or I'll call you out this very moment."

Davies's eyes popped. Many others were watching as he began to quiver at the challenge. The rules of chivalry among gentlemen went beyond the disciplinary rights of a superior officer over a junior, and Weston was entitled to demand satisfaction. Commandant Lernoult was away from the fort, inspecting defenses at Vincennes, leaving Davies himself in charge. That did not faze the defiant Weston.

Davies sputtered, "You would sully your honor for the sake of such baggage? You're a—"

Weston slapped Davies hard across the face, a cracking sound that laid a hush over the street as everyone stopped to see what would happen next. "It's you whose honor is sullied, Lieutenant. Choose your weapons."

Ella gasped, afraid for Weston, but there was nothing she could do.

Davies had no choice. He could not back down.

"Very well, Ensign. At dawn tomorrow, in the field beyond the western gate." He was shaking but governed his fury to say, "Pistols!"

When Davies spun on his heel and stamped out of the fort's gate to meet the Indians arriving for the parley, Weston calmly said with a smile, "I presume I'm off duty now. I'll get those letters for you."

Ella touched his arm. "Oh, sir, I'm so—"

"Please!" Weston wanted her to say nothing. "Your son once saved my hide. This is the least I can do."

He escorted her to the door of the tiny cabin that was his quarters, shared with another junior officer. When he came back out with the letters, Ella was almost in tears, the two children standing close to her.

"There, there," Weston said kindly. "These'll cheer you all up! And please, Mrs. Sutherland, have no fear for my welfare." He smiled in that confident, dashing way he had. "I'll expect an invitation to Valenya in return, however!"

"Ensign Weston . . ." Ella fought back a sob. "Jeremy's letters spoke so well of you that I really do feel as if I know you. I'm honored, sir!"

Weston walked with Ella to the Morely-Grey trading house and parted with her there, saying he had many matters to attend to that day. Ella watched him stride away and knew he would have to write a will and arrange affairs with Commandant Lernoult's secretary. Lernoult would be furious when he returned and learned why his officers had conducted a duel!

Ella could hardly believe this was happening, and she hurried into the trading house, where Tom and Sally had arrived a few moments earlier. When she told the others what had occurred, Tom declared he would be Weston's second, and so did James. Those two ran out to find the ensign, leaving Ella, Sally, and the children with Jeb and Lettie. All of them felt despair at the way life was becoming increasingly difficult with every passing day.

Lettie looked at Jeb, who was preparing an order for an Indian trapper, one of the few who still openly did business with the Frontier Company. He was bent over, counting out fishhooks on the Indian's blanket, which was spread on the floor to receive everything needed for the season. The Indian would come back that night to accept the goods and, as was customary, make his mark on a ledger, promising so many beaver pelts in return for this outfitting.

Trying not to be drawn into what he sensed would be a gloomy conversation with his wife, Jeb ignored Lettie's stare as long as possible. He counted out fishhooks, was distracted, lost count, and, with a sigh, stood up straight to begin again. Lettie was still staring at him. He glanced at her, then at Ella, who was sitting despondently near the iron stove, chin on her hand.

Again Jeb miscounted and this time stuck himself with a hook. He shook with annoyance and then said, "Well, woman, what is it you want to argue with me about now?"

Lettie took a quick breath, her vast breasts rising and falling. She leaned forward on the counter, saying, "We best not be ordering more stores or goods this season."

Jeb made no reply. Lettie was voicing what none of them wanted to admit. "We best be getting out. Afore it be too late."

Jeb made a fist and boomed, "Hell, wife, we ain't licked yet! They ain't got nothing against us! We got the law on our side till they prove something, and they can't prove it! We got our place here and—"

"Lettie's right," Ella said dully, too depressed even to read Jeremy's letter. She knew very well now that they were only biding their time. "It's inevitable, Jeb. Sooner or later they'll come for us. We have to be ready for that. But if we go before they come, we have to go prudently, in our own way, not be driven out."

Jeb growled, "I ain't gonna be driven!" He grumbled and strode around a bit. He and Lettie had been told of Owen's message to come to Montreal once it fell to the rebels. They also knew of the emergency plan to take shelter secretly in the Apostle Islands. Jeb had to admit that was the safest way to wait for Sutherland to come for them. Like Tom, he was neither a sailor nor a woodsman and could not lead a large party for hundreds of miles.

Loyalist Indians were the greatest threat. This coming parley would undoubtedly inspire the tribes of the northwest to support the British Army. Showered with presents, the pliable Indians would become even more belligerent to Whigs or suspected Whigs. The three of them spoke of this, and Ella said the Indians would try to earn favor with the military by abusing "enemies of the king."

"Once they're up in arms they can't be stopped before blood is spilled," Ella said—not too loudly, for Sally and the children were standing in the doorway, watching the ceremonious arrival of strutting, befeathered chiefs. "And if that Davies gives them firewater, we're bound to pay for it."

"If Davies survives the duel," Jeb observed with a nod. "It'd do us all good to have him rubbed out by that Weston fellow."

"There'll be others like Davies," Lettie said. "And yon Manoth's a bad 'un—him and his crowd of filthy pals."

Ella said, "Once we know when we have to leave, Mel and Hickory will go down to Lower Canada with a message for Owen, telling him we've gone to the islands."

Now that they knew it had to be undertaken, a plan poured out: They would stay as long as possible at Detroit, and when the moment came to go, they would slip away in whaleboats and sail to the Apostle Islands.

Lettie murmured, "Pray Owen'll come afore ice takes hold of the lake, or we'll be winterin' on them rocks!"

Later that afternoon, word of Jeremy's impending marriage in England came as a surprise, but was not a shock to Sally Cooper. She was sitting with Tom under the maple tree at Valenya, reading Jeremy's latest letter aloud, when the sentence came up, casually, as Jeremy had meant it to. She paused and read it again, silently. A cool autumn breeze wafted through the branches, rustling the dry leaves and sending down a shower of orange, red, and yellow.

Sally took Tom's hand and leaned back against the tree to gaze at the river and the rush of bright autumn color along its banks. Heera came padding through the leaves and nuzzled Tom, who stroked his big head.

She said softly, "How things change! Don't they, Tom?" She let the letter rest in her lap. "Who would've thought things would change like this?"

"I'd been hopin'!" He smiled and said, "I even asked old Mawak to do an Injun love dance for me, so's I'd win you."

They each leaned against the other's shoulder, then Sally said, "It's a good thing I didn't know about Mawak's love dances, or I'd have had him do one to get Jeremy long ago, before . . . before I knew I loved you so much."

Tom kissed her hand and then her lips. Heera pushed his massive wet nose between them and licked their faces simultaneously. They laughed and shoved the dog aside, and Tom became unexpectedly serious. He gently drew Sally's face toward his own and kissed her again, not caring who was watching. Heera lay down in the autumn leaves, tongue hanging out, seeming to grin.

"Will you be my wife, Sal?"

Sally threw her arms around his neck and said, "Oh, Tom, I'd love to! Tom, I love you!"

There came an ear-splitting howl of delight, and Heera sprang aside with a yelp as Susannah and Benjamin dropped from the tree into the dry leaves. They scrambled away, racing toward the house, yelling, "Ma! Ma! They're gonna marry! Yippee! Yippee!"

The couple laughed, and when Ella came out of her kitchen door to wave at them, Sally blew her a kiss and leaned against her man. Seeing that Tom was blushing, Sally laughed and kissed his cheek.

"Did you really have Mawak do a love dance?"

He guffawed and kissed her hard. Sally drew him close, feeling happier than she ever thought possible.

chapter 22

VICTORY

The next morning at Valenya, Ella was up and dressed well before dawn, unable to sleep because she feared for Richard Weston. Over the orchard, the sun came filtering through clouds, softly lighting her kitchen, where she sat with a cup of hot tea in her hands. The children would be down soon, and attending to them would take her mind from the anxiety.

Her stomach was twisted, and she felt cold, even holding the tea. Tom Morely had promised to come over immediately with news of the duel's outcome, but Ella feared he and James, as Weston's seconds, might be drawn into the fray. It must be taking place as she sat there.

Suddenly Heera started barking, and Ella rushed to throw open the door.

"Tom!" She ran outside as Tom Morely came bounding up from the water, waving his hat and shouting.

"Davies lost! Weston won! Weston won!"

Tom bore her into the house, Heera leaping and yapping alongside.

"Davies fired first, but too quick! Close it was, I'll say! The ball tore Weston's blouse but didn't even nick him!"

"And did Weston—?" Ella held back from asking the rest.

Tom chuckled and shook his head. "Fired into the ground. He could've plugged that bug-tit between the eyes, and I gotta give Davies credit, he would've took it like a man! But Weston— whooeee! He's a cool one! Davies'll have to back off him now that Weston spared his life!"

Relieved that no one was killed, Ella sat down at the table, and the strength drained from her. This was the best that had happened in far too long—this and Jeremy's letter, the one Weston had brought out, in which her son announced his marriage and

329

told of his plans to come home with his new bride within a year. She was excited and happy. Life was not so unrelentingly morbid after all. She hoped these things signaled the beginning of a new episode, one that meant eventual tranquillity at Valenya. It was only a hope, but the situation might be getting better now that Weston and Jeremy would both be here. How Ella wished Owen were with her. Then she and her husband could plot a course through this stormy time and confront all the dangers together.

Saint John's hung on. The only good thing that came out of those weeks was that Peter Defries regained his strength. He became his former abrasive, noisy self, cocky and funny, and always ready for a fight. He and Sutherland were valuable scouts for Montgomery, ever watchful for sign of the Indians being stirred up by loyalists. They roved the woods, sometimes going as far as Longueuil, a farming district across the river from Montreal.

It was on such a journey that they learned from a sympathetic Frenchman that British regulars remaining in the city were planning to march out with loyalists and cross the broad Saint Lawrence in a few days. With the anticipated support of many loyalists and Indians, they would make a desperate effort to attack up the Richelieu and relieve Saint John's.

Sutherland and Defries brought this vital news back to Montgomery, who promptly dispatched them and a force of three hundred Green Mountain Boys under their able commander, Colonel Seth Warner, to ambush the enemy before they could land. Sutherland brought along several light cannon, unmounted and carried strapped to packhorses. The detachment hurried along the log road leading to the Saint Lawrence across from Montreal and dug in at Longueuil, under concealment of woods.

The Green Mountain Boys conducted war the way they would a hunt. As they lay under cover at the bank of the Saint Lawrence and observed bateau after bateau over in Montreal being filled with Redcoats and loyalists, these mountain men might as well have been hunting ducks from a blind.

The morning sun was low in the sky behind Sutherland's army. It shone on the red rooftops and spires of Montreal, whose stone houses and narrow streets crowded along the far bank, with steep Mount Royal rising behind. Everyone in the ambush had orders to keep still until the last possible moment. At least forty bateaux were coming across the wide, surging river, approaching from almost half a mile off. There was some scarlet and white, but the green of hunting shirts was the pervading color, indicating the loyalist American volunteers had tried to match one another in some semblance of uniformity.

Sutherland watched them with mounting excitement and dismay. There would be much killing—and of men he knew, men he had done business with. But if this force got through to Saint John's, or raised more Canadians and Indians, the campaign was lost, the rebellion doomed when the British Army arrived here in the spring.

Poole and Lieutenant Duff manned a cannon with Sutherland. They had loaded it with three balls and a double charge of powder. When the boats came within range, the effect would be devastating, if the aim was true. Not a man moved all up and down the wooded bank of the river, and the hidden Green Mountain Boys could not be seen from out on the water. They were hard, angry men, who had sworn to avenge the recent defeat and capture of their admired leader, Ethan Allen. Allen had been taken prisoner in his bold but rash attempt to capture Montreal at the head of Green Mountain Boys and some French Canadians.

The plan had failed, and Allen was said to be in irons, on his way downriver to be taken to England and tried for treason. Sutherland knew these soldiers and loyalists coming across the Saint Lawrence would pay for that. They rowed in an arc that bent against the current, so the bateaux would land on this part of the shore. He aimed his cannon in the path of the leading vessel, which for the most part was packed with Redcoats.

The boats came on, stroke after stroke, the sun glinting off military brass and bayonets. The loyalist civilians wore drab linens, farm or work clothes, and hunting shirts. Some backwoodsmen in buckskins could be seen here and there, but not many. If there had been more they surely would have insisted on first sending scouts across to make certain the landing place was safe.

"It's a bad mistake their leaders are making," Sutherland said to his men. "We're lucky they underestimate us."

"Britishers always underestimate Americans," Lieutenant Duff said softly. "Maybe when we're done today they'll learn another lesson they'll never forget."

The boats were closer now, and Sutherland estimated they held at least eight hundred men, far more than anticipated. If they landed and were well led, the outnumbered Green Mountain Boys would be hard-pressed even to get away. He felt his mouth go dry, his heart beating fast. They must not miss, lest the British drive on despite heavy fire. The riflemen among the trees would not stand for long toe to toe with regulars and the fearful bayonet. The enemy had to be stopped cold, on the water.

Someone was moving through the bushes toward them. It was Defries who had been scouting far downriver toward Sorel. His face was blanched, his blue eyes showing great anxiety.

"Make it count, boys!" he whispered, scurrying beside Sutherland. "Fail, and we'll be caught between these and another thousand loyalists crossing fifty miles downstream."

This came as a shock to them all. That meant the other loyalists were only two days of hard marching away. If they joined with this army and went southward to relieve Saint John's, the rebels were lost.

Sutherland coolly adjusted the cannon's aim, anticipating the drift of the first bateau, which was less than two hundred yards off. Defries said the other loyalists were mostly native Scotsmen and their sons from New York and the Hampshire Grants.

"A *habitant* told me they're mostly veterans of the army who settled in the colonies after being discharged. They're known as the Royal Highland Emigrants."

Defries was gazing at Sutherland, whose expression did not change, except that he took a long, slow breath, saying, "Royal? A regiment has to earn the title 'royal.'" Sutherland said nothing more.

The first bateau was less than a hundred yards away, plodding slowly as those snub-nosed boats always did, but coming on steadily. A little closer and the first one, which seemed to have many officers, would be near enough. Sutherland had judged well: The bateau was coming gradually under the gun, its helmsman still steering slightly upstream to compensate for the current. It appeared they intended to land exactly where the ambush had been set.

Coming closer, their voices could be heard across the water, and the creaking of oars rose above the river's noise. Another twenty yards would be enough to guarantee utter rout, complete destruction—if the guns were handled perfectly.

But a nervous Green Mountain Boy fired too soon.

Sutherland swore, for his gun was not on target yet. At the single shot, the bateau's helmsman swung her nose to Sutherland's left, out of his sights. Suddenly the entire fleet began to maneuver as officers kept their heads and shouted commands. A ragged, confused fire rippled along the riverbank, bluish smoke rising from the trees, but the rebel riflemen had been too excited to aim and did little damage. Sutherland was straining at the cannon, he, Defries, and Poole manhandling it around to bear on the transport. Twenty soldiers in this bateau were already kneeling, leveling muskets, preparing to fire a wicked volley on command, for their officer had spotted Sutherland's guns. Other officers were doing the same with their own men, and in a moment hundreds of muskets would rake the woods.

Sutherland had no time to think. As the gun barrel bore on the bateau, the officer on the boat shouted "Fire!" At that precise instant, Sutherland touched the linstock to the hole. The gun boomed, jumping back on its cradle, held by ropes and pulleys tied to trees. Sutherland was swiftly yanking it back into firing position when a mighty roar went up from the Green Mountain Boys along the banks. The smoke blew away to show the bateau had been blown out of the water and was sinking. All around it were debris and floating bodies.

The other gun in Sutherland's battery had also fired, and a second transport near to shore was foundering, a hole splintered in its side. Since this boat was floating without a helmsman, and none of its men were firing back, Sutherland presumed they were all either killed or wounded.

Defries quickly swabbed the muzzle, then Poole pushed down the charge and rammed home three more balls. At this range, they would do severe damage without having to fly far. Now the Boys were calming down, concentrating on accurate fire, following the commands of their leaders. Soldiers and loyalists in the bateaux were dropping one after the other. Stunned by the demoralizing presence of rebel cannon, they returned the fire with loud but poor effect. They had no targets, and because of the cannon, dared not come close enough to make their volleys tell.

Sutherland saw three bateaux rowing hard upstream, attempting to land and get a foothold above the ambushers. Shouting to the second gun crew to follow his lead, he brought his cannon to bear and fired away. The first bateau was hit broadside and lost steerage in the strong current. As it went out of control, its men panicked and it capsized. The next cannon shots struck the second bateau, which still doggedly tried to get ashore. It was hit by the guns four times in succession, and many of the Boys picked this craft as a target, pouring lead into it. Soon, all the men aboard were down, and the bateau spun sluggishly, uselessly in the river, turning and turning slowly as it drifted toward land. The third bateau rapidly headed away from the shore.

The Green Mountain Boys shrieked with glee, because the enemy force had given up and were all fleeing back across the river toward the city. Sutherland's gunners held their fire. The enemy had two bateaux sunk, and left two other shattered boats to the mercy of the rebels and the river. As the undamaged bateaux retreated under rifle fire, these last two were driven by the current to shore. Sutherland and his men were among the first to reach them and were revolted by the carnage and bloody death they found.

Defries looked away from the bodies that filled one bateau, and even the veteran Lieutenant Duff gasped in horror. These two were not greedy for blood, but like most in the rebel army, they would defend their cause any way they must. Yet the sight of dead and dying men lying in the boat like broken dolls sickened them all.

The yelling, cheering Green Mountain Boys in buckskins and feathers came crowding out of the trees to view the slaughter, and they, too, fell silent. Those few louts who made crude comments were quickly told by their fellows to shut up. Sutherland entered a bateau and stepped into a slippery pool of blood. Then Defries came aboard to help search for survivors among the twenty Redcoats and civilians sprawled in heaps on the craft's bloody bottom. Sutherland's guns had done their work. The British were beaten, and the fall of Saint John's was only a matter of days.

"Sutherland!"

He turned, thinking one of his men had spoken, but it was a wounded loyalist, who lay against the gunwale, near a hole the cannon had blown in the vessel's side.

Sutherland felt wretched, and he knelt down to the dying man.

"Sutherland . . ." The fellow raised a sinewy hand, as though to strike, but he had not the power. The terrible, torn condition of his face and chest caused Sutherland to look away upriver, where the sun glinted off the water, bright and silvery.

"Sutherland, you . . . won't beat . . . us!" The voice was familiar—the voice of a Scot. "You won't defeat us, no matter . . . no matter how—"

The man's head lolled, and Sutherland tried to push it up, trying to make these last moments of life not so brutal. Then the loyalist gave a tremendous effort to get at a bloodstained canvas bag lying on the floor of the bateau. Sutherland lifted it for him and handed it over. With all the strength he could muster, the loyalist pushed the bag into Sutherland's arms, then fell sideways, lifeless.

Sutherland said a brief prayer, hardly knowing the words he used but remembering them from his childhood. Canvas bag in hand, he wondered sadly who this man was. After a moment, he untied the leather thong, looked inside, and found a small flask of Scotch—his own flask, the one he had given the Mohawk Valley miller, Alexander McAllister. It was McAllister lying there, but Sutherland still could not recognize him.

On November 3, Saint John's surrendered. After fifty-five days of misery, the news of the repulse of the relief force at Longueuil and the subsequent retreat of the Royal Highland Emigrants downriver was sufficient reason to give up. But the commander's resistance had cost the American rebels dearly in time, a commodity too precious to waste.

Sutherland and Defries were among the first troops to cross the Saint Lawrence and enter Montreal, which fell without a shot a few days after Saint John's capitulated. There were no soldiers or loyalists left to defend the city, for they had gone to Quebec. Governor Guy Carleton had slipped away in the night to his stronghold there, but most of the remaining Redcoats were taken prisoner by the triumphant rebels when the transports carrying the Redcoats down from Montreal were bedeviled by contrary winds. A sharp American rebel officer shipped cannon in bateaux out into the river and cut off the entire fleet of eleven small vessels—taking a general, one hundred and twenty unhappy regulars, and precious supplies of flour, beef, butter, shoes, and munitions.

To ensure that the British would not reenter the Saint Lawrence that spring, the rebels had to take Quebec, which was one hundred and fifty miles downriver. Though nearly every British regular in Lower Canada was a captive by now, Quebec was held by stubborn loyalists and a handful of Redcoats. That fortress would be difficult to take, and the arrival of winter might delay an advance by Montgomery to join Arnold's small force coming through the Maine woods.

The evening of Monday, November 13, was cold and blustery, promising another snowfall, when the ragged, weary American soldiers tramped rank on rank through the Recollet Gate to take possession of Montreal. At their head rode General Montgomery and his officers, all of them wearing their best, though patched, uniforms of blue and white. Sutherland marched with the soldiers of the York regiment, Defries at his side. The army's banner was the scarlet flag of rebellion, for there were still no Continental colors.

Unlike their officers, the ordinary soldiers were a sorry sight. Their clothing, except for a few captured Redcoat tunics, was in shreds, and many had feet wrapped up in cloth against the icy ground. They were hungry and grim, but every one had tried to clean himself and look soldierly. Though ragged, they held their heads high, proud to march as conquerors through the very same gate the British had used when the city fell at the end of the French wars.

These Americans declared they had come as friends to the French, to liberate them, to make them allies in a struggle to create a new order in America, but there were few citizens in the streets. There was no cheering, no suggestion that they were welcome at all. In they came, slogging through snowy mud in some places, finding the gray walls and shuttered windows as chilling as the weather, as hostile as the dark storm clouds overhead. But the city was theirs, and again the British Army had been defeated by untutored volunteers who once had been scorned by Redcoats as worse than useless.

That evening, Sutherland and Defries visited two elderly French who were minor partners in the Frontier Company. Dr. Michel Devalier and his wife, Marie, were aged, bent, kindly folk Sutherland and Defries had known for more than ten years. They were especially dear friends to Defries, who with his wife had been close to them during their own years living in the city.

The Devalier residence was in a small side street near the harbor. Sutherland and Defries knew the place well and went up a narrow flight of stairs to the door of the apartment. When it was opened to them, they were given a welcome that was sorely needed after so many harsh weeks in the dismal swamps of the Richelieu.

Mrs. Devalier greeted them, astonished that they were among the invaders, and overcome by turbulent emotion, she began to weep. They tried to comfort her and soothe the agitation that swept her after so many weeks of uncertainty and fear. At the old woman's side, Sutherland and Defries entered the bright, airy apartment, its walls covered with oil paintings by the doctor. This first room was part of the office in which Dr. Devalier still practiced medicine, although he was eighty years old.

"Mon Dieu, mon Dieu!" declared Mrs. Devalier, gripping the arms of the two big men as she led them into the living quarters behind the waiting room. "How relieved I am that you're here, my friends, for I know you'll protect us from the rebel pillagers! *Mon Dieu!* I am so very relieved!"

Before Sutherland could explain that there would be no pillaging allowed, Mrs. Devalier brought them to her husband. He was ill, swathed in blankets and sitting in a rocking chair before an iron stove. Like his wife, Devalier was short and bowed, but when he saw his old friends, he nearly sprang from the chair in joy.

Sutherland insisted he remain seated, and the doctor sank back down again, softly laughing and squeezing their hands. Though he was pale from prolonged illness, Dr. Devalier looked alert, his white goatee lending him a pixie quality that had not faded with age.

Sutherland and Defries sat down while Mrs. Devalier went to the small kitchen to brew coffee and fetch homemade cakes. The men immediately talked of the war, of the reluctance of the French to join either side, and of the intentions of the rebel army with regard to the city.

"Do not ruin us!" Devalier pleaded.

"Listen, Doc," Peter declared, "if there was gonna be pillagin' it would've happened already! Our boys're starvin' and half naked, but they let them Britishers at Saint John's go happily down to prison in Connecticut carryin' tons of personal baggage, coats, extra shoes, blankets!"

Defries did not mention that the British had kept their goods only because of Montgomery's fierce opposition to a York regiment's attempt at ransacking the private belongings of the soldiers. The rebel troops could well have disobeyed their commander, however, and it was testimony to their improved discipline that they heeded him.

"Pillaging will be punished," Sutherland said. "We've come to Montreal as friends, not enemies, and we want your people to join us. We need allies, not a conquered foe."

"There are a hundred and fifty thousand French in Canada, Owen," the doctor said in a hushed, almost hoarse voice, "but they are not the warlike race of fifteen years past. They have been at peace for almost a generation, and they want to keep it that way."

He said the population of what once had been called New France was just beginning to thrive under British rule. Governor Carleton recognized French needs and was trying—though awkwardly—to achieve a better social system for the French in Canada. Carleton represented a British Parliament that desperately needed the French to join government forces against the colonial rebels, or at least to remain neutral.

"Don't you see, my friends," Dr. Devalier said, "that your Congress and your rebellion and your cries for liberty frighten us? Yes, we are afraid you will take what is ours in the name of liberty, and destroy our Catholic faith, our French language, and our way of life!"

Mrs. Devalier set the table with a crisp white linen cloth, china cups, and a silver coffeepot. As she worked, laying out plates of biscuits and cakes, she said, "The British demand we aid them, and the Americans do the same. We are caught between you, but we are different from you both, and we will not destroy what we have rebuilt since the war."

It was clear the French of Lower Canada did not trust American rebels, whose mainly Protestant Congress had opposed Parliament's laws to permit Catholics in Canada to vote. Yet without the active support of the French population it would be difficult to hold this fourteenth colony against a British counterstroke.

Devalier declared, "Why, the only American who seems to understand us is your stepson, Jeremy!"

"What's that, Doctor? You've received a letter from Jeremy?" Sutherland expressed surprise, for he himself had not heard from the young man since he had left for England.

"Letter?" Devalier was astonished that Sutherland had said this. "You mean you don't know he was in the city for two weeks?"

"Jeremy? Here? Where is he now?" The idea of his stepson being back in America thrilled Sutherland. It meant they could unite to meet up with Ella and get her safely to Montreal.

Devalier said, "He's gone away with his lovely young wife; they've taken whaleboats to Niagara and just got out before your outlaws took the city!"

"This is wonderful news, my friends," Sutherland said happily, "though I wish he were still here! Anyway, I'm glad he's back, and safe. With a wife, you say? Hah! Tell me all about her!"

Mrs. Devalier replied, "Such a lovely girl he has married. She's strong, though she might not look it. Did fine on the crossing."

They said Jeremy had visited them with Penelope several times

during their brief stay in Montreal. The couple had been impatiently waiting for a vessel heading westward, but there had been
no available shipping because the British Army had commandeered
everything for war purposes. Not knowing Sutherland was with
the rebels, Jeremy and Penelope finally had barely escaped Montreal in company with a dozen whaleboats under sail. They were
now well on their way to Niagara, which was about ten days to
the west, across Lake Ontario.

The Devaliers related what they knew, including the sad news
of old Sniffer's passing in England. By the time they had finished,
Sutherland was satisfied the lad was well but gathered that Jeremy
did not yet support the rebel cause.

"Well," Defries mused, munching on cake, "he don't have to
fight for us to doctor us. He may be neutral. That's all right with
me, long as he can chop off legs and bandage heads—not like
these damned army surgeons who're convinced it's the other way
round! We're best to keep away from army surgeons if we want
to live, and let gunshot wounds and bayonet holes plug up on their
own rather'n let some army surgeon carve away at us like we was
harvest turkeys! But Jeremy's a real, educated surgeon, and havin'
a doctor like him is worth celebratin'—mind if I have another
cake to do it, Mrs. Devalier?"

Sutherland was thinking about Jeremy. He understood Defries's
point and also knew a doctor must obey an oath to save lives, but
something in Dr. Devalier's tone suggested the lad might not even
serve the revolution as a physician. That gave Sutherland an unexpected chill in his spine. The thought that his stepson could join
the other side was painful and set off a thousand conflicting emotions and considerations that were better ignored until he saw
Jeremy again and talked things through with him.

"He's got a head on his shoulders, for an *Anglais*," Devalier
said. "Must be from living with all those *habitants* at Detroit. He
knows what's right and wrong, and he won't be swept away by
rebels who call for invasions of lands that want no part of their
rebellions or so-called liberty!"

Sutherland replied, "He's been away from the northwest for a
long time, Doctor, but it won't take much to explain to him what
we're fighting for. He'll understand the cause and support it. I
know he will!"

Defries said softly, "Let's hope his pretty English wife does,
too."

*   *   *

Very early the following morning Sutherland went to Montgomery's headquarters in a stone house on the corner of rue Saint Jean and rue Notre Dame. The night before he had received a note from the general asking him to come first thing. On his way he saw American soldiers lounging about their quarters, filling doorways, and sitting on fences. They looked nothing like conquering heroes.

Nearly the entire army's enlistment was up—including that of Peter Defries—and of the fifteen hundred who had come into the city with the general, nearly half were expected to go. The soldiers were grumbling that they needed to be paid so they could buy decent clothes, feed themselves better than the army could feed them, and acquire the many things a man needed simply to survive. They had been promised by their officers that they would be reequipped, but most residents of Montreal absolutely refused to accept the promissory notes Montgomery offered in exchange for essentials. Few in Montreal would risk being ruined, and they refused to sell, except for hard cash. Hundreds of homesick, disgusted rebel soldiers would never reenlist for another tough campaign against Quebec, and Montgomery would be hard-pressed to take that city with so small a force at his disposal.

Thinking about this, Sutherland entered the headquarters building, glad to be out of the chill. He saluted the two well-clad sentries stationed at the outer door, and inside he found the hallway lined with officers and city residents hoping to have problems solved, needs filled, and questions answered. Sutherland was directed past them by a young officer serving as the general's secretary. A few men made envious comments at his preferential status with the general, but most knew him well enough to respect what he had done at Saint John's, Chambly, and Longueuil.

Sutherland went down a dim hallway, and the officer knocked on a closed door. Montgomery called out, and the Scotsman entered a large, bright chamber with windows facing westward to immense Mount Royal, which almost glowed in the pale winter's sunrise. In this room were a writing desk, three comfortable upholstered chairs near a roaring fire, and a Persian rug that was quite new.

The general welcomed Sutherland warmly, getting up from one of the high-backed armchairs facing the fire. Sutherland realized someone else was sitting in another of those chairs, but could not tell who, for its back was to him.

"Please join us, Mr. Sutherland," said Montgomery, offering the third chair that stood between these two. "But first, I have the honor of introducing an acquaintance of yours. . . ." He motioned Sutherland to the man in the other chair, who stood up slowly as the Scotsman held out his hand and came around.

It was Bradford Cullen.

chapter 23

HEAR OUR CRIES

Sutherland was so amazed to see his archenemy with Montgomery that he did not pull back his hand when the fat, bespectacled Cullen accepted it. Neither mañ said anything at first, but their handshake was brief while they scrutinized each other.

It had been ten years since last they were in the same room together, and in that time they had engaged steadily in deadly combat, sometimes from half a continent apart. Sutherland had won the first battles, but wondered how this next conflict would begin. Then he realized it had already started, and Cullen had chosen the ground and the moment of collision.

In that momentary silence, Montgomery observed them closely, but had no idea of the depth of their bitter enmity, or that it had spilled much blood of both good and evil folk.

The general nodded for them to be seated and said, "I well understand that you've long been rivals in the pelt trade, gentlemen, but as supporters of Congress, I'm sure you'll put aside all hostility for the sake of a higher, glorious cause."

It was only with great effort that Sutherland did not leave the room. He wanted no part of Bradford Cullen, but at the same time did not wish to embarrass or insult Montgomery.

Cullen grinned boldly and said with a wheezing voice, "It's as strange to me as it is to you, Mr. Sutherland."

"No doubt," the Scotsman said. Then to the general he said, "Sir, I've come in order to submit my resignation or to request a leave of absence in order to—" He halted, not wanting to reveal anything about Ella and the children in Cullen's presence. "I believe sir, you know my intentions, now that the city is ours."

"Quite," said Montgomery, looking stern. "I've requested you join Mr. Cullen and myself in order to settle several matters related to holding Montreal and conquering the rest of Canada, which cannot be considered ours until Quebec has fallen. Will you kindly be seated, gentlemen? And then, Mr. Sutherland, I'll be only too happy to approve your furlough for personal matters."

They sat down by the fire, and Sutherland quelled his anger. It was Cullen who spoke next, smoothly, sure of himself.

"Mr. Sutherland, it was I who asked General Montgomery to arrange this meeting with you, because I knew you wouldn't come to me if I asked."

"You have asked, through your man Meeks," Sutherland replied. "He got the answer already."

Cullen sighed and shook his head slowly. "For once, sir, put aside your hatred and consider the gravity of what I have to say. For the sake of the cause."

"Don't speak to me of the cause." Sutherland turned to Montgomery. "I wish to go, sir, with your permission."

Visibly upset, Montgomery sat back and tapped the arms of his chair, saying, "Can't colonials do anything but quarrel? Day in, day out, that's all my men have been doing—and now you two, when we so desperately need your alliance!"

Sutherland said, "You don't need me, General."

"But we do, damn it!" Montgomery slapped his leg and clenched his fists in frustration. "Mr. Sutherland, you know these French better than anyone, and most of the Indians, too. And considering Mr. Cullen's expertise in supplies and acquisition and his familiarity with British traders in Canada, together you can persuade the people here to support us. I'm sure of it!"

"I'm not," Sutherland said, and stood up. "Forgive my rudeness, General, but I can serve the cause in other ways, sir."

Montgomery looked bleakly at Sutherland, and although he did not know why the Scotsman was so against cooperating with Bradford Cullen, he could tell it was useless to argue.

"Perhaps, General," said Cullen, his rasping wheeze sounding almost soothingly sweet, "perhaps if Mr. Sutherland will be polite enough, I can persuade him... in private."

Cullen was smiling at Montgomery, but when Sutherland gave a curt laugh of irony, the Boston merchant suddenly took on a vicious look.

He hissed, "The life of your stepson is at stake!"

Sutherland's heart leaped. How did Cullen know this, and what was he after? If Jeremy was in danger, he would sit down with even this devil, but he knew there was some cunning at work. Cullen gave nothing away.

Steadying himself, Sutherland said, "We'll talk."

Montgomery excused himself from the room, and Sutherland sat down on the edge of the general's chair, a few feet from the merchant.

"Make light of nothing, Cullen. Cross me in this and I'll kill you."

Cullen was impassive, though his left eye twitched once involuntarily. He wheezed, set his jaw, and leaned toward Sutherland.

"I have spies at work in this city. In fact, I've been here for a week myself, and even Governor Carleton didn't know. Nor did your French friends, the Devaliers, for they would have told you so when you visited them last night."

Sutherland sat back in the chair but made no reply. He would never be surprised by the tentacles of Cullen's network of conspiracy and crime. He realized, also, it must have been Cullen's man who had shadowed him in Albany.

Cullen's face was complacent as he said languidly, "Your stepson and his new English wife were in this city waiting for a convoy to take them westward. As you know, American rebels are everywhere these days, and loyalist vessels are in danger."

Cullen said Jeremy and Penelope had set off during an American bombardment of river craft two days earlier and had barely escaped with their lives. Jeremy hoped to meet the Frontier Company ship *Trader* at the landing in eastern Lake Erie, and then go on to Detroit.

"How do you know this?" Sutherland demanded.

Cullen chuckled. "I have my ways, and I have my allies in the city's postmaster's office. Your boy sent letters to Detroit, explaining his intentions." Cullen chuckled, his piggish eyes squinting half closed. "I can show you copies of them, if you have the time."

"Go on!" Sutherland was taut, as though he would snap. "What're you getting at? Why are you telling me this?"

"Because, my dear rebellious compatriot, I want to prove to you my sincere desire to . . . ah, 'bury the hatchet' is how your red friends put it, isn't it?"

Sutherland knew there was more, and he waited.

Cullen became serious again, almost reverent, as he said with much clucking and sighing, "I hate to see a fellow like Bently, who has so much promise, murdered!"

Sutherland nearly sprang from the chair. Cullen held up his

plump hands and quickly shook his head.

"Not my doing! No! Believe me, I only want to help! I only want to prove to you that everything in the past can be forgotten!"

Sutherland stood up and from his leggin produced a sharp Scottish dirk. Cullen's eyes widened behind the spectacles, and he went pale. Sutherland did not brandish the knife but toyed with it.

"Call off your dogs, Cullen, because if not, I'm going to drag you with me out on the lakes, and you'll pay for anything you've begun."

"I swear it!" Cullen was losing composure at the sight of the blade. "I swear it! Listen, Sutherland, I mean only well to you! I'll tell you what happened. Please sit down, and put that nasty thing away!"

"Speak, Cullen, and quickly."

"Hugh Meeks! It's that villain, Hugh Meeks! I fired him, you see, because of certain indiscretions. Yes, cut him off completely. I have my standards, and he went too far! Never mind what, but he was here with me in Montreal, and when he heard about your son going off, he went after him in his own whaleboat! Meeks hates you! But he can't hurt the boy as long as he's in convoy with so many others. Yet I fear that once Bently gets aboard the *Trader*, he'll be in mortal danger."

"How? Meeks's whaleboat won't catch the *Trader*."

"But my ship, the *Helen*, will. Meeks intends to commandeer the *Helen* on Lake Erie, and no one will stop him because he stole certain documents that'll prove he has the right to take the ship wherever he wants. No customs officer will interfere as long as he doesn't go to Detroit, where he might be arrested for involvement in that unfortunate killing last year."

Standing over Cullen, Sutherland realized with shock the gravity of all he had heard. If Jeremy was unsuspecting, he would be attacked and boarded by Meeks, with no chance to resist. Though Sutherland presumed Cullen had some darker motive for revealing all this, he did not care what it was. What mattered now was that Jeremy and his bride were rescued. He asked some pointed questions about Meeks to learn the man's suspected movements, and Cullen was very precise.

"He aims to intercept the *Trader* at the Apostle Islands, at the usual stopping place just before the straits. There are coves there where Meeks can keep out of sight from passing army boats for as long as he wants."

Sutherland was thinking hard, then Cullen grasped his arm. "This is proof of my good faith, Sutherland. Believe it! And when you cool down you'll come to your senses. Good Lord, man, times are changing, and so must we if we mean to survive! We're on the same side now, and I want to work with you, to rule the northwest from Montreal or from Detroit, I don't care! Tell me how you want to do it and—"

"Why, Cullen?" Sutherland pulled his arm away. "Why do you want my alliance when it seems the Whigs'll let you have free rein up here, because they need your money and your influence?"

Cullen's jaw worked, and he looked out the window seeing nothing. "Because your friend Franklin has convinced enough delegates in Philadelphia that I must be watched until I prove myself true to the"—he wheezed the word—"cause! They won't give me any real authority because they don't yet trust a dying old man who wants only to do something good for this world before leaving it." Glancing sidelong at Sutherland, Cullen leaned back and wheezed once more, as if dejected and hurt.

He said, with a plaintive sigh, "Don't you see I've had a change of heart? I know now our country's destiny is to be free, to be a republic, and I want to help shape that destiny in whatever way I can!"

Sutherland believed none of this.

Cullen peered at Sutherland, who could not see his eyes because the light from the window glinted off the spectacles. The Scotsman looked hard at him, knowing in his bones these were lies—except for the fact that Jeremy was in danger. He knew Cullen had revealed that danger in order to make him believe that a truce was really possible between them. Yet whatever else Cullen's motives were, Jeremy must be saved immediately.

"Ah, Sutherland," Cullen rasped, "have pity on an old man! Let's talk about it all when you return."

Sutherland said nothing, his eyes ablaze, thoughts whirling. He would buy a whaleboat and dash after Jeremy before it was too late. If he could, he would intercept Meeks and end it then and there.

He said, "If this is true, Cullen, I'll come back to parley; but don't think I'll ally with you unless the cause is at stake!"

Cullen nodded once, slowly.

Sutherland strode away, leaving the door open. The merchant sat gazing at the fire, while outside Sutherland wished Montgomery success at Quebec.

"If need be, I'll join you there in December or January," Sutherland said, his voice echoing in the hallway. Montgomery bade him farewell.

Cullen smiled evilly and hardly heard. He was considering his own scheming and muttered to himself. Farley Jones had done well, reporting much of value about both Sutherland and Hugh Meeks. So far, everything was going exactly as planned. Sutherland and Meeks soon would collide, head to head. It was true that Cullen needed Sutherland's partnership to dominate the northwest—as long as the Scotsman was alive, at least. In time, Cullen would get rid of Sutherland, after wresting control of the northwest commercial system and installing his own men in positions of power.

No matter who lived or died in the inevitable battle between Meeks and Sutherland, Cullen would profit. If Sutherland went under, Cullen would have him out of the way at last. If Meeks was killed, Cullen's daughter would no longer whine to have the unworthy rogue as a husband, and Meeks would have paid for his crude seduction. Furthermore, Sutherland would have to admit that Cullen's warning had been genuine, and undeniably in the Scotsman's best interest. Cullen had set up the unsuspecting Meeks, and Sutherland would do the merchant's dirty work—and be thankful to do it!

Cullen laughed softly. If he was really fortunate, both Sutherland and Meeks would die. But that was almost too much to hope for.

After a long, hard journey from Montreal, Hugh Meeks arrived at Fort Erie, which stood at the western end of the Niagara portage road. His whaleboats had slipped past Jeremy Bently's convoy one night, getting far ahead of the slow-moving flotilla. Meeks had disembarked at Fort Niagara, showed the customs men and soldiers documents that said he was a law-abiding loyalist—he had papers identifying himself as an employee of Cullen, who was not yet known as a rebel—and now was prepared to take command of the sloop *Helen* once more.

The portage road emerged from the woods above the fort, which was a small masonry affair, squat and solid, housing a dozen soldiers. As Meeks's cargo wagon lumbered out of the trees, he took in the expanse of Lake Erie, which opened out to him.

"There she be, lads!" he bellowed. "It ain't the Spanish Main, but it'll yield up the loot we want, ye may lay to that!" He looked back at five following wagons drawn by oxen and, like his own, driven by hired French teamsters. Sitting on the cargoes in those wagons were thirty-five rough, hard-bitten men, who peered at Lake Erie as though to see across the horizon to Detroit. These were toughs Meeks had handpicked at Boston and Montreal after Cullen had told him of a plan to rule the lakes. They were good seamen and brave, but he wished there were a few old hands from his younger days—real Brethren of the Coast, as pirates called themselves.

The wagons jounced and rattled down the slope, and Meeks cried out, "No, it ain't the Caribbean funnel of gold, but you ain't no buccaneers!" He roared with laughter at that, saying he would soon make them fighting fit.

"But for now," creaked a thin voice from behind, "behave like ordinary honest seamen, or these Redcoats won't let us have the *Helen,* papers or no papers!" Farley Jones tried to stand up in the last wagon, but fell down as it swayed and lurched along. A reedy, frail creature in a dingy coat, Jones was lost among these strong, confident sailors.

"Tell 'em, Farley!" Meeks blared. "And we'll splice the mainbrace soon's we get aboard! I mean to work ye, lads, but ye'll feed and drink well and ye'll have a chance to show what ye're made of!"

Raised on timbers well above the beach, the sloop *Helen* stood on dry land beyond the British fort, which was close to the cove and anchorage. Meeks knew the ship was already well appointed and equipped with spare rigging and hardware, although his laden wagons seemed to be bringing more of that sort of stores and chandler supplies. When the soldiers did the usual cursory inspection, they would never see that beneath the piles of running gear, tar buckets, paint, canvas, and line were a dozen cannon barrels. Such heavy armament would have stirred up suspicion, but so far Meeks had not been stopped, for these wagons had been loaded after dark by his own men from their whaleboats at Niagara.

The *Helen* would be awesome, for no other ship on Erie, Michigan, Huron, or Superior carried a cannon as powerful as the twenty-four-pounder barrel hidden in Meeks's own wagon. Two of his men were skilled carpenters who could construct wooden gun carriages rapidly, and after the *Helen* took to the lake, the cannon would be mounted. The *Helen* already had two light three-pounders, and with the one twenty-four and six nine-pounders in position, Meeks would rule the inland waterways. The extra cannon barrels he had brought would be fitted to captured vessels, with the speedy *Trader* being the first quarry.

Meeks had revenge to take and would take it at the islands. He would patrol the channel where nearly every vessel that crossed Erie passed. He would lurk between the islands, and when the *Trader* sailed into range, would pounce.

There she was now! The Frontier Company's ship was anchored in the cove before Fort Erie, along with a few fishing boats and a smaller sloop belonging to fur traders who lived up at Michilimackinac. The *Trader* was a sleek, fast vessel, trim and well built. She would be faster than the heavily armed *Helen*, but if he closed on her by deception, she would have no chance to run.

The *Trader* had been sent down to Fort Erie to be taken out of the water before winter, but when Jeremy Bently appeared here in a few days, the sloop would carry him up to Detroit. Traveling westward in the sloop was faster and safer than going by whaleboat, so there was no doubt Jeremy would take this ship. The *Trader* would be alone by the time it reached the islands.

After taking revenge on Sutherland's stepson, Meeks would make for the harbor at ruined Fort Presque Isle, on the south shore of Lake Erie. From there he could sally out and capture booty at his pleasure. By the time winter set in, he would have prepared a comfortable pirate's haven at Presque Isle, living in cabins or in the ships, which would be kept out of the water until spring. Then he would again launch his force. Once Detroit was taken by rebels, there was nothing to prevent Meeks from claiming to be on their side. Then he could pass the fort's guns and run up to the other lakes. He would terrorize commerce from Fort Erie to Stinking Bay on Lake Michigan, and soon would be a very wealthy man.

Neither Meeks nor his partner, Farley Jones, knew that Cullen had betrayed them to Sutherland. Meeks believed he was to terrorize the lakes for Cullen, and enrich himself by pillaging and capturing prizes. He fancied himself a privateer—one who is licensed to prey on enemy shipping and keep the spoils. Though Congress had issued him no official letter of marque as yet, it would do so soon enough, through Cullen, and the name Hugh Meeks would go down in history alongside naval heroes like Raleigh and Drake. Meeks would win control of the Great Lakes for whoever paid him well enough to do it, but no one would cross them without his leave.

"A regular Barbary vayzeer!" he yelled at the top of his lungs, startling the sentries down by the fort, who turned to watch the wagons approach. Meeks laughed, took a long pull at a bottle of rum, and began lustily to sing an old ballad about the pirate Captain Kidd.

> Oh, you captains brave and bold,
> Hear our cries,
> Hear our cries:
> Though you seem so uncontrolled,
> Don't for the sake of gold
> Lose your souls!

This song gave Farley Jones the creeps, for he wanted no part of pirating, even under the honorable name of privateering. Cullen had insisted he go along with Meeks, so he went, but he considered it small gratitude for all he had done in Cullen's service at Montreal. Jones deserved better treatment for exposing Meeks's intention to win Linda and for keeping track of Jeremy Bently. Since Jones knew Bently, however, and Meeks did not, Jones had to be there to see that Meeks did in the young rascal.

Jones wanted no part of roving, gunsmoke, or adventure, but it pleased him to think he would see Jeremy Bently killed, and killed slowly.

On a windy, cold evening, someone rapped sharply on the front door at Valenya, and Ella stopped playing her spinet. She took the rifle from the mantelpiece and, with Heera at her side, went to see who it was.

The children were upstairs in bed, and Sally was at her loom, weaving. Mel and Hickory were sitting by the fire, he reading, she beading moccasins. They both rose as Ella called, "Who knocks?" The voice of Reverend Lee could be heard outside. Quickly unbarring the door, Ella let in the minister and his wife, both caped against the late November weather and appearing very frightened.

Surprised to see the couple out so late, Ella knew there must be trouble. She was about to close the door when Lee said, "Wait, there's someone with us!"

Richard Weston materialized from the darkness, his scarlet uniform concealed by a woolen cloak. Sally came out of the weaving room as Weston bowed to Ella in greeting.

"Forgive this unannounced intrusion, Mistress Sutherland," he said, "but you'll understand why when you hear what I have to tell."

At that, Matilda whimpered, breaking down and almost collapsing into Ella's arms. The woman was led to the settee, where her cape was removed, and Sally brought her a cup of mint tea. Reverend Lee could do nothing to solace his wife, who was so upset and afraid that she shook uncontrollably. The minister sat down heavily beside her, his hands rising and falling helplessly in his lap. He did not remove his cape, but leaned forward, elbows on knees, head in hands. Weston sighed and hung up his own cloak on a peg near the door. He was resplendent in his red tunic, and Ella thought how strange it was that a British uniform should be an uncommon sight in her home. In the past, when she had lived in the fort with her officer brother, soldiers had come and gone all day long, and she had spent many hours washing scarlet broadcloth. Now, as he took a chair from near the table and sat down, Weston seemed out of place, almost too grand for this cozy room. Sally and Hickory brought a pot of tea and more cups, but except for Matilda, everyone was too preoccupied with harrowing thoughts to have a cup. At first the visitors did not even want to talk, but Ella could stand the tension no longer and sat down beside Matilda, asking what was wrong.

The plump woman stammered, "It—it was a big, ugly Indian! So ugly! Oh, Ella, I'm afraid they'll come to kill my Angus! He has to get away! Please help us!"

Matilda pressed her forehead on Ella's shoulder and wept. Her husband said Indians had been prowling around their cabin in the fort these past few nights. At first they had done only small mischiefs, damaging things, but it was far worse now. Just before dawn this morning one came bursting in, breaking down the door, and threatened to brain the minister with a tomahawk.

" 'Foul rebel,' he called me," Lee declared, almost overcome by his own anxiety. "We were half asleep in bed, and the redskin came leaping in, painted like a hound of hell!" Matilda wailed, and Lee leaned toward his wife and tried to comfort her, then murmured, "They said we have to go—I have to go, or they'll burn us out the way they"—he gulped nervously—"the way they mean to burn you out, Ella, and anyone else who supports the Congress."

Lee fell silent, and Matilda sat back, sniffling, wiping her eyes with a soggy handkerchief. Sally and Hickory drifted into the kitchen, where they stood in silence near the hearth.

Mel stepped forward and said, "We can talk to the Senecas. They're not all as cruel as Manoth, and they'll listen to us."

Ella spoke up. "It's me they want to intimidate by frightening the Lees, my friends, but I fear it's only the beginning of a final effort to drive us all out. They won't listen to you, Mel—not the ones who are ordered to abuse us."

Ella's family, the Greys, Tom Morely, and Reverend Lee were the only Congress party folk left on the straits. She realized that if they refused to allow themselves to be pushed out by threats and raids, they would be attacked and destroyed.

She looked at the doleful Ensign Weston, who was pale and sober. "Why have you come tonight, Ensign? Are you on army business?"

Weston shook his head, eyes on the floor. "After attempting to get to the bottom of what happened to our friends the Lees, I learned that you are all in mortal danger." He restlessly crossed and uncrossed his legs, then slapped his boot and said, "They won't stop at this. They won't stop until you're slain!"

"Who?" Sally cried, with more distress in her voice than she meant to show as she came running into the common room, defiance and anger in her eyes. "Who, Ensign? That nasty Mark Davies? Manoth? Surely not Commandant Lernoult? He at least is decent and—"

Weston, seeming very sad, held up a hand to hush the distraught woman. Then he looked at Ella, stood up, and walked around as he gathered his thoughts. After a moment, he stopped pacing and said in a low voice, "Montreal has fallen. Saint John's, Chambly . . . my own regiment's colors have been taken— Damn it! I shouldn't be here at all, except that I don't want to see the Lees hurt, and I don't want to see the rest of you hurt, either!"

Ella quivered with fright and astonishment: Montreal taken by rebels! This was the news Owen had told her to wait for. This was the news that meant the moment for leave-taking had come.

Ella understood why Weston was so upset. She was the wife of a known Congress supporter, and that meant she was the enemy, no longer simply a political opponent. She, her family, and friends were sympathizers of a dangerous foe that would no doubt make Detroit its next target, perhaps laying siege to it and starving it out. The hundred and twenty soldiers and the hundreds of loyalists at the straits would permit no potential rebel spies in their community. To them, Valenya was a lair of enemies and could not be left untouched.

She looked at Weston, who was gazing back at her, concern and fear showing plainly on his handsome face.

"You must go," he said. "I have not the power to stop them. Yes, it's Davies, and the Seneca Manoth. They'll commit murder if they can." He stepped toward Ella, pleading, "Tarry no longer! Go wherever you may, wherever you must! But go soon!" He spun and strode away, to lean against the mantelpiece, head bowed.

Ella looked at Matilda and then at the minister, who spoke softly. "I have to go with you, Ella."

Matilda's lip was quivering, her eyes running with tears. "I'm going, too!" She gazed at her husband and took his hand, as if to say she would never leave him. "What shall I say to my father?"

Weston answered that. "Tell him all, Mistress Lee; your father and I have been conspiring to aid the escape of you misguided folk for some time now."

The officer walked into the middle of the room and nodded as he spoke. "Yes, Mr. Merriwether knows well of your plight, and of the threat that hangs over you. We'll do all we can to help you go in secret. I pray we can do enough to keep you safe from Davies's savages, for if they know you'll try to get away, they'll surely follow and—" He needed to say no more.

So it was finished. Ella looked at her trembling hands and slid them beneath her gown. Only the thought that Jeremy and his new bride would be coming home within a year gave her the hope that Valenya was not lost for good. She said to Weston she was grateful for all he had done for them.

"But you must not know where we're bound, Ensign, for that way no one can say you abetted our flight."

"There's another reason I'm here tonight." Weston's pain was apparent as he spoke. "I'm sorry to say, Mistress Sutherland, that word just came in: Your husband has been seen with the rebel troops at Montreal."

Ella and Sally caught their breath. Matilda and Lee groaned in dismay. Things were even more serious than they had realized.

Weston said, "Commandant Lernoult also knows, and I fear he won't leave you undisturbed here. Mistress Sutherland, you must go, you and your friends. Go before every loyalist in the fort finds out your husband has taken up arms as a rebel against the king."

*   *   *

Ella and her friends secretly readied for their escape from the
straits, and three days after Weston had come to Valenya, they
were prepared to go. Two whaleboats had been loaded with supplies and equipment sufficient for a long-term stay at the Apostle
Islands.

Plans were made to remain in their concealed island camp rather
than risk the long journey across open water, where they might
be followed by Davies or Manoth and attacked with no hope of
aid. Their aim was to stay together: the Sutherland family, the
Greys, Lees, and the Morely brothers. Mel and Hickory had already gone away by canoe to find Owen down at Montreal and
bring him to where his family was as quickly as possible.

Though James Morely was still not a supporter of the rebellion,
he worried for his family and friends and joined them as one more
fighting man who might be needed. He had given the care of the
company warehouse in the fort to Jean Martine, who, as a neutral
habitant, would probably not be persecuted by the British. James
meant to help Sutherland and his own family reorganize commercial affairs in Montreal, with that city as new company headquarters. But everything was uncertain, and what mattered now
was getting them all away safely.

Tamano came out the low door of the skin lodge that he had built
near the Sutherland barn as a temporary residence from which he
could protect the family. Behind him were Lela and their six-year-
old twins, Catherine Bright Star and David Running Wolf.

The Indian family sadly watched Ella and her children loading
a whaleboat down at the wharf. This was a moment Tamano had
known would come sooner or later, and he was sorry that his
dearest friends must leave. Ella had insisted that he not come
along, for there was no need for Tamano to become accused of
sympathizing with rebels. When it was time for the group to depart,
however, he intended to accompany her as an escort. Of late he
and Ella had talked much about what she was doing, and he had
not tried to change her mind. There was no other choice, for he
had heard rumors among the tribes that Manoth had sworn to
avenge himself on the Sutherlands.

Tamano was a tall, regal figure, standing with arms folded.
He, more than anyone, knew that a way of life was coming to an
end. He had seen the excited parties of Chippewa, Ottawa, and
even Sioux come paddling or riding down to Fort Detroit to receive

presents from the soldiers who wanted their allegiance. He had heard the boasts of untried warriors, brave and eager to prove themselves in war. He knew their desire for raiding, their hatred for whites—all whites. If the British Army called on such men to fall upon settlements of rebels, much evil would be done by both sides, and the killing would not stop as easily as it had begun.

Though there were sincere promises to protect innocent women and children while war parties struck only known rebels, Tamano had no illusions that those promises could or would be kept by warriors maddened by bloodlust. He was against the Indians being used at all to fight rebels. The settlement at Detroit would be the main base for such raids, and that would make it an object of hatred and a prime target of the rebels. One day, his own country might be overshadowed by an enemy tomahawk and torch, and he knew well the outnumbered soldiers would be powerless to protect Indian villages if Whigs were determined to strike in force. Redcoats fought from forts, but rebel settlers along the frontiers fought like Indians, and they were brave and numerous—a dangerous foe, better-armed and supplied than the northwestern tribes ever would be.

The departure of Ella meant Owen Sutherland would not come back for a very long time, if ever. Indeed, this was the end of an era, of a time when there were trusted white men who could reason with warriors, and who respected and understood the Indian.

Lela asked, "Will they ever return, my husband? I believe they will never be happy elsewhere."

Tamano looked at Ella, who paused in her labors and stood up in the whaleboat as though she heard Lela's question from forty yards away. She gazed back at her friends, held their eyes for a moment, then again set about her work.

Tamano said, "If they return, nothing will be as they once knew it. Not the people, not the land, not even us."

They labored feverishly to pack what they could, and before first light on the morning of departure, Ella was exhausted, for she had not slept in two nights. Throughout that time she had refused to cry, and had fought sorrow with work, for there were many chores to make sure they would be fed, clothed, sheltered, and armed on the islands. Lettie and the others did the same in their own homes, and by prearrangement, they all gathered in the common room at Valenya on that final morning. Outside, a stiff northwesterly wind blew through the gloom, and the cold air was biting.

Ella had said her farewells to those who could be trusted to keep the secret of the departure: Mawak, Little Hawk, Dawson Merriwether, Ensign Richard Weston, Jean Martine, and Tamano and Lela, who would stay behind and guard Valenya until Jeremy returned. Martine's daughter, Angélique, and her husband, Jacques Levesque, were up at Michilimackinac.

Yet she had been careful not to tell them the precise moment of their departure—especially Tamano, who would have come no matter what the risk. Ella thought it better to keep the others from becoming too involved. If they were accused of aiding the flight of rebels, it might go badly for them, including the Indians. Accordingly, there would be no last-minute farewells, no poignant leave-taking of close friends. What had to be done must be done in darkness, and that made Ella all the more upset. She was a proud woman who believed her new course in life was honest and good and should not begin with a stealthy flight from her beloved home. Yet for safety's sake it had to be so.

At four in the morning, those who would leave were in the house, all dressed warmly against the chill of the two-day journey that would lead downriver and across the end of the lake to the Apostle Islands. The brisk wind had raised a steady chop in the straits, promising rough passage for some distance, but although it would be windy, there was little likelihood of a storm breaking before they reached the Apostles.

In the house conversation was hushed, and those gathered in the common room said little as they drank hot coffee and chocolate against the cold. Ella fed the children porridge and thought it amazing that she simply had to wash those dirty dishes and put them away, even though she might never see them again. She had chosen a few of the things that were most dear to her, but what must remain would be fondly remembered and missed—especially the spinet. She had left a message in an envelope on the writing desk, full of a mother's helpful hints so that whenever Jeremy and Penelope arrived, they might make the most of what was here and know how to care for certain things in Ella's absence. Benjamin and Susannah had struggled bravely to select a few treasures of their own, but earlier that night Ella had found them in their room, weeping in silence because of the well-loved possessions they could not take. The others were surely experiencing the same sense of loss, the emptiness and finality of what had to be done.

Ella had taken a German clock, but the grandfather clock in the hallway must stay. Her prized Persian rug, the small kind that

Dutch folk laid on tables, had been wrapped around the clock and covered by waterproof cloth before being stowed in the boat. But the large rug she had bought in Philadelphia and most of the rugs Sally had woven were to remain. At Ella's neck dangled the cylindrical silver pendant Owen had given her when first they fell in love, and she touched it, grateful that at least their family would be intact to begin again.

At that thought, Jeremy came to mind, and Ella sighed. She was standing near a western window, watching a few lights twinkle on the distant bank, lonely and mysterious. What would her son do in this conflict? Ella closed her eyes and wept softly, head bowed, so that the people gathered in the kitchen did not notice— except for Susannah, who knew her mother so well. Susannah came to stand beside her and take her hand.

Ella drew the girl close and stroked her long, fair hair. Susannah was not crying, but her self-control was possible only because she had cried so much when alone in the past two days that she could cry no longer. She hugged the terra-cotta doll, which was also dressed in traveling clothes Sally had made. Susannah would hold it tightly to her until they were safely on the islands.

Recovering, Ella went into the kitchen where they were all washing cups and putting them away. Jeb joked about it, knowing they were right to go on as though they meant to come back soon. There was no other way.

They went toward the door, a few taking oil lamps for light. Ella stood a moment at her spinet, running a hand over it. Lettie tugged her arm, saying, "Come on, girl, thee best not dawdle here: I'll lock up, and see to it all's closed tight! Did thee take thy kettle from the fire? Good. Come on, I've already gone through this with my own darlin' home, and well know what's on thy mind. Don't dawdle."

Leading Ella out into the darkness, Lettie sniffed, then blew out the last oil lamp, which stood on a table near the door. Ella stared into the lightless interior until the door was closed. Lettie locked it, then turned to hand Ella the key.

"Don't lose it! We'll all be back one day to take what's ours."

Then Lettie shambled off, following the others to the river's edge. A mist lay on the water, and in the east a suggestion of lighter blue was in the sky.

Ella whispered, "Good-bye, Valenya," and touched the door Tom Morely had made for them. "Until another time."

As she hurried to the river, the wind changed, swinging around to the north. A cold gust rushed between the standing stones, which loomed as shadows a little way off. Ella stopped and listened. The swirling wind whistled through those great stones, lamenting as though Valenya knew her aching heart. They echoed the grief that Ella would not allow herself to utter.

She began to run, heading toward the clatter of oars and the creak of masts being stepped. The children called, and she did not look back.

chapter 24

THE COVE

Sutherland and Defries made good time from Montreal but were slowed by the need to take to the woods and bypass the Niagara portage. They could not risk being checked by soldiers there, who might know them as rebels. They had traveled for eight days, stopping no more than a night or two on dry land. In that time they crossed Lake Ontario, left the whaleboat with an obliging *habitant* fisherman, then slipped unseen along an Indian trail that came out close to Fort Erie.

There the *Trader,* a sleek two-masted sloop with a black hull picked out in white trim, could be seen lying at anchor. It had a skeleton crew of four, who intended to live nearby in a cabin all winter, guarding the vessel after it was taken out of the water to prevent damage from the ice. These sailors could be trusted to assist Sutherland and Defries once they were aboard. They had to get out to the ship, but they needed to find a boat without being seen by anyone who might report them to the soldiers.

Sutherland and Defries were unshaven, dirty, and tired, but as they lay concealed on a flat rock overlooking the cove, they were overjoyed that Jeremy and his wife were safely aboard the ship. Sutherland observed them through a telescope, seeing his stepson and Penelope strolling on deck as crewmen prepared the vessel to sail westward. The icy wind was in the west, so the *Trader* would be delayed until the breeze swung around more to the north.

It was just after dawn, cold and raw, with a gray sky that spat sleet. The two friends had not slept that night, and they were ravenously hungry. Earlier, they had munched on bits of hard army biscuit and handfuls of raisins, but they needed more, for it might be a long wait before they could get on board the *Trader* without being noticed from shore.

As they considered how best to get to the ship, Defries spotted a small garden and went down to search for potatoes and turnips they could cook. Before he could take anything, however, an elderly *habitant* farmer came on the scene and furiously accused him of trying to steal produce. Defries, of course, was dismayed, almost hurt at such a suggestion. He explained that he merely wanted to find someone to row them out to the *Trader*. He tossed a gold piece into the old man's wrinkled hands, and that did the trick. With a wink, the *habitant* declared he would row them all the way to Detroit for this much hard money, if they wanted.

They arranged to meet in another hour down in the cove, out of sight of the fort. The Frenchman understood that they desired secrecy and presumed they were smugglers. He went to get his boat, saying he would be ready at the prescribed moment. After the man left, Peter dug up some turnips and hurried back to where Sutherland waited at the edge of the trees. Soon they would be with Jeremy and would plan how to battle Hugh Meeks on their own terms.

Under cover of darkness, Ella's whaleboats had slipped past Fort Detroit, apparently unnoticed. Though Ella had been nervous, and since dawn had been haunted by the creeping feeling of being watched, they were not challenged, nor did they cross the path of anyone else on the water. The worst was over now that they had left the settlement, and Ella was relieved that they could not be tracked over open water.

They made good speed, and by the time the sun was up were gliding under billowing sails down the eastern channel of the river, with the low, forested mainland to their left, and long, rocky Fighting Island on the right. *Habitant* farms and Indian villages were not to be seen in this wild and lonely stretch of water, and although the hushed woods that covered the shoreline seemed ominous and threatening, no one lived in the vicinity to spot them from the shore. Cabins were scarce here, where the ground was too steep and stony to farm even the meager subsistence plots of the French, and there were few beaches where canoes could be drawn up.

It was a long, hard way to the Apostle Islands, and they pressed on quickly, stopping only once to answer the call of nature and to give the seasick children and poor nauseated Matilda Lee a chance to recover. When they embarked again, Ella's boat was first, its sharp prow steadily rising and slapping down again. James steered at the stern, which was pointed, like the bow. In the center, an unhappy Matilda laid her head in Ella's lap, and the children were sullen, so swathed in blankets that only their bleary eyes could be seen.

Also in Ella's craft was Reverend Lee, who was almost as miserable as his wife but managed not to show it. Heera lay on the floor, patiently accepting this uncomfortable means of travel.

In the following whaleboat were Sally, Lettie, and Jeb, with Tom at the tiller. Jeb kept a lookout along the shoreline for danger, and each boat had several firearms ready at hand. Straight ahead lay Turkey Island, which was densely forested and occupied the center of the channel. They must pass to the right here, between Turkey and Fighting islands, through a slender gap where the water was turbulent. The river rushed hard against the shore, sweeping around rocks and outcrops that threw tricky currents at the boats from unexpected quarters.

Suddenly Benjamin gave a yell of fright. He pointed to the right at a hidden cove sheltered by pines and scrub oak. Ella could not tell what he meant at first. Then James cried out, "Senecas!" and Heera began to bark.

Ella saw them: three canoes loaded with warriors, at least twelve men in all. Manoth was there, with his flowing scarlet plume. He was in the stern of the lead canoe, which was shooting swiftly out into the channel to cut off the whaleboats. Matilda awoke from a fitful slumber and sat up dizzily. When she saw Ella and James scrambling for rifles, she gasped and fainted into her benumbed husband's arms.

Ella waved to the following boat, and they also saw the Indians, who were three hundred yards to the right, slicing across their path. Ella, who was a good sailor, dropped sail. Benjamin and Susannah secured it on the lateen yard, and James heaved on the tiller, turning the boat until it slowed and closed with the other, which also let its sail down.

Tom was loading a rifle as he cried, "They must've been watching us all the time and knew we'd come out this way; we've got to fight!"

Ella quickly told the children to stay below the gunwales. Reverend Lee laid his unconscious wife on a blanket, took the tiller, and with a look of quiet desperation told Ella to give him commands.

Jeb Grey secured his boat's sail, and the two craft were joined by lines tossed fore and aft. Sally and Lee kept the tillers in position to prevent the boats from going broadside to the current.

The canoes were coming on strongly as the whaleboats drifted downriver. The gap rapidly narrowed. Ella and the men, except for Lee, armed themselves, and Sally took a rifle as well, while Lettie steered her boat. The Indians were just a hundred yards off.

Tom leveled his rifle and said, "I'll try and pot one or two before they get close enough to do any damage." Indians were notoriously poor shots and would be most dangerous if they managed to board the whaleboats or drive their quarry up on land. James agreed with his brother and prepared to fire, but Benjamin gave another yelp, and they looked around to see an additional canoe racing downstream.

"Tamano!" Benjamin screeched, recognizing the Chippewa's canoe, with the orange sun painted on its prow. "Mawak and Little Hawk, too! They're coming to help us!"

Tom and James held off from firing, for it was no use starting a battle that might be avoided now that they had support. If these Senecas were driven off and lost men, their hunger for vengeance would be greater than ever, and they would surely stalk Ella's party to the bitter end. The arrival of Tamano might induce them to back off instead of attack.

There came a burst of gunfire from Tamano's canoe, but only a volley that was meant to warn the Senecas. Still, Manoth's force continued to paddle upstream, for they far outnumbered both the whites and Tamano's group. Ella could see the Indians had rifles across their knees as they paddled hard, singing a chanting war song that kept time with their plunging strokes. They were fifty yards away; Tamano was much farther but moving faster in the current.

"Keep an eye on 'em," Jeb shouted, his rifle at the ready. "I got the big ugly one."

"I'll take him!" Tom cried. "Ex-soldiers don't shoot no better'n Injuns!"

The Senecas approached, their faces painted red, black, and white, the colors of war, and over each brawny chest was the traditional armor made of reeds worn by every Iroquois warrior. In Manoth's hand was a great war club carved of solid ironwood, with a massive knob on the end, and decorated with feathers and tufts of human hair. On they came, apparently unimpressed by the dash of Tamano and his friends.

James said, "Let's all shoot the big one at the same time! I'll wager the rest will run if he's rubbed out!"

Jeb declared, "I'd bet against that, but I hope you're right!"

Tamano was close, but the Senecas were closer, their grunting chant louder now. Then the three war canoes split off, two to the left and the third, with Manoth, to the right of the drifting whale-boats. Heera snarled, showing his teeth. It seemed every warrior was glaring right at Ella, and, spellbound, she watched them come.

As Tamano reached shooting range, the Senecas had almost surrounded Ella's group, and she saw their guns begin to come up. She had to hold her own rifle steady and show no fear to the impressionable Indians. The Senecas were coming abreast on both sides, their fierce chant thundering in her ears as her heart beat in time. The dog was barking wildly, eager to attack.

Suddenly there was a fusillade of musketry from upstream. Back beyond Tamano came four more canoes, loaded mostly with white men, who had fired in the air simultaneously, gray smoke wafting over their heads as they hurled downriver to the rescue.

The Seneca war chant abruptly died. Ella stared at the wild-eyed Manoth, and everyone else looked at him in that same mo-ment—Tom, James, Jeb, and the other Senecas, all waiting to see what he would do. His men held their paddles in the water, drifting backward as the whaleboats slid downstream. Then Tamano was alongside the whaleboats. The canoe and the lashed whaleboats drifted together with the Senecas, all at the same speed, as though they were motionless, the rest of the world moving.

Another volley of salute was fired from the group of canoes that had come down from the settlement. Then Tamano spoke harshly to Manoth in a tongue Ella could not understand, and the Seneca's face contorted into an ugly leer. He shook the heavy war club and screeched so loudly at her that Ella's ears rang. He howled at his paddlers, who lunged ahead, forcing their boats upstream against the current. They dug in so vigorously that they seemed to fly across the water. A guttural fighting chant, very quickly shouted, accompanied their angry retreat.

Tamano watched them go, then turned to Ella. "Why did you depart without asking me to come? Am I not your brother? Would I not mourn with all my heart if you were killed?"

Shaken and relieved, Ella reached out to touch his strong, dark hand, which held the canoe to her boat. "Do not be cross with me, Tamano, faithful friend, but I did not want to draw you into this difficulty for fear our enemies would hurt you, or drive you away, too."

Tamano understood, but was glum and annoyed. "Donoway's woman must call on Tamano; I will not fail you."

Just then the other canoes arrived, and in the first was Dawson Merriwether, anxious and upset, calling his daughter's name. In another canoe was the cheerful, portly Jean Martine, wearing his scarlet stocking cap and waist sash, a pipe stuck in his grinning face. In all there were twenty others, French, American, British, and Indian, who had been hastily assembled to head off the Senecas.

As Merriwether's craft came alongside, he clutched hands with Matilda, who had regained consciousness and was sitting up. "We have something to discuss, Mistress Sutherland," he said to Ella. "Let's go into that cove there, and we'll talk before you go on."

The craft put into the same cove the Indians had used to waylay Ella's group, and there they disembarked. Everyone found seats on rocks and logs, and broke out some cold food and drink. They dared not remain long enough to light fires lest Manoth come back with Davies and soldiers to arrest them.

Merriwether explained that late last night Ensign Weston had overheard Davies order Manoth to ambush Ella's party. Apparently the Indians had been constantly spying on Ella and the others and had seen the final preparations for flight. Since Weston could not act to aid Ella without being disciplined as a rebel sympathizer, he had called on Merriwether to gather men for an escort out of the straits. But Ella's group had been gone an hour or so by the time Merriwether's party reached Valenya.

Merriwether was leaning against a pine tree, his wan, frightened daughter sitting on a blanket at his feet. Ella's children were beside Matilda, waiting for their mother to give them bread and cheese, which she was cutting on a tree stump.

The Virginian looked down at Matilda, then said to Ella, "I'm coming to your refuge until I see my daughter safely on her way."

Ella gasped. "But, sir, it'll be many days without decent shelter—"

Merriwether shook his head and continued, "The others will go back to the fort, with none of them actually knowing where you'll go. The army can ask, but they won't be able to tell."

Tamano was standing with legs apart and leaned on his rifle as he watched Ella give her children food. "I go on with you, too, Ella; I stay until Donoway comes back, for I believe he will come soon."

"I believe so, too," said the tall Sioux, Little Hawk, who was wearing a modest version of his tribe's typical many-feathered headdress and carried his dead father's coup stick—a pole like a shepherd's crook, decorated with feathers and used to touch an enemy in battle, thus showing great bravery. "Mawak, Tamano, and Little Hawk will guard you lest those Seneca dogs come back."

Ella was grateful for their kindness and said, "I am sorry not to have asked your assistance earlier, my friends, for I see now we needed you."

Then she looked at Merriwether and said, "You've been wonderful through this, sir."

Merriwether smiled wistfully, taking Matilda's hand. "You have done much for us, Mistress Sutherland. Incidentally, I've posted dependable men to protect Valenya for you, and when I go back I'll see to it that things are kept shipshape for your son and his new wife to move into the house."

The Virginian knew Jean Martine and Tamano had already agreed to keep an eye on both Valenya and the Grey residence; but neither of them had the weight with the army or British-American loyalists that he carried as a staunch supporter of the king and the wealthiest man in the settlement.

Ella was overjoyed to hear this and hugged Merriwether, who blushed and chuckled, as she declared, "I hope we'll all be back home soon, not just Jeremy!"

Those words dropped into a gulf of silence. Merriwether looked pained and made no reply. Martine, who stood nearby, took the pipe from his mouth, turned away, and said they should get going. Ella forced herself to move, kissed the Frenchman's cheek, and with the children in hand, went to her whaleboat. The three Indians got into their own canoe, which would also carry Merriwether. He helped a shaky Matilda join her husband, who was at the water's edge, where he was reading a Bible and seemed exceedingly melancholy.

They said a sad good-bye to Martine and the others who had come down to help, then pushed off. Soon the river widened, and Ella was again on her way to meet Owen. She ached to see him, longed for his arms, his strength. He would lead them to a safe country, where their own kind were preparing to defend themselves against Parliament's soldiers and the likes of Manoth and Lieutenant Davies.

Several days later the *Trader* plowed westward through dark, icy water, in sight of the Apostle Islands, where Ella and her company were camped. The weather was windy, damp, and cold, the sky hung with gloomy storm clouds, and occasional gusts of sleet made the vessel's deck slippery and wet.

Standing in the *Trader*'s bow, Owen Sutherland stared ahead at the jagged islands in their path. He knew Ella should be there, because with him were Mel and Hickory, who had met the *Trader* near Fort Erie. Anxious for his people's safety, Sutherland gazed across the water, sleet lashing his face. He had told Jeremy and the others of the danger from Meeks, and had kept a sharp eye out for the pirate's ship. So far not another vessel had been sighted on the lake.

For the past four days Sutherland had talked and talked, argued, and debated with Jeremy. No matter what Sutherland said, the young man was immovable, dead set against joining the rebellion. Sutherland had reasoned with him, saying England gave America no other choice but to fight. Attempts by Congress to compromise had been spurned by Parliament that summer, and Americans who stood up for their rights were called traitors, guilty of the vilest treason. Even the king himself said so, although Americans were only demanding rights due them as subjects of the Empire.

Jeremy had rejected Sutherland's position and had declared himself as free as any man could be. War could be stopped only if American rebels laid down their arms, recognized the authority of colonial governors, and returned confiscated loyalist properties to their rightful owners.

Sutherland had objected, saying it was too late to turn back. The rebellion was like an avalanche, with these first rocks tumbling down being a prelude to a fierce and violent clash no one could avoid or ignore.

"Pa." Sutherland turned to see his stepson come up on the forecastle with him. Both were thickly garbed against the December cold, muffled in scarves, hats, and gloves. Jeremy leaned on the railing, looking toward the islands.

"We'll be there soon, and your mother'll be glad to see you, son," Sutherland said. "Give her a little while before you tell her where you stand. Don't spoil her joy right off."

Jeremy had already told Sutherland he would travel on beyond the Apostles, back to Detroit, and would not go with them to Montreal as long as it was held by rebels.

He said, "I'll hold on to everything of ours that I can, and when this is over, I hope you can return to the straits again; you'll always be welcome—"

With a sound of disgust he turned abruptly away, for his words sounded as if someone else were speaking, some stranger, civil and hospitable, not a son who loved his family.

Sutherland gripped Jeremy's shoulder, and both men bowed
their heads, nearly overcome with sorrow at what was happening.
It might well be that they would never meet again, that this brief
reunion on the island would be a last farewell.

Just then Penelope came up the steps, dressed in Jeremy's red
stocking cap and a dark-green riding coat, struggling against the
lurching rise and fall of the bow. Jeremy put his arm over her as
she moved against the railing and looked out at the lake. She was
as miserable as they at their situation, especially because she had
immediately liked Sutherland and was already a friend of Peter
Defries's. To consider them rebels against her country was absolutely dismaying, and it had been impossible to shake off the
unreal, dreamlike quality of this journey across beautiful, wintry
Lake Erie.

Trying to be encouraging, she said, "It's a wonderful land, and
I love it already! So wild . . . so free!" She looked at Sutherland,
who was on her right, with Jeremy at her left. "It's so big that I
can't understand why there's not enough room for everyone, Whigs
and Tories!"

Sutherland smiled at that and gazed across the water toward
the mass of an island steadily growing larger. "This country's not
big enough to hold our differences, because we're used to open
space. It's not the same in Britain, where you have so many kinds
of folk all living close together, that there's no other way to get
along but to compromise."

Jeremy added, "In the northwest our neighbor can be someone
who lives a hundred miles off, but if he's not a good neighbor,
or doesn't look at things the way we do, we don't like him even
at that distance, and he's much too close, you see."

He had intended to be light and casual about this, but somehow
it came out too seriously, too near the truth, perhaps. Penelope
puzzled over it and shook her head.

Sutherland interjected, "That's what we call a tall tale out
here—you know, a story that's not exactly in perspective."

Jeremy added, "Speechifyin', they say down in Fort Pitt."

Sutherland said, "Grandiferous eloquating."

Penelope nodded. "Combobbolating on the subject, like the
frontiersman who speaks so loud that one might see his words?
Shaves with sheet lightning? Eats pickled thunderbolts for breakfast—"

"For dinner," corrected Sutherland, with a laugh. "Aye, you've been given a good start in understanding us frontier folk."

"Bodacious," she answered.

Sutherland chuckled, saying, "I'm glad Jeremy brought back something good from the other side . . . I mean from the other side of the ocean! Well, I suppose I mean it both ways."

Penelope smiled at her husband, whose eyes were full of love for her. Then, to her father-in-law, she said bluntly, "Do you blame me for Jeremy believing what he does?"

Sutherland slowly shook his head. "Your man would have good reason to spurn our cause for love of you, lass, and I would understand that better than the other reasons he gives." He looked at Jeremy. "I'm proud you've got yourself a good woman, son, and I hope we'll find a way around our differences."

Jeremy replied, "Let's hope things get no worse than they are, Pa. Let's hope we're not driven farther away from one another."

"Let's hope." It was Penelope who said that, and she took their arms and drew them close. She was staring hard out at the water as though the answer were to be found on the island. "The way things are going, hope is all we have left."

Ella was alone, strolling along a pebbly beach a few hundred yards from the encampment, which huddled at the edge of the pine trees that bordered this quiet cove. She and Owen had often come to this island, to picnic, pick berries, fish, and now and again to be alone together for a few days. The cove was a deep semicircle half a mile across, and at each end were high bluffs of limestone, wooded with pine and windblown scrub oak. The steep bluffs and the high ground behind the cove sheltered the anchorage from the westerly gales that were so frequent at this time of year, making it tranquil, even in early December.

Thousands of ducks of every shape and size paused here in their migrations, and the many pools and inlets pushing into the line of trees were alive with them. The forest was close to the beach, like a dark wall of green, and that made the cove all the more serene. It seemed the world beyond could never penetrate this place, where gulls called and dived, swooping down to skim across the rippling water. Unafraid of Ella, the gulls strutted close to her, marching along the beach through gentle rushes of waves that slowly lapped at the sand.

The soaring promontory ahead of Ella was unoccupied, but the one at the other side of the cove always had someone posted to look for the *Trader*'s sail. There would be few vessels on the lake so late in the season; as soon as one came into view, they could almost be certain it would be Owen's.

Ella was relieved that Dawson Merriwether had agreed to protect Valenya for as long as he could. He was back at the camp with the others, a comforting, grandfatherly figure for the children. Benjamin and Susannah, both of them cheerful and energetic after almost a week of sleeping in lean-tos and eating campfire meals, looked upon all this as a wonderful adventure. The nightly cold was not bothering them, and they did not have the recurrent, nagging fear of discovery that haunted Ella and sometimes kept her awake, sitting before the fire.

There was a shout from far back along the beach, and she turned to see her people pouring down from the camp. Bracing herself against the wind, she looked out at the lake. The *Trader* was bearing down on the cove! Owen was here at last! A thrill coursed through her, and she laughed despite all her worries. Owen was back and they would get on rebuilding their life. She watched the fine ship come sailing into the cove, water foaming under the bow, men climbing through the rigging to take in sail. She thought she saw her husband in the bow, waving his hat. Although the vessel was two hundred yards away, it seemed Jeremy was beside him! Were her eyes playing tricks? She looked closer as the *Trader* came about and dropped anchor, to be greeted by a canoe going out to meet it. Owen was swinging down on a line to the canoe, Jeremy and Defries close behind.

Joyfully, Ella began to run along the stony beach, wind blowing sand sharply into her face, almost blinding her. Suddenly the gulls screeched in fright and flapped away. Someone grabbed savagely at her wrist, and she was spun cruelly around to look right into Manoth's terrifying face.

Ella screamed and tried to pull away, but the Seneca just laughed and squeezed her arm, painfully. A few warriors were with him, and they had been watching for just this chance. Ella shouted toward the ship, but the wind gusted, and her voice was lost.

Manoth snarled at her. "You mine now!"

He wrenched Ella off her feet and dragged her, kicking and screaming, into the dense woods, where they vanished in the shadowy pine.

Not far away, Tom and Sally were in the woods, walking hand in hand, and when they saw the *Trader* through the trees, they yelled for joy and ran out to wave to it. Heera was with them, and at that moment, the great husky gave a loud howl and set off pounding along the beach. Tom looked down the cove and saw Manoth capturing Ella. He cried out, racing after the attacking dog. It was a long run of a hundred yards, and the loose stones and sand were maddeningly hindering, but Tom sprinted ahead, though he carried only a tomahawk and hunting knife. Sally rushed toward the *Trader* for help.

There everyone was laughing and joking, welcoming Sutherland, Jeremy, and Defries, who had been brought in by Tamano's canoe. Sutherland was hugging his children, and when he saw Sally come flying to him, he dropped them, preparing to catch her.

"Indians!" Sally screamed before she reached him. "Manoth has Ella! Get her! Get her!"

Spotting Tom just before he disappeared into the woods, Sutherland did not wait to find a rifle and ammunition. Armed with only his claymore, he darted away. Jeremy and Defries dashed behind, also lightly armed, for there was not a moment to spare if Manoth had a waiting canoe or if he was bent on murder. Tamano immediately organized the others and ordered them aboard the ship, because there might be more hostiles who would fall upon them.

On board the *Trader* were the four seamen, Mel, Hickory, and Penelope. They quickly threw over rope ladders as the boats came to them, and helped the anxious women and crying children come up. Jeb, Lee, and Merriwether followed, while James and Mawak remained on shore to scout around for sign of other attackers.

Tamano and Little Hawk hurried along the beach, carrying extra rifles slung over their backs and pistols stuck into belts. They knew it was best to be cautious in case Owen and his men ran into an ambush. It would do no good to have them all taken by surprise, so they entered the trees through another path that would take them behind the track Sutherland and Manoth were using.

Penelope was the first person the distraught Sally met as she clambered over the railing, and for a moment the two women faced each other, searching and appraising, even before they introduced themselves.

Penelope spoke first. "I've longed to meet you, Sally, but . . . this is not—"

Sally took her hands, and they held each other, expressing immediate affection. "I'm glad to meet you, Penelope." Then dread for Ella made Sally shudder and turn very pale, and the Englishwoman gripped her hands more tightly.

"Come to the cabin," Penelope said, then spoke to all the
women and children. "It's warm in the cabin, and it's safer than
standing on the open deck if there are enemies abroad!"

Sutherland was frantically crashing along the trail, heedless of
danger that might spring out from the trees at any moment. He
was wild with fear, and nothing would stop him taking on any
number of Seneca for Ella. He held the naked claymore close to
his waist, to keep it from being caught in branches and bushes
that crowded the path. Tom and Heera were nowhere in sight.
Now and again Sutherland could hear awful, heartrending shrieks
as Ella shouted his name.

The trail led higher and higher, toward the unoccupied lookout
point at the far end of the cove. The water and a sheer drop were
on Sutherland's left; the path he was on narrowed rapidly—a
perfect place for an ambush. Where was Tom? He must be close,
for the cries of Ella were less than forty yards away. Blood pounded
through Sutherland's head as he strained every muscle to get up
that steep slope. He was muttering Ella's name over and over as
he ran, horror tormenting him. Ella cried out again. He was so
close!

There was another scream, and then another, but not Ella's.
Rifles cracked nearby. Voices were cursing and then came Heera's
vicious snarls of attack. Tom must be fighting just ahead. Sutherland crashed through the undergrowth, spun beneath lashing
branches, leaving the trail to push through trees that sheltered a
noisy, brutal battle.

He heard Tom's wild roar of defiance and Heera's growling.
They were here! He howled the Highland war cry and leaped
through tangled bushes into a clearing where Tom was battling
three Indians hand to hand, another lying at his feet. They were
trying to hack him to pieces with tomahawks, and Tom took several
wicked blows. He staggered, but gave as well in return. He would
not fall, though blood ran down his face and covered his chest.
Heera was at the throat of a fifth Indian, who was on the ground,
kicking and yelping. Was this Manoth? As Sutherland charged,
he looked for Ella, but could not see her. He ferociously crashed
into a warrior attacking Tom, knocking him down, and the others
scattered.

The man tried to scramble into the bushes, but fell, head split
open by the claymore. The Indian battling Heera managed to yank

out a tomahawk to strike the dog, but Sutherland sprang at him and knocked the weapon away. He was not Manoth. Leaping clear of the husky, the tenacious warrior made for Sutherland. The point of his sword flashed at the man's throat, and the Indian stopped short, terror in his eyes, bite marks on his hands and chest. Heera growled, but Sutherland ordered the dog to heel.

The Scotsman hastily demanded, "Your leader! White woman! Where?"

The Seneca was impassive. Sutherland had no time to waste. He roughly shoved the sword point under the Indian's chin and drew blood. The Seneca winced and backed off, his black eyes widening. Sutherland threatened again, and the warrior curtly indicated a steep climb up the rocks, through straggling trees.

"Watch this one, Tom," Sutherland said quickly, not looking around at his friend, not seeing he had collapsed near the two dead Senecas. "Stay, Heera! Help Tom!"

Then he scrambled away up the incline. Hearing Jeremy and Peter coming along the trail, he did not call to them, for he was certain Manoth and Ella were very near and did not want to give himself away as he approached. Manoth was trapped up there, with no other way back but by this stony path—or straight over the cliff. The lookout point was a limestone tower, eighty feet above the water, which surrounded it on three sides.

Sutherland shook with fear for Ella. Sweat poured from him as he moved silently, climbing up and up the narrow path that curved through brush to the very top.

Then he heard something. Loose stones came clattering down. They were just above. Why did Ella not cry out? He leaned back, holding on to outcropping rocks. Looking upward, he saw her! Twenty feet away, almost straight up, she was struggling with the Seneca, who had his big hand over her mouth, the other gripping her arm. Ella's blond hair flew as she fought. Her clothes were torn and stained with blood. Sutherland gasped, horrified, but made no sound, even when Ella was yanked back, out of sight.

Manoth would be watching the trail, which wound around the lookout. A bullet or tomahawk blade would meet Sutherland if he continued to follow the path. There was no choice but to leave it.

Sheathing his claymore, he climbed over the edge of the trail and onto the rocky cliff face. As fast as he could, he began to work his way up, not looking down at the water far below. The limestone was brittle and loose; footholds were dangerous, but he forced himself up, foot by precarious foot. It was a sheer, dizzying drop into the lake. Ella's name pounded over and over in his mind as he held on to slender ledges, sometimes pulling his whole weight up by one hand. If there was a sturdy bush to be used, he heaved himself up by it, and as he climbed, found the cliff was angled dangerously outward, so that he actually leaned back. Wind buffeted him, stone gave way under his probing toes, but up he went, thinking only of Ella, Ella, Ella.

Inch by inch he climbed, pressed hard against the rock, scraping upward, silently cursing as he battled toward the top. At the brink of the precipice, he got one hand over. This would take all his strength, and if Manoth saw him, he was done for. He reached up with the other hand and pulled. Rock came away in his hand. His body slid back. He grabbed desperately. There was nothing to hold. He was slithering backward, falling. He began to drop, but a scrub oak snagged him, breaking the slide. He hooked one leg around it, his hands scrabbling and scratching to get a hold of jagged stone as he skidded down. The oak held and stopped him. He paused, panting, closing his eyes briefly, then went up again. He longed to shout Ella's name as he fought his way up to the brink. He hauled himself up and had one leg over the edge when he saw her.

Ella! She was lying on the flat rock, the breeze idly flapping her coat. She moaned. She was alive! Sutherland struggled over the brink and whispered, "Lass? Ella?"

By speaking, he had risked too much.

He sensed Manoth had heard him. With the same final thrust that threw him up over the edge and onto solid rock, Sutherland hurled himself to one side, rolling. A rifle blasted just inches from his head. Then the claymore was out, biting, slashing blindly, striking flesh and bone, though Manoth did not groan in pain. Sutherland rolled and slashed, taking a brutal thud from the rifle butt against the side of his head.

Half dazed, he leaped to his feet, ducking another clubbing, and dived forward. His shoulder rammed into the Seneca's stomach, and the rifle clattered to the ground. They crashed down together into a thick tangle of bushes, and Manoth let out a ferocious yell of anger and pain. Arms, knees, elbows, hands, and the hilt of Sutherland's claymore did the close-in work. Sutherland tried to get the sword free for a killing stroke, but Manoth was too strong and fought his way clear, kicking mightily and getting free. Then both were on their knees, eye to eye, in the dense bushes. Manoth yelled a war cry and brought his tomahawk down, slicing at Sutherland's head. The claymore blocked it, and another, and another rapid, clanging stroke that quivered against the blade, inches from his face. Then, as the tomahawk struck again, he absorbed the blow enough to make the weapon hang just an instant on the sword. In that same movement Sutherland deflected the tomahawk, and Manoth went off balance, the stroke sliding to the side and downward. Manoth could not avoid moving into the full force of Sutherland's claymore hilt. The vicious crack stunned him, smashing his nose to a bloody pulp.

But the Indian shook it off, berserkly chopping again. Sutherland was gaining the edge and coolly parried a wicked blow, and another. A third he ducked, but the frenzied Manoth flung the tomahawk from close range. Sutherland moved slightly, and it grazed his ear, thudding into a tree trunk, leaving the Indian unarmed. Both men running with blood, they faced each other, still on their knees.

"Come on," Sutherland panted, brandishing the claymore. "Come now, and die."

The unflinching, breathless warrior expected no mercy. Sutherland had never killed a man in cold blood before, but this must be the first time, for Manoth would not surrender. The warrior's enormous hands could tear Sutherland apart if the claymore was not hovering between them. Still, it would take several well-aimed blows to kill Manoth, who glared insanely, blowing and gasping for air.

It was the moment. Sutherland readied himself.

Then Ella screamed and rolled toward the edge of the cliff, unaware where she was. He shouted at her, and in that moment Manoth sprang, and the jarring impact knocked Sutherland back with stunning force. Manoth jumped on top of him, but the Scotsman fought with shrewd instinct, keeping his enemy's momentum going by kicking his own legs mightily to throw himself free. He screeched the Highland battle yell and whirled around to face the man, claymore again ready. To his dismay Manoth was breaking through the branches, making for Ella. Sutherland leaped after him, but was a fraction too late. Ella was almost over the edge. Manoth was a step away from her.

chapter 25

BATTLE IN THE COVE

Suddenly the Indian was rammed from the side and knocked back. Jeremy was there, locking his arms on the Seneca's head. Manoth whipped around, crashing them both down hard on the rock. In that instant Sutherland dropped the claymore and dived onto his belly, grabbing for Ella, who was slipping over the edge. Howling her name, he caught at her coat as she fell, but it tore, and her legs dangled in air. Snatching with his other hand, Sutherland attempted to get a solid hold, but he was losing her; she was almost gone.

"Ella!" he screamed. "No! Ella!" He lurched forward and, in that desperate effort, would have died with her. But she clutched at him, her fingers clawing at his sleeve, hooking a cuff. He threw himself ahead, almost over the brink, and somehow had her. He yanked mightily, roaring with the strain, and she came up. He dragged her back, embraced her for the briefest moment, and then spun to see Jeremy and Manoth on their feet, grappling at each other's throats. They, too, were at the brink, tottering back and forth, each trying to trip the other, to force his enemy off balance.

Sutherland gave another shout and went for the claymore. Manoth saw him and broke free. With two steps, the Seneca darted over the edge of the precipice and flew through the air, his blood-curdling scream of challenge ringing out.

Peter lumbered up just then, Heera at his side. Having seen the Indian's leap, he went carefully to the edge of the cliff and looked over, muttering in amazement.

Sutherland and Jeremy did not watch. They rushed to Ella, whose eyes were clouded. There was a nasty, bluish lump on her forehead. The palms of her hands were cut from resisting her captor, and she was badly beaten, her clothes torn away, blood trickling from her burst lower lip.

"Ma?" Jeremy said in a hushed voice. "It's us, Ma. It's all right now." Heera whined and nuzzled Ella, who was motionless, her eyes closed.

Sutherland had no idea how badly hurt she was, and he held her against him, cradling Ella's head and talking softly to her. The wind whipped about them, cold and sharp.

Defries came back and said, "That Injun made it."

Sutherland looked up at him but did not care anymore, even when Defries told them Manoth had survived the leap and was plucked out of the water by his fleeing companions, who had hidden canoes down below when they had slipped onto the island. Defries dropped to his knees and looked at Ella, a sigh escaping him.

Jeremy pursed his lips, mastering his anguish, and took off his coat to wrap her. He said, "Tom's hurt bad, too, Pa." Sutherland listened, eyes closed, Ella's face against his cheek, as Jeremy said, "Tom was tomahawked. Tamano and Little Hawk are with him." Jeremy was badly shaken. "We have to get them back down to the ship."

Sutherland lifted his wife and stood a moment with her.

"Ella, my love. Ella."

Her eyes fluttered open. She saw him. Jeremy said, "Ma?" and came to her side. Ella blinked as though she could not believe what she was seeing.

"Is it really you, my son?"

"Really," Jeremy said, kissing her forehead. "You'll be all right now."

Sutherland breathed in relief, smiled, and closed his eyes as he held her close. "Thank the Lord. . . ."

She said, "I think I can stand, Owen." He set her gently on her feet, and though she was a bit uncertain, she insisted on making her own way. "I'll be fine." She smiled and embraced them. "I'll be fine now that you're both with me again."

Suddenly Defries said, "Listen!" He looked around. "Hear that! Someone's singin'!"

They all heard the song, carried on the wind, but could not tell where it came from.

> Oh, you captains brave and bold,
>   Hear our cries,
>   Hear our cries:
> Though you seem so uncontrolled,

Don't for the sake of gold
Lose your souls!

Then they saw below them the *Helen* sailing around the point,
two hundred yards off. Hugh Meeks's ship was tacking against
the wind, her deck crowded with fighting men. The pirate himself
was on the quarterdeck, blaring out his favorite song, confident
of victory and revenge.

"He's come," Sutherland said. Momentarily hypnotized, they
watched the ship sail toward the entrance to the cove. In the
direction from which the *Helen* approached, the wind was troublesome, and Meeks would have to take her back out to get the
breeze astern. Then he could drive the vessel straight in from the
east. The *Trader* was anchored well inside the cove, and it would
take Meeks ten or fifteen minutes to bring the *Helen* in and lay
her alongside for boarding.

"Come on," Sutherland said grimly. "We mustn't lose the only
advantage we have: Meeks doesn't know we've been expecting
him. He'll think to take the *Trader* by surprise."

Carrying Ella, Sutherland hurried away down the steep path
with the others, Heera bounding ahead. They came upon Tamano
and Little Hawk, who were weaving a stretcher made of leggin
thongs, belts, and roots for the unconscious Tom Morely. Tom
lay nearby, covered with Little Hawk's hunting shirt—the Sioux
was bare-chested despite the gnawing cold. Jeremy quickly examined Tom, who was pale, almost lifeless, his head swathed in
bloody strips torn from Tamano's shirt. He did not move when
Jeremy put an ear to his chest.

"He's just alive," Jeremy said. "Not much more! Come on,
we must get him aboard the *Trader*, where at least it's warm!"

Sutherland muttered, "It'll be too warm when Meeks comes at
us." He looked through the trees and saw the *Helen* coming about,
a mile away. Soon she would sail for the cove. There was no
escape.

The *Trader*'s deck was alive with a nervous bustling, but everyone
was orderly and courageous. They knew why the *Helen* was coming at them, because Penelope and the sailors had told them all
of the danger from Meeks. They worked rapidly to prepare to
defend themselves as best they could. James and Mawak by now
had come aboard to help.

The sailors were readying the two four-pounders on the port

side, facing the *Helen*. The cannon were secured by heavy tackles, which held their wooden carriages in place and could turn the gun side to side for aiming fore and aft. Beside the guns were swabs, ramrods, and a handspike to help force the carriage into position for firing.

Lettie Morely struggled with a heavy bucket she had just filled by tossing it over the side on a line. She poured the water into another pail near the cannon, to be used to keep a sheepskin sponge at one end of the rammer wet enough to clean out the muzzle and extinguish any sparks before reloading. Lettie also worked at filling a cask of water standing in the middle of the ship, meant for fighting fires.

Up on the quarterdeck, James was loading the swivel gun, the smallest cannon of all. Mounted on the railing, it could be turned in every direction, and when filled with musket balls, it was incredibly destructive. Near James, Mawak was methodically loading rifles and pistols. Forward, at the ship's bow, Dawson Merriwether stood with Jeb Grey, watching the *Helen* through a spyglass, sometimes running the glass along the beach in search of Sutherland's group.

Matilda and Reverend Lee were near the cannon, stacking ten-inch-long cylindrical canisters filled with powder and small iron shot. Reverend Lee was singing softly, and his wife joined in. They seemed as composed as anyone on board, their very presence comforting the others. They were directed by a seaman who was in charge of preparing the cannon, and followed orders perfectly. Before long, each cannon had neat piles of canister, grapeshot— iron in the form of a cluster of grapes that would blow apart and wreak havoc when fired—and cannonballs laid neatly inside a square framework. The minister and his wife had done well and done it quickly.

Mel and Hickory were prying open a wooden crate with a crowbar, and when it creaked open, it was the loudest sound to be heard on the ship. Mel gave a pleased exclamation and gently lifted out a black grenade the size of a small melon. A slow fuse stuck out of it, and after that fuse was lit, the grenade would be thrown, to explode in half a minute. In Oneida, Mel spoke of an idea to Hickory. Dismayed at his plan, she looked up at the high crow's nest on the top of the mainmast and was about to protest. But Mel was methodically stuffing a grenade into each coat pocket and more into a canvas haversack. He had made up his mind. Hickory obediently fetched a tinderbox from the cabin. Her husband took it, then patted her hand, telling her not to worry.

Next, Mel was awkwardly, though gamely, dragging himself up the rigging, hand over hand, his feet slipping and tangling in the ropes as he forced himself higher and higher above the deck. Merriwether and Jeb Grey took note. Mel was in a dangerous place, but if he was able to do what he intended, the pirates would be surprised when they tried to board.

In the after cabin were the children, Sally, and Penelope. Susannah and Benjamin were frightened, but remained calm because of the courageous example of their elders. The cabin was sixteen feet wide and ten deep, with a built-in bunk on the left as one entered. Part of a broad window that ran across the ship's stern was pushed open to let out the steamy odor of soup Sally and Penelope were cooking on a charcoal brazier. There was no telling how long the encounter with Meeks would last, and hunger had to be satisfied quickly as soon as there was a respite.

Both women were about the same height and carried themselves erectly and with grace. They were dark and beautiful, their long hair pinned up, but there the similarity ended. Sally wore no makeup; her loveliness was like a wildflower's, free and easy. She wore a plain linen apron over a flannel skirt that came only to her knees, Indian-fashion, and had leggins on her calves. Her fingernails were short, the better for work and for playing the violin.

Penelope wore an apron to protect her fine riding coat of forest-green velvet that reached the floor. Penelope's light makeup was tasteful, but compared to Sally, she seemed very much a refined and cultured creature in a raw, primitive land.

They had talked little since Owen and Jeremy had abruptly rushed away to rescue Ella, and both were worried, intensely quiet as they ladled soup into wooden bowls and set out spoons and bread on a table that folded down from the wall.

As Sally sliced the bread, she watched Penelope work and could tell the Englishwoman was no pampered snob. Moving quickly, decisively, without wasted effort, Penelope was aware that Sally was observing her, but was too busy to pay much heed. She realized she must be a curiosity to these people, and to Jeremy's former sweetheart in particular. When the last soup bowl was ready, Penelope lifted the heavy teakettle from the brazier, then took thick towels and asked Sally to help her carry the brazier and its coals outside.

"What for?" Sally asked. "We'll have to cook again later on."

"In case of fire. If a cannonball hits the cabin and upsets the ashes, we'll all be burned to cinders."

Sally admired such common sense. "Have you been through this before?" she asked as they lugged the brazier out onto the deck to heave the coals overboard.

Penelope nodded. "I used to sail with my father, and we were in fights with pirates more than once. I learned a few things then, the hard way." They laid the empty brazier down to cool, its stand keeping it off the decking.

Penelope hurried back into the cabin, and Sally thought she should not be so surprised that this woman was a special person. If it were otherwise, Jeremy would not have chosen her for his wife. Returning to the cabin, Sally went to Penelope, who was folding hammocks and laying blankets on the floor to be used as bedding for the wounded.

"I wish—" Sally hesitated. Penelope turned to face her. "I wish we could have given you a better welcome to our country, Penelope."

They embraced, holding each other tightly. After a moment Penelope stood back and said, "I'm glad to be here, Sally, and truly happy to meet you at last."

Sally smiled faintly, for the fear that pervaded both of them would permit no more than that. "We've a lot to talk about."

In this brief exchange, these two young women were brought together, and each knew that what Jeremy had told about the other was true.

Penelope said, "My husband thought we'd be great friends. I think so, too."

"So do I."

Then they heard the voices of Sutherland and Jeremy outside, and with the children crying for their mother, they all hurried from the cabin. There they met Owen climbing over the rail, and he leaned down to lift the unconscious Tom, suspended in a netting as he was raised from the canoe below.

Sally wailed and ran to Tom, seeing the blood and his wan, sickly face. She almost wept, but fought back overwhelming anguish and took her lover's hand. Ella was brought aboard with her son's help. She nearly fell into Lettie's arms, weak and shaken from the ordeal. Defries, Tamano, and Little Hawk boarded next, bringing Heera with them in the netting.

Sutherland had led his people through the woods so that Meeks would not see them and get a better estimate of the force that would meet him when he struck. The Scotsman's group had come to the *Trader* by canoe, making sure they were behind the vessel as they paddled out to it. Already Sutherland was devising a plan, and as soon as he was aboard, he called for a council of war. The women took Tom and the children into the cabin, and Jeremy hurried down the hatch to fetch his medicines and surgical instruments to care for Tom.

Sutherland and the other men gathered on the far side of the ship's dinghy, which was on a rack in the center of the deck. They were out of sight but could see the *Helen* running into the cove, less than six hundred yards away, sails billowing white against the gloomy sky. Time was precious now.

Gazing through the glass, Merriwether said, "They've cleared their decks of most fighting men, and they're showing only the normal crew to deceive us into thinking they're peaceful."

Jeb said, "Mebbe we should put a couple of rounds into her to show 'em our teeth; they might back off then!"

Sutherland shook his head, taking the glass and examining the pirate vessel. "No, they'd lie off and blow us apart if they thought they couldn't board without heavy loss, and they'd just dog us if we tried to get out of the cove. Our best chance is in coming to grips now."

"Against so many?" Merriwether exclaimed. "We've far fewer fighting men! How can we match their manpower?"

Sutherland looked at Mel, high above in the crow's nest, partly concealed by a furled sail. They waved to each other, and the Scotsman said, "Like that—with our wits!" A knot was in his gut, but he quelled his doubts and declared, "Lads, we'll beat that pirate at his own game!"

In the after cabin, Jeremy cleaned Tom's wound and saw how deadly it was: The bone above his left ear was cracked, and he had taken several less severe chops on his shoulders and arms. It was the head wound that worried Jeremy most, for it required delicate surgery to remove chips, cleanse the gash, and stitch the skin together. But there was no time for an operation now, for Jeremy was needed on deck to defend the ship. All he could do for the moment was stanch the flow of blood and apply proper bandaging. At his shoulder Sally hovered over her man, watching every move Jeremy made and helping as best she could. Sally and he had hardly spoken, for they had thrown themselves into the task of saving Tom.

Jeremy drew the bandage about his friend's head, then he

looked up and his eyes caught Sally's. She said, "We're to marry."

Jeremy's worried expression gave way to one of surprise. "That makes me glad, Sal! You're right for each other. I guess perhaps we should've felt it all along."

Sally looked at Tom and touched his shoulder. "But we didn't know it—except for Tom." She drew a trembling breath. "How I love him, Jeremy."

Jeremy took Sally by the shoulders. She was weeping. "You'll marry! Have faith! We'll get him through this!"

Into the cabin came Ella and Penelope, returning from a round of the deck, where they had quickly passed out soup and cups of tea to the men. Matilda and Lettie were doing the same with bread and cheese.

Ella liked Penelope's looks and her courage. There had been no need for them to speak as they served the hot food, and now they were back in the cabin, their work done. Benjamin and Susannah came to their mother's side, glad she was not seriously hurt, and they looked up at Penelope, who was watching them as curiously as they observed her. Ella told the children to stay out of the way when the trouble started, saying they should remain low, near the bunk, on the side away from Meeks's attack.

Penelope said, "They're beautiful children. I can see Jeremy in them, and you." She gave a little laugh and shook her head. "Strange to talk of such things at a time like this, isn't it?"

Ella said, "I wish we could have given you a better welcome—"

"I already said that," Sally told Ella, a faint smile crossing her face, and then she returned to Tom.

Jeremy was finished and hurriedly rolled down his sleeves. He looked at Ella and Penelope, who were self-consciously facing each other, as though not sure what to say. How alike they were! Once he had thought Penelope similar to Sally, but now he could see his mother's English character in his new wife. Penelope came from the same place as Ella and from the same sort of people.

He went to them and took their hands. After a moment Ella gave Jeremy's hand to Penelope, then went to comfort Sally.

"Take care," Penelope said to Jeremy, and kissed him.

He nodded, kissed her again, then was gone, leaving the three women with the children and Tom. They said nothing until Lettie and Matilda came bustling back in. Then the spell was broken, and they were ready for the worst.

* * *

A short while later, Sutherland stood alone on the quarterdeck, watching the *Helen* reduce sail and drift slowly into the placid cove. No one else was in sight on his ship as he leaned casually against the loaded swivel gun mounted on the railing. The gun's muzzle was aimed at the *Helen,* which was now within a hundred yards. Sutherland was gambling that Meeks wanted the *Trader* as a prize and would try to take it with as little destruction to either vessel as possible.

The *Trader*'s two gunports were draped with canvas suspended from the railing. An experienced hand like Hugh Meeks would take note of that and be suspicious enough to be careful. It would not be the first time a canvas tarp concealed unexpected guns that promptly spat flame and ball.

Meeks stood out on his own quarterdeck, three pistols in his belt, and the heavy cutlass at his side. He could not have expected to see Sutherland here, but if Meeks had thought the Scotsman was in Montreal, he showed no surprise. As the *Helen* came within fifty yards, he called through a speaking trumpet, "There's nowhere to run, Sutherland! Strike yer colors afore I start throwin' iron!"

The *Helen*'s sails were swiftly furled, and she immediately lost headway. Her anchor was dropped and cable played out as the helmsman obeyed an order from Meeks to put the ship hard to port. This caused the vessel to swing broadside to the *Trader,* drifting closer until she was no more than twenty yards away.

Meeks bellowed again, "Strike yer colors, I say!"

"I have no colors, pirate!"

Meeks chuckled at that. "Don't make no nevermind! Surrender! Or do I sink ye here and now?" He nodded to his crew; four gunports were raised, and black barrels thrust out at the *Trader.*

Meeks hoped Sutherland would think there were only fifteen crewmen on his ship; then, if Sutherland was reluctant to surrender, Meeks would call out the other fifteen fighting men who were hidden below. The intent was to intimidate the crew of Sutherland's ship at the sudden change in odds—a common pirate tactic. But Meeks suddenly realized there was no *Trader* crew in sight, only Sutherland and that menacing swivel gun, aimed right at him.

Meeks roared, "Yer in my power, damn ye! Fight, and I'll grant no quarter! Allow yerself to be taken without further ado, and I'll swear not to harm a hair on yer head! I just want yer ship, see?"

He laughed at that, and so did his men, who hooted and whistled as they brandished pistols and cutlasses, the best tools for close killing on a deck.

"Come and take it!"

The ships were less than ten yards apart. If the pirate gave the order, a dozen bullets would fly at Sutherland, and those big guns would rake the deck with grapeshot and canister.

But Meeks had survived so long in perilous places because he was just as cautious as he was brave. He strongly suspected some trick, and would not fire the first salvo, lest the second be Sutherland's, and have as devastating an effect on his own ship. Meeks wanted to board and wipe out Sutherland's people without unnecessary damage from cannon fire. Yet he smelled trickery. That made him itchy.

"Come and take me yourself, Meeks, if you're man enough!"

The pirate glared, eyes narrowing, and he rubbed his mouth. He was not willing to fight Sutherland in single combat—not after what had happened last year, when the Scotsman nearly slew him.

Meeks gave a signal, and three large iron grappling hooks attached to lines were thrown through the air to catch on the railing of the *Trader*. With a heave, the pirates hauled the two vessels closer together; men clung to the rail and rigging, eager to leap across once the *Trader* came near enough. Still Sutherland made no move. Meeks stared, wide-eyed; he was red in the face, and that white rope-burn on his throat stood out starkly. He knew something was not right. It was all too easy. Or perhaps Sutherland had made an error in judgment. In another moment the pirates could swarm aboard and take Sutherland prisoner. Even if the Scotsman fought back, he would be killed, or captured and tortured to death. If Sutherland's handful of men were hidden on the ship, they would be overwhelmed as well, for he had allowed Meeks to come too close.

Gaining confidence, face aglow with excitement and anticipation, Meeks leaned forward on the balls of his feet, staring right into the black muzzle of the swivel near Sutherland. Meeks was a bulwark of strength to his men, showing no fear even while looking down the barrel of a cannon, for he knew if the Scotsman brought up a match to fire it, he would have enough time to spring aside.

Sutherland had indeed just made some movement with his hand. He had not gone for a match, though. The only thing he had done was make a slight wave. But to whom?

There was a dull thud on the deck of Meeks's ship. Then another. A pirate screamed "Grenade!" and crewmen scrambled for the railing, which was not yet against the *Trader*. In the same instant that Meeks saw those two grenades thrown down from the rigging by Mel, they both went off with a loud clap, spraying lethal iron splinters everywhere. Meeks sensed that Sutherland was touching off the swivel and dived for cover. He was right. The swivel's blast from only a few yards away nearly deafened the pirate, singeing his clothes as he leaped from the quarterdeck. Unharmed, he landed heavily on the deck and screamed for his men down in the hold to come up and attack. But he was answered by three dull booms, as of grenades going off below among his men. Impossible! How could Sutherland's crew have tossed grenades through closed deck hatches?

A hatch cover was immediately thrown open, and screaming, wounded men came pouring out, acrid blue smoke erupting from the hold at the same time. With a growl, Meeks spun to level his pistol at the Scotsman, who was rapidly hauling on a line attached to a pulley. This line drew a thick, strong netting up in a screen that ran the entire length of the *Trader* and hung between the two ships. It was a method frequently used to delay enemy boarders, who would become easy targets if they tried to climb over the net and drop down onto the deck. Meeks had to stop Sutherland from securing that line on the far railing. Taking careful aim, he fired.

Sutherland staggered and went down. The line sagged, and the net began to go limp. The pirates gave a shout and rushed forward, but Sutherland heaved with all his might, and the net went taut again, blocking their attack. Cursing foully, Meeks clambered back onto his quarterdeck, shouting through the noise and smoke for his fighters to cut their way through the net. He grabbed another pistol and aimed at the wounded Sutherland, who was lying against the far gunwale, desperately trying to tie the line that held up the netting.

Suddenly there was a tremendous boom of cannon, and Meeks reeled. Peter Defries and a young sailor had waited until the last minute, then sprang from their concealment beneath sailcloth to touch off the two cannon shrouded by canvas. Fiery blasts spewed canister in a swath through the crowded pirates, who fled back from the rail in confusion, leaving mates lying on deck, wounded and dying. Meeks roared in fury and fired his second pistol, and the sailor with Defries clutched at his chest, falling to the deck. As bullets sang around him, Defries whisked the fellow away, scurrying for the ship's bow, where others were hidden behind a hasty defense of barrels and crates.

Meeks snatched a third pistol from his belt and again sought out Sutherland. Through smoke he saw the Scotsman vanish into the cabin, but there was a puddle of blood where Sutherland had lain. Before escaping, Sutherland had lashed the line that ran to the netting, temporarily hindering the boarders.

"Have at 'em, ye scurvy dogs! Have at 'em!" Meeks screamed like a demon at his startled men. "Away boarders! Away, I say!" His men wavered, for their deck ran red with blood, and the wounded were shrieking in pain. Sutherland's tactic of not raising the strong net until the battle was almost joined had worked to its discouraging best. The pirates had not expected a stiff fight, but at least twenty were still on their feet, and Sutherland's force could not match that. "Cut 'em to pieces! Are ye lubberly yellow dogs? Follow me!"

With that he leaped onto the railing and swung his cutlass at the rope nets, slashing gaps in them. Other pirates did the same, and though Sutherland's defenders fired at the attackers, the pirates took heart at their captain's courage and surged over the rail. Meeks was grazed in the thigh as Merriwether fired from the cabin through a loophole, but he ignored the flesh wound and ordered his men to root out the defenders.

Sutherland was also in the crowded cabin, his left shoulder badly wounded by the ball from Meeks's pistol. As Sutherland sat on a table, Ella quickly wrapped his torn shoulder; the bullet had not struck bone but had passed through. Fighting the awful pain, he watched her as in a dream. The silver pendant at her throat sparkled as it swayed. Neither spoke, even after Ella finished her work. Lettie improvised a sling, and he urged her to make it tight so his wounded arm would not get in the way.

Sutherland glanced around to see his children sitting on the floor, against the wall opposite the enemy ship. With them were Penelope and Matilda, and all were calm, though their eyes showed anxiety. Lee was there, pouring tea. His hands were steady, and he did not spill a drop as he meticulously poured cup after cup, enough for twenty people.

Sally was silently ministering to Tom, who lay in the dimness on the bunk. He had not stirred. Mawak, Merriwether, and another sailor were firing through the loopholes; they did not waste shots, because gunsmoke filling the cabin was harsh on the eyes and made breathing difficult. Hickory loaded for them, no sign of fear on her impassive face. A steady patter and thud of bullets struck the door and wall as the pirates came aboard and took cover to blast away at the cabin.

Sutherland stood up, and dizziness caused him to sway. But he forced himself to go on despite the wound, for it was time for the next stage of his plan. He hoped Jeremy, Tamano, and Little Hawk could carry through their own part. It was they who had slipped around the *Helen* in a canoe and tossed grenades into portholes, killing and wounding pirates hiding belowdecks. In the confusion and darkness of the *Helen*'s hold, survivors of the attack would not have been able to tell where the grenades had come from, so Jeremy and the Indians were probably still undetected down in their canoe.

At the far end of the *Trader*, two crewmen were forted up behind barrels and bales, along with Jeb, Defries, James, and Heera, who was kept tied for his own safety. High on the mast, Mel had thrown his last grenade and was hunched low in the crow's nest, hoping no pirate came up after him.

Sutherland cried, "Hold them off for a little while yet!" Then he went to the stern window, opened it, and tossed out a rope that was secured to a ring on the cabin wall. When he was gone, Ella shut the window once more. Merriwether and Mawak went on firing out at the pirates on deck, but it was obvious the enemy eventually would beat down firearms aimed through the loopholes, then break the door open. For the moment Meeks's men were caught in a crossfire between the two groups of defenders and were forced to take cover. It was a standoff; but at nightfall, if matters had not changed, the pirates would have the upper hand.

Outside, Meeks ducked under the dinghy stowed amidships on the *Trader* and cried to a man nearby, "Get back to the ship and fetch over some stinkpots! We'll smoke these bastards out! And none of 'em's to get away!"

The man scurried off, lead whizzing past as he leaped like a monkey aboard the *Helen*. He was after large earthenware jars filled with a noxious combination of saltpeter, sulphur, decayed fish, and gum resin. When the wicks of the stinkpots were lit, the jars would be tossed near the locked cabin door and the resulting overpowering fumes would force those inside to come out and be shot down.

Meeks thought Sutherland was in the cabin along with most of his people. He had his men keep up a steady fire at the loopholes to worry the defenders, while other pirates pinned down the men at the bow of the ship. The deck of the *Trader* was a deadly place to show one's head.

It was a credit to Meeks's choice of a crew that the skinny fellow he had sent for the stinkpots came hopping back over the railing, bobbing and flinching at lead that struck all about him. He gained cover between the two cannon on the port side, and no one needed to tell him what to do next.

The pirates opened a fierce, coordinated barrage against the cabin to cover their comrade, until he leaped out with a lit stinkpot and rolled it against the door. As the man darted aside, a bullet from Mawak's rifle knocked him flailing to the deck, but his work was done. The stench of the thick, black smoke that poured from the stinkpot was almost too much even for the pirates on the open deck. For the people inside the cabin it was unbearable.

The foul, burning fumes seeped beneath the door and through the loopholes. Mingling with acrid gunsmoke, the stinkpot's gasses smothered the defenders of the cabin. The coughing children lay flat on the floor, and Sally threw open all the cabin windows at the stern. Blankets were stuffed against cracks around the door, but nothing could stop that disgusting odor from choking them. Coughing roughly, eyes and noses running, they were unable to see or breathe. Soon they must give up or leap out of the cabin window into the water. The beach was fifty yards off, and to get to it was their only chance.

"We have to swim to shore!" Ella cried, gagging on foul smoke, eyes afire. She grabbed her two children. "Get to the land, my darlings! Swim, and don't stop! Swim as you've never swum before!"

Feeling her way, because her eyes were blinded, she tugged off her children's outer clothes. Others were doing the same to their own garments.

Penelope rushed to Ella, a rifle in her hand. "I'll swim with Susannah!" She gasped. "We'll get ashore!"

Ella hurried to the window, where Merriwether and a sailor grabbed hold of Sutherland's rope, which hung down where he had left it when he had slipped away. The two men began to swing out, about to let the children down, but Meeks had expected this. A rough laugh came from above, and Merriwether looked up to see Meeks pointing two pistols at them. The first went off and struck the sailor, who screamed and fell into the water, but before Meeks could fire the second, Penelope appeared and shot the rifle at him. She missed, but forced Meeks to recoil, giving Merriwether the time to get back inside before the pirate fired again.

Meeks was mad with rage, for the bullet had grazed his face, drawing blood. He shouted down at the stern window, "Open that cabin door and surrender before we blow you to bits!"

The noxious gas from the stinkpots came billowing up out of the cabin, where most now lay on the floor, retching, spitting, coughing uncontrollably. Even Meeks had to back off a minute, and as he stepped away from the railing, he had another idea. He called for his men to lash ropes to the rail and go over the side.

"We'll get 'em, one way or the other! Shoot into the cabin and spare no one!" His pirates came up with pistols, ready to pass them down to their mates, who were girdled with ropes about the waist and thighs and lowered down to the cabin window.

Benjamin and Susannah held hands. Like the others, they could hardly see for the smoke, and breathing was almost impossible, but they did not complain.

A pirate swung past the window and Benjamin was first to see him. As the boy shouted in warning, the man fired blindly into the smoky cabin, then scrambled up the rope. Another pirate hung down, this one with two pistols, but before he could discharge them, Mawak howled and hurled a pike into his chest. The pirate screamed and went completely limp. Then the first pirate was there once more, and he tossed a lighted grenade into the cabin.

Susannah saw it bounce past and shrieked "Grenade!" Her brother bounded after it, but the many legs of people frantically rushing to find the explosive knocked him aside, and he lost it in the darkness.

chapter 26

CLAYMORE AND CUTLASS

Ella scrambled across the floor, seeking out the light of the sparkling fuse. There it was, under the table! She dived to grab the grenade; however, Penelope reached it first, snatched it up, and ran to the window. She hurled it outside, but at that instant the same pirate swung past again and shot his pistol, screeching in triumph as Penelope staggered back into the cabin. Ella hardly heard the grenade explode harmlessly in the water. Panic-stricken, she cried out Penelope's name and caught the woman before she fell to the floor.

Another shot rang out, and Reverend Lee muttered, "Lord have mercy on his soul!" Ella glanced at the window and saw the man who had wounded Penelope dangling, dead. Lee was holding a rifle, still aimed.

Penelope's eyes were open, and she gasped for breath as Ella laid her on bedding in the corner. No one else had seen Penelope fall, for they were stuffing everything they could against cracks and loopholes facing the deck, in order to stop the flow of poisonous smoke and fumes.

"Ella," Penelope whispered.

"Lie still, my dear one!" Ella said, trying not to break down. "Be still; it's all right! You'll be all right."

But Penelope's blood ran over Ella's hands, flowing from a wound high on her left breast. Penelope smiled weakly. "I don't feel any pain." She closed her eyes.

"Penelope! Penelope!"

She opened her eyes, saying softly, "No pain. It'll be all right, Ella. Don't worry."

The cabin was a hellish world of brimstone and blood. Even with the window thrown open, they could hardly breathe, and the stench was not subsiding. As the darkest smoke drifted away, the horror and misery deepened when they found Ella with Penelope.

Lettie groaned. "Poor little thing! Poor little thing! Dear Lord, it ain't right. It ain't." Lee and Matilda knelt by her and began to pray.

There came a savage pounding at the door. Axes bit and splintered furiously through the wood. It would be only moments before the enemy broke in. Meeks had given up trying to get into the cabin through the window, for no more of his men would risk ending up like their two dead companions who hung down at the stern. Gazing at Penelope, Ella heard gunfire and shouting outside, the clatter of feet above them as pirates ran back and forth on the quarterdeck.

Where was Owen? Had he been killed?

The pirates kept smashing the door, wielding axes with demonic fury. Already light filtered through a long gash, as did fumes from the stinkpot. The filthy, billowing smoke shielded the pirates from Defries and the others at the bow. Unless Owen succeeded soon, there would be no one left in the cabin to save. Even now some thought it was too late.

Sally grabbed a loaded musket, her face contorted with sorrow and rage. Like all the others, she was streaked with tears and dirt, sweat and blood. Panting for air, unable to hold back, she cried, "I won't die easily!"

An ax cracked through the door, and Mawak grabbed its head, dragging it inside. At the same moment, Hickory pointed her rifle out at the man holding the ax and put a bullet between his eyes. That did not slow the other pirates, who chopped at the door with renewed fury. A hinge creaked, soon to give. The pirates shouted and swore, their axes driving through the wood with every stroke.

"I'm going out!" Sally declared.

Merriwether and Hickory grabbed sturdy pikes, and Mawak readied his tomahawk. Ella took a pike of her own and then looked at the children. Fighting back a sob, she kissed them tenderly and said, "Stay with Penelope, children! Stay until I come back!"

Lee stood by the children, unable to speak. He picked up two pistols, and Matilda resolutely took one of them. Sally went to Tom and kissed him. Benjamin stood up, taking a small knife to protect his sister.

Merriwether, Lee, and Matilda fired through the door simultaneously, driving the pirates back, if only for a short while.

Then the sagging door was unbarred by Merriwether. They crowded forward. Mawak hurled the door wide and sunlight and smoke poured into the room. He shrieked like a young warrior, driving back a startled pirate, skewering him as he would an animal. The others were close behind him, raging, screaming wildly. The pirates rose from their shelter and prepared to cut them down.

Just then, resounding blasts came from the two swivel guns on the *Helen*'s quarterdeck. Sutherland and Jeremy fired grapeshot that cut down pirates as a scythe cut wheat. In that instant Tamano and Little Hawk howled and leaped across the railing from the *Helen*, tomahawks chopping and battering; Sutherland and Jeremy charged with them, claymore and tomahawk wielded left and right at reeling enemies. With a wild scream, Mel Webster came sliding full speed down a rope to ram against a surprised pirate, who went down hard under the impact, face slamming on the deck. Hickory was beside Mel, her long pike stabbing as they joined Defries and the others who attacked from the front of the ship. With Heera in the lead, they drove the retreating pirates into a knot in the center of the deck.

Sutherland's injured left shoulder was agony, but he went right for Meeks, who had dashed back onto his own ship. Sutherland leaped across the rail after the rogue, who was trapped on the quarterdeck.

"Stand and fight, Meeks!"

The pirate raised his hands, cutlass high above his head, an expression of terror on his face. "Spare me," he whined, and as he spoke, came forward. Sutherland reached the top of the steps, claymore pointed at the man's chest, just three feet away.

"Drop the sword!" Sutherland demanded.

Meeks brought the cutlass down slowly. Back on the *Trader* the noise of battle was fading as pirates surrendered or died.

"I yield!" Meeks cried hoarsely, his head inclined back slightly as he stared at Sutherland. "My sword's yers, mate! I got no fight left in me." Blood soaked Meeks's leg, where the bullet had grazed him, and his face had another wound, received when Penelope had nearly finished him off.

"The sword," Sutherland hissed. "Drop it where you stand, or you'll die now!"

Meeks glared, teeth clenched. He opened his fist to drop the cutlass, and tipped the weapon slowly forward. It was shoulder high and coming down, the hilt resting in the pirate's hand, when Sutherland saw, too late, it was aimed at him. With a flick of his forearm, Meeks hurled the sword like a spear. It shot at the Scotsman. He ducked, and it grazed his cheek, then was instantly jerked back by a leather thong secured to Meeks's wrist. In a twinkling, the pirate had it again and slashed at Sutherland's legs.

Sutherland sprang over the stroke and in the same motion drove his claymore at Meeks. It thudded into a rib, digging in an inch as Meeks recoiled and backed off.

"No quarter!" Sutherland roared.

"None given or asked!" Meeks replied with a snarl and a tremendous swing of the cutlass.

Sutherland stepped aside, then came in. Meeks parried thrust upon thrust, heavy cutlass to sturdy claymore, ringing crash after crash against the other's blade. Gradually the pirate gained the offensive. The wounded Sutherland was hard put to keep his footing because there were cannon, tools, cordage, and buckets all around. Meeks, though, could have walked here blindfolded and not once misstepped. The Scotsman might have backed off and found a rifle with which to kill the man, who would have been at bay, for all the surviving pirates had surrendered on the *Trader*. But there was always the chance a doomed Hugh Meeks would go below to torch a powder keg and blow them all up.

Also, there was vengeance to be taken. Even though his shoulder was terrible agony, Sutherland concentrated on the cutlass, the other man's hot eyes, and on his own footwork. They fought back and forth across the deck. No fancy swordplay, just slash and cut, duck, chop, and dig, short punches with the hilt and fierce grappling when they came close in.

Meeks had nothing to lose and fought with reckless ferocity. He was a dead man even if he killed Sutherland. Desperate, unafraid, he was fighting the last battle of his cruel life. As he stroked, blocked, cursed, and kicked, the lust for danger and violence flamed up in him, and he began to cackle in a mad frenzy.

Sweating and bleeding, they drove each other back and forth over the quarterdeck, from railing to railing. Sutherland had the advantage, the claymore stabbing, drawing blood from his enemy's sword arm, but Meeks fought back as though untouched, leaping and swinging, his thick frock coat flying about like a demon's wings.

The Scotsman slowed and tried to become poised, but pain and weariness sapped him. He was weakening from loss of blood, while Meeks was growing stronger as insanity took hold. Suth-

erland looked for the villain to charge, wanting to meet Meeks
head on, taking a glancing stroke if he must, but getting a killing
stab into the man's vitals.

Meeks had not yet harmed Sutherland with his huge blade, but
only one stroke finding its mark would be the end. Sutherland
began backing down the stairs of the quarterdeck, a delirious
Meeks driving him with hack after hack that barely missed. Retreating across the main deck, Sutherland fought off a headlong
attack and found himself driven back against the railing. Mind
spinning, he felt rather than saw the curved blade whisk down.
He narrowly managed to slide past it, hearing steel dig into the
wood.

Meeks pushed full force against him and squeezed Sutherland's
throat, bending him back, trying to hold his head steady as the
cutlass came down again, missing by a hairsbreadth. Sutherland's
feet came off the decking. His bad arm was pinned against his
body, but his free hand punched the hilt of the claymore at Meeks's
head again and again. The pirate was intoxicated with rage, furious
that he could not land a killing blow.

"Die! Die, you dog!" Meeks's voice was a banshee shriek, his
red face the vision of evil. "Blast ye for a—" He grunted, blood
splattering, as Sutherland caught him full in the face with a shat-
tering whack. In the next instant Sutherland kneed the stunned
Meeks savagely in the groin, and the pirate gasped. The claymore
sped across in a short, hacking arc, staggering the pirate as it
glanced off the side of his head, sending him stumbling, to fall
heavily to the deck.

Following swiftly, Sutherland came on, claymore raised. He
looked into the man's coal-fire eyes and saw a sudden gleam in
them, something sly. Meeks scrambled quickly backward, like a
crab. Blood ran from the gash on the side of his head, but he held
on to his cutlass and got to the cabin door, which was ajar. Sutherland went after him, meaning to finish his foe.

Meeks clambered to his feet, his back to the cabin, then lowered
his cutlass, putting the point on the deck. He was daring Sutherland
to strike. Fury and hatred boiled over in Sutherland, who was
willing to oblige.

Though suspecting some cunning, Sutherland was so angry that
he ignored caution. He feinted with the claymore, twice right,
once left, then struck right. Meeks parried the blow, as Sutherland
had anticipated, and their swords locked. But before the Scotsman
could pull back the claymore, Meeks grabbed his sword hand in

an iron grip and hung on with all his might.

Meeks cackled like a lunatic, his crude power locking them together, swords jammed at the hilts. Sutherland's bad shoulder made it impossible to break away. The pirate might have heaved Sutherland back and followed with a merciless attack. Instead, he used his free hand to clutch Sutherland's shirt front, holding him close, their swords immobilized between them. Sutherland smelled the foul breath, sweat, and blood, and stared into those malevolent eyes. Too late, he realized someone was in the cabin, partly concealed by the door, a pistol in hand, and Meeks knew it.

Sutherland would make an easy target if only Meeks could turn him slightly more toward the door. Meeks realized Sutherland knew what was happening, and laughed gleefully. It was a good revenge in exchange for defeat and certain death. With a grunt, Meeks tried to turn Sutherland, who fought against him. Heaving back and forth, they trembled with every ounce of strength. Meeks was too strong, however, and Sutherland could not break away.

The Scotsman put all he had into getting back from that pistol, which was coming down slowly, leveling right at him. He could not get clear. Meeks's face was running with blood, turning the scar on his neck red. One hard wrench and he would have Sutherland just where he wanted him, to take a bullet in the spine.

Only seconds had passed, although the struggle seemed endless, but still the shot had not come. The pistol was aimed, waiting for Meeks to position his victim. The two men were locked even more tightly, but the pirate was irresistible and, with a final roar of triumph, whirled Sutherland around, back to the door.

Meeks shrieked, "Shoot! Shoot!"

Sutherland twisted, unable to get free.

"Shoot! Damn you, Farley!"

There was a loud report and gunsmoke. Meeks screamed and lost his hold as Sutherland hurled him away, to crash against a cannon. Then the Scotsman thrust once, through the heart, and with a long, moaning gasp, Hugh Meeks breathed away his evil life.

The pirate's cutlass fell clanking onto the deck. Sutherland stepped back. He turned to see Dawson Merriwether standing outside the cabin door, looking down at a dead man. It was Farley Jones. A smoking pistol was in Merriwether's hand, and as he leaned against the doorjamb, he whispered, "Now Claudia is avenged."

Sutherland staggered to Merriwether and pulled him away.

They were joined by Peter Defries and Tamano, who helped them get back to the *Trader*. Weak, swaying on his feet, Sutherland went into the cabin. There he found Jeremy kneeling by Penelope.

"No!" Sutherland groaned, putting a hand on Jeremy's shoulder and falling to his knees. "It can't be . . ."

Jeremy looked at him through tears and said, "It wasn't worth this! Nothing was worth this, Pa!" Jeremy laid his forehead upon Penelope's shoulder and wept. She was dead.

Sutherland slowly shook his head. How could it have come to this? He wanted to tell Jeremy that Hugh Meeks had nothing to do with the cause, that this day's horror had not occurred because of the rebellion. He wanted to say this and much more, but could not.

Jeremy left the cabin, carrying Penelope out into the daylight. Sutherland remained on his knees, overcome with sadness, remorse, and disbelief that it all had ended so tragically. His eyes filled with tears.

Then a cool hand touched his cheek. Ella was there. He rose and drew her head against his chest. Ella had been spared. She had been spared, and outside, the children were crying. But they were alive.

Across the room, a sorrowful Sally was with Tom, slowly rubbing a wet cloth over his feverish face. The head wound above his ear was not bleeding, but it seemed very grave. Sutherland came to Sally and took her trembling hand. He could hardly look at Tom, for it seemed the lad was also lost.

Sally bit her lip as her fingers ran over Tom's beautiful face. He did not respond.

Then Ella spoke, her voice loud in the stillness. "We'll get medicine, bandages, hot water . . . whatever we can do." She went outside to arrange for a fire to be lit in the brazier.

Sutherland stood with Sally, wishing he could have prevented all this. Perhaps he should have returned to the northwest instead of going to Philadelphia. Perhaps he could have saved Penelope—

Sally gripped his hand and said, "Don't blame . . . anyone, Owen. You did all you could do."

Sutherland felt hollow. His exhausted body and many wounds ached, but he did not care. Tom was what mattered now.

He whispered, "We won't let him die, Sally."

Then Jeremy was beside them. He stood next to Sally, looking down at Tom. Sutherland saw the lad was cool, almost cold, and that the color had drained from his face. Jeremy had closed off all emotion. It was a wonder that he was standing there at all. A lesser man would not be.

Jeremy bent over to examine his friend, then he began to do things decisively, precisely, with the movements of one who knew his calling.

"I want a table set up here, and plenty of bandages and hot water; Pa, please lay out my surgical instruments, and Sally, get sponges and some basins, and keep everyone away until I want them."

Ella stood at the door, gazing at her son. It was she who had called him back into the cabin. There was a pause as they all looked at one another as though they were strangers. The moment passed.

"Please look lively," Jeremy said, and began to take the bloody bandages from Tom's head. "We have to aid the living, and there's no time to lose."

Sally touched his arm. "Is there hope?"

Jeremy did not look at her. "There has to be hope, Sal. Hope is all we have left."

In the gray light of dawn the dead were buried on the island. The surviving pirates took care of their own, and Sutherland's crewmen were buried not far away, Lee saying a service over them. Then another funeral procession wound its way up the high bluff, to a windswept clearing that viewed the magnificent expanse of Lake Erie. Here Penelope Bently was laid to rest. Before departing, they sang "Amazing Grace" over her, then left Jeremy standing alone with Heera by the fresh grave.

Penelope had felt about life the same way Jeremy did, and now she was gone. He was alone on a road that would take him—he did not know where. Standing in the wind, he contemplated what he could sort out, but found no meaning in any of it, no meaning except that this was the way of life and of death. He did not blame Sutherland's rebels or the cause, for Penelope had died at the hands of evil men—men who bore no allegiance to anything except their own idols of power and wealth. For Jeremy, there was no sense of right or wrong, of justice, or even injustice. It simply had happened. Penelope was gone.

Jeremy did not know how long he stood there by the graveside, eyes empty. Heera lay beside him all the while. It seemed his family and friends were just ending the hymn, for he could hear it yet, but when he looked at the sky, he realized hours had passed.

He had no desire to leave this place, no desire to go anywhere. else at all.

"Jeremy."

He looked around as Sutherland approached, the wounded arm inside his frock coat. They stood side by side, heads bowed, the cold breeze blowing their hair and flapping the collars of their coats. Sutherland might have tried to say many things to comfort him, but what Jeremy needed most was time and love, and, as the lad already knew, hope.

After a while Sutherland said, "Come join us in camp, son."

Jeremy closed his eyes, then opened them.

Sutherland put an arm around him. "I know what you're feeling."

Jeremy's anger flared up, and he glared at his stepfather, saying, "How can anyone know?"

Then he was struck, remembering that Sutherland had lost his own beloved wife just as suddenly. Sutherland stood in a completely different light now. Jeremy felt he was seeing his stepfather for the first time, understanding the deeper man he was, the burden he carried.

Jeremy sharply turned away to stare at the lake. Then he looked at the grave and again at Owen. He said, "You do understand."

"Will you come with me, son? They want you; Tom's asking for you."

Tom Morely and Sally Cooper sat side by side on the beach of the cove. Jeremy had saved his life, removing slivers of bone from his skull and stitching up the ragged wound. Bandages swathed Tom's head and went right around his chin. He looked clear-eyed, but was weak, for Jeremy had bled him, a medical procedure commonly employed to awaken stunned patients.

Everyone was gathered around a large campfire, waiting for Jeremy and Sutherland to come down. Out in the cove the *Trader* and *Helen* lay side by side at anchor. It was expected that Merriwether and the Indians would return to Detroit on the *Trader* and tell all that had happened—including the fact that Hugh Meeks was a freebooter with no allegiance to the rebels. After what Bradford Cullen had said, no one could prove that the pirate had anything to do with the merchant.

Sutherland and the others—Ella hoped Jeremy, too—would travel across Lake Erie on the *Helen*, taking the prisoners, who would be put in the hands of *habitants*, later to be turned over to the Redcoats at Fort Erie. Sutherland's party would avoid British-

held Fort Niagara and go to Montreal in the whaleboat left with
the Frenchman on the shore of Lake Ontario. Ella sat on a log,
watching the fire. There was nothing more to be said as far as
Jeremy's joining the rebellion was concerned. He would not. Last
night, after a poignant discussion, he had made it plain to her that
he was following another course. His calling was to be a doctor,
with responsibility to all the people of the northwest. Ella only
prayed her son would not take up arms against the rebellion and
one day find himself in combat with his family.

Sitting around that roaring blaze, they talked of the past, of
the future, and of their dreams. No one complained or voiced inner
doubts. Everyone wanted to think only good. Mel and Hickory
would go to visit her father in the Mohawk Valley, to see whether
they could stay in the village of Oneidas until the war ended. They
were still neutrals, wanting only to live peacefully.

The other Indians also intended to keep out of this white man's
conflict. Tamano had told Sutherland plainly he would not take
sides in the fight. Their long friendship would not end, but it might
wither unless Sutherland returned one day in peace to the northwest. Little Hawk and Mawak would go back to their village near
Detroit and try to persuade the young men to remain quiet no
matter how loudly the British called upon them to fight rebels.

The Sutherlands, Tom and Sally, the Greys, the Lees, and
James Morely would try to make a go of it in Montreal. Whether
any kind of trade could be carried out was a question, but there
was plenty of money now that Sutherland had sold the pelts in
Albany. Merriwether would see to it the partners of the Frontier
Company in the northwest—from Detroit to Michilimackinac—
would receive their fair share of this money, and he would be
reimbursed by a promissory note Sutherland had drawn on a neutral
trading firm doing business in Montreal. Sutherland would now
be headquartered in that rebel-held city, where existing Frontier
Company warehouses would serve as a new base of operations.

Peter Defries would go back to Albany to rejoin his family.
Later he would return to the rebel army in Lower Canada and offer
his services until the war was brought to an end. Owen would do
the same.

As for Sally and Tom, they were the only bright spot in this
grim picture. They sat on a log together, Sally's head on his
shoulder. They were not cheerful but considered themselves blessed
to be alive and together.

Defries took note of how much in love they seemed. He had

Benjamin on one knee and Susannah huddled against his left side. Looking across the fire at the young couple, he said, "When do you mean to marry?"

They looked up, and Tom glanced at Reverend Lee, who was sitting on a blanket with Matilda, reading his Bible.

Tom said, "We'd marry right now . . . if only things wasn't so damned awful!"

Sally agreed. "We don't feel right to be so happy, if you understand."

Defries looked at Lee, saying, "Maybe you can join 'em on the ship, once we're in Montreal."

Tom said, without thinking, "I only wish Jeremy could be my best man. Ah! That's a danged fool selfish thing to think at a time like this, ain't it?"

"No, it's not." It was Jeremy's voice.

They turned to see him, Owen, and Heera standing at the edge of the trees. They rose, and Jeremy came to Tom and grasped his hand.

"In times like these, Tom, you mustn't wait." To Sally, he said, "I'd be honored to be there when you make your vows, but I'm going to Detroit with Tamano to protect Valenya . . . for as long as I can. So we'd better get on with the marriage right now."

Sally was smiling, but the tears escaped anyway, and she kissed Jeremy's hand. Tom took his other hand, and the three friends embraced. An inner strength brought them through sorrow, beyond despair, into another realm that could be described in one word:

"Hope," Sally said. "Whatever else we share, it's hope that will endure no matter what happens to us after we part. We can't go on at all without hope."

The marriage was arranged. Overcoming her grief for Penelope and her sadness that she must again part from Jeremy, Ella gladly supplied a temporary ring. Lettie and Matilda set to preparing the modest wedding dinner, but there was no feasting, no revelry, no dancing or merry singing. Still, everyone's spirit was lifted.

In a ceremony full of love, Sally Cooper and Tom Morely were wedded on the beach, and Owen Sutherland gave the bride away just as the last rays of sundown glinted orange and golden over the island, sparkling on the water of the tranquil cove.

A Special Preview of the
Opening Chapter of
Book 5 in the
Northwest Territory Series

CONFLICT

by
Oliver Payne

*On sale July 1984
wherever Berkley books
are sold*

Chapter 1

It was Christmas morning in the year 1775, and a drizzling mist obscured the straits between Lakes Erie and Saint Clair. The pale light of wintry dawn merged water and sky into a gray mass, shrouding a birchbark canoe that made its way upstream to Fort Detroit, five miles ahead. The three paddlers—two women and a man—were unaware of the danger that bore down on them from behind, just minutes away.

Like a lonely firefly lost in the fog, the yellow light of a bow lantern signaled the approach of the last merchant ship to sail for the fort before winter set in. Cutting through mist and water as though they were one and the same substance, the sloop *Trader* drove straight for the unsuspecting canoeists, invisible in the dimness ahead.

Unless someone on the sloop's deck spotted the canoe in time, it would be rammed like so much stray driftwood. There was even a chance that no one on board the ship would hear the cries of the paddlers, who would be thrown into the icy water and lost. Mist darkened everything that morning, and it was no wonder a tall young man standing in the bow of the sloop could not see the canoe in his ship's path.

Peering into the grayness, Jeremy Bently was alert for rocks and snags, not canoes, because no experienced folk of the northwest would dare take such fragile craft out in this mist. Indeed, it was dangerous for any boat on the river in such weather. This late in the season, however, a good following wind was not to be wasted, and Jeremy was not overly worried. There was enough visibility to make out the dark outline of the eastern shore to the right, and he knew these waters well. By now the *Trader* was north of Grande Isle, where the straits were a safe thousand yards across. Besides, he was anxious to reach Fort Detroit, for then he would be home, after five long years away.

Wearing a thick scarlet stocking cap and a dark blue frock coat, Jeremy Bently was a remarkably handsome young man, with long legs and arms. He had broad shoulders and a thick neck that told of immense physical strength. His blond hair was clubbed in back, where it hung over his collar, and drops of water gleamed on a scraggly beard of two weeks' growth. His high cheekbones and square jaw took on the light of the lantern that hung before him on the bowsprit. Eyes narrowing as he stared upriver, he could not penetrate the gloom far enough to see the canoe, now less than two hundred and fifty yards off.

A following breeze blew gently, hurrying the two-masted sloop along, and Jeremy took pleasure in the hushed atmosphere. He listened to the soothing rush of foam past the bow; overhead, spars creaked steadily, rhythmically. It was like floating through some dreamworld, and he found his mind wandering. Memories came and drew him away.

Though Jeremy appeared serene as he stood there, lost in thought, within him there was a deep emptiness, and the memories were not welcome ones. In his imagination were visions of death and suffering, tragedy and loss. In his twenty-two years, he had never before felt so alone.

The water was smooth, hardly ruffled by the breeze as the *Trader* pressed blindly on. Jeremy wondered whether that lovely bluff on the island where Penelope lay at rest was also shrouded in mist this morning. He remembered the solitude there, and the difficulty he had felt in leaving that place a few days ago. Standing next to her grave, one had a wide view of the lake, and of the sunrise. Was there a sunrise to be seen there just now? Perhaps, for the island was far to the south. Perhaps the sun was breaking over the horizon, golden . . . Penelope would have loved that tiny island, that beautiful hillside.

He realized his eyes had been closed. Opening them, he sensed that the morning light shimmered more brightly through the drizzle. The mist was thinning.

Even with his eyes open, however, he could still imagine Penelope, dark of hair and eyes, smiling at him the way she had the first time he knew he loved her. They had been riding together over an English meadow, and she had laughed often that day. How fortunate he had been to have had Penelope's love, if only for a few short months.

He did not know how the words came into his mind, but it was as if Penelope had spoken them: "Have hope. Share that hope, and do good for your people in this difficult time."

Have hope. More than ever, Jeremy knew that he was meant to return here. He would be the sole trained physician for a thousand miles or more; that alone was good enough reason to remain neutral in the bitter struggle being waged by rebel Whigs and Tory loyalists who were arming themselves in the eastern colonies, preparing for all-out civil war. He prayed the rebellion would be stopped before it spread into a hellish nightmare of slaughter and destruction that would prevent peacemaking until one side or the other was utterly defeated. Such a war, he knew, might rage for years before the British Army and Navy managed to bring the rebels under control once and for all.

He prayed peace terms would be reached between Parliament in London and the Continental Congress in Philadelphia long before the army began a decisive campaign against the half-trained, ill-equipped rebel militias. Jeremy had just spent several months in Britain, and he had been brought up out here at Detroit as the nephew of a British officer. He well knew the vengeful fury of the British Army, which already had lost so many men in the battles of Lexington and Bunker Hill. If the war continued much longer, the suffering in America would be appalling and might even spread into the wilderness, perhaps as far as Fort Detroit, the most remote major outpost in all the Empire. There would be hardly an American or Briton who would not count friends or relations among the casualties.

Something caught in Jeremy's throat. He sighed, feeling an uneasiness within that did not belong there—not if he was to get on with the business at hand and begin another life. His duty now, he reminded himself, was to the ship. For a fleeting moment he thought perhaps they should anchor until the drizzle lifted, as it would surely do before long. But no one else would be on the straits at this hour—particularly not on this morning. He had almost forgotten what day it was!

To himself, Jeremy whispered, "Happy Christmas . . . peace on earth . . . goodwill—"

"Ahoy in the bow, Doctor Bently, sorr!"

Jeremy turned to look back at Simon Clancy, the swarthy Irishman who stood on the quarterdeck at the helm. The handsome sailor called out that Jeremy should look lively for any sign of the river swinging eastward, as it would do soon. Jeremy waved in acknowledgment, glad to have the likes of Simon Clancy at the wheel. Clancy was the only real seaman in the crew, and the bloody bandage wrapped around his head recalled the battle on Erie, where three other sailors who normally manned the *Trader* had been killed.

Clancy was wiry, of average height, and the same age as Jeremy. Broad across the chest, he carried himself with a kind of aggressive pride that matched his quick wit and courage. He was a dependable comrade in any situation.

The Irishman stood beside another man, whose homespun smock and red kerchief for a cap made him seem a common deckhand. But Dawson Merriwether, who sat on a barrel and calmly smoked a long-stemmed white pipe, was no ordinary seaman. He was the richest and most influential merchant in the northwest now that Owen Sutherland had been driven into rebel country. As a staunch loyalist, the aging, paunchy Merriwether was looked upon as a bulwark to others of his political sympathies, and his upbringing as a Virginia planter and gentleman made him well suited for the role of a leading Tory. This morning, however, he was simply a sailor.

Clancy called again. "There'll be no room for error, Doc, not with our two topmen down in the cabin, shakin' rattles and throwin' bones to make medicine to chase away the bad weather! Fog spooks 'em."

Jeremy waved again. He knew Indians did not like to journey on the threshold of winter. In this season most stayed close to the dozen scattered northwest trading posts, such as Detroit, and tried to keep from starving to death. Though living in a land of plenty, Indians were notoriously poor at providing for the cold months, and often only the charity of Redcoat commanders kept them from being wiped out by a bad winter. Of course, the generosity of Parliament's soldiers served to keep the redskins loyal to the king. The government supplied all their needs, and thus year after year kept them trapping peltry for wealthy British merchants, who made huge profits each spring, when furs were shipped across the sea.

No, Indians would not step outside their lodges so early on a winter's morning, and none would risk paddling canoes through such fog, which they considered an act of demoniac power and full of peril. Nor would the few hundred French and half-breed *habitants* who dwelt along the straits and up at the fort be on the water. By now all were surely at mass in the Church of Sainte Anne's at the fort. These simple, strong folk were as devout as their forebears, who had come to this country with the permission of the Indians two hundred years earlier.

As for the Redcoat garrison of one hundred rank and file in the stockade, most would have a day off from normal drudgery and drill. They would keep to their barracks or the alehouse, drinking and gambling, whoring if they could find a willing squaw, fighting if they got drunk enough on their frugal pay and watered holiday grog.

The several hundred British and American civilians living at Fort Detroit were mainly Protestants, as pious as the Catholic French, and certainly not the kind to go boating on Christmas morning, when they, too, should be in church.

Jeremy wondered what changes he would find at Detroit after five years, but he was sure the people would not have changed much. The turbulent outside world of civilization, culture, and philosophy seldom touched this isolated community, where the latest fashions and newest ideas came with the government mail—a year late.

Here, life was brawling, rich, and bountiful in the warm months, hard and spare in the cold. Folk who chose to live out here were tough, set in their ways, not easily given to social change or political idealism. Survival in the wild required a cool head and practical genius as well as a strong back and ready courage. The strife that afflicted the three million people of the eastern colonies had not troubled Detroit very much. Those residents who had ambitions to change the order of things—such as the Sutherlands—had been forced to depart, perhaps forever, or for as long as King George III ruled the British Empire.

Fort Detroit would repose in half slumber this winter, as ever it had, with only the regular round of weekly parties and dances to liven dull spirits. No doubt the place was already dozing, as though the tumult and killing of the last few months had never occurred to the eastward. An impenetrable wall of forest kept the rest of the world far, far away, and even the war was almost unreal to many of the people of Detroit.

"Are you thinking about Valenya, little brother?"

The voice from behind spoke in Chippewa, deep and melodious. Jeremy turned as Tamano joined him in the bow. A middle-aged warrior, lean and well-muscled, Tamano was almost as tall as Jeremy, and though past his prime, he more than made up in intelligence and experience for what he had lost in sheer physical strength. Like Jeremy, he wore a heavy frock coat against the chill. He had no hat, and his long black hair hung in two braids upon his chest. A single eagle feather flickered at his ear as he stared forward into the curtain of mist.

Jeremy turned to lean on the railing. In the softness of lantern light and gray drizzle, these two were sharp contrasts—the Indian dark, solemn, with eyes black and penetrating like some bird of prey; the white man fair, with delicate features and a firm mouth that told of good breeding and of civilized manners.

Tamano spoke again, his voice gentle and slow, once more using the tongue of his people, which Jeremy knew so well. Tamano had taught him much about the Indians and the forest, and was like an uncle to him.

"I have no drawings or magic needle to guide me, but we are close to home, for I can smell my Lela's cooking fire." Tamano shut his eyes, raised his face, and breathed as though savoring a wonderful aroma. "Ahhh. Beaver tail, broiled and spiced! Lela knows her man is near."

Jeremy smiled. "Your little ones will be at it first if we don't get clear of this mist and catch a stronger breeze, my brother."

Jeremy's voice was of medium pitch, but he spoke the Chippewa language with all the throaty guttural of a native son. His elegant, wealthy friends back in Britain would have marveled at his transformation as he expressed himself in Chippewa. They knew him only as a refined and educated gentleman, comfortable in the most sophisticated company. Jeremy had changed their former narrow ideas about the character of Americans who came out of the forest lands, but they would have been confused to see the physician just then. He looked almost like a Chippewa as he spoke, hands moving freely, head tilted back.

"Aiee," Tamano replied with a grin and a nod. "The little ones are not so little these days; you have not beheld them in five years, and you will be pleased to see how they grow like green corn and eat beaver tail like *carcajou,* the wolverine!"

Tamano proudly said that his twin children, a boy and a girl of six, favored the clothes of whites, and longed to learn all they could in a white man's school.

"They will bring the best of your people to my people," he went on, gazing thoughtfully into the mist. "And they will assure my race a stronger position in the bad time that is to come, when this rebellion is past and the whites come to take our land, as I know they will. This no red man can prevent."

Jeremy considered his friend's words closely. For years, Tamano had been the close companion of Owen Sutherland, and had taught Donoway—Sutherland's Indian name—when the Scotsman first came to this land twenty years earlier.

Tamano, too, had bade a sad farewell to Owen Sutherland after the battle on the lake, and Jeremy knew that like most northwestern Indians, Tamano feared the rebel cause that Sutherland supported. He was about to ask Tamano who he thought would eventually prevail, but just then the ship lurched and momentarily lost headway. The canvas snapped loudly.

Back at the helm on the quarterdeck, Simon Clancy shouted in his thick brogue to the cabin below. "Hands on deck, me hearties! We've some sailin' to do! Wind's swingin' round, me redskin boyos! We'll get home in style if you handle her right. On deck!"

He cried at two figures who came bounding out of the cabin door, both reeling awkwardly with the sudden roll of the ship.

"Steady, there! I'll make ye Jack Tars afore we reach anchorage!"

The first man was lumbering and portly, had long, braided hair, and was wearing buckskin leggins and several layers of colorful trade shirts. This was Mawak, an aged Ottawa medicine man, who insisted on lending a hand at sailing the ship. The other fellow was a slim and muscular Indian in his late twenties, and like Mawak, he had never before been a sailor. Little Hawk was a tall Santee Sioux from west of the Wees-konsan, a brave and dashing warrior determined to prove no white man's skill was too difficult for him to master.

Clancy cried, "Sheet home the mains'l boom, and pay no mind to the gaff for now. Then lay forward and take in the—" Seeing that the Indians had stopped short, with no idea what he meant, he cursed, pointed, and tried another approach. "Pull on that rope there, Mawak. You, Little Hawk, unlash that line—" But before he could finish the sentence, Little Hawk shrilled a savage cry and sprang into the rigging, scurrying up the foremast shrouds like a monkey.

"No! No!" Clancy yelled. "Not the fore course, Little Hawk! The main topsail! Come down! Just help Mawak on the sheet tackle! Come down now, afore the wind throws you into the drink!"

In one fluid motion, Little Hawk stopped his rapid progress up the rigging, leaped onto another rope, and slid lightly down to the deck. His reckless agility made even the hard-bitten Clancy whoop with admiration.

"Ye'd do for a dandy topman, me boyo!"

In the bow, Jeremy and Tamano watched, chuckling to see the Indians haul away in unison and sing a seaman's chant Clancy had taught them. The flapping canvas mainsail caught the breeze again and filled, billowing in the mist. The *Trader* leaned over, quickening its pace across the water.

Tamano cried in Ottawa to Mawak, who was securing a line at the stern of the ship, "You'll never be content in your bark canoe again, old uncle! Perhaps you should become a captain in the great white father's navy!"

Jeremy laughed to hear that. He understood a half-dozen Indian tongues, as well as French. He watched with admiration as the bulky Mawak deftly tied a bowline with a flourish, ending with his gnarled hands palms-up in the air.

Mawak cried back, also in Ottawa, "Indeed, Tamano, Mawak is too enormous for his canoe! Maybe our white father across the sea will lend me a winged boat like this one, and I'll find him the passage to the northwest ocean, eh?"

Little Hawk laughed and swung back up the rigging, just for the fun of it, kicking his legs high over his head and around the mainstay, until he dangled, with hands free, swaying to and fro.

"Better than my pony! Hoka hey! Blow, old woman wind!" His friends laughed along with him. "Dance with me, wind! Hoka hey!"

Jeremy leaned back against the railing. He was home again. Here were his Indian companions of boyhood, and this was the country he knew and loved. He wished the weather would clear so he could see the familiar, low-lying shore better. But the feel of the driving mist, the smell of the wind, and the sound of the Detroit River spoke to him. For the first time since Penelope died, he knew there really was hope, and there was a future for him here.

Then he was distracted. He thought he heard singing in the distance. It was a beautiful sound, the sort that might be enchantment, like the voices of elusive, bewitched sirens luring sailors to doom, as in the old myths. He turned his attention from Little Hawk's daring antics and listened, wondering whether he was the only one who heard it. But Tamano, too, hesitated. Yes, women were singing nearby. Was the ship too close to shore? Was the wind playing tricks, carrying the song far over the water? No lights from campfires or cabins were in sight.

It was an English song on the wind, melodious and gay, in perfect harmony. Jeremy glanced at Tamano, then at the dark eastern shore, before peering ahead into the distance.

"You hear it, my brother?" he asked.

"It is close," Tamano replied. "But where?"

The wind in the rigging and the creak of the ship mingled with the rush of water surging past, making the song difficult to pin-point. The other three men on deck seemed to hear nothing, and went on with their banter as the *Trader* drove onward. The song rose higher, closer now. It was the popular tune "Drum Major," the tale of a young woman who enlists in the army to be with her sweetheart soldier.

> Young men and maidens and bachelors sweet,
> I'll sing you a song that is new and complete,
> Concerning a damsel that followed the drum;
> For the sake of her true love for a soldier she's gone.

The voices were pure, haunting in the mist. Jeremy suddenly knew someone was on the water, and very near.

"Halloo!" he cried out, attracting the attention of the others on the *Trader*. "Halloo, out there! Where are you?"

The song died instantly. There was a shout of dismay—this time a man's voice, followed by the clatter of paddles on a canoe's gunwales.

"Where be ye, b'gad?" It was a rough, deep voice, just yards off, dead ahead.

"Sloop!" Jeremy roared, and then the mist gave up the canoe, revealing it almost under the ship's charging bow. "Helm to port! Helm aport!"

Simon Clancy heard and spun the wheel over, but it was too late. Women in the canoe screamed, and the man bellowed in fury. The craft sprang aside as paddles flashed. Jeremy and Tamano gaped helplessly as the ship scraped the stern of the canoe, the wash raising the fragile vessel and slewing it sideways. Its paddlers—two women in scarlet cloaks, and a lanky, gray-bearded man in a floppy brown hat—struggled to keep from capsizing. But water sloshed in, filling the canoe quickly. The rush of foam left the paddlers hip deep. The craft was sinking.

"Get the dinghy!" Jeremy yelled to Tamano as the *Trader* swept past. The Chippewa sprang away to unlash the rowboat stowed along the center of the sloop's deck. "Hold on!" Jeremy cried to the white man in the stern of the canoe, but the birchbark craft was swamped. It could last only minutes.

The man below almost stood up in his anger, and shook a fist at Jeremy. "Blackguard! Scoundrel! Save us! Save us so I can thrash you within an inch of your worthless—"

"Uncle Cole!" shouted the woman who sat in the center of the canoe. As she spoke, her hood fell away, revealing honey blond hair and a pretty face that seemed to radiate in the dusky light. "Just bail, Uncle Cole! Bail! Use your hat!"

The man named Cole growled and yanked off his hat, briskly dipping it into the canoe to battle with the river. The two women were rapidly using wooden bowls to throw out the icy water, which already came almost to the canoe's gunwales, soaking gear and clothing. They worked quickly, but without panic. As Jeremy stripped off his frock coat and kicked off his shoes, he knew they would have no hope of surviving in the icy river unless someone came to their aid, and soon.

By now the *Trader* had drifted past, but Clancy had turned her bow into the wind, and she was steadily losing headway, beginning to drift back downstream toward the canoe. But the canoe was also drifting downstream. Jeremy was joined in the bow by Little Hawk, whose black hair hung down over his shoulders. Both men had stripped to the waist despite the chill of early winter. The canoe already was thirty yards away, nearly lost in the mist. The slightest gust of wind or trick of the current would be enough to send it to the bottom.

"I should've been watching closer!" Jeremy declared, angry with himself that he had been idly lost in thought while the ship had sailed at the canoe. "They're done for if we can't get them aboard the *Trader*!"

As he stripped down, Jeremy looked around to Tamano and Mawak, who were hurriedly unlashing the dinghy, which would be lowered over the side within a few moments. Almost naked, with only an undergarment over his loins, he snatched two coiled lines from where they hung on the railing. Dawson Merriwether, puffing and nervous, joined Jeremy and Little Hawk, who were prepared to leap into the water. Both young men had slung the coils over their shoulders.

"Help Tamano lower the dinghy!" Jeremy yelled at Merriwether. "We'll try to keep them afloat until you reach us!"

"Take care, but hurry, lads," Merriwether declared. Then he scurried away to assist Tamano and Mawak with the boat. At the same moment, Jeremy and Little Hawk dived overboard. The bitter-cold water was a shock as they struck, surfaced, and swam toward the canoe. It was as if the river clamped itself cruelly about their limbs while they labored to reach the birch boat in time.

Jeremy heard the defiant shout of the bearded man called Cole. "Come on, ye scoundrels! Come on so I can drag yer worthless hides down with me!" Then, apparently thinking better of it, he cried, "Save the ladies! Never mind me! Come for the girls! Oh . . . this end's sinking! Damned Injun boats! We should've took a whaleboat! Hurry, you two! Hurry!"

Cole Ross's voice had changed from angry to anxious, and he spoke rapidly to the two women. Through the murky, dense cold, Jeremy heard the man say, "Grab one of these knaves, girls, and don't let go! Here they come! Don't panic! Here they come! Oh . . . I'm done for! Annie, Gwendolyn, take care of yerselves! God go with ye!"

Jeremy reached the swamped canoe. Looking through water that streamed down over his face, he saw two very beautiful women—the blonde with the shining face, and a young woman with long auburn hair and dark eyes. The canoe was nearly under by now, but there was still a chance of saving it. Jeremy removed the coil of rope from over his neck and threw part of it to the blond woman, who came up with one end, and immediately seemed to understand her rescuer's intentions. Jeremy dove under the craft, no easy task in such freezing water. His strength was sapped with every passing moment, but he surfaced on the other side and took the end of the rope that was in the blonde's hands. Tying it to complete the loop, he pulled the line taut around the canoe, which might be kept from sinking if the *Trader* came back soon enough to winch it out of the water.

Little Hawk did the same, with the muttering Cole Ross taking a grip on the other line. Then Jeremy's worst fears came to pass: The canoe tilted, stern down, and took in more water.

Ross clutched the blond woman by the shoulders and demanded she abandon the canoe. But she was impassive, shaking her head.

"Gwendolyn, Annie—grab hold of those fellows! Quick, now." Ross screamed, "Gwendolyn! Save yourself!"

"Not yet!" she cried. While the auburn-haired Annie sprang into the river and Jeremy's arms, Gwen took up the line Little Hawk had brought, and rammed it through an iron eyebolt fastened to the canoe's left gunwale. Water poured over her legs as she battled to secure the rope to another iron loop on the right side. The craft was going down.

"Give it up!" Ross bellowed, ready to leave the canoe.

Struggling to stay afloat in a mass of petticoats and the cloak of the other woman, Jeremy shouted, "Get overboard, woman, or you'll be sucked down with the canoe! Get overboard! Don't be a damned fool!"

For an instant, Gwen glared at Jeremy, and he felt her tremendous force of character and courage. He knew she would not give up—not until it was too late.

The bearded Ross shouted, "We're lost..."

The canoe went completely below the surface. Sputtering and gagging, Cole Ross fell out of the stern, flailing with arms and legs, obviously a poor swimmer.

The woman in Jeremy's arms, who smelled of fine perfume, screamed, "Papa! Help him! He can't swim! Help him, please!"

Little Hawk made for the burly man, who was near to panic, going under suddenly and surfacing twice more before the Sioux got a grip on him. The fellow might have been too much even for Little Hawk to manage had Gwen not swum at their side, calling for her uncle to calm down and stop struggling. With the Indian and the woman helping, Ross lay back in the water, gasping for air and grunting that life was too cruel to him.

"All we have in the world..." he mumbled, sputtering for air. "Lost! Oh, woe! Why should we have to suffer so?"

Gwen tried to soothe him, and held up an end of the line she had lashed to the canoe. "It's not sunk yet, Uncle Cole! See, it's not all the way to the bottom. We still have the line! There's hope!"

Jeremy admired her incredible bravery, but knew she would soon have to let go of the line, which would be dragged down with the sinking canoe. He held on to his own line, but once it went taut, he would have to let go rather than be pulled under to certain death. If he and the blond woman tried to keep the canoe afloat without the aid of the *Trader*'s dinghy, they both would drown in the icy water.

Then he heard a welcome shout from nearby. Out of the fog came the rowboat, Tamano and Simon Clancy pulling hard on the oars. Annie Ross, the beauty in Jeremy's arms, called and waved.

"We're saved! Thank God! We're saved!" Then she screamed, "Gwen!"

Gwendolyn Hardy had gone under. The canoe yanked her down. Jeremy realized Gwen's line was far shorter than his, which was yet playing out. He was dismayed that she had not let go. The dinghy was upon them, and Jeremy took the startled Annie by the waist and pushed her up out of the water. She landed heavily in the boat. Cole Ross was nearly unconscious from cold and shock, and did not know his niece was going to the bottom with his canoe and their belongings.

Jeremy threw his line aboard the dinghy, and Clancy ran it over the bow, then lashed it to a thwart; but the force of the canoe going down was too much, and the Irishman had to play the line out gradually. Still there was no sign of Gwen.

In Chippewa, Little Hawk shouted to Jeremy, "The girl must let go! We can save her canoe, but she'll be dead before we get her back up!"

Jeremy saw the bubbles rise where the woman had gone down. With a swift gulp of air, he dived for her.

ROMANCE, WAR, HONOR AND ADVENTURE AT THE DAWN OF A NEW FRONTIER!

NORTHWEST TERRITORY

Not since John Jakes' <u>Kent Family Chronicles</u> has there been a series of books like the NORTHWEST TERRITORY, which vividly chronicles the forging of America and the men and women who made this country great. These are the stories of the Sutherland family and their founding of a great trading company along the frontier and in the cities of the Old Northwest—America's heartland. Facing the perils of Indian attacks and the threat of Revolution, the Sutherlands fight for what they believe, helping to shape America's destiny.

_____ 05452-7/$2.95 WARPATH (Book 1)

Owen Sutherland—Scottish-born frontiersman, soldier, and trader—leads the men of the Northwest in putting down the most brutal Indian uprising in America's history. In the midst of this turmoil, he meets and falls in love with Ella Bently, a beautiful young Englishwoman at Fort Detroit.

NORTHWEST TERRITORY